Dame Fiona Kidman OBE is one of New Zealand's most highly acclaimed novelists. *New Zealand Books* said of Kidman, 'We cannot talk about writing in New Zealand without acknowledging her.' Born in Hawera, she has worked as a librarian, radio producer, critic and scriptwriter. Her first novel, *A Breed of Women*, was published in 1979 and became a bestseller. She has since written more than 25 books including novels, poetry, non-fiction and a play. Fiona Kidman lives in Wellington, New Zealand.

## Also by Fiona Kidman

**Novels**
*A Breed of Women*, 1979
*Mandarin Summer*, 1981
*Paddy's Puzzle*, 1983
*The Book of Secrets*, 1987
*True Stars*, 1990
*Ricochet Baby*, 1996
*Songs from the Violet Café*, 2003
*The Captive Wife*, 2005
*The Infinite Air*, 2013
**Short story collections (as author)**
*Mrs Dixon and Friend*, 1982
*Unsuitable Friends*, 1988
*The Foreign Woman*, 1993
*The House Within*, 1997
*The Best of Fiona Kidman's Short Stories*, 1998
*A Needle in the Heart*, 2002
*The Trouble with Fire*, 2011
**Short story collections (as editor)**
*New Zealand Love Stories: An Oxford Anthology*, 1999
*The Best New Zealand Fiction 1*, 2004
*The Best New Zealand Fiction 2*, 2005
*The Best New Zealand Fiction 3*, 2006
**Non-fiction**
*Gone North*, 1984
*Wellington*, 1989
*Palm Prints*, 1994
*At the End of Darwin Road*, 2008
*Beside the Dark Pool*, 2009
**Poetry**
*Honey and Bitters*, 1975
*On the Tightrope*, 1978
*Going to the Chathams*, 1985
*Wakeful Nights*, 1991
*Where Your Left Hand Rests*, 2010
*This Change in the Light*, 2016
**Play**
*Search for Sister Blue*, 1975

# ALL DAY AT THE MOVIES

Fiona Kidman

AARDVARK
BUREAU

# ALL DAY AT
# THE MOVIES

Fiona Kidman

Aardvark Bureau
London
An imprint of Gallic Books

An Aardvark Bureau Book
An imprint of Gallic Books

First published in 2016 by Random House New Zealand
Copyright © Fiona Kidman 2016
Fiona Kidman has asserted her moral right to be identified as the author
of the work.

First published in Great Britain in 2017 by
Aardvark Bureau, 59 Ebury Street, London SW1W 0NZ

A CIP record for this book is available from the British Library
ISBN 978-1-910709-34-4

Typeset in Garamond Pro by Aardvark Bureau
Printed in the UK by
CPI Group (UK) Ltd, Croydon, CR0 4YY
2 4 6 8 10 9 7 5 3 1

For Vince and Helen and Kirsty

# CONTENTS

# 1

# The smoke harvest

# 1952

It was like moving to another country. The city of tram lines and crowded houses left behind, and now this wide open landscape. The bus lurched around another corner, hitting corrugations in the road. Irene Sandle perched on the edge of the slatted wooden seat and put her arm around her daughter's shoulder. The child was six going on seven, a freckle-faced girl, who her mother suspected would grow up to be plain, but it wouldn't matter because she was clever. Like her father, the airman, who had died so close to the end of the war. Irene tried not to dwell on that, the unfairness of it, him coming home for that short sweet halcyon leave and going back to a conflict that was due to end soon. He was lost over the Pacific but he had left her Jessie.

They had departed from Wellington early in the morning, a storm tossing them around as the ferry made its way beyond the heads. Walls of water had drenched the city and the wind slapped at the eaves of her mother's house as they said their goodbyes. Now here they were on the other side of the strait, the sea ironed as flat as a linen tablecloth when they arrived in Picton. As the bus wound its way through country roads the sun glittered between the leaves of beech trees. The greenness of the countryside astonished Irene, used as she was to living in streets of houses side by side, with neighbours talking over back fences while they hung soggy washing on their clotheslines. And ahead of them lay a shining estuary, a silver swathe across the landscape, and before they knew it, they had arrived in the main street of a small town: a few tall houses, but most of them modest wooden dwellings with flower beds around them, some churches, all the shops you would expect — butcher, grocery, dress shop. Everything about Motueka was awash with glowing light.

'Where are we?' Jessie asked, her thin face puckered in an anxious frown. She had been sick on the boat and still seemed listless, as if the bus ride had drained the last of her resources.

'Nearly there, pet,' Irene said. They were stopping at a depot where the driver signalled the passengers to alight. Alongside it was a large building with a tall clock tower ornamented with glass panels, and the tobacco company's name emblazoned on what looked like the reception area of a factory. Shiny Buick and Studebaker cars were parked in a row in front.

Irene was so concerned about Jessie she hadn't studied her fellow travellers. As she waited her turn to step into the aisle, she saw among the men a handful of young women like herself, carrying their suitcases. They were dressed more casually than she, several with hair tied up in scarves, wearing slacks, something women did more since the war. None of them were accompanied by children, although one woman looked older, and full-figured, as if she might have had some. She wore a thin wedding band and although she, too, was dressed casually, her make-up was heavy, her lipstick bright red.

Irene was embarrassed by her cream blouse adorned with pearl buttons, her navy blue pencil skirt, white gloves and polished shoes. But after all, she was going to a new job. It wasn't exactly an interview, because she'd already been told that there was a place for her, and that she could bring a child if she wanted. But still, it was beginning again, meeting a new employer.

A man stood holding a clipboard that he glanced at as each person stepped from the bus and gave their names. He ticked them off one by one. Irene waited to the last, or so she thought. The man looked her up and down. 'Name?'

'Irene Sandle.' She held out a gloved hand. He studied it in silence before extending his own.

'Jock Pawson. The kid?'

'Jessie.'

'Same name? Sandle.'

'Of course.' She hesitated, not thinking she would have to explain. 'I'm a widow. Jessie goes to school.'

'I understand. I have to keep a record. So you want to work in the tobacco fields, Mrs Sandle?' He had faded ginger hair and a frayed beard that he tugged with his free hand as he studied her. His fingers were tobacco-stained.

'They said there was a place for me. I've got a letter. They said I could have a house.'

'Och, aye, don't panic. If you've got a letter, nobody's saying you can't have it. I'm just wondering if you can manage outdoor work. Picking tobacco's hard work.'

'I'm willing to work hard.'

'I daresay you are. They all say that. Fourteen hours a day. Did you do farm work in the war?'

But she wasn't going to tell him what she did in the war. She didn't care for this ruddy faced man with his stomach beginning to billow over his trousers, the crumbs in his beard. He made her think of plantation overseers in books she'd read. It was hard to tell his age — she guessed mid-forties at least. She noted, though, that he had powerful-looking arms beneath his checked shirt and something about the set nature of his

13

expression suggested that he liked to get his own way. There seemed little point in telling him that she had worked in a city library throughout the war, a job she'd loved more than she could ever explain; that shelving musty books and choosing ones to take home had offered her a world of endless possibility; or that she had dawdled over morning tea so that she could read an extra chapter before resuming her duties, and that her fellow workers had often said, 'Quit dreaming, Irene, there's customers waiting at the desk.' Not that she hadn't done her fair share of work and, because she knew so much about the books, she'd been the one whom the customers liked talking to anyway. Irene didn't think all of these things at once, but she had thought about them, and other matters, often enough to know that her life history was her own and none of this was what she wanted Jock Pawson to learn. Besides, the war was beginning to seem a long time ago. The world around them was changing already. She was aware of him staring at her. Something in her recoiled. Jessie was tugging at her skirt, and the child's white frightened face tore at her heart.

The whole awkward moment was broken when Jock's attention turned to a movement behind her. It was the stealthy action of someone trying to slide past without being noticed. Jock's hand shot out.

'And who are you and where do you think you're going?' He was holding the arm of a man Irene had seen boarding the bus in Nelson. He must have gone right to the back. The man wore a battered leather jacket, worn into soft folds, with unusual buttons. He was thin as a whip, his eyes the colour of strong black tea, his skin swarthy. Irene detected threads of grey in his soft unruly hair.

'I heard there was work here.'

'What's your name?'

'Butcher. Bert Butcher. I've worked in the mines over the

West Coast. I'm just after a change.' Irene thought she heard the trace of an accent. 'I could be useful around the place. I did some electrics in the mine.' He tamped down a slim pipe as he spoke, preparing to light up.

'Where did you come from?'

'I'm a Maori fella. Sir.'

'You look like a Jew boy to me.'

'Not me, no sir.'

Irene said, 'Is there anywhere I can get food for my daughter?'

There was a grocer's shop where she could buy provisions, Jock told her. Everyone else had headed that way already, so she'd better be quick. The bus would be leaving for the fields any time now. She needed to stock up.

He gave a curt nod in the direction of the man who called himself Bert Butcher. 'Go on, then,' he said. 'You'll have to bunk down in the single-men's quarters. That's if you can find a bed.' Irene saw how Jock's eyes followed the man.

Before he moved on, Jock thrust a parcel in her arms. 'Overalls and boots,' he said. 'They get deducted from your last pay before you leave.'

A workers' bus came round and picked everyone up from the grocer's shop. Irene bought bread and butter, some bananas, milk and tins of baked beans. She couldn't think what else to get. The woman with all the make-up introduced herself. Her name was Margaret, although everyone called her Dixie. 'You know, like the song.' She warbled a line of 'I Wish I was in Dixie' and hooted with laughter. 'Yeah, I wish all right. It's been a long time between drinks,' she said. 'You're in the next bach to me. I can tell you the last fella in there was a dirty bastard. You'll need some Lysol, and a scrubbing brush. Get some eggs, too, they've got them here.' She glanced at Jessie. 'She always as peaky as this?'

On the crowded bus, Dixie sat herself across the aisle from

Irene so they could continue their conversation. 'I'm a regular, I come here every season. The kids are old enough to look after themselves. My hubby died at the beginning of the war. Silly bugger, he didn't need to go — he was thirty-six and we had two kids. I said to him, "Bob, you're more use to us here than dead." "Well," he said, "conscription's coming in, I'll have to go. I don't want any white feathers poked through my letterbox." I let it go, what could I do? You get used to it, being on your own. You have to, don't you? Well, you're young, you'll find somebody else without any trouble. Be glad you're not fair, fat and forty. I like the singalongs here, and we go to the dances. You like square dancing? No? Oh, you'll get the hang of it. You get to meet some fellas, too. You met Jock? Yes, now he's a card, but he doesn't dance — not the type.'

The bus pulled up at two rows of small shacks that were almost as close to one another as the houses in Wellington. One row was for women and the other for the men, Dixie explained. 'If you do meet any fellas, best keep it to yourself. The owners are a bit funny about stuff going on, know what I mean?'

Irene saw a homestead not far away. An old man sat on the verandah in what looked like a wheelchair, wreathed by smoke. Some of the tobacco farmers had been here a long time, she would learn, built the farms up from scratch and worked until they were done for. Now they needed managers, men like Jock Pawson.

The one-room bach allocated to Irene and Jessie was more like a wooden hut than a house, with a corrugated-iron roof and a lean-to containing an iron bath. A tank stood on a stand outside. 'You need to watch how much water you use. It doesn't rain much here,' Dixie said. 'Though, thank goodness for that, or we'd all be out of a job.' Dixie said she was lucky they had the power on; further along the line the baches hadn't been hooked up. They put the Maori fellas in there, they were used to going without. Irene saw that they were hooked up to a pole that carried electricity to larger buildings towering beyond. These were the kilns, standing twenty feet high, that housed the furnaces where the tobacco was cured. Before them lay fields of tobacco plants, their coarse broad leaves like a green sea rolling across the plains. The air was filled with a strange shimmering scent.

The man who called himself Bert Butcher had helped Irene to carry her groceries to the door, without saying a word. When she turned to thank him, he was gone. She thought he looked foreign.

The room held a rank fetid smell. There was a mattress on an iron bed and another one on the floor. A pot and a kettle stood side by side on an iron stove.

'Mummy,' Jessie said. 'Mummy, don't cry.'

Irene glanced around. 'Andrew,' she said aloud, 'why aren't you here?' She still sought him in moments of despair. He had always known what to do.

Andrew and Irene had met at the technical college where they were both in the A-stream for English. She was doing the academic course and he was in engineering, and neither of them had ever looked at anyone else. He'd gone into the air force before war was declared. She was so proud to be seen out with one of the boys in blue, Irene who always had her nose in a book, transformed by love. First love. Only love. Dead love. They had to get their parents' permission to marry, they were so young, but it was wartime and that made a difference.

She would still be working in the library but for Jessie's birth. When she went back to ask for her old position after the war, it had been filled. The land girls who had worked in the countryside came flocking after jobs in town. She did have a war widow's pension after all and a roof over her head, the head librarian explained. It wouldn't be fair to take her back. That wasn't exactly the point, because the roof was over her parents' house. For a time that was all right, but it wasn't any more.

Now, when Irene looked at the scared little girl beside her, whom she had named Jessie after her dear love's late mother, she was overwhelmed all over again. Jessie lit up her life, had made it possible for her to go on, to live without Andrew. She didn't care about the lost life at the library, or the years spent under her parents' roof, nothing at all really, except that she and Jessie might at last have a place where they could be alone and safe and free. At this moment, she wasn't sure that she'd found it. The flight from Wellington, and all that was familiar, was fast becoming a nightmare.

'It'll be all right, Mummy,' Jessie said, a sudden smile illuminating her face. She clapped her hands. 'Our very own house, Mummy,' she said. 'Just like you said.' Her daughter, comforting her.

Irene gave Jessie bread she had torn from the loaf and some milk. She didn't feel at all hungry, and after she had drunk the milk, Jessie didn't want the bread either. Her eyes were heavy. Irene scanned around the room. There was so much to do. First, she opened a suitcase. She had known to bring sheets and a blanket; the letter had told her that. She smoothed a sheet across the mattress, then lay down on it, pulling Jessie alongside her. Once she got her settled, she could make a start on things.

There were some things that, in time, Jock Pawson would tell his future wife, and then only once. He wasn't a man given to small talk. And there were things he would keep to himself.

It was young flesh Jock hankered for. It was beginning to look as if it were too late for what he was after, that perhaps young women would never be interested in him. His older sister, Agnes, who lived up north, had said to him, time and again, Jock, you'd better get moving. Goodness knows, I tried to have bairns but I never could. The end of the line. Think how our parents went through all they did to bring us out here. We'll all be gone before we know it, if you don't find yourself a woman soon.

At times Jock did question whether their parents had made the right decision, bringing them from Scotland. He was a boy at the time, just thirteen, and the Great War not long finished. You need more education, lad, his father said. You're not going to get it here in Glasgow. They lived south side of the Clyde and his father had spent his whole working life on a factory production line, making munitions. That is what would become of Jock, too, and Agnes would marry into the same sort of life, was what he said. We want to be in charge, not just the bloody workers, we need to be able to say what's what for ourselves.

When they arrived, his father worked for a year in the mines. He earned enough money to set up a dairy in Dunedin, a place he thought would do them because there were kinsmen there, other Scots. Jock stayed at school until he was fifteen. Now that was an education. You would nae have got that in Glasgow, lad, his father said. Agnes married a young man who came to the university to train as a dentist. Those should have been good times.

They hadn't counted on the Depression. Jock had to choose between relief work or going down the mines where there was still work to be had and his father knew someone. It was a job but it got to him, the dark tunnels, the soot that stayed under his nails even when he scrubbed himself raw, the cold mists that hung in the West Coast valleys. He wanted a woman then, but the women were already taken, or on the make, or they wouldn't look at him. There were plenty of men in the mines who had their own wives. He didn't ask for much, a feed at night, a warm bed, a woman. He paid for flesh now and then but that wasn't the answer, furtive encounters that began on street corners, and the chance of getting caught. He got the clap once, and when it was cleaned up he knew he wouldn't go down that road again. The doctor had stared at him with distaste when he asked for sulphonamides. You brought it on yourself, man, the doctor said.

Back in Dunedin, his mother had died, his father was struggling to pay his suppliers. You're still working for the bosses, his father said, bitter at how things had gone. That was when Jock got his ticket to become a mining inspector, helping his father by day, studying at night. Next time he went down the mines it would be on his own terms. It wasn't just the workers he could tell what to do, but the bosses, too.

He went down all the mines in the south — Seddon, Blackball, Roa — over the years he inspected the lot, donning his helmet, pulling his beard, pointing out equipment faults, his senses attuned for the smell of gas, the drip of water on the rocks. Jock made ten quid a week and he felt rich. He put money in the bank, week after week, compounding interest; soon he had a thousand and money seemed to grow after that. He loved it, never spent a penny more than he could help. At nights, instead of going in search of women, he would take out his bank statements and read them to check there were no errors, no missed entries. On pay days he would take his pound notes out and count them, their texture silk beneath his fingertips. His job was essential work, and he wasn't drafted. There was a shortage of men during the war. He thought he might find a woman then, but he didn't. It was the mines that did it, he decided. He still had the smell of soot on him.

Like the dark man who had emerged from the bus, he needed a change. He mightn't know much about women but he knew what made workers tick. There was money to be made in the tobacco fields.

The night the woman came with the child, he felt an excitement, something that announced itself as a churning in his stomach, almost like a sickness.

When Irene woke, cold and stiff, night had fallen. Jessie slept quietly beside her. Irene stumbled in the dark, feeling the wall near the door for a switch. By the weak light from the bare bulb she found the two blankets she had folded in the bottom of one of the suitcases and placed one over her sleeping child. Jessie resembled Andrew. He'd been a scrawny kid when they first met at school, his straight hair spiky where the barber had shorn it. He was never a looker, she'd be the first to admit it, but he made her laugh, right from the beginning. And he knew all sorts of things from the reading he did; they were two of a kind. One day we'll travel the world together, he'd said. We'll go to the Taj Mahal and to Egypt to see the Pyramids, and to Canada to see the Niagara Falls.

There was nothing in the room except the mess she had made on the dirty bench where her groceries were still stacked, and the spilled-open suitcases. Even though it was summer there was a chill in the air, but she couldn't see any wood to make a fire in the range. Perhaps there was some stacked near the door, she couldn't remember. As she stood, hesitating, there was a light tap at the door. At first she thought she had imagined it. But it happened a second time, a soft insistent knock. 'Who is it?' she called.

The silence was unbroken. After a minute or so, Irene pulled the door open with a sweeping motion as if preparing to stand up to whoever was there, pulling herself up to her full height, though she had barely come up to Andrew's shoulder. There was no one to be seen. On the step stood a pot of steaming stew.

The silence held fast. 'Thank you,' she called into the rustling night. 'Thank you.'

'Thank you,' she said to Dixie when she saw her the next morning. It was Sunday. They had one day to get settled in before work began. After this there would be no let-up. Can you work seven days a week? the advertisement had asked.

Dixie looked at her blankly. 'Thank you for what?'

'The stew. I thought it was from you.'

Dixie put her hands up. 'I'm not the fairy godmother. You'd better come in,' she said. 'You look all wrung out. I'll make us a brew.'

The inside of her bach appeared comfortable, with a white coverlet on the bed, some photos of children propped on a gate-leg table, a couple of chairs, each with a cushion. 'I leave my stuff here year to year,' she explained. 'I've told Jock to keep an eye on it for me. Old stick in the mud that he is.'

'Perhaps it was Mr Pawson.'

'What? Brought you the stew up from the cookhouse? I'd have heard him. Anyway, I can't see him bringing you a feed if he didn't drop by with one for me.' She glanced sideways at Irene. Something shifted in her eyes.

Irene caught her own reflection in a mirror tacked on the wall. Beneath it a plank was supported by two stacks of bricks, serving as a dressing table for a row of cosmetics. She saw the dark wave of her hair, the eyes that Andrew had said were green although she would have described them as hazel, sunken a little in the pallor of her complexion. In his letters home, he would tell her that she was the prettiest girl in the class and the smartest, too. He saw her the way others didn't. You will still be beautiful when we are old, he had written to her. That was in his last letter, after he had gone back to the Pacific, the one that arrived when she had just started throwing up with Jessie, and wondering what she had eaten. She was twenty-eight now, but she thought she looked older. Beside her Jessie had picked up a lipstick.

'Don't touch,' she said.

'Don't worry,' Dixie said, seeming to relax. 'Here, I'll put a bit on you, make you a pretty girl, eh? My kids used to love it when I dollied them up.' She was drawing a red mouth on Jessie, tweaking her hair up with a comb. 'Bit of powder on your nose, you like that, don't you? You need a pretty bow in your hair, that's what. You get Mummy to buy one next time you're in town.'

Irene felt powerless to complain. Jessie looked like a clown, but the child was delighted with herself, jumping up and down to view herself in Dixie's mirror.

'There, see, she likes it. A little bit of powder and a little bit of paint, makes a girl just what we ain't. Didn't you say that in school? Boys used to write it in your autograph book.'

Jessie had become excited by all the attention. 'I'll take her out to play,' Irene said.

'She'll have to learn how to look after herself, with you in the fields. Don't worry, it's safe as houses round here. What brought you anyway?'

Irene shrugged, not knowing where to begin. 'My father's a wharfie,' she said, as if that explained it all. The waterfront lockout that had brought the country to a standstill had ended only months earlier.

'Oh, one of the Commies,' Dixie said. 'You'll have seen it all.'

'We had pretty good times after the war,' Irene said. 'Dad's wages were good.' She described the old-fashioned house in Kilbirnie where she and her brother Ray had grown up. It had space to spare when they were kids. There were high ceilings and stained-glass windows that made dancing lights. But after the war every room began to fill, first with her and Jessie, because she was a widow, then Ray, who'd been injured, so he and his wife came to live with them while he had rehab, and then they had a baby, too. Irene's mother said if Irene was living with them, it was only fair that her brother did as well, so they all stayed.

'Whenever I said I'd find somewhere for me and Jessie to live, Mum went on about the kind of places I might be able to find in Wellington on my pension. Rat-infested dumps over the Courtenay Place shops, was what she said. Besides, if I could get a job, who did I expect was going to look after Jessie? But there, she's at school now.'

Dixie was curious. 'So Sid Holland wins the election and you're all on the bones of your backsides?'

'Something like that. They'd taken Ray on at the wharves, too. They wanted the wharfies to work longer hours. Well, you'll have heard about all of that. Things were getting really dangerous for the men. Next thing they were on strike, and Dad and Ray were out demonstrating or else holed up at home. The only money coming in was my pension.' Irene shivered, pulling her cardigan around her, not sure whether the woman would sympathise or not. There were plenty who didn't. A hundred and fifty days of no wages and a simmering rage in the house. How did you explain that to people who weren't part of it? Each day in that house had turned into a battlefield. Irene's mother was going through the change, and she said that one more night of Ray's baby grizzling or Jessie running up and down the passageway would drive her insane. The smallest *sound* was really too much for her to *bear*, that's what she said. She'd had years of kids living in the house, helping bring them up.

24

When the strike was finally over, Irene said she really was going, she'd find a place for her and Jessie to live. Somewhere with fresh air and freedom under the wide open skies. You always were one for being *romantic*, her mother said, but she seemed pleased. Though this wasn't true either; Irene wasn't romantic these days, not since the telegram came to say that Andrew Sandle wasn't coming home.

'You don't want to let the boss know you're a Commie,' Dixie said.

'I didn't say I was.'

'Jock's not a union man. He only puts up with them because he has to.' She flicked out a packet of cigarettes and offered them to Irene. 'Tailor-mades. Enjoy them while they last. It'll be all home brew from here on, and the boss only lets us have so much of that. It's the rules. Mind you,' and here she leaned forward in a conspiratorial way, 'Jock smokes tailor-mades. If he's in a good mood he'll drop me off a couple. You want to get on his good side.'

'I don't smoke,' Irene said. 'Asthma,' she added hurriedly, seeing the look on Dixie's face. 'When I was a child. I just don't want it to come back.' All her family smoked. The house in Kilbirnie was always choked with smoke. And here she was, coming to pick tobacco, the weed she'd inhaled since her childhood. It wasn't lost on her.

Dixie shrugged. 'People like you that put us out of a job.'

Outside, Jessie had climbed an apple tree that grew near the huts, and was swinging from a branch.

'Come down, monkey,' Irene called, excusing herself.

Dixie blew a perfect smoke ring, watched it drift towards the ceiling.

When she got back to her place, Irene considered the pot left at the door the night before. She had washed it, ready to return to its owner. The best thing, she decided, was simply to leave it where she had found it on the step. That night, after dark, somebody put a stack of wood at her front door. She must have been asleep because she didn't hear a thing. If they had knocked, she had slept through it.

'I'll start you on topping the flower heads,' Jock told Irene. He showed her how they formed at the top as the tobacco plants matured. The petals had to be picked out so they wouldn't fall and scorch the leaf below. At the junction of each plant, between leaf and stalk, suckers had to be nipped out, too, to increase the leaf size. She was surprised how patient he was with her. He often shouted at other workers who were slow or not catching on fast enough, but not at her. All the same, she was in agony at the end of each day, her arms covered in a tar-like substance that itched, even when she had washed herself down. Her hands swelled, the backs of her legs ached and her face burned in the sun.

'You're doing well,' Jock told her. When she had been there for a week, he got her picking. She learned the different types of leaf; the leaves nearest the ground were called lugs, above them the best leaves were cutters, all the way up to the tips. He would come often and stand near to her, giving a running commentary on the different stages of the whole process. She longed to tell him that she understood the work, that if he would just leave her to it, she would manage. When he was watching, she felt clumsy and made more mistakes, often mixing one leaf type with another. It must be that he was pushing her to work harder, she thought. When he moved on, she would catch her breath, falter for a moment before resuming the endless motion of picking the leaves ready to be taken away and dried, then cured.

The dark quiet man, Bert, who had been on the bus the day she arrived, came and worked alongside her one day. She had hardly seen him since she had come to the tobacco fields.

She knew he worked in a shed gang, feeding the kilns. This was dangerous work. The furnaces, fuelled with coke and coal, sent tremendous heat up through flue pipes. A cure took five days, and during that time there was no rest for the people who worked in the kilns. On this day a cure had just finished and preparations were starting for the next one. She thought he must be weary, but his movements were very quick and sure as he moved steadily through the row she was working on. He stood close to her and said, 'You need to rest.' His breath near her cheek smelt smoky and intense.

'I can't,' she said. 'I'm slower than everyone else now. They'll notice.'

'I'll finish this row for you,' he said. Again she heard that slight inflection in his voice and she didn't think it was Maori. A foreign mother, perhaps? His dark eyes were hooded, set deep in his head. She allowed herself to be propelled to the end of the row.

Jock was watching, and somehow she had known that he would be.

'Mr Butcher,' he said, a false note of civility in his manner, 'you're needed in the kiln shed.'

Irene called in sick for a day. It was up to her to decide whether she stayed, knowing she wasn't really strong enough for this work. There was, too, an atmosphere she didn't like. It was hard to define, especially in the evenings when some of the workers who had brought guitars began to sing, harmonising in the blue fading light, old melodies that people had sung through the war. It looked and sounded like a country idyll, something Chekhov might have written about. How to explain her unease? She told herself it was just her, the misery her body was experiencing, the lack of people to talk to about things that interested her.

Yet Jessie was happy. The child had never looked so healthy. When she wasn't at school she played in the apple trees with other children who had arrived at the field, climbed, ran races, and was teaching herself to read way ahead of her class. She had read all the books Irene had brought with her, intending to read to her every night just like at home, not that she ever did because she was dead on her feet at the end of each shift. When Jessie dropped off to sleep, Irene sat beside her, absorbing her child's face, wanting to touch the delicate veins in her eyelids, greedy for these moments when she possessed her. Already she had money in her bank account, and a dream was beginning to shape itself, of going back to Wellington and setting up on her own with Jessie. Sooner or later, she believed she would get her job back in the library. She wouldn't have to excuse herself to her mother who said that reading books all the time was bad for a girl. There was that girl Iris who wrote books and had babies *when she wasn't married* and her life was just all sorrow, mental hospitals and ... but her mother couldn't bring herself to say the word *suicide*. In the end, dead, anyway. Irene's mother had known Mrs Wilkinson, the mother of Iris, although she called herself something else, and it had been a terrible thing for her to have to lose a daughter to books. And, Irene's mother had said, she hoped that Irene wasn't thinking of writing books. It brought disgrace on a family.

Irene reflected on this, on her idle day, while she lay on the lumpy mattress. Her mother wouldn't like what was going through her head right now. She had, in fact, had the idea for some time that she might write a book. Here, in the tobacco fields, was the perfect setting. She hadn't read Caldwell and Steinbeck for nothing. Perhaps she needed to stay a little longer, get to know the people better. She should go into town to the dance where the workers went. Dixie always did, and she said it would do Irene the world of good to let loose a bit. The kids went along, too; they could always have a sleep on the cushions out the back of the hall.

She was dozing, half asleep, half thinking about how she might start her novel, when a figure appeared in the doorway.

'You got the cramps today?' Jock Pawson said.

Irene sat bolt upright, pulling the blanket over herself, aware that the buttons of her blouse were partly undone. Jock came in without being invited and sat on the rickety chair near the bed.

'Well, some women get them worse than others,' he said. 'So I'm told.'

'Yes, well, I suppose so,' she said, her face prickling with shame. She wasn't bleeding, it was just that she was so tired but she didn't want to tell him that. 'I'll be all right in the morning. I always am.' It was hard to tell what was worse, concocting this lie, or having to talk to the man about her periods. To her horror, he was stretching out his hand to stroke her bare arm.

'You sure you haven't come down with a fever? We can't have someone infectious around here. The workers can't afford to let up.'

'It's just what you said, Mr Pawson,' she said, her voice strangling in her throat.

'You don't have to be formal with me, Irene. The name's Jock.' Still the persistent finger touched her arm. 'You must get lonely, a widow like yourself.'

'Yes, yes I do.' Anything to appease him, and where was Jessie when she needed her? She was due home on the school bus very soon.

'I can understand that. I'm a man who gets lonely, too.' He hesitated. 'It's not going to be easy for you, with a kiddie and all. The men can take their pick of the girls these days,

29

they've been so long without fellows around. No doubt you'll be thinking about a father for her again.'

'No,' Irene said. 'No, I'm not.' And it was true, she had never had the faintest stirring of desire for another man since Andrew. She hadn't even tried to imagine another man's body. Yet here was this man, sitting beside her, touching her, and she knew that he was asking her to think about sex. Worse than that, by the sound of it, marriage. She gave a long shudder.

'I'm sorry,' he said, standing up, his manner abrupt. 'I'll leave you to it. I hope you're well enough to work in the morning.' At the doorway he paused. 'There are plenty of workers out there who'd be glad of a place.'

In the evening, she heard a soft knock on the door, the same as she had heard on the first night she arrived. As before, there was nobody to be seen outside, although she thought she detected a shadow. In the distance, someone was playing a guitar, and men were singing 'My Foolish Heart', something about the moon. From their voices, she guessed they were the Maori workers who had come from way up north. And, as if all that were not enough, there was a full moon rising, seemingly providing inspiration for the singers. On the step stood a pot of tomato soup that had a delicate, herbal scent, suggesting it had been cooked with care. In a flash, she guessed where it had come from, and wondered why she hadn't worked it out before. Somewhere inside her, despite the day's events, she recognised an old lost chime. The delicious food, the flickering lights of kerosene lanterns, the singing in the distance were arousing and unsettling. It wasn't Jock Pawson her thoughts were turning to.

When she and Jessie had eaten, and homework had been done, Irene put the light out and lay down. Her hand strayed between her thighs. She tried to summon Andrew's face, the loved contours of his body, but he was gone. She had lost sight of him. But still the feeling persisted.

The day following Jock's visit was a Friday. A bus took the workers to town for shopping, the only night the shops stayed open. Everyone got dressed up. Dixie wore polished cotton dresses with flaring skirts and coiled her hair in rolls over the top of her head. After the shops closed, the workers flocked either to the picture theatre or the dance hall. The High Street turned into a tide of people. You could almost pretend you were in the city.

An hour or so before the bus was due to leave, Jock appeared, wearing fawn slacks and a woollen pullover with a fresh blue shirt. Dixie was sitting on her step, painting her toenails scarlet. Jessie sat close to her, hoping that Dixie would dab her nails, too.

'Well, well, Jock,' she said, her face lighting up. 'You're never coming to the dance tonight, are you?'

'I was thinking about it.'

'Well, how about that? You told us all you couldn't dance.'

'I'm no good on foxtrots, I've got two left feet. But I can call, if you're doing a square dance. Allemande, promenade to your left, all bow,' he cried, clapping his hands to demonstrate his talents. 'Altogether now.'

'You old dog,' Dixie said, shrieking with delight. 'Where did you learn those tricks?' She leaned over and popped a splash of colour on Jessie's fingernails.

'Oh, you know, over the Coast,' he said, assuming a modest pose now that his secret was out. 'Anyway, I was wondering if Mrs Sandle was coming to town tonight?' He glanced at Jessie. 'You need to put your shoes on, lassie, if you're coming with your mother.'

31

'Irene?' Dixie said. 'You're looking for her?'

Irene had come to the door wearing a blue and lemon print dress with a nipped-in waist. Jock's face reddened.

'The bus is due to leave soon, Mrs Sandle. You coming into town with us?'

All thoughts of going to the dance and meeting more people fled. 'Not tonight,' she said. 'I got enough groceries to last me last week.' She stood there, trying to pretend that wearing a pretty dress was what she did every evening.

Dixie's eyes had clouded over. She put the cap firmly back on the nail polish. 'You'd better go home to your mummy,' she said to Jessie, her voice none too friendly. 'Perhaps Bert Butcher will come calling while we're out.'

'Is it true?' Jock asked.

'No, it's not,' Irene said, her cheeks stinging.

Jock turned on his heel, without a word.

'Dixie,' Irene said, after Jock had gone, 'I'm not — it's not like that.'

'Oh no? The whole camp knows he comes here at nights.'

'He's never set foot in our bach.'

Dixie just raised her eyebrows, her expression sour. 'I know pipe smoke when I smell it.'

When the bus got into town, Jock went to the phone box on the street corner. He had a handful of coins. He rang the operator and asked for tolls. The number he gave was on the West Coast, in one of the mining towns he knew so well. After that, he worked through another list of numbers, all to mining bosses. He pushed one coin after another into the slot and for once he didn't think about how much money he was spending.

Irene knew this was the moment she really should leave. She would pack up her few things. In the morning she would go to the owner's house and ask to use his phone and ring for a taxi. She and Jessie would be gone.

But Dixie was right. While Jessie lay sleeping, and the camp of huddled baches lay empty, Bert Butcher did come to her. Very quietly, so as not to wake the child, they put their arms around each other. He whispered her name in her ear, and some endearments she did not understand. It seemed, suddenly, that she had wanted him from the beginning, the moment she had seen him alighting from the bus. Her body, so slow to warm, was overcome with heat. She followed him outside, as if mesmerised. They lay down in the grass together. The sky above them was a plain of stars. An echo of caution signalled in the back of her head, but it was too late for that, her mouth and all of her so hungry she was taking him in, in great gulps. He took her with almost foxy stealth, knowing she would be there for him, that she wouldn't ask him to stop.

Afterwards, they sat on the step together. 'I've been thinking of leaving here,' she said.

'I can't lose you now.' His jacket lay beside them. He picked it up and dug his pipe out of his pocket.

'We could both go,' she said.

'People would notice.' In the flare of the match, as he lit the pipe, she saw his anxious frown.

'Does that matter?'

When he made no reply, she asked him, 'Who are you? Really?'

33

'We should wait a little while,' he said, evading her question. They could leave separately. He would meet her in Wellington. Or they could travel further north. Auckland was a good place. They had to be careful.

She didn't understand this. But she knew she wasn't going to leave this man any time soon.

'Are you afraid of Jock?' he asked.

'I don't think he would hurt me,' she said, as evasive as he had been.

'I'd kill him,' Bert said. 'With my bare hands.' He held them up for her to see in the moonlight, long sinewy hands; she felt the power in them when he touched her.

In the still distance, they heard shouting and laughter, the noise of an engine, the bus returning from town.

'I'll see you again soon,' he whispered. 'As soon as the way is clear.'

'You sound like the highwayman,' she said, and laughed.

'Who is that? This highwayman?'

'A poem. Never mind.'

'You're a poet?'

'Just go,' she said.

Towards dawn, she slept, just a sheet covering her nakedness. She dreamed she was a child again, and all of life lay ahead of her still. She half woke, remembering Bert's touch, running her hands over her body again, reminding herself of what had taken place in the night, that it was true.

A few days later, Jessie got into Dixie's nail polish when Irene and Dixie were at work in the fields. She sat on Dixie's white coverlet and opened the bright polish in order to paint her toenails. With the bottle propped beside her, she painted one toe after another. Then the bottle tipped over. The red varnish spread like blood, a swelling stain across the ocean of Dixie's bed.

Irene was preparing dinner, two lamb chops and a tin of peas, when Dixie arrived at the door, the coverlet in her hands. 'Where's that child of yours?' she spat.

Deep in her own thoughts, Irene hadn't noticed that Jessie was missing. She went outside and called. Just as she was beginning to panic, Jessie appeared from behind a clump of bushes, her face tear-stained. Her small toenails gleamed. 'I wanted to be pretty, Mummy,' she said. 'Pretty like Dixie.'

'Pretty like me. You want to give this kid a bloody good hiding. I'll hold her while you do it.' Dixie reached for Jessie.

'Don't you dare touch her,' Irene said, stepping between them. She snatched the coverlet from Dixie's hands. 'So what's so fine about this that it can't be replaced?'

'Slut!' Dixie screamed, lunging at her.

Irene smacked Dixie's face hard then, a thwack that made the woman stumble backwards. 'It's just a bit of cheap material. I'll get you another cover on Friday night.'

'You bitch, you can't even say sorry. You can't control your brat.' Dixie had her fists up.

Irene picked up the frying pan and lifted it. 'Don't you touch one hair on her head,' she said. Dixie's eyes bulged with sudden fear. 'You were the one who taught my kid tricks like this. You know what you look like? An old whore, that's what.'

As soon as the words were out of her mouth she knew how big her mistake was. 'I'm sorry, Dixie,' she said. 'I didn't mean that. I said I'll buy you a new cover on Friday.'

This was how she came to go to town on Friday night, instead of waiting in for Bert. The next time he saw her, he turned his face away, as if they were strangers.

The days followed one other. The sun shone with harsh bright constancy, not letting up. Irene lost a layer of skin and then another, and then it started to harden. The pain that had been so intense at the beginning had become bearable. When she looked in her pocket mirror she saw that she was ripe and brown. At night her breasts tingled, her nipples hard, as she thought about Bert Butcher. The harvest was a good one, the days lengthening as the labourers worked longer and longer hours, filling the kilns. She thought perhaps it was difficult for him to get away. He hadn't been near her again and she hadn't had a chance to explain why she wasn't there on the night she went shopping.

The cover she bought Dixie was better than the one that had been ruined but the words between them hadn't gone away. The older woman was withdrawn. She had taken to drinking with a group of workers at the far end of the camp. One night she stood between her bach and Irene's, and puked. Irene offered to get her a cold cloth. She'd seen her father puking more than once during the strike.

'What do you care?' Dixie said, gasping for breath. 'I know a thing or two about you.'

'You said. Just let me get you cleaned up. Go to bed and I'll make you a cup of tea.'

'Oh, bugger off,' Dixie said, turning and staggering towards her door.

One night, Irene put Jessie to bed and told her to be a good girl, that she would be back in half an hour. 'You're not to go outside,' she said. 'I want you to stay awake until I get back. Read a book or do some colouring in.' Already she was worrying about the consequences before she had gone, but she couldn't stop herself.

'Where are you going, Mummy?' Jessie asked.

'I have to see someone.'

'Is it Mr Butcher? He likes you, doesn't he, Mummy?'

'Who said that?'

'Dixie told my friend Laurel. What if Dixie comes?'

'She won't, she's gone down the camp to see her friends.' She leaned over and kissed the top of Jessie's head. 'I'll be quick, darling. I have to go.'

She walked along between the rows of baches towards the singing and drinking. It was a colder night than she expected, the sort that made the tobacco growers anxious. A late frost would ruin them all. She wished she had worn a cardigan. Men whistled as she emerged in the circle of light where they were gathered. Some of the women signalled for her to come over. A couple of the girls were doing a hula, holding enormous tobacco leaves in front of their knickers, pretending they were skirts, swaying their hips. Somebody offered her a beer. *Have a brown bomber, sweetheart. C'mon.* Bert was sitting on the step of his bach, tamping tobacco into his pipe. He was wearing his battered leather jacket. She knew that he had seen her and kept on walking towards the rustling fields where work had stopped for the day. When she was far into the rows, she stood still, and waited. Soon she felt his footfall behind her. She didn't turn around. 'I had to go to town that night. I couldn't help it,' she said.

'I know about that.'

'Oh, surprise me,' she said. 'Is there anything anyone doesn't know in this place? Is that why you haven't come back?' she said. 'Didn't you like what we did?' This newfound assertiveness surprised her. But then, she thought, perhaps I'm behaving more like a spurned woman in a nineteenth-century novel. They always came to grief. She turned to leave.

'I'm being watched,' he said. His hands had closed around her elbows, holding her back from walking away.

'Why?'

'It doesn't matter.'

'An excuse. I don't believe you.' But as soon as the words were out, she thought, he isn't lying.

He kissed her hard on the mouth, and drew away. 'You're being watched, too.'

'Why should anyone watch me? You and I have done nothing wrong. You think we're the only ones who do things?'

It was a black night, stars hiding under cloud cover that suggested the possibility of rain, rather than frost. She could hear the singing from the camp: 'Smoke Gets in Your Eyes.' *Yet today my love has flown away.* She thought fleetingly of Andrew. Flown away all right. *I am without …* Without. Jessie was without her.

'I have to go,' she said.

He spoke as if he hadn't heard her. He pulled her close to him, nuzzling the back of her neck, his hands cupping her breasts. 'The woman who lives across from you told Pawson you were up to no good, said you couldn't look after your kid. I heard her.'

'What did he say?'

'It was none of his business, he said. So she told him you were a Commie.'

'A what? Oh, for God's sake.' She was aware of a strange smell in the air, that she couldn't yet identify. 'My father was a wharfie. He was in the strike. What does he think I am, a trade union official in disguise?' She laughed, wildly, a little madly. Something else had just occurred to her: her swollen tender breasts and the period that hadn't come.

'He said you'd get over it in time. He thinks you'll go with him.'

'I never would.' She stood for a moment, thinking. 'I'm going to tell him I'm leaving here tomorrow,' she said. 'If you've got any sense you'll come away, too.' She lifted her head. 'Burning,' she said, 'something's burning.'

Behind them smoke was rising and the singing had turned to cries of panic. From one of the kilns a coil of flame was rising in the sky.

'Jessie!' Irene screamed.

Bert was racing ahead of her, faster than she could run.

Beyond the tobacco fields, everyone was running. This was the disaster that could strike — the furnace out of control, the kiln burned down, the harvest lost. The fire was snaking higher and higher, green and yellow flames, the air heaving with the smell of nicotiana. As she sprinted down through the camp, Irene saw Jock Pawson outlined against the burning building. Above him the power line that linked the kiln shed to the pole outside the baches was arcing above his head.

He saw Bert. 'Butcher.' And then, putting his hands to his mouth to form a trumpet, he screamed, 'Bottcher, where are you, Hans Bottcher? You're needed.' He gestured towards the twisting power line. Go up the pole and disconnect it.'

Already Bert was clambering up the pole. That was the moment Jessie appeared from the bach and began running towards her mother.

'No,' shouted Bert, and as the line fell he threw himself from the pole, trapping Jessie in his arms and rolling her free.

'Run, Jessie!' Irene shrieked. 'Run fast.'

Jessie threw herself into her mother's arms, the power line danced like a skipping rope and Bert caught it as he fell, tearing it from the pole, his body arching in a terrible writhing motion before he lay still. As Irene ran forward, Jock Pawson threw her to the ground so that her body didn't connect with that of the dead man. And still plumes of flame pierced the night sky, curling and licking and caressing the hurrying clouds, and there was nothing anyone could do except watch the crop burn and stare aghast at the blackened body of the man who had called himself Bert Butcher.

The owner had come down from his house, leaning on a stick. 'Who was in charge of the furnace?'

Jock's head snapped around, as if caught in a trap. Then he collected himself, pointing at the dead man. 'It was him.'

Someone had fetched a wooden-handled broom so they could push Bert's body away from the line without getting electrocuted, in case it was still live, for it seemed to the watchers that his blackened body was still twitching. Soon the police came from town, bringing men out from the power board. By that time the kiln was a pile of golden cinders.

There wasn't much left to **DO**. The police interviewed everyone there. Irene didn't say that she had been in the fields with Bert when she noticed the fire. She didn't believe that it was Bert who had been left in charge of the furnace. It was hard to credit that he would have been sitting there tamping down his pipe that night, but the story that he had left his post satisfied them all. He was, in the end, a hero, they said, as if that excused everything. He saved the little girl's life. There was a brief story in the newspaper about the fire and the death of a worker.

> *The identity of the man who died has been difficult*
> *to establish, as he was carrying no papers, and has*
> *no known next-of-kin. He matches the description*
> *of an Austrian called Hans Bottcher, who was*

*sought as a ship deserter before the war. This man was a German, perhaps with Jewish ancestry. It was thought he was seeking asylum from Nazi Germany. When faced with the possibility of detention and subsequent deportation, he found work in the West Coast coal mines throughout the war. Inquiries are proceeding. His remains will be buried.*

'I don't forget a face,' Jock said. 'I knew I'd seen him before.'

Irene waited for the body to be moved. Jock went to town with the police when they left with it. The workers had retreated to their baches, a pall fallen over the place. She went to the spot where Bert had died. The area had been cleared; there seemed nothing to see except scorch marks on the bare earth. She began to walk away, through the long grass that led beyond to the apple trees, then stopped. At her feet lay some small objects, things that must have flown from Bert's pockets and from his clothes. She picked them up and wrapped them in her handkerchief.

An evening or two later, when everyone was packing up to leave, Jock came to see her. Dixie had already left, without a word to her neighbour. Jessie was at the farm owner's house, being cosseted and fed blancmange by his wife, the miracle girl who had been saved, one less statistic on a very bad night. Irene would tell herself that, in time, Jessie would forget, that she would not recall having seen what she had, she would not remember that her mother had failed to care for her well enough, although this is something Irene would not forget and it would haunt her all her life.

She was expecting Jock Pawson to come to her. She saw her own body now as a gateway to safety. It surprised her how easy it was, looking at it like this.

# 2

# Clay particles

# 1963

Over and again, Belinda replays scenes that have stayed with her for a lifetime, ones that prickle behind her eyelids just before she wakes, no matter where she is. There's an ocean at the end of the street where she lives, with a bright dark sea washing against a wall in summer, a sea that turns violent when the wind turns to the south and spume fills the air, a small deserted island lying offshore. Often, in the evenings, Belinda walks to the front gate, and on a good night nothing can hide the sweep of brilliant sunsets that settle over the strait, the saddle of water that lies between this tip of one island and the beginning of the other. On clear days she can see the mountain caps of the far island, shimmering in the distance, gleaming like wedding cakes. Near at hand, fishing boats bob up and down on the water. Early in the mornings the fishermen will swing past the gate to the house where she lives; later they return with their catch. Their voices throb as they pass, sometimes in song, a snatch of Italian, it depends on the weather whether they are happy or not. Belinda's mother had taught her a rhyme, *We'll weather the weather together, whatever the weather may be*, and it's a refrain that still surfaces on rainy days.

Before the fishermen leave, they collect bait from a red shed that stands on the rocks above the waterline. The stench of the bait on hot days catches you in the back of the throat, although this is something Belinda can't describe when she writes this scene. She is a film maker and smell cannot happen in the movies, it can only be implied. But if she breathes deeply, it is there, and it is this, perhaps most of all, that brings it all back to her. What happened.

The house where Belinda lives is a wooden bungalow, built close to its neighbour. At night she can hear the sea crashing on the sea wall. There's a patch of earth at the back of the house that consists of heavy clay soil, where things don't really grow. Belinda's mother once planted a rose bush that struggled through the summers, sprouting occasional light maize-coloured blooms. She tried tomatoes, because they grew so well up the road at the Italian houses, but the fruit never ripened. Another year, it was a row of cabbages. She was bent, for a time, on providing the family with fresh healthy vegetables. Near the fenceline stands an incinerator.

Belinda lives with her mother and father, her younger brother and sister, and for a time an older half-sister. It is in this house that she has her last clear memory of her mother, even though she was taken to visit her in hospital in her dying days.

She sees her mother, hair wispy and uneven, head bent over a book, and hears a small exasperated sigh escaping as she closes it, readying herself to prepare a meal. Irene never captured the knack of coping. There was always wet washing hanging over wooden racks, sticky benchtops and a litter of open library books. Irene read books all the time when other women did the ironing or were starting dinner. Dinner was often late, as if Irene really didn't care much what they ate. Belinda thinks later that her mother just wasn't hungry, that her taste disappeared as she got sicker.

She remembers, with at times a touch of bitterness, the way Irene favoured her eldest child, the one who came before Belinda, and got away with things she and the other children couldn't. 'I'll tell your father,' she might say to the three young ones, when the noise of them all shouting and squabbling got too much, only she never did. Their father, Jock, would take his belt to them if he was angry. The fact that their mother didn't tell him was, Belinda supposes, love of a kind. That, and the distracted hand that brushed her children's foreheads when they were in bed, and she read to them.

There was a particular moment, Belinda will recall, when her mother stood beside her at the gate and they looked out across the sea together, towards the mountains to the south. 'I met your father over there,' Irene said. There was something muted and despairing about the way she spoke.

It was at the incinerator that Belinda saw Charm the day after Irene died. The woman was burning her mother's clothes. Charm's real name was Charmaine but she had always been known as Charm, not Sharm, even though Charmaine sounded like Sharmaine. She had a thin face and fair hair that looked as if it hadn't been brushed out after having rollers in it, so that the curls stood out like sausages. Her nose was narrow, and her flexible lips formed a circular pout when she smoked a cigarette.

'I've known your dad a long time,' she said. 'It's just as well he's got old friends to call on at a time like this.'

Belinda hadn't known that her father had this friend, but then he and her mother didn't go out a lot. There were the three children to care for: herself and Grant and Janice. One every two years, the first years her parents were married, not to mention Jessie, the one who ran off up North just when her mother needed her.

'I'll be bound that girl has had a baby. That's always why girls go North, you know,' Charm said, while she was waiting for the flames to die down enough to drop in another load. 'Although you're too young to know about things like that. How old are you? Eleven? You want to be careful when you get older.' She looked with disgust at a burnt oven mitt and some torn stockings as she threw them into the fire. 'Your mother was no housekeeper, was she?'

'Mum got tired,' Belinda said.

Charm checked her over. 'You're like her, aren't you? One of those dark little things that watch you from behind your back. You don't look much like Grant and Janice. I wonder where your mother found you? You'll get your periods in a year or so. Then you'll need to look out for yourself. Won't you, eh?'

'I guess so.' Belinda followed Charm back into the house, hoping she might yet protect her mother's belongings. But Charm was taking every single thing her mother had ever owned out of a chest of drawers and from the wardrobe: a silky though well-worn dressing gown that had lost its belt years ago, a rope of fake pearls, a handbag, a home-made floral print dress, panties with stretched elastic. Charm picked them up by her fingertips, dumping them in a large hemp sack, preparing to take them to the incinerator, which was burning fiercely with its last consignment of jackets and blouses. She emptied out the make-up drawer, with its shreds of powder and vanishing cream, and threw a tube of red lipstick after them, having tried a little on her own long lips and grimacing.

'It's probably got germs. We used to live a couple of doors along from you, me and my husband. Well, he's dead now — fell down the stairs and knocked his head. He wasn't much loss, never did an honest day's work. I collected his insurance money, so that was useful, not that it was enough to cover the mortgage. Your dad was a great help, getting it all sorted out, selling the house. Your mother never made the effort. Well, she was usually pregnant. You were a real screamer as a baby. Thank God I never had kids.'

Charm had come upon a pile of books. She snorted. 'That was Irene, always had her nose in a book. Thought she was better than the rest of us.'

'Could I keep some of those?' Belinda asked. She held a worn copy of *The Grapes of Wrath* to her chest.

'What would you do with them? You'll get enough books at school and, besides, your Aunt Agnes won't have room for them all.'

'Are we going to live with Aunt Agnes?'

'Your father can't look after you lot. Come on, help me take this stuff to the incinerator.' She picked up a pile of novels and a slim book of poems. 'Trash, if you ask me,' she said.

The books followed the clothes unceremoniously into the bag. Lots of Steinbeck. Out. *War and Peace.* Out. *Check to Your King.* A worn copy, well loved. Charm turned it over, wrinkling her nose with distaste. 'Robin Hyde. That stupid girl who killed herself,' she muttered, as if to herself. Out, too.

'You'd better start packing,' she said. 'I told you, you're off to Masterton to live.'

It was news to Belinda that she and Grant and Janice were to be sent away. 'I beg your pardon?' she said.

'Don't beg, you can always sell matches,' Charm said. This was one of the innumerable smug sayings that Charm would trot out over the years Belinda knew her. In the kitchen, her father's sister Agnes was rattling pots and pans, preparing the next meal. People from along the street had brought covered casserole dishes, even though none of them knew the Pawsons all that well. An Italian neighbour from one of the fishing families had brought a large pot of hot pasta swimming in creamy sauce, dotted with mussels. She was dressed in black, her face respectful and sad. The food had been accepted with nods and what passed for smiles from Aunt Agnes, while Charm grimaced behind her back. The pot had since been placed under the sink, covered over with a tea towel. 'We'll decide what to do with that later,' Agnes said. She had put potatoes on the stove to boil.

Belinda didn't dislike her aunt, but was a little afraid of her. Like Charm, she was a widow, although a much older one. She shaved her upper lip when she remembered, and when she didn't a dark shadow appeared, just like a man. Her Scots accent had never left her, although she and her brother Jock Pawson had lived in New Zealand more than forty years. She lived alone in a large house in a small town 'up the line', as she liked to call it.

Outside in the narrow garden, smoke was curling and spreading between the houses. The afternoon was drawing in. Charm stirred embers in the incinerator, bringing the fire back to life as she hurled Irene's books into the rising flames. Belinda couldn't understand why everything that remained of her mother must go, and it shocked her that she was so powerless to stop it happening. In the flames, she imagined she saw her mother's face, pale, intense, pleading, as though asking to be saved, to keep something of her alive. She saw scraps of paper that carried her older sister Jessie's handwriting. Charm was still going on about Jessie.

'She couldn't even come when her mother needed her. I hear she's condescended to come to Wellington and grace us with her presence for the funeral. I've packed all her stuff up. Her suitcase is in the passage waiting for her.'

Agnes was calling from the house that dinner was ready. And, in that moment, when Charm was distracted by the leaping flames, Belinda remembered that there was something of her mother's that Charm hadn't yet discovered. In the drawer of her sewing machine table a box of buttons was stowed, a random collection pulled from discarded clothing. Some must have come from a much earlier time in Irene's life, for among black fly buttons from Jock's trousers, and navy ones from his shirts, there were glass buttons that sparkled, pearl ones that might have come from gloves, red, blue and silver buttons, a big copper button and a large hand-made one covered with tiny strips of black woven leather with threads hanging from it. It had a strange rough texture as if it had been left on a stove. Belinda's mother used to let her count the buttons and make patterns on the floor with them, in the days when she still sat and sewed for them all as best she could. Once, though, she leaned over and plucked the leather button from the floor and put it back in the tin. 'Not that one,' she said.

Belinda raced off into the house, without a word of explanation to Charm. She darted up the passageway, past the sitting room where her father, Jock, had sat slumped for days. It was odd to see him huddled in a frayed old jersey and grubby pants. He worked in an office in town, and most days he wore a crumpled suit and a tie. He hated the unions but, right now, he could see the point. At least he knew his rights when it came to a death in the family. He was stirring himself in response to his sister's call from the kitchen to 'hurry and eat while the food was hot'.

Belinda kept going. She slid her hand into the drawer and there it was, the tobacco tin box, stamped 'Riverhead Gold'. She plucked it out, slipping it in her cardigan pocket. As she walked, as smoothly as she could so the box didn't rattle, she saw Charm coming towards her. For an instant she panicked, a scene unfolding before her eyes, the woman trying to take the tin from her, her kicking her in the shins or biting her.

But Charm had entered the sitting room. Her father had

risen from the chair and now stood leaning his head on his arm against the mantelpiece. Charm's hand was resting on his, implying there were some intimacy of sorrow that excluded others. The two of them turned as Belinda stood hovering, uncertain of what to do, to explain why she had been walking along the hall of the house she had lived in since she was born. She had the weird feeling that she was a stranger in it now.

There was a distraction in the doorway. Jessie had arrived. Belinda thought, fleetingly, that she and the other children might be saved.

Jessie was nearly eight years older than Belinda, a tall angular girl who, in better times, Aunt Agnes had tried to liken to Jock Pawson, as if she might really be his daughter. Likenesses, that's what these older women talked about, always searching for clues and genealogies, ropes of generations that would bind them to the present and a future they would never see. When she was grown and long gone from this house of sorrow by the sea, Belinda would think back to those conversations in which everyone was likened to every other person they might or might not be related to, and wonder.

The kitchen was full of insults and shouting between Jessie and the older women as the evening wore on. Grant and Janice had been sent to bed. Grant didn't want to sleep in the same room as his sister, Janice, but his father said, 'You'll get a thick ear if there's any more of that.' These two did resemble Jock, no doubt about that, gingery brown hair and fair skinned, freckled at this stage, which Aunt Agnes said was just like their father when he was a child. Belinda knew Grant's shameful secret, the reason he didn't want to sleep in the same room as Janice. He wet his bed more nights than not, especially when his dreams were bad. She knew because, since her mother had fallen ill, it was she who washed his sheets and hid this from his father. Both the little ones had secrets that only she and her mother knew.

Janice was seven and still couldn't recognise the words in her *Janet and John* reader. 'Look, Janice,' Belinda would say, 'Janet is jumping. See that word "jump"? Can you say the letters for me? "J", it's a big letter, the same as you put at the beginning of your name.' But Janice would look at her with a dumb-mutt expression that made Belinda want to shake her. What was the point, she asked herself, when Janice still couldn't spell her own name anyway?

Charm produced a bottle of sherry. 'You need strength for tomorrow,' she said, even though Agnes was disapproving.

The insults were directed at Jessie who, when she had left earlier in the year, had gone to work in a café up North in Rotorua. 'Or so she says,' Charm reiterated, and Agnes nodded in agreement.

Agnes added that it had been the day after Jessie's birthday and, to think, Irene had talked her brother into taking them all out to dinner, and paying, the night before.

'I gave her a present,' Agnes said. 'You remember, Jessie, I gave you my special Milford Sound teaspoon from my collection. I found it in your room when I was packing up your stuff. A lot she cares about that, was what I thought. I've taken it back.'

Charm said, 'Jock, you should say something. Don't just sit there and let this girl take over.'

In fact, Jessie had sat without saying a word up until this point. 'I don't know who you are,' she said now, 'but I don't think it's any of your business.'

'There, you see what I mean? And a university girl, too, only you threw that all away, didn't you?'

'Yes, yes, I suppose I did,' Jessie said. Her face was set in harsh lines, as if she were much older.

'Your name's been in the papers,' Jock said. 'The police are looking for you. A good thing your mother never knew.'

Belinda was piecing together, as much as she could, what had happened. There had been a boating accident on a lake up North. The people who had died or disappeared were people from the café. Jessie had been with them on the night of the accident. There had been a quarrel in the café and the victims of this tragedy had taken to the boat when the weather was rough. Instead of waiting to be interviewed by the police, Jessie had left town straight away. It was nothing she had done, just evidence she might possess, perhaps a witness to what had occurred.

'That's what you do,' Jock said. 'You just leave when it suits you.'

'I thought I was supposed to come home,' Jessie said. 'Wasn't that the idea? My mother is dead.'

Jessie walked out of the kitchen to the bedroom, shutting the door behind her. The adults looked around at one another and shrugged their shoulders. Charm was putting on her coat, readying herself to go along the Parade and catch a trolley bus home to what she called 'her digs' in Wellington. Jock said he would walk with her. A woman wasn't safe on the streets these nights.

'Time you were in bed,' Agnes said to Belinda. 'Go on, off you go.'

Belinda had never shared a bedroom with Jessie before, but now that Aunt Agnes was staying over, a mattress had been brought up from the basement.

Jessie was sitting on the edge of the bed, her shoulders hunched over.

'Just tell me what happened, Belinda,' she said, her voice thick with suppressed tears. 'You're the oldest. What happened to Mum?'

'She was in the hospital. I was only allowed to go once,'

Belinda said. 'Dad took us on the bus to Newtown.'

Belinda wanted to tell Jessie about the dark tunnels of the corridors, the floors that squeaked, and the wards where the beds seemed jammed together. It had been hard to find where her mother lay. The way Grant had frowned up at the signs, reading them as he went.

'Why is there a Clean Linen Bay,' he asked Belinda, 'when there isn't any water?'

That was Grant for you, he took things so literally. Where they lived was called Island Bay, and there was Houghton Bay along the road, and Lyall Bay beyond that, and here was Grant finding another one in the hospital corridor, as though their mother might be lying on a curling wave washing her into shore.

Belinda had imagined that her mother would be lying in a bed just like hers at home, but when they found their way to the right cubicle, it was an iron-framed bed, covered with a starched white sheet. Her body so shrunken it hardly made a dent beneath, her lank hair sticking to the pillow. And her mother could no longer speak her name, her mouth struggling to form words but no sound coming out.

'Did she ask for me?'

Belinda shook her head. It was impossible to explain.

Jessie turned out the light, even though Belinda hadn't undressed, and Belinda sensed that she had lain down with her back to her. In the dark, she thought she heard Jessie sob, though she couldn't be sure. Jessie never cried.

'Were they your best friends, Jessie? The people in the boat?'

Jessie made a muffled noise.

Belinda said, 'Jessie, can you stay with us?'

There was a silence in the dark room.

'Shut up and go to sleep,' Jessie said.

On the way to the bus stop, Charm stopped at a lamppost, as if to do up her shoelace under the light. As she straightened up, she ran her hand up Jock's leg, until she touched his crotch.

'I think you've been missing something, Jock.'

'Not here, not in the street,' he said, his voice thick.

'I can't see Agnes caring for all those children. Can you, Jock?'

A wind came off the sea the morning of the funeral. Summer hadn't hit the city yet. Jock had ordered taxis for them. He didn't believe in owning cars, not when he could ride a bike to and from work. He told his son to count his pennies under the pillow at nights, so that he would always know how much pocket money he had, and how much of it to save.

First there was a service at St Hilda's on the Parade.

'Anglican,' Aunt Agnes said. 'If we must.'

'What was I to do?' Jock said. 'She never took to being Presbyterian.'

'I suppose I can't hold it against her. I mean, how long is it since you were inside a church, brother? I can tell you, the children will be going to Sunday school when I get my hands on them. And none of this fancy stuff.'

Not that it was fancy at all. The vicar hadn't known Irene. Grant and Janice didn't know what to do, whether to sit or stand, and Belinda wasn't too sure either, although she could follow the service. Charm was sniffling into a handkerchief. She was dressed in a black woollen coat and a green felt hat with a crimson feather like a streak of blood running down its side. When the children looked about to bawl, she grabbed their hands and stood in a proprietary way as if they were really hers. The vicar delivered some short, crisp comments about the love of mothers for their children and how they were sometimes required to answer to God's higher calling. The twenty-third psalm was delivered, a prayer said. The vicar called on Jock to say a few words if he wished. He shook his head.

Jessie moved towards the front of the church. Jock went to grab her arm, but Jessie pulled away from him. She looked around the small group of Brighton Street neighbours who made up the congregation. Instead of speaking, she walked out.

*Walking out, that's what she does.* Belinda heard the words buzzing in her head. When they got outside, Jessie was nowhere to be seen. Charm had let go of the children. Janice, the baby of the family, came over and put her head against Belinda's waist. She was a tubby little creature, her face tear-stained and frightened. Someone had put a pink bow in her wiry curls; the Fair Isle cardigan that Irene had knitted was buttoned up over her chest. The sleeves were getting short. Belinda put her arm around her. I am eleven, she thought. I need to look after the children. The idea terrified her. No wonder Jessie had run off. Grant stumped along behind them, his face screwed up as tight as a bag of walnuts so that you could hardly see his eyes. His hair was combed into a cow-lick.

When they got to the graveside, among the narrow paths of the Karori cemetery, Jessie was there already, her face still set in its rigid expression. Her mother's favourite child. Belinda knew this in her heart. But now, Jessie had been joined by an elderly couple, the man bent over almost double, supporting himself on a walking stick. They were helped by a younger man. Belinda didn't recognise them, but the woman was holding Jessie's hand and weeping.

The family trooped in silence towards the grave, a shaft of space cut out of the earth, the neighbours acting as pallbearers for Irene's pine coffin. It was lowered down and down and down, into the clay soil, the wreath Jessie had ordered, without consulting anyone, of sweet peas and late poppies slipping out of sight. Belinda's mother disappearing for good, not just her clothes and books and poems that she read out loud to her, but all of her. The flames of the fire Charm had made in the garden leapt in front of her again, but this time she couldn't see her mother's face at all. It was gone. There was just a hole in the ground with a pile of damp earth beside it. A weak sun appeared. The children were instructed to walk around the open grave and throw clods of earth down onto the coffin, to be part of this erasing of her mother. Jessie hesitated before moving to join them. Janice and Grant began to wail, Grant in spite of himself and his determination to act like a big boy.

'My hands are dirty,' he said, trying to brush the earth from his clothes.

Aunt Agnes grabbed him firmly by the arm. Jock took a handkerchief out of his pocket and passed it over to him.

And then, a surprising thing happened. As the grave digger began to rain down more spadefuls of earth onto the coffin, Jessie took Belinda by the hand. It was just for a moment and when Belinda raised her eyes she couldn't decide whether Jessie was offering comfort or needed it herself. She looked back to where Jessie had stood with the old people, and they had gone. Jessie offered no explanation as to their presence.

The wake was held in the sitting room in Brighton Street. Charm and Aunt Agnes had arranged for some sausage rolls and sandwiches to be brought in. Charm had ordered beer to be delivered as well, plus a couple more bottles of sherry, although Aunt Agnes said it was not a habit she wanted to be getting into but she supposed they had a duty to the neighbours who had helped out. While they were all nibbling and sipping in the front room, a young man appeared at the door. His mother was wondering if they wouldn't mind if he picked up her big pot as she was making dinner for the family. Charm and Agnes exchanged frozen looks. The young man was wearing a black waistcoat over a white shirt, as if out of respect for visiting a house bereaved. But the shirt was open at the throat, revealing a gold chain quivering among curly black hair. His complexion was olive, and muscles bulged beneath the soft fabric of his garment.

'Antonio!' Jessie exclaimed.

He looked at her, his face intent. 'Jessie Sandle,' he said, 'Jessie, all grown-up.'

'That's enough,' Jock said.

'We haven't had time to clean the pot,' Agnes said, all politeness. 'Do you mind if one of the children drops it over, perhaps in an hour?'

'I'll bring it back in a few minutes,' said Jessie.

When the door was closed, she glared at Agnes and Charm and said, 'You didn't have the guts to tell them you hadn't eaten their pasta, did you? God, you're a bunch of plebeians.'

Agnes said, 'I think she means she's cleverer than the rest of us. She'll learn.'

'I told you, Jock, that girl needs a few good slaps,' Charm said. 'Eyeties. Catholics. I'll bet they need a big pot.'

'There's ten of them, or thereabouts,' Agnes said.

'That's Catholics for you,' Charm said, only she pronounced it 'Cartholics', as if it were some kind of joke. 'They're putting Jack Kennedy away today, too. There's another one.'

Jessie could be heard tearing up newspaper, and running taps, disposing of the food, cleaning the pot.

'We're lucky we're not at war with Russia,' Agnes said darkly. 'Goodness knows what would have happened next time if someone hadn't shot him dead. Some things are meant for the best.'

The neighbours were beginning to drift away, unsettled by the appearance of the Italian boy and this loose talk. Some of them worked for the boy's family, setting out on the fishing boats with them in the early hours of each morning.

Charm began brushing her coat, which lay over the back of one of the chairs. 'I got dirt on it at the cemetery. It should be dry now.'

'Clay,' said Agnes. 'It sticks like the devil.'

Jock roused himself, as if he had been sleepwalking all day. 'They made clay corpses in the auld country,' he said.

'Jock,' Agnes said, in a warning older sister's voice.

'It's true, I saw it once when I was a lad. It was what witches did.' The room had fallen silent. Jock's voice was slurring with the beer. 'It was done to get revenge on those who did you harm. You made a figure of the man or woman you didnae like out of clay, and placed it in a stream where the water would run over it. The water wore it away as though it were the flesh of the person you wished gone.'

'Witchcraft,' Agnes said. 'People went to court for things like that.'

'Ah yes,' said Jock, 'if they found out. Otherwise they'd like as not get sick and waste away.'

'Like Irene,' said Charm.

Jock looked at Charm with heavy eyes.

'You've got me wrong, I wouldnae do that to the lass.'

Belinda sat very still, in case anyone in the room noticed she was still there. The kitchen had fallen quiet. There was the soft click of the front door being closed as Jessie let herself out.

In the morning Jessie took the children on an outing. There was a soft indefinable expression in her eyes. She had come in very late the night before. Belinda half woke when she heard her sister come in, but she was too sleepy to see what time it was.

Jessie had been humming under her breath.

'That's kind of you,' Agnes said, surprised. She was ashen-faced with exhaustion. The children's shrill voices in the sitting room next door all but drowned out their conversation. The two younger children had always been noisy, the sort who people hushed in public. They were beginning to return to their everyday selves.

'You had a lot to do last night,' Jessie said, 'clearing up and all.'

'No thanks to someone I could spit on from here,' Charm said. She was smoking a cigarette, her hand clasped around a tea cup. She looked at ease, almost as if the kitchen belonged to her.

'Well …' Jessie began.

'What's the use of a well if you don't have water?' Charm said, cutting past her.

'Well,' continued Jessie, as though she hadn't heard Charm, 'I thought if I took the children out for the day it would give you a break. We could go to the zoo.'

Agnes heaved a sigh of relief. 'We thought about sending them back to school today, but their father reckoned that wouldn't look right. Mind you, he headed off first thing, but then someone has to provide. I'll give you money for the tickets.'

'I have some,' Jessie said. 'It's all right. I'll look after them.'

That was how the day passed, walking from cage to cage, feeding the ducks, gazing at the elephant. They bought lunch from the kiosk, sandwiches and meat pies, and sat on a wooden seat watching the monkey enclosure. Baby animals wound themselves around their mothers' backs and necks, absurd little grins on their faces as the parent creatures swung through the branches.

'Kids, I'm leaving tomorrow,' Jessie said. 'I'm going away.'

Belinda's heart clenched itself into a fist in her chest. She should have known. She didn't ask where Jessie was going.

When Belinda tried to tell her father, Jock Pawson, about the way their stepmother treated them, he simply shrugged. They'd been talking rubbish at school, kids always said their stepmothers were monsters. They had food on the table and clean clothes, didn't they?

Jock led a different kind of life with Charm from the one he'd had with Irene. The house was as neat as a pin, as Charm often pointed out, and dinner was on the table every night at six. As soon as Jock arrived home she opened a flagon of sherry. We deserve some treats at the end of a day's toil, she would say. Jock sat there, his tie askew over his paunch, looking as if heaven had hit him in the face. There would be a period of animation as Charm warbled and sometimes whistled, then a slide into melancholy between her and Jock, and it would be time for bed for everyone in the house.

Belinda tried showing her father the rope burns on Grant's wrists where Charm had tied him to a chair because of the wet sheets, and bruises on Janice's arms where she'd been smacked for not doing her homework.

'You kids knock around with the wrong sort,' he said. 'You want to get decent friends, bring them over.'

There wasn't much to show for hair pulling, or getting your nose twisted, but there was all of that, too. Janice got head lice and Charm shaved her head and put kerosene on it. When Janice screamed and tried to get away, Charm lit a match and threatened to hold it on Janice's chemical-smelling head. None of them got school lunches if they answered her back. You couldn't always tell when you were answering back anyway. Just the way you said please and thank you was enough to set her off some days. *Please*. Pleased with yourself, are you? Whack. *Thank you*. Thank you for what? Calling you a liar? I'll get the belt to you. Janice's face was a mask these days. Grant started setting the clock and getting up every hour through the night so his sheets would be dry. There were big circles under his eyes. Belinda often thought about Jessie and the way she just left; most days she hated her.

On a summer day when the holidays seemed interminable, because at least when there was school there was somewhere to go, the three of them sat on the sea wall, staring out at the ocean. Sometimes Antonio came along the beach and he always seemed to have toffees in his pocket. He'd come over and offer to share them. Don't tell Charm, Belinda would warn the children.

Charm went to town that day and left Belinda in charge. Belinda was thirteen by then, and trying to hide from Charm that she had her periods, but she knew that her stepmother had guessed. *You can take that insolent look off your face. You might think you're grown-up but you're not. You can put your donkey saddles in a bucket in the wash house, but don't think I'll be cleaning up behind you.* She had said it that morning and Belinda wanted to vanish through a hole in the floor. Her stomach was hurting right now.

'I wish she was dead,' Grant said. 'We could just sneak up and kill her when nobody was looking.'

Janice drummed her heels on the wall. 'We could all hold her down and smash her head in,' she said.

'Well, we can't,' Belinda said. But, remembering what she had wished only that morning, she said, 'We could make her disappear.'

She explained about the clay corpse, how if they made an effigy of Charm they could take her to the beach and let her wash away, and soon she would die. It was like a lucky charm. They all giggled at that. Lucky charm, lucky charm, they chanted.

Irene's rose bush was in flower, with a burst of unlikely blooms on a plant given up for dead. Belinda thought it was called 'Peace', and the showy creamy flowers flushed with pink made her want to laugh, as if things were suddenly on their side.

They dug with furious haste, filling the laundry bucket as fast as they could and taking it to the beach each time it was full. Belinda organised them into a chain, so that one was always digging, taking it in turns to run to the beach and tip the clay at the water's edge. When she thought they had enough, they all went to the beach and began shaping their corpse. Hurry, Belinda told the children, she'll be back soon. Besides, soon the tide would turn. If they were to dispose of Charm today they needed to be quick.

'It's like plasticine,' Janice said, as they kneaded the sticky stuff into shape on the wet sand.

Belinda had a sudden thought. 'Wait,' she said, 'I'm going back to the house.'

Grant and Janice jumped up and down. Hurry, it was their turn to shout. But Belinda knew what she was after, it had to be right.

She reappeared in a few minutes, carrying a brown paper bag. 'Just wait and see,' she said. 'It'll be perfect.'

A loose shape was the best they could achieve, just a head that kept floating away because Belinda said they needed to make sure the water got to Charm's brain first, then a mound of clay for her body, two wriggly lines where her arms were supposed to go, and then a wave would come before they could put feet on her legs and they ran away, splashing and shouting with laughter. Happiness, the three of them together, bent over with mirth, the first time they could remember since their mother got sick.

And then Belinda produced her master stroke from the paper bag, some buttons from one of Jock's old overcoats, to plant in a row on the corpse's chest. (Belinda had saved the special leather one.) Finally she placed Charm's green hat with the red feather on its head. The three of them danced, holding hands, shrieking into a rising breeze. A wave came and flicked the hat away almost as soon as they had put it on, dragging the clay beneath it out to sea. As they stood back, the waves rushed in and overtook the whole effigy and Charm seemed to dissolve before their eyes.

Belinda looked back to the sea wall. Charm was standing there, in a red dress, a cardigan pulled over her low-slung breasts. There was no knowing how long she had been there.

But she had seen. Belinda knew that she knew.

# 3

# Blue Monday

# 1970

The wind tore the sea apart at the entrance to the Campbell Island harbour, turning it into wild loops of spume that spun across its surface. Young sea lions played in the kelp at the water's edge while huge dark birds wheeled overhead. Seth Anderson loved the giant petrels. His blood soared when he looked skywards and saw them lifting their wings, their feathered capes. Some of the men called them stinkers, as if they couldn't see the beauty of their flight, nor understand the tenderness with which they raised their young for months at a time. He watched when they laid their annual egg, just a single one, in a nest made of moss on bare ground.

It was several months since he'd come south to Campbell Island to work at the meteorological station. There were eight men on this remote outpost, hundreds of kilometres to the south of New Zealand. Their job was to measure the temperature of the upper air, its pressure and humidity, and report back to New Zealand by radio telephone. As well, they would make scientific observations of one kind or another about the environment. On the whole, the men were mates, although there were days when the weather got to them. At twenty-three, he was the youngest, and it had taken him a while to get to know the men.

Some had wives and children at home; they'd come away for a year for the money, not the adventure. They saw him as a kid, the clever brat who'd been foisted on them. His degree was in science. He'd done honours in physics and passed with distinction. When he went back to the mainland he would do a Master's.

That didn't make him practical, they said, and set traps for him, some of them small and silly. On one of the first nights, after they had moved into their timber huts at Beeman Cove on the island, they played a pointless game. The married men started counting the handkerchiefs their wives had put in their bags when they were making up their clothing kits. For those who'd been before, it was a standing joke — whose wife loved him the most. One guy called Mike had twenty and was declared the winner.

'How many handkerchiefs have you got, Snot?' he asked Seth, who had been silent during the exercise.

Seth did a mental calculation about what was expected of him. Half a dozen, he told them and the older men jeered.

'You can use the back of your sleeve when you run out,' Mike said. 'You got a girlfriend?'

Seth hesitated. 'Not really,' he said.

'Go on,' Mike said. 'You have. What's her name?'

'No, I don't. Honest.' He didn't want to tell them that he liked quite a few girls, but he hadn't picked any of them as special. Not yet. Most of these girls wore skirts that reached just beneath their bums, and pale make-up with heavy black eyeliner and lashes like a flock of mosquitoes. They twisted their little bodies before him, knew all the words to 'Come and Get It' and sang them at parties. All the parties.

And yet they were so clever, as dewy as freshly cut melons when they turned up for lectures, regarding exams as mere exercises that interrupted their real lives. He'd slept with several, and that was part of the problem. He didn't think they should have let him — not if he was going to settle down with any of them. It wasn't right that they were easy. He couldn't visualise taking any of them home to meet his mother.

There was a young one who seemed different. She wasn't a university girl; he would see her at old-fashioned dances in the local hall at Masterton when he was home on vacation. He'd met her a few times, a girl with pale skin and dark hair, a little soft around the chin but she had big brave eyes. She was about seventeen, perhaps, although he didn't get round to asking how old she was.

'Save the supper waltz for me,' he'd murmur against her ear when he arrived. She had an odd way of looking as if she had been expecting him, and she always seemed ravenous.

'Keep the last dance for me,' he'd say, before they both moved off to find other partners. But as often as not, she sat the next dances out until it was time to go home. Seth would take her in his mother's car to park up along near the public gardens, his fingers slipping into the top of her stockings and gently letting her suspenders go. When he touched her she would dissolve into a helpless needy creature. No, she would say, and no again, until one night she gave in.

At a certain junction in the street she would ask him to stop the car and let her out, so that he never knew where she lived. All he knew for certain was that she worked in a plant nursery and was applying to go to teachers' training college next year. She had had good marks in English, she told him with a certain shy pride.

At Beeman Cove, in the long nights ahead, as the elements battered the huts, Seth often found her pale face swimming before him, her body's hungry desire, her urgency, the bright, slightly startled expression in her dark eyes when she saw him across the dance hall.

He left without telling any of the girls he was seeing that he was off south. His mother cried about him leaving and said it was all very well having daughters, but he was her only boy and that he had to take care of himself. In fact, she had put twenty-five handkerchiefs into the kit she was making up for him to take south.

When eight months had passed since the men were put ashore at Beeman Cove the supply ship came and went. Some of the men eyed its departure in a covetous way, as if longing to be on it. It won't be long now, they said to each other, glad for fresh food but yearning for meat of another kind, as they put it. Jacking off was all very well, but it wasn't the real thing.

Seth was ready to leave, but he was determined not to show it. His father had told him before he left that where he was going was a job for hard bastards, and did he think he was up to it? Being a man, that was important to his father. He took Seth pig hunting in the ranges, and bivouacked in the snow, taught him how to build a camp fire — better than any boy scout, he boasted. When Seth looked in the mirror, he saw a man not unlike his father, just younger, with a thatch of fair straight hair and light blue eyes. There was Scandinavian heritage not far back. His father earned his living putting roofs on houses; he had a head for heights, could carry big weights, hammer nails straight. He was used to hard work, another of his proud claims. When Seth took up hockey, not rugby, his father sighed and rubbed his chin. That boy is full of surprises, he told his wife. He was pleased when he heard Seth was going south.

After the ship left, Seth decided to walk across the cliff tops to see how the baby petrels were doing. There was a hen that had injured her wing. He'd taken to going most days, carrying food scraps to where she was nesting with her chick. He had to advance carefully, in order, as best he could, not to frighten the other birds. At first, the mother of the chick tried to fly at him, but the bad wing failed her. It surprised him that she had survived for as long as she had. The other birds' mates appeared to bring them food. He found himself worrying that the mother would be abandoned by her mate, the chick left to die. After he had been there a few times, the bird seemed to accept his presence. In an odd sort of way, she reminded him of the girl. He smiled to himself: his 'bird'. Kneeling near the nest, he placed the food down, and walked away so he could watch her stretch her neck, peck and gather it towards her.

He wondered if this is what hard bastards should be doing, going out feeding scraps of meat from the mess to a bird, and feeling sentimental about them. As he straightened, pain stabbed him in the abdomen. Cramp and the cold, he decided.

Back at the huts, there was mail, an accumulation of real letters from home. His mother had written to him every week: about flower shows in Masterton, coffee mornings she had gone to with her friends, books she had read (she took six books from the library every fortnight, unlike his father, who read little more than the newspaper), what his sisters were doing. They were younger than him. The older girl, Emma, had gone to Auckland for her first year at university, and Rebecca, a late baby, was still at school. He was struck by sudden inexplicable longing when he saw other men around him reading their letters, taken out of envelopes that had kisses on the back of them, or spilled pictures drawn by children.

Mike looked up. 'No letter from your girlfriend, mate?'

'I haven't got one. I told you.' Seth's voice was more terse than he intended.

'I reckon you have, Snot.'

'We're not going steady.'

'Ah ha, so there is one. What happened? Did she ditch you before you went away? C'mon, what's her name?'

'Belinda,' he blurted, before he could stop himself. 'Her name's Belinda.'

Mike lowered the letter he was reading. 'Okay, now we're getting somewhere. Tell me more about this Belinda.'

'Nothing much to tell.' Seth was furious with himself.

'What's her second name?'

Seth looked at him with a feeling of loathing. 'That's my business,' he said. He had no idea what Belinda's second name was.

In the night, he woke with the pain like a giant wound in his right side. He lay clutching his stomach, trying not to groan, until his room mate got up and called in the head officer on the station.

Appendicitis, the officer reckoned. Just as well the supply ship was still in range. With luck, and some calm weather, they could get Seth out of here in the morning. With even more luck, he'd last long enough to get to a doctor in time.

Belinda was living in a farmhouse with a huge kitchen bordered by long wooden benches. The floor was polished linoleum. The men who milked the cows on the farm came in after early morning milking and ate enormous breakfasts of fried bacon and eggs, usually with a steak thrown in, and mountains of toast washed down with tea. The teapot was so large and heavy Belinda could hardly lift it when it was full, or not when she first arrived, although she had become used to it. The men took off their gumboots when they came into the kitchen, padding around in thick woollen socks that bulged where they had been darned and redarned. They had large chafed hands. For the most part, they didn't look at Belinda, although the youngest, a farm cadet not much older than her, stole sideways glances now and then. The older men were brothers, who had farmed together since they were young. They talked to each other in low voices, occasionally interrupted by bursts of mirth. When they addressed Belinda it was in a series of grunts. This house belonged to the oldest brother and his wife.

One of Belinda's jobs was to clean up after the meal, before scrubbing the benches and the floor. The smell of bacon fat and egg yolk still made her feel sick. When that work was done she would cut up beef and onions, in readiness for the farmer's wife to make stew for the evening meal. Her name was Marie, a small woman with tightly permed hair, and cool blue-grey eyes. Belinda had imagined that a farmer's wife would be buxom and cheerful, not this quick sharp creature. She moved deftly in the kitchen, preparing food and organising the household, but she didn't do cleaning. Belinda soon understood that she was one of a long line of girls in predicaments like hers who had worked on this farm. Every Friday, Marie went shopping in Palmerston North, usually bringing back a new dress or skirt, or shoes, once a pair of golfing shoes. Her golf handicap, and her breasts which were still pert, gave her great satisfaction.

'You'll get your figure back eventually,' she said. 'It takes time, although I always kept myself fit when I was carrying. You spend too much time moping around. If you're wondering who the father is, you've left it a bit late for that, my girl.'

She had tried to extract the information from Belinda several times, usually when she was inspecting the benches with a critical eye and declaring them not clean enough.

'Look, can't you see the blood stains there in the cracks? We'll all get food poisoning if you're not careful.' It was the same when Belinda was making a bed. 'Didn't anybody ever teach you how to make a bed properly?' she would ask. 'You fit the corner under the mattress, just so. You do know it would help the social worker place this baby of yours in a better home if you came clean? People don't want just any old pig in a poke.'

Belinda had looked away.

'It wasn't your father? Something like that?'

'I haven't seen my father in years,' Belinda said, sullen, on her hands and knees scrubbing the red and brown squared linoleum.

'There's nothing wrong with sex,' Marie remarked one morning. 'I mean, it's a changing world, isn't it? Bruce and I have our little flings on the side, things we wouldn't have thought of ten years ago.' She was smoking a cigarette, watching Belinda out of the corner of her eye. 'I've had a bit of fun in my time, I can tell you. Does that shock you? Surely not? You're a girl of the times. You just got caught.'

'I don't care what you do,' Belinda said. It was the nearest she'd come to rebellion.

'Oh, very high and mighty,' Marie said. 'I reckon this guy was a darkie. One of the shearing gangs when they've come to town. You're going to have a tar baby, is that it?'

'He's white,' Belinda shouted. 'He goes to university.'

'Well, you don't say? Really?'

The silence thickened around them.

'You could say, Miss, that we're getting somewhere. So he dumped you?'

'He doesn't know.'

'Why ever not? A one-night stand, perhaps?'

'I don't know where he is,' Belinda said miserably.

'So *you* don't know who the father is?' the social worker asked Agnes Rattray. Agnes had put out her best fine china, the Shelley tea set given to her on the occasion of her long-ago marriage: she had been a widow for thirty years. Her white hair surrounded her face in short frizzy waves. She and the social worker sat opposite each other in chairs with curved wooden arms, the seats covered with moquette fabric that had seen better days. The woodwork in her sitting room wore dark varnish.

'I wouldn't have a clue. Don't think I didn't ask her,' Agnes said, her fingers fretting in her lap. 'I did try, you know. I'm her aunt, I took her in when she and her stepmother didn't get on. They said she was a wild girl, but I thought I could straighten her out. The neighbours said I was a saint taking her in. I thought, Well, I never had children, it wouldn't hurt me. Oh dear, I'm so ashamed.' Her voice faded into silence.

'It's not your fault, Mrs Rattray,' the social worker said. She had introduced herself as Kaye Borrell, a slim woman in late middle-age. Her bobbed hair was flecked with grey that matched the padded shoulders of her suit. A purple silk scarf was settled around her throat, as if to announce a soft side to her business-like approach. 'You'd be surprised how many girls from good families get into trouble.'

'I should have picked it sooner. I thought she had a problem with her weight — she was always a solid girl for her height. I gave her plenty of vegetables, no cakes, I thought she'd be better off without that stuff. I didn't notice.'

'You did a wonderful job, Mrs Rattray. Before long she'll be back and nobody any the wiser. You haven't told the neighbours?'

'Of course not. I don't look stupid, do I?' Agnes sat up straighter in her chair, holding her cup between two fingers. 'But I'm not having her back.'

'I see.'

'I mean, who's to say she won't start breeding like a rabbit

71

again?' Agnes's face contorted with disgust. 'She started getting airs and graces, you know. They made too much of her at school. She wanted to stay on until the seventh form, or whatever it is, but I said, "Look, I let you stay past turning fifteen. My family came out from Scotland where you were lucky to stay until you were twelve years of age, aye." You can have too much of a good thing. I'm a pensioner now, even if I do have my own little house. I said to her, "You need to get out there and work for a year, find out what the real world's all about."'

Spittle had begun to fly from the corners of Agnes's mouth.

'She let me down. I was only charging her ten dollars a week in board while she got a start at the plant place when they took her on. She'll be paying a lot more than that when she finds somewhere to live. I hope to God it won't be in this town. Can you let her know that?'

The social worker leaned forward, her manner confidential.

'I understand, Mrs Rattray. I shouldn't really be asking you this, but if you could just help me out with who the father might be, it would be a great help. People have preferences about the babies they choose. Little boys and girls with fair complexions are very much in demand.'

'Oh, who knows what colour it'll turn out. Her father's got red hair, and her brother and sister are a bit gingery.'

'Well, that's a help.' The social worker made a note. 'I might just have a match there.'

Agnes sighed, her face clouding over again, as if unconvinced by what she'd just said. 'It could be dark for all I know. She's turned out quite dark herself. Too much of her mother in her, that girl.'

'Something in the family?'

'No,' Agnes said, her voice faltering. 'No, of course not. Forget it. Belinda could have been with anyone, for all I know. Black, brown or yellow.'

'But she's told the lady where she stays that it was a boy of European descent who goes to university.'

'Has she now? Well, I don't know where she'd meet someone like that.'

'Someone at the plant nursery, perhaps? Working on vacation?'

'I can't tell you. I'm sorry. All I can say, plain and simple, I'm pleased to see the back of her.'

Miss Borrell sighed and put her notebook back in her satchel.

The couple Kaye Borrell had in mind were called Sheila and Monty.

'We've started going to church again,' Sheila told her, when she came to visit. 'You know, if we're going to adopt a baby we promise it'll be brought up right.'

It wasn't that they weren't God-fearing, but they'd slipped up a bit lately, just so much on at work, but Sheila would stay home if they had a baby. Sheila had been brought up Methodist, and Monty's family were Baptists. Sheila found the Baptists a bit hot on God, a bit much for her, although she did respect his family's values. They got married in her church all the same, because the couple's families both agreed it was respectful to acknowledge the slight differences in interpreting the Bible in favour of the bride. Sheila had worn a white dress with lace panels, and a veil over her face. She told the social worker all this in a great rush, as if they had written a list of their virtues in order to present their case.

Miss Borrell nodded, full of reassurance. 'I'm sure that won't be a problem,' she said, and smiled. 'I can see you're very respectable people.'

Sheila didn't add that she hadn't been a virgin: there was no point in advertising that, and it was her and Monty's business what they'd got up to before the wedding. She reckoned they'd got lucky because she hadn't fallen, like so many of her girlfriends. It was odd, the way you moved away from the girls who'd had babies. She felt she'd failed a test of friendship because it could just as easily have been her. Now it felt she and Monty had failed God, not worshipping after they got married. There was so much to do in those first years: their jobs, buying a section, getting their house built in one of the new subdivisions near Wellington. She liked that their address wasn't quite Lower Hutt, even though she went to school there. Wellington was just a better address.

They used contraception in those first years. Sheila wore a diaphragm when Monty was keen on having a bit, as he called it. How about we have a bit, old girl? he would say, and they'd start cuddling in the kitchen, and next thing they'd be in bed. The diaphragm was a rubber dome that she had to use with sticky jelly, and it always made her aware there was something *there*. It was a relief when they began trying for a baby and she didn't have to put the damn thing in any more.

The trouble was, nothing happened. She went on getting her periods every month, regular as clockwork, and all the headaches, and feeling sorry for herself. Her job was in a typing pool in the city. There were days when the clamour of all the typewriters going at once made her want to scream. The doctor said there wasn't a thing wrong with her, and they should just keep going. If she could relax and enjoy herself a bit more, it would be sure to happen. That didn't make sense to Sheila: there was nothing wrong with their sex life. Or not that she could tell, not having had much experience beyond Monty. One evening, Monty stood up and turned off the television, a firm look in his eye that meant they were going to have a serious conversation.

'We can't go on like this,' he said. 'You're upsetting yourself too much over this baby thing. We can do without kids if we have to.'

Sheila thought of her spotless house, the three bedrooms laid out in a perfect floor plan that would make it easy to reach the children at nights, the rumpus room that lay in wait for when they were older.

'The doctor said it might be you. You know, your sperm count or something.'

Monty gave a heavy sigh. 'I've had a test.'

'You did? Why didn't you tell me?'

'I'm telling you now. I'm fine.'

Sheila twisted her wedding band round on her finger. They had had it made to match with her engagement ring, a tiny crust of diamonds inset in the gold. She took both her rings off when she washed up in the evenings in order to keep them sparkling.

'It's been five years,' Monty said. 'Five years of banging on and nothing happening. Ten years since we got married. The doctor, well, he said the chances are getting less.'

'I know,' Sheila said. Her thirty-fourth birthday had been and gone. The camellia bushes they had planted when they built the house were sturdy shrubs that massed with bloom in early winter. 'Do you want a divorce? Is that what you're saying?'

Monty looked at her then as if she really were mental. 'Of course not. Dumb cluck. We can adopt. There're plenty of babies out there that need a home. I reckon we'd be sitters.'

Sheila felt her heart lifting. Her husband, with his red hair and fair skin that burned so easily in the sun, was excited. 'I never thought you would,' she said. 'Oh golly, I wonder if we can get a redhead?'

'It doesn't matter.'

'Boy or girl?'

'It's not important. Well, you know, it'd be nice to have a boy to kick a ball around with.'

So she could see then, that he had been hiding it all these years, how much he wanted a kid. He was a joiner with a building company, not always one to tell you what he was feeling. He worked long hours and lived in a man's world. But he had his little ways of showing that he cared about her, turning up with a bunch of flowers or a box of chocolates on a Friday, springing surprises for her birthday. Come to think of it, he treated her like a princess.

'We'll have to see the welfare people,' she said. 'Do you think they'll like us? Do you think we'll be good enough?'

He laughed, as if he could see every thought in her head, pulling her down close beside him on the sofa. 'Of course they'll like us, you're meant to be a mum.'

'I'll have to spring-clean. Monty, we should pray.'

After that, she had started making a list of things they had to offer: the house, a tick for that, income, yes, they had good jobs, saved money, they would have enough when she stopped working. She wasn't sure if they were well enough educated, but perhaps it didn't matter, so long as they took good care of this child, who was already taking shape and substance in her imagination. Well, there wouldn't be any problem about that.

'The mother's a clever girl,' the social worker told Sheila and Monty when she came around to check out the house.

'We're not clever,' Sheila said, all her doubts rushing to the fore. 'Well, you know, not *clever*, if you know what I mean.'

'She's a girl with a difficult background,' the social worker said carefully. 'But I'm sure you and this baby will be up to each other.'

She added that, of course, they could have a look at the baby before they made a decision, but she had reason to believe it would turn out a light-skinned child and might have had a well-educated father. The girl wasn't very forthcoming. She could have been with more than one boy, of course, so there were no guarantees, but Miss Borrell had them at the top of her list for this child. And apparently red hair ran in the girl's family — now wouldn't that be a nice surprise?

When they saw the baby, it was love at first sight, never mind that he didn't have red hair. It was Monty who picked the child up first, his face alight with joy.

'Hey, little guy,' he said. 'Are you ever coming home with me?' He handed the boy over to Sheila. 'Don't you reckon, old girl?'

Her hands trembled as she received the shawled bundle into her arms. Sheila didn't need to answer. She kissed the top of his head with its soft fontanelle, the smell of baby shampoo in the fair hair. Her face was radiant. 'When can we take him?' she asked.

'You could take him tomorrow if you like,' Miss Borrell said. 'We can get the paperwork done this afternoon. Can you come back then? The sooner the better, actually; the mother's a bit of a handful at the moment.'

They stayed in a motel for the night, so they didn't have to drive all the way home to Wellington again, and back the next day. Monty chose the nicest place he could see on the drive into town, one that had an extra big bed and fluffy white pillows stacked up high. Sheila said they should get takeaways, but Monty said that they should celebrate with a good dinner and wine. After all, this was the last night they would be able to go out without getting a baby-sitter. They looked at each other, amazed laughter bubbling up inside them.

Over dinner, they talked about names. Up until now they had avoided this, because there had been so many disappointments that it felt risky. Nothing fancy, they thought. A good strong name. He was a sturdy boy. 'Peter,' Monty said, his voice almost shy. 'Well, it's a saint's name.'

'It's perfect,' Sheila said. 'He looks like a Peter. You're clever, Monty, getting it right straight off like that.'

They made love in the big bed when they got back to the motel. In the morning, Monty kissed the tip of Sheila's nose.

'Wake up, Mummy,' he said.

Sheila held Peter close to her all the way home the next day. She couldn't believe how peaceful he was. It's as if he knows he's going home, she remarked to Monty.

'It's a boy,' Belinda heard someone say. They let her hold him for a few moments, then he was taken away so quickly she didn't really know what he looked like. She struggled to clear her brain, to retain the image of him, as though she could somehow stamp it on her retina and summon it up whenever she wanted, for the rest of her life. She didn't think he resembled her, or her own dead mother, or, thankfully, her father Jock Pawson; just a small complete person who was entirely himself, but beautiful, his skin unmarked, ivory pale, fuzzy tufts of fair hair covering his scalp. It seemed to her, thinking back, that he had stared at her, fierce, demanding, willing her to take care of him right there and then. But she had dozens of stitches to be inserted where he had torn his way into the world, and while that was done, her son was whisked away. For months she had talked to him, her small companion, kicking and squirming. She was sure it was a boy. At night, in her bed in the farmhouse, she had placed her hands around her belly and whispered to him. 'It'll be all right. You and me, we're in it together.'

It seemed to her now that parents lied to their children from the beginning, made them promises they could never keep. She had said to her unborn child that she would love him and care for him for her whole life. What on earth had possessed her to say that to him, and what would he make of it when he was grown-up? Because she knew he would remember, how could he not, the fierceness of her love? And then her abandonment of him.

They kept her in hospital for two weeks while the episiotomy healed. Two weeks in a long ward with ten beds, each with a new mother in it, their babies brought to them from the nursery at feeding times. The other mothers, who wore wedding rings, could go down and see their babies in the nursery. As she lay and cried silently behind the drawn curtains, one of the new mothers pushed her way through and sat down beside her. 'Why don't you come and look at your baby?'

'I'm not allowed.'

'They can't stop you. I saw your baby this morning. He's gorgeous.'

'You don't understand,' Belinda said.

'Well, I do, that's the thing. They thought I was going to lose my baby, but she's come through all right. It would have killed me to lose her.'

'Miss Borrell told me if I tried to go along there, they'd lock the doors. She said it would just make it worse if I saw him.'

'Do you believe that?'

'Yes, no. Please, just leave me alone.' She had rolled on her side, unable to control her sobs.

But the following morning, after a sleepless night, Belinda got out of the bed, pulled on her dressing gown and made her way to the corridor of the maternity wing. She took small painful steps, because her stitches were still sore and her vagina ached whenever she moved. At that moment, the matron appeared, almost as if she had been expecting this, and had been lying in wait.

'He's gone,' the matron said. 'He went first thing this morning, straight after his early feed.'

'You didn't tell me.'

'We didn't have to tell you. You had all of that explained to you. Now go back to bed, Belinda.' As if she were a child who had strayed from a classroom. She fainted in the corridor. That much she remembered.

She worked now in a toy shop in Palmerston North, where mothers came every day with toddlers in pushchairs, new babies strapped on their backs, or in front-packs. 'They like to feel their mother's heartbeat after they've come out,' one mother told her. 'They get lonely and scared if they don't feel you near them.' It was as stupid a job as she could possibly have taken, but it was all that was going in the town right then because students were on vacation and wanting work. Christmas wasn't far away and business was picking up so the shop was busy.

It was ten weeks since she had given birth to her son. Aunt Agnes had sent twenty dollars to cover her first week's rent. Her father, she wrote, would send another twenty the next time he got paid. It was money intended for Grant, a bright lad with a good future. With luck, Jock had written to Agnes, he could get the boy a cadetship in the public service after he'd been to university. He would do better than his sister; he'd always known she was no good. Charm had tried to tell him what a bad lot she was, but he'd given Belinda the benefit of the doubt. From now on he wanted nothing to do with her. She was on her own. Her brother and sister didn't want to see her again either.

Belinda wrapped up Barbie dolls. She demonstrated the way that Buzzy Bee toys with their brightly striped wooden bellies whirred their wings when pulled along by a string. Quite often she thought about dying, putting herself to death. There were several ways she could do this, but jumping off a cliff seemed the least complicated. Trouble was, there weren't many high cliffs in Palmerston North, a city that sat on rolling plains of grass. She started considering bridges. There were not many tall buildings in the town.

Late one afternoon, she stood behind the counter watching fat rain on the pavement outside. She would have to make a dash for it to the boarding house where she was living. Perhaps Julie Felix would be on the television in the lounge, although she would have to share her with other residents, an older woman, a man who was usually half-cut, and a couple of forestry workers. She liked Julie. She would follow her to San Francisco with flowers in her hair any day if she could. Earlier in the day, Marie had come into the shop with her daughter-in-law, up from Christchurch, in search of a teddy bear for her granddaughter. Belinda had glanced at pictures of children in the farmhouse sitting room. Marie had never spoken of her grandchildren, as though they and the photographs might be sullied by Belinda knowing of them.

'Hello,' Belinda had croaked. She was about to call her Marie but caught herself in time, and addressed her as Mrs Norman. Marie looked through her as if she'd never seen her. Belinda thought about dying again with a fresh sweet yearning. It wouldn't be long.

Then a young man entered the shop. At first she thought he was a new father, come to buy a soft toy for his baby. You could tell them, they were flushed and nervous and excited all at once. They wanted to tell you all about the birth and how the baby's eyes had followed them the moment it was born, its weight, all those things.

She took a second look and recognised him.

When Seth emerged back into the world things had changed. The better part of a year had passed since he left for Campbell Island. After his emergency operation, he went home to

Masterton to recuperate. First, though, on the day he left hospital, he took the cable car from Lambton Quay up to the university, just to get a feel for the place again. He hung about at the student cafeteria, hoping to see some of the girls he knew. But the term had ended and there was just a handful still around, picking up exam results, returning books. As he sat sipping slowly at a coffee to make it last, he did see some girls, and they were familiar but different, the miniskirts gone, replaced by ugly flared jeans, their sleek bobs standing out in Afro curls. None of them spared a look in his direction. He supposed that, in his checked bushman's jacket and the beard he'd grown on the island, he looked like some hillbilly come to town to gawp at girls. His head felt strange, as if floating. The night before, when he spoke to his mother on the hospital phone she had said, 'Now don't do anything silly, will you? Dad and I will be at the hospital at two to pick you up. We'd be there earlier but your dad's got the roof off a house right now.' Seth laid his head in his arms on the table and planned his way back to the hospital.

While he had been in the south, the night he nearly died, his home town had felt like a place he might not see again. The quiet main street, the wooden houses with their graceful verandahs, the town clock and the park were just the same, as though he'd never been away. His mother's chicken soup warmed him, his sister Rebecca, recently finished school, tiptoed around him, and even his father appeared subdued, unable to resist patting Seth on the shoulder whenever he passed, as if to check that it was really him. The villa was furnished in style by his mother, maintained to perfection by his father. Sunlight fell in comfortable nooks all over the house, bay windows with deep armchairs, shelves of books that his mother had collected over the years, her library she called it, tall vases of flowers picked from the garden. He loafed around, read and felt his strength coming back.

After some weeks had passed in this way, he made his way to a plant nursery near the gardens. He wasn't sure it was the right place, but he thought it worth a try. 'I'm looking for Belinda,' he said, trying to sound nonchalant, when approached by a woman wearing a large apron and wielding pruning shears.

She gave him an odd glance. 'Belinda's not here now,' she said.

'Okay, where would I find her, then?'

'I've got no idea,' the woman said. There was a disagreeable note in her voice, as if he had said something wrong.

'Do you know if she's still in town?'

'I doubt it. Look, I'd be inclined to leave that poor girl alone if I were you, unless you know something about it.'

'About?'

'You don't know?' She had begun attacking a shrub, snipping off faded leaves, trimming it into shape ready for sale.

'Know what?'

She turned to view him carefully. 'Nothing. There's nothing I can tell you about Belinda Pawson.'

So this was progress. The girl had a surname he could check.

'I'll look her up in the phone book,' he said, as if it were such an obvious thing to do that she might have suggested it.

'I don't think you'll find her in the phone book,' the woman said with finality, finishing the conversation.

'Do you happen to know a girl called Belinda Pawson?' he asked Rebecca, that evening.

'Belinda? Oh yeah, she was a year ahead of me at school.'

'What was she like?'

'Brain box. Top in everything. She left school early. The teachers were really wild — they said she was a scholarship girl, or that's what I heard. My friend Gayleen's mother was her English teacher. She lived with her auntie, old bat. Why, what do you want to know about Belinda? She got in trouble.'

'What sort of trouble?' But he knew already. He just knew.

Welfare said that Sheila and Monty could keep Peter over the weekend and the social worker would pick him up on Monday. Monty said the child should just go because it was too hard on his wife, but Sheila begged for him to stay.

'What did I do wrong?' she asked Kaye Borrell when she came round to tell them the news. At first Sheila thought that she had come to check up on them, to see how well they were doing. Miss Borrell had been reticent when she rang to arrange a visit, but Sheila picked up something in her voice that told her they were not going to receive good news.

She had made up six bottles of scalded milk and put them in the fridge, twenty-four hours of feed. Peter was a hungry little boy, but provided he had his bottle every four hours, regular as clockwork, he didn't grizzle and, miraculously, didn't cry through the night. He had been like that since they brought him home from the hospital in Palmerston North.

Sheila said, after Miss Borrell had phoned, that she wondered if Monty should stay home from work. Peter was nearly three months and smiling every time they looked at him.

'It'll just be routine,' Monty said.

'They didn't say they'd be checking up,' Sheila said, her voice uneasy.

'It'll be like Plunket, I expect. You know, just seeing how we're coping, all that sort of stuff. They'll think you're brilliant.' He had a big job on at the factory, a run of joinery for a new building in town.

Sheila was unconvinced. 'She said she'd like to talk to us.'

In the end, Monty agreed it made sense for him to stay home in the morning. If he could get away straight after lunch he could catch up, perhaps even do a bit of double-time tomorrow, it being Saturday. Miss Borrell was due at 10.30.

Her knock came on the dot. Monty let her in. As soon as she entered the house, Sheila knew there really was something wrong. She was sitting in an armchair, Peter over her shoulder as she burped him after his bottle. A little spill tumbled from him, curds on her shoulder. Sheila gave an apologetic smile, but Kaye Borrell didn't seem to notice. The social worker's eyes swept around the immaculate sitting room with its cushions neatly squared on the sofa. It seemed to Sheila that she was taking an unusually long time to say what she had come for. When Monty offered her a cup of tea, she shook her head and spoke gravely.

'Bad news, I'm afraid.'

'He's really well,' Sheila said, a sudden knot of fear tightening in her stomach. 'The Plunket nurse comes every week and she says he's great. He's put on weight. She said his milestones are good. I know he's only three months, and it's too early to tell us much, but she says he's very alert for his age.'

'It's the mother,' the other woman said, after a halting silence. 'She wants him back.'

'She can't. I'm his mother,' Sheila cried out.

'I know, but his birth mother has the right to change her mind for the first six months. We explained that to you at the beginning.'

'But she can't look after him, you told us that.' Monty's voice was aggrieved.

'Where's this girl going to keep him?' said Sheila. 'In a garage somewhere?'

Miss Borrell regarded her with genuine pity.

'I'm sorry, we've gone into it very carefully. It seems she can look after him. She got married to the baby's father last week. His family is very supportive. The couple have gone to live with his family for the time being.'

'Where? Where do they live?'

'I can't tell you that.'

'You mean,' said Sheila slowly, 'that we won't ever see him again.'

The social worker nodded, picking an imaginary piece of fluff from her skirt as she did so.

'Take him away,' Monty said, his fury rising.

'I thought you might like him for the weekend. I need someone to come with me when we pick him up.'

'No,' Monty said, 'we don't want him.'

'Yes, we do,' Sheila said. 'Please, please don't take him now. Monty, don't do this, just let him stay.' Peter had begun to cry in her arms. She swaddled him and kissed his forehead, his little smooth-skinned face, until he calmed.

The social worker looked at Monty, who shrugged and turned away. 'He'll be safe with you?' she said, an edge in her tone, recovering some ground. 'If you want another baby, we have to know the child is in good hands.'

Monty glared at her as if she were mad. 'Another baby?' he said, and shook his head. 'What do you think this is? The chocolate factory.'

'I take it that's a yes,' Kaye Borrell said. 'He'll be all right with you, then?'

As she stood to leave, Sheila said, 'What about us? Doesn't this girl care? She doesn't sound fit to have a baby.'

The social worker picked up her gloves and let herself out, down along the pathway edged with petunias.

'So it seems we're the fucking baby-sitters,' Monty said, as he picked up the keys to his truck and walked out.

Sheila thought he would refuse to look at Peter again. He didn't ask after him when he came home. She could tell he had had a few beers.

But when Peter cried during the night, one of the few times

86

he had, it was Monty who got up and changed him. When he had done with that, he brought the baby back to bed and for a little while they lay there with him between them, before returning him to his bassinet, with all its mobiles dancing above. They did this again for the following two nights. Monty told him silly funny stories as if Peter could understand them, ones he had been saving up for when his son was older. Sheila recited some nursery rhymes and tickled his feet and played this little piggy, but very gently, so as not to frighten him.

Monty didn't go into work on Monday, just waited for the social worker and her companion to arrive. When they had gone, when Peter had left them, he sat with his arm draped around Sheila's shoulder and neither of them said anything.

# 4
# Telling lies
# 1972

The bell signalling the end of class shrilled so loudly through the school that Linda Morley put her head between her hands to shut out the noise. This cacophony disturbed the rhythm of each working day. Linda had been a guidance counsellor for the past ten years, and she had heard it a thousand times before, but today it seemed worse than usual, a clangour so piercing it felt as if her eardrums might burst. In a moment hundreds of feet would rush through the corridors, shoes scuffing on the high polish of linoleum, the voices of students, and that of teachers admonishing them to be quiet. Order, girls, order.

Her day had started with a bad omen, not, she reminded herself with impatience, that she was superstitious. In the bathroom she had dropped her hand mirror, one given by her godmother as a twenty-first birthday present. The mirror had a pretty silver backing that matched the brush, her initials engraved on the surface. When she picked up the mirror and turned it over, her face was reflected back to her with a deep fissure, the glass cracked. A splinter fell out. Seven years' bad luck. She tried to banish the thought. Still, the dressing-table set was a treasure, and it was spoiled. The twenty-first birthday was well in the past. She was thirty-four, although she knew she could pass for younger. Her figure was tight and trim, her skin as flawless as that of many of the girls in the corridor.

But her lover, Philip, had left early, as he did every Friday, as if to cram as much into the day as he could before getting out of town for the weekend. First he went to the gym and did fitness exercises for an hour. When he finished work at the university, where he was a lecturer in English, he would catch the train to the place he still referred to as home, where his wife Sylvia lived. Only, last night, she had felt him lying awake beside her, wired as if ready to get out of bed hours before the alarm went off.

She cooked him an egg, soft-boiled the way he liked, and made toast with wholemeal bread, pale tea without milk. A man who was small but neatly packaged in his body, he wore blue cotton shirts, and woollen jerseys Sylvia had knitted for him, with moleskin trousers, nothing to indicate that he carried the weight of knowledge on his shoulders. Pretension in the lecture theatre was a thing of the past as far as he was concerned. So he said. He pushed his breakfast aside, barely touching it.

'Oh, hon,' she said, 'just calm down. You know you always get het up when you're going to Sylvia's.' She never said 'going home'.

This morning he had said, 'Don't fucking counsel me, Linda. Just don't.'

It rattled her, she had to admit it. Part of her wanted to crawl back under the bed covers for the day and just stare at her pale ceiling above the mezzanine floor where they slept. She had created what she described as a capsule of cool lemony light in her apartment, space that made no claims on personhood, where people could just find themselves. Philip didn't entirely agree with this concept. A bit of a box, isn't it? he'd said, the first time he visited her. You need a bit more colour in here, don't you? She thought he'd become accustomed to it, but she added a turquoise bedspread because it reminded her of the sea. Although they could see Wellington Harbour through a slit window above the bed anyway, a line of blue-green light flecked with white caps.

To calm herself, she had chosen her clothes with even more than her usual care. A cream mohair jersey with a paisley pattern, a straight blue skirt, platform heels — an outfit representing, she felt, both sensitivity and authority. She flicked the silver-backed brush through her big hair, streaked with gold lights.

As if Philip's moodiness was not enough, she had a particularly difficult case to deal with. She had been counselling a girl for the past two years and getting nowhere. Today, she hoped, would be her breakthrough day.

Ed Carter, the physical education teacher, came into her office, without knocking. This irritated her, although she had the open sign on her door, so that any student seeking her advice would feel welcome. He brought with him a swelling surge not just of noise, but of the smell of girls en masse: the soggy odour of uniforms dampened with rain and dried again, some not cleaned from the beginning of one year to the end, muddy shoes, cheap perfume, armpit and crotch and menstruation smells. You could talk to girls a hundred times about hygiene yet some never got the message.

'Shut it, Ed,' Linda said, meaning the door.

He took this as an invitation to perch on the edge of her desk. 'TGIF.'

He meant Thank God It's Friday, the day the staff would go to the pub after work and not go home till it shut at ten. Teachers needed time to relax, they told each other. Linda used to go, before she met Philip and Sylvia. She knew the conversations off by heart. They were all about what kid had done what to whom, and how this had been dealt with, and which parents had been called in and which kid was smarter than they thought, and so on, endless talk about the jobs they were supposed to be leaving behind for the weekend. Nobody talked about their families. Teachers were families of their own, speaking a language they didn't want to take home.

'What can I do for you, Ed?'

Younger than her, he looked pretty much how a gymnasium teacher should be — a tall, rangy man, big shoulders, an oblong jaw (lantern-jawed came to mind, but that sounded so Victorian romantic she dismissed it as unworthy). Girls fought for his attention. She remembered his wife had left him recently, taking the two children with her, and softened. Teachers, she often thought, needed counselling as much as their charges.

He had shifted himself to a chair, straddling it back to front.

'You stay at home on your own on Friday nights these days,' he said.

'No, I don't. I go to the movies.'

'On your own.'

'Not always.'

'Liar. You're fooling yourself, Linda.'

'Life's complicated. You should know that.' She guessed there was an invitation in the offing and sought to stave it off. She picked up a folder.

'Janice Pawson,' she said. 'You come across her?' She knew he must have, because once a week he got to see every girl in the school.

'Janice.' He screwed up his cheek, then shrugged, as if to rebuke himself. Linda recognised the dent in the girl's face that made it asymmetrical. Forceps delivery that had never straightened out.

'Poor little kid,' Ed was saying. 'I made her cry doing handstands. I said, "Come on, you can do it, Jan." And I kept on and on at her. I wanted to shake something out of her, make her do better than she thought she could. And then she started to cry. You know, just that dumb expression, and tears rolling down her face. I felt like an arsehole.'

'Oh God, that's awful, Ed. I know what you mean, though, there's something there you just can't reach.'

Ed's face brightened. 'But you know what? All of a sudden, while she was still boo-hoo-ing, she stands there and does a perfect handstand. Just like that. And when she'd done it, she was proud of herself. You could see it in her face. If she never does another handstand in her life, she's done that one.'

'Wow, really? She did that for you? I'm full of admiration.'

Ed looked modest. 'Stick at it, you'll find the spot. She wants to be a hairdresser.'

Linda glanced at the open folder in front of her. 'Yes, she told me. Might be a bit ambitious. It says she's got siblings. A brother and two sisters. You must have come across the older girls?' Although he was younger, Ed had been at this school longer than she had. She had held positions at other schools.

'Well, there was Jessie, of course. Jessie Sandle, dux of the school. You must have seen her name on the honours board — 1962, or thereabouts.'

'I didn't make the connection. A half-sister?'

'That's right. Mind you, she wasn't much good at handstands either. Well, there you go, Jessie wouldn't take shit like that from me. She knew she was smart, in fact so smart she managed to avoid coming to phys ed most days. I doubt if she had much to do with Jan. She was, oh I reckon, ten years or so older. I heard she went to Oxford, and now she's a journalist. Famous old girl. You see her by-line in the world news section.'

'I have. Fancy that, Janice Pawson's sister. What about the next sister?'

'Didn't come here. Some trouble at home I heard. She left to live with a relative in Masterton and went to school there. I think she's had a baby.'

'Trouble at home? I've asked her parents to come in; they never do.'

'You'll crack it. Gotta go. Don't forget: TGIF.' He stopped at the door. 'What's Janice been up to this time, anyway?'

'Truanting. Again. Her specialty. '

When Ed had gone, Linda sat and stared at her notes. Janice wasn't due in for half an hour. Of course, she had supposed there was trouble at home. She thought Ed might know more than he'd said. Or he was guessing at something, but wasn't sure enough to tell her. Linda couldn't imagine how she might persuade Janice Pawson to stand on her hands for her.

She had reports to write up. It was a matter of pride that she finished each week with her desk tidy and her work complete. Instead, she picked up the phone and rang Philip at his office. This was a rule she was breaking. Their working lives must be kept separate, he had told her. He needed space to think. His train of thought before he gave a lecture must not be interrupted. There was an energy flow between him and his students, and getting ready for their interaction was like practising for an athletic event.

Linda thought he might not pick up but he did. When she said, 'It's me, Linda,' he asked quickly if there was an emergency, his voice brisk, a trifle sharp.

'Please stay with me tonight. You don't have to go to Sylvia's.'

'What are you talking about? Are you sick or something?'

'No.'

'You're not pregnant?'

There was an edge of fear in his voice.

'No.' She guessed it was a competition now, to see who put the phone down first, and decided to win.

Philip and Sylvia owned a cottage in Pinehaven. It was surrounded by a garden that wouldn't be out of place in a magazine, wisteria round the verandah in spring, hollyhocks and roses blooming all through the summer. It was the herb garden that was truly impressive, overflowing with sage, parsley, rosemary, lavender, basil and borage and other plants Sylvia described as of the medieval variety, tansy and nettles. In her garden shed, which she called the factory, she concocted creams and potions, natural remedies of all kinds. The business was flourishing. Just recently Sylvia had taken on an assistant and was considering building larger premises. Linda knew all of this because she and Sylvia used to be friends. They first met at a weekend retreat devoted to pacifism, and Sylvia and she knew they were kindred spirits straight away. Sylvia said she must come home and meet her husband and all their friends. She was ample-breasted and broad in the bottom, but walked with a swaying grace. Her skin was unblemished, testimony to her products.

Before things changed, Linda had visited the couple often. All of them, she, Sylvia and Philip, and friends of theirs, would sit in the conversation pit that Philip had created in the living room, a space heaped with big soft cushions, and talk until it was nearly morning, and drink wine, the Beatles playing in the background. They wore Campaign for Nuclear Disarmament badges, recoiled with disgust from South African racial policies, always signed petitions to stop whatever they didn't think was right with the world: aluminium smelters, the Vietnam War — although they hoped the tide was turning there.

Linda wasn't certain if Sylvia knew that most of Philip's weeknights were spent with her, but stayed away from her, just in case.

Janice met Darrell when she was fourteen. He was twenty-two years old and worked for a time on a fishing boat at Island Bay, until he was sacked for being late to work once too often. The boats left very early in the morning, according to the tides, and they couldn't wait for stragglers. It meant they were a man short at sea. Darrell said it was because the fishermen were a pack of shits, always asking for more from a man than they were willing to pay and he was glad to be out of it. Janice wasn't sure about this, because the Italians had always been good to her. When she was little and got hidings from Charm, one of the older Italian women would call out to her and invite her in for hot soup, or a piece of thick lemon cake with a syrupy crust on the top. Janice liked the warmth of their kitchens, the colourful rugs, a cross with Jesus suspended from the wall with his arms spread out. The men, when they came in, said 'Hi, Jan', as if seeing her there were nothing out of the ordinary, and went about their business. Janice wondered how they knew Charm belted her, because she never cried or made a noise. It was the one strong thing about her, she believed, not to give Charm satisfaction. There were other things in her life that were worse but nobody knew about those, except her father.

She thought the Italians were smart people, but Darrell wasn't the best decision they had made. Not that she had worked this out yet. What she did know was that, one morning, she found him sitting on the sea wall smoking, when she was on her way to school. The hem of her uniform was down, her shoes unpolished; she knew she must have looked a sight. She rarely glanced in the mirror because she didn't want to be reminded of what there was to see. She hated the way her cheek hollowed in like a little cave. She can't help it if she's plain, Charm said to her Aunt Agnes when she visited from the Wairarapa.

'Never mind plain,' Agnes would say. 'Count it as a blessing, as long as she's a good girl. If you'd been let down the way I have by her sister, you'd know what I mean.'

This was before Belinda had married the father of their baby boy. Agnes did speak of her a little more kindly after that.

'Not that I see her,' she sniffed. 'She seems to think she's better than me now she's married into *that* family. University and all that. The father only mends roofs — I don't know where the money comes from.'

Besides, Belinda was the one who had turned out to be attractive, unlike the other Pawson children. Strange, Janice thought, that she and Jessie both had curly hair that turned into corkscrews in the wet, even though their dead mother's had been dark and wavy, and they had had different fathers. Some throwback, Charm said, as if her mother's past were bad karma, whatever that was. It was whispered that her grandfather had been a wharfie, and an Irishman to boot. It was Belinda, an ugly duckling of a different mould, who had turned into someone, if not beautiful, at least easy on the eye, just like in stories. Janice wasn't expecting any miracles of her own.

And Janice was the one Charm described as a dumb mutt. The girls at school were no kinder. In the corridors, between periods, when teachers couldn't catch them at it, they would say things like *Did you know two and two make five?*, a dig at her inability to make sense of letters and symbols on the page, and the fact she was in a special class. Or *Someone's fish is off. Wonder whose it is?*, as if she hadn't changed her sanitary towel, although it could be anybody's, or just *Hi, Lazybones.*

When Darrell said 'Hello, gorgeous' in a special voice, and swept his hair, short back and sides and long in the middle, heavy with Brylcreem, away from his forehead, Janice thought he must be having her on. She was lying low at the time because she had just seen Charm walking up Brighton Street. Not that she thought Charm would notice her - she was hobbling along, holding one high-heeled shoe in her hand and using her umbrella as a walking stick. Then she leaned over and tucked something in the grass. Janice was sure she was falling over, but she righted herself and moved on. Pissed again, Janice thought, and who cared, except that the night before the house had been empty, except for her and her father, and that thing had happened again. She was sure Charm would have laughed if anyone told her that her presence protected Janice, but in a sense it was true.

Darrell smiled, a crooked smile because half of one tooth was broken.

'So what are you up to?' he asked. 'Want me to carry your books to school?' He threw up his hands before she could reply. 'Joke. Spare me from schools.'

'Me, too,' Janice said.

'You want a ciggie?'

'Sure.'

She had practised smoking Charm's fags several times and thought she was getting quite good at it. She dragged on her cigarette and blew a long plume of smoke into the sea air, so that it swirled and eddied around their heads.

'Cool,' Darrell said. 'You want to come for a ride? I've got my car parked along the road.'

The car was an old streamlined Chevy, painted red and cream, vintage 1950s. There were imitation tiger-skin rugs over the seats, big dice bobbing on strings from the roof between the driver and passenger sides.

'Where are we going?' Janice asked.

'Miles away. You never know, we might drive all day. You game for it?'

'Yep. So long as you don't want to muck around, you know what I mean?'

'Muck about? Oh yeah, that. You might like it.'

'I don't,' Janice said. 'Anyway, you know I've got my pinny pain.' This was a fact; it had started that morning and she was relieved, the same way she always was. 'So?'

'So what?'

'You still want to take me for a ride?'

'Get in,' he said.

So they drove all the way up to Waiouru, nearly two hundred kilometres, State Highway One unpeeling itself before them. Darrell let her pick a station on the car radio and she found what she wanted, the hit parade playing 'I Did What I Did for Maria', about a man being executed for shooting the man who killed his wife. When the song was finished, she switched the radio off, and sang a version of it to herself, her voice low and sweet but relentless in pursuit of the tune, *I did what I did, I did what I did did did did,* until he started drumming on the steering wheel with one fist and laughing like crazy, over and over, the pair of them as mad as rattlesnakes in heat, as Darrell put it.

'That's our song,' he said, so that she saw that they had some sort of future before them.

They drove on and on, to where they could see the navy blue mountains with their frosting of snow, and the tussock grass feathering against the breeze. He pointed out the road that led to the military camp. For a while he had been in the army, but he didn't like rules and saluting people, all that rubbish.

'Yeah, I reckoned it'd be the life for me,' he said, tapping out another cigarette on the steering wheel. 'I thought I'd get to tell the new recruits what to do when I'd been in for a bit.'

'So what happened?'

'Ah, they kicked me out.'

'Why was that?'

'Dunno really. CO picked on me, so I let him have it one day.'

'Oh yep, I know what that's like,' Janice said. 'I mean I can understand that sort of behaviour. People like that, they're everywhere.'

He stopped and bought pies and doughnuts. She got out of the car and felt the crisp air, saw purple heather growing on the roadsides, brambles bright with rosehips. 'I like it here,' Janice said. She had never felt happier.

On the way back to Wellington, they stopped overnight and slept in the car, parked up in a layby. Darrell didn't try anything on with her, not that time.

The crazy thing was, nobody reported her missing. It was almost as if Jock and Charm hadn't noticed. No, perhaps that wasn't true. Janice reckoned to herself that sooner or later she'd have been reported missing at school and they would have had to do something. In the meantime, Jock would want to keep the police out of it for as long as possible. Neither he nor Charm would want the police sniffing around. After that, Darrell picked her up most days when school was finished. They slept together sometimes, though he wasn't pushy about it. She knew quite a lot about sex; she could take it or leave it. There was an inevitability, the price of having a boyfriend. It wasn't much different to the dark pressure she understood, a similar toss and tip, a heave and it was over. In a grim way, she believed she knew more about her mother's life than her clever sisters thought they did, or ever could. Nevertheless, she looked at herself in the mirror more often. What she saw couldn't be all bad if it was enough to catch a grown-up boyfriend of her own. When other girls saw her getting picked up in the Chevy, there was a change in the atmosphere at school. 'Have you done it with him, Janice?' they asked her, but she just popped some gum and laughed. Janice Pawson laughing.

Darrell had money on and off. She didn't ask where it came from. Sometimes he bought her small gifts, a pair of clip-on earrings, some lipstick. At night she lay in bed holding each new gift to her, along with a tooth she kept in a pencil case. It was one of her own milk teeth, which her mother had pulled out for her with a piece of cotton, not long before she went to hospital. The cotton was still tied around it. This was a memory that took her back to her mother, the concentration on her face, Janice her whole focus for those moments, the sharp pain of the tooth being pulled from her gum, something coming apart.

Charm knew they hated her. She was a stepmother, after all, and stepmothers were supposed to be horrible. She didn't set out to be. Charm was brought up by a stepmother herself, a wizened shrew with her hair pulled back in a knot, a bitter tongue in her head. Nothing she did was ever good enough. Now she was behaving just the same, and she couldn't stop herself. What had she wanted when she married Jock Pawson? A roof over her head, she supposed, a man she could walk out with, some children — even if they weren't her own. None of it had worked out the way she imagined.

She had been married to Jock for going on ten years. When Janice and her older brother Grant were in high school, she took a part-time job cleaning at one of the pubs, four days a week, finishing in mid-afternoon. Friday was her day off. It was at this job that she met a woman called Sandy who became her best friend and introduced her to the crowd at the Duke. At the end of a shift, she and Sandy would sit down in the staff quarters and have a smoke and talk about their lives.

'If I counted my mistakes, one by one,' she confided to Sandy, 'I reckon they'd go back to the day Jock's wife died. I burned all her stuff. You should have seen the way those kids looked at me.' She still saw their faces as she tried to erase their mother from their lives, their panic as the flames consumed her belongings in the backyard of their house.

'You were doing the right thing,' Sandy said.

'I thought it was for the best. Best for them not to have to think about her every day. You know what I mean?'

Sandy nodded. 'I'd have done the same.'

'I reckoned on giving them a fresh start. I cleaned the house from top to bottom. I shone all the pots and pans in that bloody dirty kitchen, scrubbed the toilets down, washed the filth off the windows. It was a proper pigsty.'

She shivered, remembering the sour smell of neglect and sickness that had permeated the house.

'They didn't appreciate it?'

'No thanks at all.'

'You don't want to take it to heart. My kids tell me I ruined their lives all the time. I didn't, of course. They just do it to make you feel bad.'

But Charm couldn't explain how she didn't know what a fresh start meant for the children. She had no models in her head for new beginnings. She had made a life, in her first marriage, with a man who drank too much, until the day he fell down the stairs. People said she pushed him. What she thought was that he had pushed her to drink, in order to keep him company.

'I thought he'd get over Irene — that was his first wife, you see,' Charm said. 'I didn't think he even liked her very much. We'd had it off a couple of times while she was still alive. He came round to my house after my husband died. A bit of nookie won't do you any harm, that was what he said, cheer me up a bit.'

'Well, he was no saint, was he then? He meant it wouldn't do *him* any harm.'

'He reckoned I was a cocktease. I guess I shouldn't have done it.'

'Oh, there's lots of things we shouldn't do,' Sandy reassured her.

'So it's like she was nothing to him when she was alive and now she's a saint. As if she was the great romance.'

'So he's gone off the boil?' Sandy said. 'Well, you said he was getting on. It happens to lots of blokes when they get old.'

That was when Charm told Sandy what was going on. She hadn't told anyone, but it was bursting out of her, the need to tell someone, to know the right thing to do.

Sandy sat back, shaking her head. 'You need to do something,' she said. 'I mean, that's not right.'

Charm wished, afterwards, that she hadn't told Sandy because now it was hard to face her when she still didn't do anything. She didn't know what would become of her when she could no longer live in the house in Brighton Street, but that wasn't the reason in itself she couldn't bring herself to do the right thing. This was something she couldn't explain to her friend, the dread of confrontation that had seemed easy when the children were smaller and she had control in that house. Now she didn't know which way things would spiral, what Jock would do, what would happen to Janice. And what would be said about her to all the welfare people she suspected might become involved.

What she did say was that Sandy wouldn't notice there was anything wrong if she were to meet Jock. He was getting on in years and had taken to wearing a good tweed coat in winter, scarf and nice leather gloves, brogues, a trilby hat that he tipped to people when he passed them in the street. He liked his shirts ironed in a certain way. His fingernails were shiny and well trimmed, their white rims spotless. He was sucking the life out of her and taking it into himself. Charm learned by accident, when she found a letter from an insurance company in an old coat of his at the back of his wardrobe, that his late wife Irene had a policy that was paid out on her death. She waited for him to tell her he had money, but he never did.

Not long after they married, he began attending night classes in photography. He met a group of men he referred to as his chums. Some had darkrooms at the back of their houses, or in little sheds tucked away in their gardens. They met at the weekends. A blokes' world, he said, like the old days down the Coast before the war when he kept an eye on the coal mines. When he and Charm were first together he liked a drink or two. Now he never drank with her. He didn't bring his chums to meet her, and she didn't see his photographs either. They were, he said, wildlife photographers. They took pictures of nature and tramped around Red Rocks by the sea on fine days. Nothing that would interest her.

There was just the one girl left at home, although the boy had stayed longer. Charm had stopped laying a hand on Janice, who was big, and strong enough to fight back. In her heart, she knew that the girl hadn't deserved it, that she'd reaped the blame for the disappointments of Charm's marriage to her father. Charm remembered Janice at the registry office on the day of the wedding, holding the bouquet while Jock put the ring on Charm's finger, the only one of the children who would agree, although her little freckled face was puzzled. Jock hadn't wanted a fuss, but Charm had wanted some kind of ceremony. His sister had come over for the wedding, and the children had stood awkwardly in the plain room where it took place.

The girl regarded her with insolence these days, as if to say, I'm doing your job. Janice knew that she knew.

She found out one night when she came in earlier than expected. There had been a punch-up in the Duke, and the barman had heaved all the patrons out after the police came. She let herself in quietly, not wanting to disturb Jock.

The door of Janice's room was slightly ajar. Charm heard her say: 'I'm sick of this. You've got a wife.'

Charm felt her heart freeze.

'I've got two, haven't I?' he said.

The girl stifled a noise, either a cry of pain or a sob or both.

'I'll tell her,' Janice said. 'I'll tell Charm.'

Charm heard him laugh.

'A lot of good that'll do you. She doesn't care sixpence for you.'

'You don't know.'

'You think anyone would believe her? Anyway, I'd kick her out as quick as look at her.'

'Then who'd iron your shirts?'

Charm knew she should go in, break up this post-coital conversation, but she was immobilised, as if her feet were stuck to the floor.

His voice was savage then. 'You would. And I'll beat the tripe out of you if you tell her. Or anyone else.'

As she heard him move from the bed, Charm slipped off her shoes and retreated down the passage towards the front door, opening it and turning back round, as though she had just walked in. She called out, 'Hello, I'm home.'

Jock appeared in the doorway of Janice's room.

'Hello,' he said. 'Just checking on Jan's homework.' As if tucking his shirt in his trousers as he walked out of his daughter's bedroom were perfectly normal. He looked at her deadpan. 'Have a good evening, did we?'

In the morning, Charm sat with her head in her hands, elbows on the bleached wooden kitchen table, thinking about the night before. She shivered, lowered her hands, ran the tip of her index finger down a crack at the edge of the table, searching out dirt. That must be it, her and her dirty mind, seeking out muck. She must have imagined it. She must have had more to drink than she realised. But in the harsh light of that and many mornings that followed, she knew she wasn't wrong, and that it had been happening for a long while.

She knew what needed to be done but she still couldn't. It was easier to head for the Duke, where there was boozy laughter and cigarette smoke and a few yarns, and in the morning, when she woke up in the room where the older girl used to sleep, there was a hangover, and Jock gone to work. If she squeezed her mind shut, she could almost go back to the place where it wasn't really happening. Like when an earthquake struck, so awful at the time, but so long as you escaped damage or injury, you got over it. Only, in the back of your mind, you were always waiting for another one.

She was thinking about all of this around lunchtime on a Friday, the remains of a cheese sandwich in front of her, the first food of the day she could face, when the phone rang. It was the woman from the school who sent letters to Jock, asking him if he would please, please come in and talk about his daughter.

'Mrs Pawson? Janice was due in my office half an hour ago,' Linda Morley said. 'It appears that she's staying away from school again.'

'I'm her stepmother. There's not much I can do about her.'

'I see. You've no idea where she is, then?'

'Out with that boy, I expect.'

The teacher sounded surprised. 'Janice has a boyfriend?'

'Oh yes. She thinks we don't know, but she's a proper little tearaway, that girl. She hangs out with a no-hoper. Darrell, his name's Darrell.'

'I don't suppose you could come in and have a chat with me, could you?'

Charm hesitated. This, after all, might be what she could do. 'Yes,' she said, 'all right, then.'

After she had put the phone down, she uncapped the bottle of gin she kept in her room. Hair of the dog — it might help. She rang Sandy and asked her what she should say, because Sandy's children hadn't always been saints.

'Just don't let her get high and mighty with you,' Sandy said. 'They always do.'

'Okay, thanks.'

'Charm,' Sandy said anxiously, on the other end of the line, 'you haven't been on the booze, have you? I mean, well, you know, there's a time and place.'

'I'm fine,' Charm said, 'just fine.'

She dressed herself in a plaid skirt, put on a white blouse with a brooch at the throat that her first husband had bought for her when they got married, and a cardigan. She spent a few moments hesitating over whether a red or a blue one looked more respectable, and settled for the blue.

Linda hadn't had time to imagine what Janice Pawson's stepmother might be like. Her day had accelerated as it went along. There was a fight in the school grounds at lunchtime, two girls who acted like mud wrestlers, slinging each other around by the hair. They had been disciplined by their dean, but one of them was hysterical and full of hate. The dean had packed her off to Linda to try and talk sense into her. There was a mother on the phone who thought she knew what was best for her daughter. Mothers usually did, and mostly they were wrong. They thought that what was abnormal was normal and that their children were always right; it was a tiring business trying to talk sense into them. They said things like *You haven't got children of your own, have you Miss Morley? You'll see it differently then.* Or *How dare you interfere with the rules we make for our girl?* It was tricky stuff, especially the ones who got pregnant and hadn't told their mothers, and she had to break the news to them that their princesses were fallen angels. The ashen faces and the whimpering, mothers and daughters. So many tears. She'd had one of those before lunch.

Just before Charmaine arrived (Charm, in brackets on the

contact form, but Linda couldn't believe anyone would call themselves that), Philip had rung.

'We need to talk,' he said. 'I'll meet you at the Pencarrow after school.'

The Pencarrow was a tearoom on Lambton Quay, decked out with fishing nets and shells. Linda thought it kitsch, but Philip liked the date scones.

'I'm going out,' she said. 'TGIF.' This was a lie, or it was until that moment, it was not what she planned to do at all.

'You won't go,' Philip said, his voice confident.

'I might,' she said, and hung up. It might be true after all. Philip might think she was hoping for kind words but, wearing her counsellor's hat, her intuition told her that he intendedto announce that he was going back to Sylvia. He wanted it to happen over date scones where she wouldn't shout or throw his things into the street, like in the movies, or even cry in an obvious way.

The woman facing her in the chair was in her fifties perhaps, not unattractive in a blowsy way, wisps of blonde hair escaping around her face from under a woollen beret, her lipstick a bit on the thick side. A smell of toothpaste and musky perfume masking alcohol and cigarettes hovered in the air.

'Jan's a bit of a loser,' Charmaine Pawson said, 'but you know she's not a bad kid.'

'She's hardly ever at school,' Linda said. 'You think she's with a boy?'

'Well, I thought you people would know,' Charm said. She sucked in her breath. 'Myself, I'm a working woman. You don't expect me to babysit a fifteen-year-old, do you?'

'I don't really know what to expect,' Linda said, trying to keep her voice even. She hadn't realised how tired she was. 'We need to know that she's in a safe environment.'

'What are you getting at? Why wouldn't it be safe?'

'I don't know.' Ed Carter's words came back to her. 'Is there any trouble at home?'

As soon as the words were out, Linda knew she had spoken too soon, that this woman needed time and patience if she was to get to the bottom of things.

'That's very rude,' Charm said. 'Rude. That is very rude, you know, Miss Morley. I keep a good home. I have treated those children like my own. My own, you understand. What I want to know is why this school can't teach Janice to read and write proper. Proper*ly*.'

From her careful movements and enunciated speech, Linda gathered that Charm was drunk. The whole conversation was pointless.

This was the moment Janice chose to appear at the door. Her face closed.

'What the fuck?'

'Language,' Charm said. 'You see what I have to put up with.'

'What's she doing here?' Janice said.

'You were supposed to be here after second period this morning,' Linda said. 'That was several hours ago.'

'Yeah, well, I came to say I'm sorry. I got held up.'

'That's thoughtful of you, Janice,' Linda said. 'But the school is responsible for you during school time, as Mrs Pawson has just mentioned. So we have to find out what's happened to you.' This was a sop for the woman, who was already presenting herself as the problem in Janice's life. It might not be too late to extract something from her. 'Janice, tell me, how did you get held up?'

'I told you, it'll be that boyfriend of hers,' Charm said. 'He's a grown man and she's just a kid. He can get had up for that, you know.'

'Why don't you just shut up, you stupid bitch.' Janice's face was contorted.

'Enough,' Linda said, raising her hand in what she hoped was a pacifying motion. 'We're here to sort out problems, not to make them. Janice, were you trying to avoid phys ed? I think if we talked to Mr Carter he could sort something out for you.'

'You just wait until I tell your father,' said Charm.

'You can tell him what you like. I'm outta here. Youse can tell him all you like. I'm old enough to leave school. Me and Darrell are heading north, he's got a construction job up the line.'

'Don't talk rough,' Charm said.

'You're under the age of consent,' Linda said.

'I'm what?' Suddenly Janice appeared to be almost laughing.

Linda said, in a patient quiet voice, 'You're too young to live with your boyfriend, Janice. You do know that, don't you?'

Janice had stopped laughing. She spoke across Linda as if she had barely heard her.

'You're a liar, Charm, that's what you are. You keep your nose out of my business. I can tell my father a few things about you. Has he caught you hiding the bottles in the grass where you go back for them? She does that you know, Miss. My father won't let her bring her piss home, so she goes back for it when he's out. Look at her, three o'clock in the afternoon, and she's fonged.'

Charm tried to lunge at her, but her feet got tangled in the legs of the chair. 'You little cow.'

Linda said, 'I'd like to bring this meeting to a close.'

Janice turned to her stepmother again. 'You're jealous.'

Linda saw Charm hesitate.

'Go on, tell Miss why you're jealous. '

'Is there anything you want to tell me, Mrs Pawson?'

The silence lengthened.

'Jealous? Me jealous of a boy with jug ears? Hardly.' Charm fumbled for her handbag, tried to muster some dignity as she lurched out the door. The girl watched her go.

'Janice?'

'Yes, Miss?'

'You still want to be a hairdresser? I might be able to get you into a salon in the city. You'd probably have to start with sweeping up after customers. You'd still have to pass some exams. It would be a good incentive for you to overcome your learning difficulties.'

'I'll be gone.'

'We'll talk about this on Monday.'

'Miss, you want to know what she's jealous about?'

'I think this is between your stepmother and you.'

'Sure, Miss. Bye now.' At the door she turned and said, almost under her breath, but just so Linda could hear, 'I'm a better fuck than her.'

A wave of disgust passed through Linda as the door closed behind the girl. And then, when it was too late, she understood. Trouble at home. *Tell* her. The girl had laughed when Linda said she was under the age of consent. I'll tell your father. *Tell her.* Two women, slugging it out over a man. Forget the boyfriend.

And what had she said? Do you still want to be a hairdresser? In her firm, calm counselling voice. There had been so much truth swirling around the room, offered up to her on a plate, and she had only listened to the lies. She must stop Janice. Linda turned to the window. From where she stood, she saw Janice climbing into a car.

Linda sat and wept. She wept for the girl she didn't expect to see again, and whom she'd allowed to escape into darkness. She cried, too, for the man who was going home to his wife. Most of all, she was crying over such virtuous patter when she was no better than some she could count in an afternoon.

During the night, Philip would ring and shout down the phone, 'All right, all right then, you proved your point. I sat and waited for you at the Pencarrow. I saw dozens of women better-looking than you walking down the street. I was just going to

110

tell you I'd get my stuff on Monday. No special reason, except I woke up this morning and thought what am I doing there in your stupid yellow room when I've got a nice house and a garden and a wife who puts a decent casserole on the table? Did I tell you that you're a lousy cook, Linda? Because you are.'

She would turn to Ed Carter in the bed and say that it was nothing. Nothing at all. Old baggage, everyone had it. And she would think that perhaps she would be loved after all, and in the morning she would think that this mightn't happen. Not yet anyway.

Not long after her night with Ed Carter she will meet a man who will cherish her always, not a genius, just a man who is consistent and solid in his ways. When Linda is in her sixties, and then her seventies, and she has grandchildren, she will think back to the frivolities of her own early life. That day will return now and then like a comic-book ghost, pale, shapeless and mean, a day when she looked evil in the face and did not recognise it. People talk about moments that changed their lives, not always seeing that there are many moments that add up to the time when they are ready for change. But, Linda will think, there is something that defines the moment, something to hold onto and remind yourself that change is possible. She will stop giving out advice, or not in any official sense. Linda is a good listener, her friends will say.

Janice will ride in Darrell's car, away from Brighton Street, away from the lights in the Italian houses, the fishing boats bobbing in the water. She will wish that she'd had time to say goodbye to the good women wearing black who'd taken her in when she was a child. She won't look back with any other regrets. They have yet to come.

# 5

# How high the sky
# 1974

On what was supposed to be the best day of his life, Grant Pawson found himself upside down in a suburban garden, hanging from his seatbelt, in a Piper Cub aeroplane. Or that's as far as he can remember because, when he woke up, it was the next day and he was in hospital. An account of his disaster was splashed all over the newspapers, complete with details of how he had called out for his mother in the moments leading up to the crash. None of the journalists covering the incident had managed to discover what his mother had had to say about that. This was because she had been dead for almost ten years. But there are certain scents that will haunt Grant without him exactly knowing why: daphne in bloom, the first spring flowering of damask roses, damp earth, plant fertiliser and hen shit, leaking fuel. And there was some other smell, but in the last drifting seconds of consciousness, he thought, surely not.

He won't forget, either, the sound of sirens, nor the white fear on the face of the woman whose garden it was. 'Are you all right?' she said in a thin reedy voice, when it was obvious that he was not.

In a very short time, two police cars arrived, then an ambulance, followed by fire engines, grinding to a halt outside, a steady stream of men, variously carrying stretchers and hoses.

'We've been following him on the radio,' the first officer said to Joan Moody, whose house it was. 'The guys at the control tower knew he was in trouble ten minutes ago. His first solo flight and he freezes at the controls. He's been up there in the sky yelling blue murder over the radio.'

'Poor boy, poor boy,' Joan said.

The wing tip of the plane was wedged in the shattered remains of the gazebo her late husband, Dugald, had built for her. As she surveyed the destruction, the plane tilted on her lawn, a boy, or that's what he seemed, fading away, perhaps dying for all she knew, she covered her mouth with the back of her hand, remembering afternoon teas she and Dugald had shared in the gazebo, during the last days of his life. Three more women appeared from inside the house, a respectable-looking bunch, mostly wearing tweed skirts and scarves knotted at the throats of cashmere sweaters.

One of the police officers cleared his throat, eyeing them curiously. The women were shaken, but there was, too, something furtive about them that was hard to interpret.

'I told them to stay inside,' Joan said, as though reading the man's mind. And indeed, she felt a light-headedness, a hallucinatory quality as though the air had somehow become clearer, and her feet were not attached to the ground. She held onto the birdbath for support. 'I thought it mightn't be safe to come out.'

The women stood in a huddle.

'I guess you ladies have had a nasty shock,' the policeman said. 'Go inside and have a sit down if you want to.'

Joan's friend, Ivy Mason, said that it was probably best if they got along now. They didn't want to get in the way.

'No, ladies, please just wait right here,' the policeman said. 'I'll need to take statements from all of you.'

Grant was being examined by an ambulance officer.

'I reckon I can smell a bit of the old waccy baccy round here,' the man said.

'That would explain a lot. Anyway, they'll sort that out at the hospital. We need to get him out of here.'

'Help yourselves to a sherry,' Joan said to her friends. 'There's some in the decanter on the dresser. Go on now, I'll see to this.'

It was Ivy who led the women back inside. One of her nice brogues caught on the edge of the path, causing her to stagger, though she recovered herself just in time.

'Oh my, I nearly did go arse over kite, didn't I?' She chortled as if she'd been really funny.

'Ivy, stop it,' Joan said. 'Officer, we had a little wine at lunchtime. We're all just so upset. It must have gone to Ivy's head.' The words seemed to hover above her, like balloons.

Ivy said, 'We'll go in and pray for him. Poor lad, what was he doing up in the sky by himself?'

Allan Johnson chose that moment to appear around the side of the house, shoving fronds of unruly hair behind his ears, his mouth loose as he approached Grant.

'Fucken hell, mate, what've you done?'

'You his mate, are you?' the police officer said. 'We need to have a chat with you, too.'

Allan tried to back away. He seemed about to turn and run.

'Pick him up,' the officer said.

Grant met Allan when they were working together on the Wellington rubbish trucks. The truck was driven from gate to gate, the two young men hanging onto a bar at the back. At each stop, they rushed up steps to the back doors of the nearest houses, seized a bag of rubbish put out by the householder and sped back to the truck. They ran non-stop, the truck driver urging them to get a move on, hurry up, for Chrissake, we haven't got all day to hang around here. There was talk that back-door rubbish collection would be cancelled soon, and go kerbside. Men couldn't be expected to work like this, picking up slops and scraps, often jagged glass that the householder hadn't bothered to wrap, the detritus of lives. Not all were careless and some left out bags of biscuits and bottles of beer for the men. It was a job, and Grant was accumulating money. He'd had a year working in a hardware store, but the money was peanuts; he was no further ahead and was losing his fitness. True, it nearly killed him when he started on the trucks — the backs of his legs on fire, and never enough hot water at home to wash off the muck. His stepmother made him sluice himself down with a cold hose before he entered the house.

'You're a smart little shit, aren't you?' Allan said one morning before the run began. 'I picked it up straight away. Why would you want a job like this?"

Grant explained how he wanted to get into the air force, and that he took a train north every weekend, for weekly flying lessons. He could get them cheaper up the line.

Allan nodded his head wisely. 'Yeah, good luck, mate. I reckon fair enough. You know, I thought you might be a right wanker when you turned up. Tell the truth, I didn't reckon they'd give you a job. But you're bloody good, mate. You reckon on being a pilot then?'

Grant nodded. He didn't say that he just missed a university scholarship when he left school a year or so ago. He had put that behind him. 'I want to get into the air force. I'm going to volunteer. What about you?'

'You won't catch me volunteering. Best thing Norman Kirk ever did was getting rid of conscription. He'll go down in history for that. Who wants to fight in wars?'

Grant was uncomfortable. The Labour government had come in on a promise of making military training voluntary, rather than on a ballot. There'd been talk about this at home. That's what you got with these left-wing outfits, his father said. So far as Grant could tell, his father hadn't been to war. When asked, he'd muttered about being a man between the wars: too young for one, too old for the next. Besides, he'd had important work to do on the home front, overseeing coal mines. They couldn't have done without me, he told his son, and that was all he had to say about it. As for Kirk, he was too tied up with the unions. Golden years, he said, bloody golden years we've had, and Kirk'll sell us all down the drain.

'I reckon it's the life for me,' Grant said. 'Anyway, I plan to be an officer. I reckon if I can fly a plane, it'll be a start.'

'I've done boot camp, already,' Allan said, his face darkening.

Grant wasn't sure what Allan meant by this. His new friend didn't seem anxious to explain.

Sooner or later, Grant's father said he should go to university anyway, be a lawyer, something like that, make a pile of money by the time he was fifty and retire. Who'd want to be like him, Jock Pawson said. Slaved all my bloody life, and for what? His son thought to mention, but didn't, that Charm failed to live up to her name, had kept Jock slaving because of all the money she spent on horses and booze, and going out with women she described as her girlfriends.

Jock said, in a temper once, that he'd met her sort before, and he thought he'd been in for a bit more than this when he married her. Where Jock had met women like Charm before, Grant had no idea. His father didn't talk about his past, or his first wife. It had all started out roses with Charm and the old man, but it hadn't lasted. Grant couldn't wait to get out of the house near the sea but, until the expensive flying lessons were complete, he felt impecunious and stranded. It was hard to tell who disgusted him more, his father or his stepmother. His stepmother, who had become slatternly, seemed the obvious choice, but there were things about his father that Grant couldn't bring himself to think about. They didn't happen, he told himself, when the thoughts sneaked up on him in idle moments. In the evenings, on week nights, he got out of the house and went to the pictures. He liked that. He could lose himself for a bit. Night after night, just queuing up, taking his ticket, sitting in the dark, watching the movie and slouching off home when everyone had gone to bed. It was hard to wake up some mornings in time for his early start to work, but it was worth it, not having to stay in.

Allan said, 'You reckon I could come up and watch you fly?'

At first Grant was inclined to say no. He wasn't used to having friends.

'Think about it, mate,' Allan said. He'd collected up a couple of dozen beers on the run that day. They were supposed to share them with the driver, but Allan had dumped some behind a warehouse. Later, when the run was over, he'd come back for them. 'Come round to my place. We can knock these back, have a smoke or something.'

He inhabited a room of slime and torn curtains. There were three other men, all a little older than Allan, living in the run-down house. It was great they had their own place, Allan said.

When Grant looked startled, Allan said, 'Boys' home, that's where I grew up. I tell you, this place is a palace, man. These are my mates. They looked after me, eh.'

The men's names were Willie, Snort and Ripper, or that's how Allan introduced them. They had stubble on their chins, rough tattoos on their arms. Snort had one on his forehead of a word that looked like 'Fuct', written vertically. There was also a girl, who sat motionless in a corner. While Grant was there, she stared ahead of her with seemingly blank eyes. Grant

117

understood that if she was to be introduced, then he had to wait until one of the men decided on it. Her hair was stacked up in a black bird's nest arrangement on top of her head. Her face was very pale and her lips were painted white. Only her slate-coloured eyes, cool and hostile, rimmed with black kohl, provided colour in her face. He didn't dare to stare at her. The introduction didn't happen.

Ripper checked Grant over. He'd worn a clean shirt with freshly pressed jeans. In spite of the filth of his job, and Charm's cold showers, Grant had cultivated an early fastidiousness about his person. When he got inside in the evenings, he boiled a jug of hot water and took it to the bathroom where he scrubbed under his fingernails, behind his ears and knees, as if trying to clean something from beneath the skin itself.

'Who's this fancy little arsehole, anyway?'

'He's all right,' Allan said. 'He's meaner than he seems.'

'Doesn't look it. You sure he's not spying on us?'

'Nah, he's a mate.' He passed Grant a rolled joint. 'C'mon, just because he's smart doesn't make him a bad bugger. Eh, Grantie?'

'How did you end up in a boys' home?' Grant asked.

'Oh yeah, well, see my ol' man used to beat up on the old lady, always pissed. He had me pinching fags for him when I was a kid. They reckoned I was neglected. Well, yeah, I was, but it was worse in the home, eh guys?'

They talked among themselves: about getting their heads punched in by the staff and by each other, swung around by the hair, the solitary confinement, taking it up the arse.

'My stepmother used to beat the tripe out of me,' Grant said. 'She's a real bitch.'

'Your stepmother? Didn't you punch her back?'

'No,' Grant said, recognising a mistake. The men were looking at him as though he were a dead rat. 'Well, my dad had a leather strap.'

'You still living at home?' Ripper asked, incredulous.

When Grant didn't reply, Snort said, 'He's a little fairy. Stays at home with a sheila who beats him up and a daddy with a big strap. I reckon we could show you a thing or two, faggot.'

'That was when I was a kid,' Grant said. 'I'm just staying until I'm in the military.' A pincer movement had developed around him. Allan looked stricken.

'Just until I'm in the military,' his tormentors said. 'Oh yeah. What are we going to do to him, boys? Shall we smash the crap out of him?'

'Quit it,' Allan said. Out of the corner of his eye, Grant thought he saw the woman's head swivel and turn in his direction. There was just enough pause for him to shoot out the door and run. Footsteps followed for a few minutes as he ran harder and faster. In his last year at school, he'd won the fifteen hundred metres; they weren't to know that. He heard the heaving grunts of a man who had run out of strength. The footsteps fell away. A sense of exhilaration flooded through him. The stars seemed to be racing above.

In the morning he wondered whether to turn up for work or not. He had more or less made up his mind that he'd hand in his notice. He went in anyway. At the depot, he smelled the muck of the trucks, a stench never quite removed, despite sluicing at the end of the shifts. The sight of Allan's bulky frame made him hesitate. Allan turned round, his face bruised and swollen.

'Yeah, good on you, mate, you got away,' Allan said, and it took Grant a moment to register that the other youth was friendly, not taking the piss. He figured the black eye Allan sported was on his account. 'So how about it, I go up the line with you on Saturday and watch your flying lesson?'

Grant couldn't see how he could refuse. Even as he was buying his ticket at the station, he still hoped Allan wouldn't turn up, but turned around in the queue and he was there. 'I brought some grub,' he said, holding up a paper bag of sandwiches.

It became a regular thing. Grant still had three lessons to go before his first solo. Allan had a plan of his own. He told Grant, in a hesitant almost shy manner, that he was going after an apprenticeship in the public works. What had happened to him in the past (and yes, he'd done time as a youth offender for a burglary, he wasn't proud of it), he reckoned he could still come out all right. If it was good enough for the prime minister to leave school early and be a boiler-maker, he could make something of himself, too. Allan reckoned Norman Kirk was an inspiration.

'I'm all for Big Norm,' he'd say. Big Norm. Big in every way, a large man with a generous heart, that's what people said. Allan reckoned Norm'd change things for people like him.

As they hurtled through the tunnels beneath the mountain range and rushed through the countryside, trees turning red in the advancing autumn, past herds of pansy-eyed cows, the stacks of dairy factory buildings in little towns, Grant saw himself changing, viewing the world from new angles. He had thought Allan a bit of a half-wit, but it occurred to him now that they weren't so different: two outsiders, a couple of loners in a fraught world, drawn together. It was embarrassing to realise that Allan saw him, too, as a role model. Little did Allan know what his life was really like, even though he had tried to explain it on the night of his visit. He knew Allan was waiting for a return invitation, but he didn't take people to meet Jock and Charm. He would have liked Allan to have met Janice, but it was too late for that. She was a dumb kid, with her wonky face, but he missed her, the last anchor to what passed as home. She'd gone off with some bloke, he'd been told, and, in this, his sisters seemed to be much of a kind.

The high-winged Piper Super Cub Grant was learning to fly had a body painted yellow, with red wings and cowl — a regular little dragon of a machine. It had a top speed of a hundred and eighty-five kilometres an hour. There were two seats, one for Bob, his instructor, and one for him. Bob was a lean fellow, tanned and muscular, with a crew-cut, mid-forties perhaps. Grant supposed he was good-looking. Women waited for him at the end of the lessons, not always the same woman, although they treated Bob with similar mellow affection, raising their cheeks to accept his kisses. On the last lesson before his first solo, after he and Bob climbed out of the plane, they found one of these women chatting to Allan, laughing over some private joke. Allan was still a rough-looking bastard, but he'd cleaned himself up over the past weeks, his long hair clean and curling behind his ears, the stubble of feathery beard shaved, at the weekends anyway. He had big shoulders, and it gave Grant a jolt to see that women might find him attractive. Although Grant was nineteen, he hadn't regarded girls in this way. Desire of any kind was yet to touch him. He could only look in on those who professed love for each other and wonder.

Bob seemed none too friendly when he saw this banter going on between Allan and the woman. She was younger than Bob, a blonde with big white teeth and shiny gums that showed when she smiled. Her lipstick appeared part of her soft mobile mouth. Grant saw she was wearing a wedding ring, but he didn't think she was Bob's wife.

'Your mate's doing pretty well,' Bob said to Allan. 'I reckon he'll be through next week.'

'I plan to keep flying,' Grant said. 'Get some more hours up.'

'Sure,' Bob shrugged and Grant wondered if he'd had enough of him.

He told himself he was imagining it. At school, the counsellor he was ordered to see told him that his withdrawn nature was due to his mother's death. That, and his instinct to reject people's good intentions, as if he could control others by leaving them before they could leave him. He didn't believe this. The counsellor was an arsehole, spouting jargon. He had to keep telling himself this.

'Are you going to bring Lothario with you next week?' Bob said, and it was on the tip of Grant's tongue to say that no, he wanted to do his solo on his own with no distractions, but one look at Allan's animated expression told him that he couldn't do that. The counsellor's smarmy, comforting face loomed before him.

'You bet,' Grant said. 'Allan's waiting for me to get my passenger's licence, aren't you, mate?'

All the same, he wondered what Allan and the blonde, whose name was Mandy, had been talking about that made them so happy. Almost as if they had a secret.

'Cool chick,' Allan said, after Bob and Mandy had left.

Grant had an uneasy feeling that Mandy would be there the following week. Not that it really mattered; Bob would be on the ground, and he would be up in the sky, alone.

The following Saturday was overcast when they left Wellington, a hint of thunder in the air. Grant worried that the flight might be cancelled. Before he left home, he phoned Bob to check that the flight was still on. Bob's sleepy, grumpy voice answered. 'Didn't you go to bed last night?' he said. 'The weather's okay here. Have you got cold feet?'

A woman's voice, not Mandy's, said, 'Who is it?'

'Some kid wants to do his solo today.' Bob's voice was muffled, but not enough that Grant couldn't hear.

'Can't you put him off? We're supposed to be going to your mother's today.' Grant guessed that it was Bob's wife.

'Nah. I need to get it over and done with.' Taking his hand away from the phone, he said, 'Just get your arse over here, mate. I'll worry about the weather.'

So he was right. Bob had had a gutsful of him. For a moment, Grant thought about giving it away. He admired Bob, did his every bidding. He had thought himself a star, just like Bob told him. He paused at his bedroom door before packing up the last of his gear, then turned back. For years he'd kept a secret talisman, one that he hid at the back of his bookshelf, still filled with old textbooks he knew Charm wouldn't touch in her housekeeping, which had become desultory. The object filled him with both longing and repulsion, a terrible fascination. When he'd had exams at school, or run a race, he would touch it beforehand in a secret furtive manner, to bring him luck. The mangy brown fur collar had been his mother's, rescued from the bonfire of her belongings that Charm had made. He slipped the collar into his jacket pocket.

Mandy was there waiting. She flicked her hair from her face and wished Grant well. First, he and Bob would do some circuits and then, all going well, Bob would land the plane and hand over to Grant.

'Nicely done,' Bob said, when they were on the ground. He seemed to mean it, although he appeared in a hurry to get the flight over. Grant guessed he didn't want to leave Allan and Mandy alone for too long.

'All righty, then, it's all yours. Now just remember, don't go over five thousand feet. You got that?'

'Yes.'

'Good lad. What else?'

'Keep an eye on my instruments, watch out for other aircraft.'

'You got it. Remember your radio procedures. If you get into trouble, let us know. I'll be in the control tower.'

And just like that, Grant was soaring into the sky, higher and higher, and it all belonged to him, the great space he had been searching for in his life since he was a child. Or was it that the space was already there, and at last he could contemplate it on his own? He reached in and touched the fox fur in his pocket.

And it came flooding back to him, the thing he wasn't supposed to remember, the thing that had happened the night after his mother died. His vague strange mother with her head always in a book, the awful food she cooked, the way she let him and his sisters bang on the table with the handles of their knives and forks and shout when their father wasn't there. He remembered green strands of boiled cabbage, stuff they ate because they were hungry and that was what she gave them. But there was, too, the gentleness with which she placed her hand on his head every night, as he pulled the covers up, a sense she gave him of his life mattering. And the way she washed his wet sheets on bad nights and didn't tell Jock, though he knew his father had worked it out.

He peed his bed the night she died. The next night, after the bonfire, his father said, 'You'd better get into bed with me.' All the other beds in the house were full. 'If you wet it, I'll take the strap to you.'

The sky, which was overcast, despite Bob's assurances about the weather, now filled with clouds that tumbled towards him. He should have been able to see the sea in the distance, but he

124

couldn't. Had he let the plane drift outside the range of the circuit he was supposed to follow? A misty rain was developing. But still his mind was playing back some old reel of memory and he couldn't stop it.

Grant was awake when his father finally slid into bed beside him. Jock had gone out to walk Charm to her bus. He was gone a long time. Grant lay fighting sleep, so that he could control his bladder, curling himself into as small a ball as he could make himself, his mother's fur collar clutched against his chest. He sensed his father's bony frame, pouched with sagging flesh, his heavy breathing. His father reached over, telling him to keep still, for God's sake. Then his hand brushed the fur collar, and hesitated. What happened next was so quick, Grant had come to believe it never happened. But it did, and now, up here in the sky and the altimeter climbing, he knew that it was true.

His father's hand had moved among the fur, he had groaned, touched first himself, then Grant's penis, rubbing it up and down in his hand, until it stood up like a little prick of asparagus. Grant gave a howl of anguish, and his father's voice at his ear said, 'Shut up, shut up, will you. For Chrissake, shut up.'

He had let go of his son, and rolled over in the bed. Sometime in the night they had both gone to sleep. In the morning the bed was wet, and his father viewed the evidence without speaking. But Grant didn't get the strap.

Grant would remember this moment of clarity in the sky, when all the bad dreams that had pursued him since his mother died, made sense. He had long suspected that there was nobody you could trust. Nobody.

His attention, he will think, must have wandered for seconds rather than minutes, yet all of a sudden he was lost in the sky. He had no idea where he was. His altimeter told him he was three thousand feet up. He could barely see the ground.

'Airport control, this is Piper Cub ZK DODO. I'm lost,' he shouted.

'Control to ZK DODO,' Bob's voice came back. 'You're not lost, I can see you. Turn left and prepare to land.'

'I can't,' Grant said. He looked at the control panel. The controls made no sense to him. The plane began to fall towards the earth. 'Mum,' he shouted, 'Mummy, I'm lost!'

The plane roared, lurched, the ground raced towards him. He forced the nose up but it was too late.

'Mum,' he cried again. 'Where are you?'

There was a splintering thud, then silence, the scent of Joan Moody's roses, and oblivion.

Tell Ivy, tell Joan, telephone. It was the standing joke among them. Ivy, with her wig because she suffered from alopecia, her sharp tongue, her unerring ear for a good story, was the one who got in with the news first. Joan wasn't surprised when she called. She already knew what Ivy had heard, but she didn't tell Ivy that straight away.

'That boy's up in court next week,' Ivy said. She had a friend whose son was a court reporter. 'You know, the one who turned up at the crash?'

'Yes. We need to have a meeting about this,' Joan said, as if getting together were a formal matter and there would be no argument. 'Here. Tomorrow.'

The four women, Joan and Ivy, Alice and Maureen, had all known each other for what seemed like forever. For yonks, as they said. They met when their children were just starting school, and they belonged to mothers' groups. Now their children were parents, grown up and long gone. But they were still there, indestructible, as though the world would fall apart without them to keep an eye on it.

When she had finished talking to Ivy, Joan put the phone down and contemplated the pretty room that she and Dugald had decorated together. The house had a vintage style, timber beams and beautiful rimu doors they had stripped down to bare wood and treated. The dining-room table seated ten, and when the family came to visit they could all gather round it. Only, Dugald was missing now. She wanted to remonstrate when one of the children took his chair at the head of the table, but she knew this was silly. Spaces were made to be filled, and this growing brood of her descendants was doing exactly that. He would have loved to see them there. It was the thing he would miss, he said when he knew he was dying, seeing how the little ones turned out. At nights she would lie in bed and, in her head, tell him, hoping that he would hear. She wished so much that he was here now.

Joan looked around distractedly, trying to decide which room she would use to entertain her guests. Not the sitting room, it was too informal. Soon they would be lounging around and telling her which of the bottles of wine they had brought to open next and talking at the top of their voices, the way they always did.

The dining room, she decided, where this nonsense had taken place. They would see themselves for what they were, a bunch of grotesque old women who had behaved badly, and must face what they would have to do next.

On the day that Grant Pawson crash-landed in her garden, Joan had made pissaladière for her friends, swotting it up out of Elizabeth David's *French Provincial Cooking*, going to town the day before to buy the olives and anchovies. They were hard to come by, and she felt superior when she asked for them at the grocery store. She saw herself that morning, preparing the potato and flour dough for the pastry. It was Maureen's turn to bring the desserts; she had made chocolate orange custards, quivering in their ramekins when she brought the container in from the car. They looked decadent, the dark chocolate wearing a cheerful frizz of orange zest.

By the time everything was eaten, and three bottles of wine had been despatched, the atmosphere was mellow. Too mellow by far.

Maureen was the youngest, a woman who had had aspirations to write short stories but had abandoned the idea after several classes and as many rejection slips.

'It's all this avant garde nonsense,' she said when she finally gave up. 'Who reads it? Not me, I can tell you.' She was a round fair woman, with bright brown eyes.

Joan suspected Maureen may have had affairs, but this was not something they talked about. They talked about other women who had gone off the rails, but not themselves.

At lunch, Maureen gave a gentle burp. 'If we're going to be really modern, we should try pot.'

Alice, more ascetic in her appearance than the others, with her horn-rimmed glasses, and who travelled a lot, said in a crisp tone, 'Don't be silly, Maureen.' Alice was married to a lawyer, the only one who still had a living husband.

But Maureen was undaunted. She turned her flushed rosy face from one to another. 'I've got a surprise for you.'

She reached for her handbag under the table and opened it.

'*Voilà*!' She produced a roughly rolled cigarette, or that's what it looked like to Joan.

There was a silence.

Maureen said, 'Well, don't act so stricken. It's a joint.'

'Marijuana? Where did you get it?'

'I've got a lovely young gardener,' Maureen said, airily. 'He and I talk about all sorts of things. Oh, to be young.'

'Maureen, put that thing away,' Joan said, fighting her rising panic.

'Oh, come on, Joan, you need to learn something new. We need to learn how to smoke a bit of dope. I'll bet none of you have tried it.'

'I have,' said Alice.

As Ivy had remarked more than once to Joan, Alice was a cool one, the way she dressed in grey silk blouses rather than sweaters like the rest of them. At times they wondered why she continued to bother with them. Ivy reckoned Alice was still having sex. 'Can you imagine it, at our age?'

Alice said, 'It was in Mexico. That's a bit different to smoking a joint here.'

'But you did it?' Maureen said, in a pleased voice.

'Have you and the gardener been at it? Smoking, I mean,' Ivy said. A whisker on her chin quivered. Joan, looking over at her, thought, *Ivy hasn't plucked*. She would mention it to her perhaps. Ivy was letting go a little; she'd noticed it of late.

'Well, I know what to do,' Maureen said, evading the question.

'Oh, give it here,' Alice said. 'If you must.'

Maureen passed the joint over with a box of matches, and Alice lit up, as if it were nothing special. Just watching her do this, as an ordinary everyday activity, made everyone relax a little more. If Alice had smoked dope, perhaps it was all right. Joan just wished it wasn't in her house.

'Joan, you're not inhaling,' Maureen said, when the joint was passed to her.

'I've never smoked anything,' Joan said. She held it tentatively to her mouth, thinking how odd that she was tasting her friends' lipsticks after all these years. The thought of it made her giggle a little.

'You see,' Maureen said triumphantly. 'You're getting the effect already. Everyone, Joan is getting stoned, isn't she? Isn't she getting high?'

'I am not,' Joan said, and it was true she hadn't taken a drag like the others were doing, but this whole scene, with her friends solemnly passing the joint around her dining-room table, was funnier than she could have imagined.

That was the moment of the crash, and a long subsiding whine. The house shuddered, like in an earthquake.

It was just a mild concussion, the doctors said. Grant might not remember much. They'd given him morphine while they set his broken arm, a nasty break, needing a temporary pin. He slept until later the next day. When he woke up, the nurses treated him with a kind of amused compassion. One of them said, 'It's all right. They didn't find any dope on you.'

'I didn't have any,' Grant said.

'Don't get het up. They were searching for it, that's all.'

'Do you think I'm that dumb? It was my first solo.'

The nurse bit her bottom lip as if to suppress a smile, but the corners of her mouth kept twitching. She tucked something soft in the bed beside him. 'So you don't lose it,' she said. It was his mother's fur collar. He pushed it down inside the bed, ashamed.

His father turned up soon after that, a newspaper in his hand. The nurse who had been nice to him saw the paper and frowned. It was too late. Jock had already shown it to Grant. Grant read what was written there, the description of his last words on the flight, broadcast on a radio frequency heard by several in the town, including a cub reporter.

'*Mummy*,' Jock said. 'What are you, boy?'

Grant regarded his father with loathing. The next time the cleaners came around with their rubbish bags, he slipped the collar into one and rolled over, his face to the wall.

When the policeman told Joan that they would all have to make a statement, and that might take a while, she said, 'Well, if you don't mind, I'm going inside to start dinner.'

She saw they were questioning the young man who had appeared around the side of the house. It looked as if there might be a fight about to start.

'I think that would be a really good idea, Mrs Moody,' the young policeman said. 'Just try and keep everyone calm.' Her beautiful garden was covered with a foamy substance. He made a helpless gesture. 'I'm afraid the plane'll be here a day or so. Air accident people will have to come up from Wellington and investigate before it can be moved.'

Yet another man appeared, whom she recognised as a local flying instructor. A bit of a lady's man, Ivy had said once. He fancies himself, that one. He seemed to be lunging at the young man who was being questioned.

'Come along, ladies,' Joan said, taking charge.

She remembered shepherding them inside like errant schoolchildren. 'Go to the bathroom and use my toothbrush.

All of you. Then go into the sitting room, and sit down.'

'What are you going to do?' Maureen asked, in a small frightened voice.

'Didn't you hear me? I'm going to start dinner.'

She walked into the dining room, opening all the windows as she went. She stopped to collect up the evidence from among the dirty dishes on her lovely table. In the adjoining kitchen, she put a pan on the stove to heat, added oil and sliced an onion before dropping it into the pan. In a few moments, the smell of frying onion filled the kitchen, drifting through the dining and sitting rooms. She didn't turn on the fan.

'You got us out of it,' Maureen said, when they gathered for the arranged meeting. A month had passed. 'You're a heroine, Joan. Who would have thought you had it in you?'

'You could write a short story about it, couldn't you, Maureen?' Ivy said, a bit of the old acid coming back.

'They arrested that young man, the pilot's friend,' Joan said. 'It's not funny. He's up on drug charges and it's our fault.'

'Well, they must have found something on him,' Ivy said. 'I mean, if they didn't have something to go on, they wouldn't have charged him.'

'If my house hadn't smelled like Woodstock, they wouldn't have picked on him,' Joan said. She felt tears prickle behind her eyelids. Since the accident she had been so tired, lying awake at nights, racked with guilt. 'That was his friend in the plane. He was worried sick — didn't you see him crying? He's just a kid. We need to tell the police it was us.'

The silence around the room was thick, palpable. You could bend it, Joan thought. Ivy still hadn't plucked, but she couldn't be bothered mentioning it to her now.

Alice spoke up then, her voice languid; Alice who knew things because of her lawyer husband, but didn't always tell them. Client confidentiality and all that, she would murmur.

'He had a half-smoked joint in his pocket. He'd been smoking it all right,' she said. 'He's been charged with possession. Nothing to do with us at all.'

'Perhaps it was planted on him,' Joan said.

'Don't be ridiculous,' Alice said. 'You know our cops, they're decent men. He said it wasn't his, someone had given it to him. Some woman. But really, it doesn't make any difference whose it was, he was the one who had it in his pocket.'

'So that's it?' Joan said.

Her friends shrugged.

'Oh well,' said Alice, 'if you want to make proper fools of yourselves, go down to the police station. I know a good lawyer who might help you.'

'No need to be sarcastic,' Maureen said. 'We get the message, don't we, Joan?'

Joan shook her head. 'Not really.'

'You don't think you're being a bit of a prig about all this, Joan?' Alice asked.

Maureen was the first to nod in agreement. Ivy simply seemed bewildered for a moment or so. Then she said, 'Alice is right, we should let it go.'

After they had gone, Joan's tears began to spill. Such happy years, the four of them. She wasn't sure how she would fill her days without them.

Grant went to see Allan in prison. His arm was still in plaster. He caught the bus up to Mount Crawford jail, high above the harbour on a point jutting out into the sea. Only the inmates couldn't see the ocean. It was winter. The night before, he had stood in a queue that snaked all the way down Molesworth

Street, waiting to enter Parliament and pay his respects at the coffin of Norman Kirk. There was weeping in the chill late winter wind, the sound of a karanga, people looking desolate, as if everything had changed. Big Norm had gone. The scent of lilies in the high-vaulted foyer said it all.

'I went to say goodbye,' Grant said. 'I said it for you, too.'

Allan looked at him across the table that separated them, his eyes already dead.

'They shouldn't have banged you up,' Grant said. 'Didn't you tell them it was Mandy's dope?'

'They didn't want to know. I've got a record.'

'It's only three months,' Grant said. He couldn't think what else to say.

'It's a lifetime,' Allan said.

At first, Grant didn't understand what his friend meant. But as the bus descended the hill through the swirling mist, heading for the city, he thought that he did. It scared him.

# 6

## Staying up late

## 1977

'Good taste,' Belinda was saying. 'I mean why doesn't someone do something tasteless on television? Or better still, why don't they have a bit of bad taste? It's probably better than no taste.'

'Because the licence holders wouldn't pay their fees,' Daniel said.

Six of them were crammed around a table in a cubicle at The Woolshed, built to imitate a barn with wooden rafters and timber-topped tables, up steep steps from Lambton Quay. They were eating moussaka and drinking red wine.

'They'd soon come back,' Belinda said. 'They'd stop watching sheep-dog trials and *Close to Home* if they had a bit of real gutsy drama. Life and death and all that stuff. Pain and misery and a bit of suicide thrown in. The BBC could do it. But nobody risks *any*thing.'

'The dear old Beeb. So that's your yardstick of bad taste. Oh Belinda, Berlinney, they're tame, really they are,' Daniel said.

Daniel was a television producer, although none of his projects had got the green light lately. He was leaning against his wife, Carla, raising his voice above the noise of businessmen shouting at each other at the end of the week ('ze zoots', Daniel called them, in a phoney Italian accent), a few politicians, a group of writers, some who knew Daniel and waved matey greetings from the far end of the room. Daniel had intense liquid-brown eyes, shaggy grey hair held back by a headband, a gold filling in one of his front teeth. He was wearing a floral shirt and tight pants. 'So what would you put in a script if the drama department gave you the chance?'

'I'd write something about women's lives, their *real* lives.'

'Ah yes,' Daniel sighed. He signalled to Nick at the other end of the table. Nick was a director. Belinda hadn't learned the distinction between producers and directors, but she thought Daniel had more power than Nick. 'You see what women's liberation has done? They've dreamed up all these scenarios at the Women's Convention and now they want us to direct kitchen sink dramas. Girls, it won't do.'

'Don't say "girls" to me,' Belinda said.

'Because basically,' Carla said, 'you're all a bunch of wankers out there at Avalon.' She pushed a strand of her long dead-straight blonde hair behind her ear. She was dressed in a black sweater, pants and red beads. 'Belinda is absolutely right. Look at *Talking to a Stranger*, that was revolutionary drama.'

'But darling, six hours, six hours long,' Daniel said. 'It was more like a novel. You have to be Eugene O'Neill to hold an audience for that long, and this is television you're talking about. Besides, one-off dramas are over.'

'It played in four parts. It was wonderful,' Belinda chimed in. 'That young actress, Judi Dench, she was brilliant. Oh go on, tell me we don't have actresses like that in New Zealand.'

'Women actors, darling,' Letitia said, and for some reason she was laughing. Belinda thought it was aimed at her.

Letitia was the only one of the four women who were not already friends when the meal started. She was older by at least twenty years, a woman with a broad Yorkshire accent, her figure turning stout, blood-red fingernails, and make-up like pink cement. She had *experience*, darlings, more ITV than the Beeb, which was why she'd been brought out to New Zealand to show the locals how to do things.

She had tagged along behind Daniel and Nick when they said they were heading off for a meal. It was supposed to be a women's night out. Carla had sighed with embarrassment when Daniel insisted on turning up with his colleagues. He whispered something in Carla's ear, and her eyes flicked from Frances, another of the friends, to Nick. Belinda guessed he was trying to arrange a hook-up for Nick. Frances had just broken up with her boyfriend. Belinda thought men must find Frances sexy; she wore wispy diaphanous dresses that showed her curves, and there was something about her wide mouth and curious almost flat teeth that was perhaps inviting. And there was no doubt that Nick was good-looking, with chiselled features and deep set bright blue eyes. His close-cut hair revealed a beautiful curve to the shape of his head. Belinda guessed he was in his late thirties. He was directing documentaries but, like them all, he was just waiting for a drama, preferably a series, to come up.

Nick said: 'It's got a lovely mondegreen in one of its titles.' He was picking up on Belinda's enthusiasm for the play. '"Gladly My Cross-Eyed Bear". Remember? The third episode.'

'Oh yes,' Belinda said. '*Gladly my cross I'd bear*. My mother-in-law thought that was sacrilegious. A mondegreen, is that what it's called?' She rolled it around in her mouth once or twice, like tasting wine, and Nick laughed. 'You're educating me,' she told him.

Belinda, Carla and Frances had met at the United Women's Convention two years earlier. The day had been filled with the sound of pouring rain pounding on the iron roof, which all but drowned out the main speakers' voices at times. Outside the ground had turned to mud as more and more women arrived. Belinda had expected just a handful of women, but two

137

thousand turned up in the Winter Show buildings, a cavernous hall milling with ecstatic women telling each other the stories of their lives. Carla and Frances had arrived together, old friends from school days, both older than Belinda. They all got caught up in a group that was discussing the rights of mothers and children. Two lesbian women talked about being denied access to their children. So then Belinda told them her story, about how she nearly lost her baby but changed her mind and managed to get him back from the jaws of adoption and keep him. Suddenly they were all friends, each knowing someone who knew someone, putting their arms around each other in sisterhood. Belinda, they said, was incredibly brave.

Carla had a job in the library, shelving books three days a week. She and Daniel had two teenagers. Carla sighed over them a lot. Frances was a teacher who was childless but had joined the discussion group anyway, because she worked with children. Really, she confided, she wanted to work in television.

'Don't do it,' Carla told her. 'I just can't stand those men when they get together. They're sexist pigs, worst kind.'

Not so secretly, Belinda wanted to write screenplays, too, but she had her hands full, what with the children and university. She was coming up for air after studying honours in English literature. There were gaps in her education as the children grew: Play Centre groups, school trips, after-school music, activities her mother would never have imagined for her children. Some nights Belinda fell asleep with her work book propped in front of her. She wished she'd done political science because the world was changing, and literature was one thing but surely the dynamics of change were more important. It seemed to her that if she could write for the media she could alter the world because everyone had a television these days. She was sure she would never write a great novel or become a Mansfield scholar.

At the other end of the table, Daniel was telling a story about the prime minister, Rob Muldoon. 'I went to see him,' he was saying. 'Well, a group of us went to talk to him about funding for more drama. He was dancing up and down about how we needed more documentaries and he wasn't going to have the government spending money on made-up rubbish. And we needed more advertising to pay for television anyway. So we said to him we thought the advertising content was too high as it was.'

'And he said …' said Carla, yawning. She'd heard the story before.

'Oh, well, *he* said that *he* liked advertising because that was when he got up to make his cups of tea.' Daniel flung his hands wide. 'We're done for.'

'We need to change the government,' Belinda said. She heard herself speak in another part of her brain and thought she might have had too much to drink. 'I mean, essentially, ess-*ensh*-ally, wouldn't you say, he's fucking us over? That's it, we need to change the government.'

'And you're going to do that single-handedly, are you, Belinda? Eh, babe?', Letitia said in a languid drawl.

'Well, laugh all you like, women can do anything. That's what I'm going to raise my daughter to believe.' Belinda was hell-bent on making her point.

'I wasn't saying they couldn't, darling. I *am* a woman, in case you hadn't noticed. I was merely pointing out that if you're going to proclaim the equality of women, you have to get the language right. How many children do you actually have, little Belinda?'

'Three.' Belinda made her tone short. Or so she thought.

'My God, you can't be much more than a teenager, a child bride. Who's minding the children now?'

Belinda didn't answer this. It didn't seem like any of the bossy woman's business. But it reminded her how late it was, and that her mother-in-law might be worrying about her. Seth was away at a scientific conference in Auckland, and Maisie and Don were minding the children at their place in Masterton. Belinda remembered, through a haze of red wine, that she was supposed to have caught the last train of the night to the Wairarapa.

It was Maisie who first believed the girl when her son brought her home and said that she had given birth to his baby. She looked like a scarecrow, even though she was dressed in tidy, shabby clothes, the cotton blouse stained slightly in front. Maisie could see that her breast milk hadn't completely dried up. Her dark hair was lank, not because it was dirty, but because she seemed unhealthy. Those slanted dark eyes had shadows beneath them that looked like bruises. Don Anderson wouldn't come round easily to the idea that his son Seth had fathered what he termed a bastard.

'How does he know it's his?' he muttered in the privacy of their bedroom that night. 'She could have been with anyone.'

'Hush,' Maisie said. 'Walls have ears.'

The girl was in the next room. It was too soon to let her sleep in the same room as Seth. There were still so many things to be settled. Maisie was sure the walls were too thick for Don to be overheard, although they'd had to make love as quietly as they could when the children were small because Emma, next door, sometimes came in and asked if there was something wrong and were they arguing, when in fact they were joyous and enthusiastic. They were quieter these days. A happy couple. People said you never knew what went on behind the closed doors of a marriage, but theirs was a strong one. Maisie told

Don that night, in their whispered talk, to trust her; she had a feeling this was Seth's child, but they would get to the bottom of it.

This hadn't stop her quizzing Seth in the kitchen when she was dishing up dinner, scalloped veal with a light cream sauce and new potatoes, a salad in a big wooden bowl. He came prowling in behind her, and scooped a little sauce on his finger from the pan.

'You'll burn yourself,' she said, swatting his hand with her wooden spatula. She knew he was waiting for her to say something.

'When?' she said.

There was a silence from her son. The copper-bottomed pots on the shelf above the stove gleamed in this place where she presided. Blue and white cups hung on hooks from a shelf on the dresser at the end of the room above her mother's willow-patterned ashets, or *assiettes* as she sometimes called them when she was exercising her French. The house had belonged to her parents. Maisie knew every groove in the wood, the tread of the stairs that led from downstairs up to the bedrooms. Every colour, every curtain were those she had chosen over the years, as old ones bleached and faded and were replaced. There had always been certainty in her life. She knew which butcher sold the best meat, when the apples would be ripe on the trees and how to give birth without causing anxiety. It had all come to her as naturally as growing up in this house. This certainty had stood her in good stead when she decided to marry Don. Her parents hadn't wanted her to marry into trade, but she'd proved them wrong. This old house wouldn't be standing now if Don hadn't been as skilled as he was.

Seth said, at last, 'The month before I left to go to the met station.'

Maisie had been coddling him since his operation, trying to build him up to be the strong young man he had always been.

He and the girl had both been so pale when they stood in the front room and announced the birth of the girl's baby. A boy.

After it had been said, and Maisie had understood that her life was being altered, that nothing would ever be the same again, and, blindingly, that she might well be a grandmother, the girl had dissolved into sobs. There was no point in pressing for detail. Seth's younger sister, Rebecca, the only one at home, looked stunned and retreated to her room, and hadn't come out since.

'So this little boy must be … ?' She held up the fingers of one hand, counting, as she stirred the sauce with the other.

'Ten weeks. He's just ten weeks old.'

'So where is he now?'

'He's been adopted out.'

'Oh no,' she said. Then, recovering herself, 'Well, of course, what else would she do? Hasn't she got any family?'

'Belinda lived with her aunt. Agnes Rattray. She kicked her out.'

'Oh, my God.' This was an expression Maisie rarely used. She had been brought up Anglican and still went to church. Every fourth week, when it was her turn, she and the Ladies' Group arranged the flowers in the church on Saturday afternoons, in preparation for the next day's service. 'I know who you mean. A bit of an old biddy.'

A picture of Agnes came to mind, a woman she saw often at the grocer's shop, a harsh-looking woman with a strong Scots burr in her voice, a set expression. She remembered the grocer telling Agnes she was a saint, taking in a wayward girl at her age.

'So Belinda, that's her, the girl that lived with old Agnes?'

'Belinda went to school with Rebecca.'

Maisie had seen the way Rebecca had taken off when all of this began unfolding in the front room, as if embarrassed by the whole thing.

Maisie took a long deep breath. The cream sauce had begun to curdle. 'She's a very clever girl, isn't she? Alice said she won the English prize.'

'I don't know,' Seth said. 'Perhaps. We didn't talk much.'

His mother turned her gaze on him, and saw him blushing. 'Then you'd better find out, hadn't you?' she said.

When Don was finally asleep, Maisie lay awake. The night was very still. As she burrowed into Don's broad back, she closed her eyes. Only her thoughts kept churning on. She couldn't stop herself from trying to piece together what might be the truth. She remembered lending Seth her car on Saturday nights. Presumably the back seat of that car was where this child had been conceived. Like Don, she had yet to be convinced. Seth hadn't seen the baby, this child who lived with strangers. He barely knew the girl, whether she was clever or dim or just promiscuous. It wasn't even clear how they'd come to meet each other that day, some story about running into each other in a toy shop. But what was Seth doing in toy shops? At what point, she asked herself, had the decision been made to come home and shatter the calm of the household with an announcement like this? None of it made sense. In the silence, she heard a muffled noise. Through the timbers of the old house, she detected the noise of serious weeping.

As softly as she could, she climbed out of bed and reached for her dressing gown. In the hall she stopped at Belinda's closed door, undecided as to whether she should knock or just go in. This is my house, she thought. She eased the door open and saw, in the light of the bedside lamp, the girl sitting with her knees pulled up to her chin. Her shoulders were shaking. No, it was more than that, her whole body was convulsing.

Maisie sat down on the side of the bed and put out a tentative hand. 'It'll do no good,' she said. 'You're making yourself ill. You didn't eat anything at dinner.'

The girl lapsed into sullen hiccupping sobs. After a few minutes, she began to speak in a low monotone.

'They took him straight away. I wasn't allowed to go and look at him. I know he had fair hair, I do know that much. They said he was eight pounds when he was born, a good weight, and that he was very healthy. He should be a good listener, I talked to him the whole time I was carrying him. I stayed on a horrible farm. If I talked to him it meant I wasn't hearing the old bitch whose house I stayed in. And when there was nobody around I sang to him. I remembered some songs my mother used to sing to me.'

She paused and Maisie rushed to fill the silence. 'What did she sing?'

'She liked the old hits. Wartime stuff. "Auf Wiedersehen, Sweetheart." You know, "We'll Meet Again" and all that shit.'

'I take it your mother's dead, Belinda?'

Belinda nodded, running her fingers through her hair in a distressed motion.

'You were the oldest?' Maisie was trying to find a way in, to reach the girl.

'Second. I wasn't the golden girl.' Belinda hesitated, mulling over what she had said. 'Jessie's my half-sister. She was born just after the war. My mother always looked out for her. I guess she liked Jessie's father. She didn't like mine and I don't blame her. I saw Mum when she was dying. I wanted to sing something to her then, but I knew it would seem stupid in a hospital so I didn't do anything.'

'It wouldn't have been stupid,' Maisie said softly. 'But you weren't to know that. How old were you?'

'Eleven and I'd never seen anyone sick like that. Nobody told me she'd die. Then I got a stepmother. Her name was Charm. I hated her. I did everything I could to make her mad. I tried to kill her.' Belinda's voice had taken on an almost hypnotic quality.

'You did? What did you do?'

'Oh, nothing much. I didn't attack her or anything. We kids made an effigy of her and destroyed it. You know, like burning a scarecrow on Guy Fawkes, only this was different — she was supposed to dissolve into the sea. She caught us.'

'Is that why you went to live with Agnes?'

'Yes. Agnes is all right. It's not her fault, you know, that I got pregnant. I just wanted Seth.' She closed her eyes, her face sensual. 'Being with him was like eating the icing off the Christmas cake. He's sweet, you know. He was like something unbelievable. Yeah, I wanted him.'

Maisie's whole body tingled. 'You wrote to him when he was on the island?'

'No, not at all. I didn't know where he was.'

'How did you know he'd come back from the island?' Maisie asked, her voice faltering. The night felt strange, the quietness of it, the two of them sitting on the bed together, sharing an intimacy too close for comfort. Belinda's nipples had started to leak again inside Rebecca's nightgown, which Maisie had lent her, as if talking about Seth like this had aroused her milk supply. This girl, or this young woman as she should consider her, had been closer to her own son than she had. And wasn't there something they could give mothers to stop them lactating sooner than this? Sage tea, she thought, but where on earth could she get some?

Belinda seemed puzzled. 'I didn't know he'd come back from the island. I didn't even know he'd gone there.'

'But you found him?'

Belinda sat up straight, and looked Maisie straight in the eye, a rebellious expression on her face.

'I didn't find him. He found me.'

In the morning, when they were all seated at the breakfast table, Maisie said, 'It mightn't be too late to retrieve my grandson.'

So the story that Belinda told her friends at the convention had had a modicum of truth about it. But, had it not been for Maisie, she doubted that she would have had the strength to go through the whole business of getting back her son, who, it turned out, was called Peter. There was a meeting with the frosty-faced social worker who had arranged his placement and now had to tell the new parents that they couldn't have him after all. There was paperwork and a brief court appearance for the adoption to be cancelled. Most important, as far as social services were concerned, there was a wedding, after grudging permission had been extracted from Belinda's father. He had to be asked because she was too young to marry without his consent.

'Well, it's a good thing someone's taking her on, I suppose,' he said on the telephone. 'I don't want her back, that's for sure. I hope she doesn't go messing you around, that's all.'

'I'm sure she won't,' Maisie said. It was really Don's place to phone him, but she didn't think he was ready for that yet. Now she wished she'd insisted.

'She's always been a handful, you know. I don't think you know what you're letting yourselves in for.'

'Mr Pawson, would you like to come to the wedding?' Maisie had asked.

'No,' he said, his voice hardening, 'just send me the paperwork and I'll see to it.' A transaction like trading cattle, Maisie thought.

There was just Seth's family in the church, and afterwards at the house, but Maisie made sure Belinda had a nice dress to wear, a short cream lace frock, and there were flowers and a cake with hers and Seth's names written on it in blue icing.

When Belinda said 'I do' in the wedding ceremony, Seth looked so happy she couldn't believe it. He wanted her. Plain, clever Seth Anderson, promising to love and cherish her for the rest of her life.

'Do you want to change his name?' Seth asked, when the baby was brought to them by the social worker.

'Peter will do,' she said, although it wasn't her first choice.

'He's so like his daddy,' Maisie said, wanting to hold him first, but knowing this was the moment for Seth.

Belinda was pregnant within a month but still started university. Maisie looked after Peter. 'You can't waste a brain like yours,' she told her.

Belinda named this baby Dylan, because she'd been reading Dylan Thomas's poems and she liked the melody of his voice on the page, and on the radio, and also because she considered him rebellious, although Seth said wasn't he just a drunk? It didn't matter, they both liked the name. They liked everything the other liked.

At first, Belinda and Seth rented a tiny apartment in Berhampore, and Maisie caught the train in every day so that Belinda could 'go up the hill', as her mother-in-law put it. She'd always wanted to go to university, but girls of her generation didn't do that. She was making sure all her children went. Rebecca was starting a degree in psychology, Belinda must have the same opportunities, Maisie said. Besides, what a pleasure, a grandson. So unexpected, such delight.

So Dylan came a year after Peter and, eighteen months later, Simone arrived. By then Belinda was reading French feminist literature: Simone was named in honour of de Beauvoir. Seth said any name was fine by him, so long as the babies were healthy. All the same, he did ask her if she could be more careful about taking her contraceptive pill.

This led to one of their few quarrels. 'I thought you liked our babies,' she said.

Afterwards, she knew it had been a childish thing to say. She was not quite twenty-two when Simone was born. Not twenty-two and three unplanned babies.

'Don't be ridiculous,' he'd snapped. 'My mother's tired, that's all. I'd like to have sex with you without thinking when's the baby due.'

'I like having babies. I like having them with you. So okay, tell me that's unhealthy.'

'Of course it's unhealthy if you want to go to university and have a baby every year and a mortgage, too.' Don had decided that the family needed a house of their own and had come up with the deposit.

'So I have to stuff chemicals down my throat? That's not unhealthy?'

'I'll use a rubber,' he said.

'Why didn't you do that the first time, then? You took the chance, too.'

They shouted for an hour or more. Seth put his arms around her. She collapsed against him.

'Whatever you do is fine by me, you know that,' he said.

Belinda stopped crying. He spoke with such conviction that she was finally ready to consider the sense of what he had said. She could think of nothing she had done in her life to deserve this kindness awarded her by Seth and his mother. There were times when it was hard to live up to. Seth's sisters and his father might be more sceptical about her virtues — she was sure that they were — but Seth was willing to accept her on whatever terms she asked. It was frightening.

Seth kept his arms around her, holding her close. 'I know why you want to keep having babies. It's because we nearly lost Peter. That's what it's about. You need to be sure there's always

a baby. It scares me silly, too, how close we came to losing him.'
Sometimes it seemed Seth watched over Peter more closely than
she did.

'Mum's getting a bit run-down. She's no spring chicken any
more, much as she loves the kids.'

Now that the children were older (although Simone was
really still a toddler, and a fighting fit one at that), and Seth had
a good job at the science research institute, they had home-help
during the week. But still, more often than not, the children
went to stay with Maisie and Don at the weekends so that
Belinda could study. She and Seth had bought their house, up
the road from where they first lived. The new place was a doer-
upper, a narrow, older house that needed lots of work. There
was a small courtyard, big enough for Peter and Dylan to have
a swing, and a row of vegetables at the edge, which Maisie had
planted for her. Don was near retirement; he often came down
from the Wairarapa to tear out walls or replace gutterings, put
up new fences. That Friday afternoon, while he was working
on the house, Carla had rung and said they were going out for
dinner and what were the chances of Belinda coming along.

'Seth's away. I can't.'

'Oh, shame. Daniel's bringing some of his workmates.
They're rubbish, but it might be fun.'

Belinda stood in the little hallway and thought. The children
were sitting quietly, watching cartoons on television. Don put
his head around the doorway to say goodbye. 'Don,' she said,
'you couldn't put the kids in the van and take them home for
the night, could you?'

She saw him hesitate. 'I thought term had finished,' he said.

'I want to talk over a proposal for my Master's with my
supervisor. I mean, the person who'll supervise me if I get
accepted. I'll come over on the late train so I'm there for them
in the morning.'

'I guess a few hours wouldn't hurt,' he said.

After he'd got the children into the car, and she'd waved and called out 'See you soon', she dressed herself in a silky orange dress with flowing sleeves and applied two coats of mascara to her lashes. It was her eyes that people remarked on when they met her, her gorgeous eyes.

The restaurant was empty, except for the six of them, the staff waiting to go home. Belinda knew she had to get to a phone, but while the bill was sorted out and divided among them, it slipped her mind until it was too late.

They all tumbled out into the moonlit night and down the long flight of steps that led to Lambton Quay. Daniel's big Ford station wagon was parked in a side street. 'All in, I'm your taxi,' he cried.

'You're drunk, Danny boy,' Letitia said. 'You shouldn't be driving.'

'Are you in or not?'

'Not. I'll find a taxi of my own.' With that she clattered into the night. The streets seemed deserted.

'She'll have a long walk home,' Daniel said. 'She lives in Brooklyn. Good luck to her.'

'Well, good riddance to her. Daniel, why ever did you bring that snotty old biddy along?' Carla said.

'Oh, don't worry about her.'

'But really,' Carla said. 'It was supposed to be a fun night out, and she was criticising all of us, you could tell. Just because she's a Pom, she thinks she's superior.'

'Now some would say that was racist. She's got the boss's ear at the moment,' Daniel said. 'C'mon, you lot, who's first off?'

'Me,' said Belinda. Through the mist in her brain, she thought she might still be able to rescue the situation. If she could get to a phone, her own phone, it would be all right. She couldn't ring from a phone box: she would have to put coins in the slot and it would be a dead giveaway to the person who answered that she wasn't at home.

'No, me,' Frances said. 'I have to take my dog for a run. He'll pee all over the carpet.'

'This isn't in the script, Frances babe.'

Belinda guessed that this was because Frances and Nick were meant to land up at the same place. Nick's thigh was pushed hard against hers in the back seat of the car. Perhaps he would get out when Frances did, that must be it.

Frances's place, it turned out, was in Karori, the opposite direction to where Belinda was meant to be going. Daniel had sailed past the railway station, gunning the car up the hill before Belinda had time to stop him. She tried to suppress her rising panic.

Don had gone to meet the train at the station. 'Looks like she must have missed it,' he told Maisie.

'Never mind, she'll have gone home,' Maisie said. 'I'll give her a call to make sure she's all right.'

Don had gone to sleep by then. At midnight, she woke him up. 'She's not answering her phone,' she said. 'I've rung three times now. Surely she'd have heard me, she's a light sleeper.'

'While the cat's away, the mice will play,' Don mumbled sleepily.

'She wouldn't,' Maisie said.

'She might,' her husband said.

And then there were the four of them in the car, Daniel and Carla and Nick and Belinda, or Berlinney, as Daniel kept calling her. There had been a pause while Frances got out of the car, but Nick stayed put as Frances disappeared up her path.

'Two down, four to go. Let's go for a burn,' Daniel cried. 'The night's young.'

'Where are we going?' Belinda said.

'Out to the coast. What do you reckon, folks?'

'Where do you live?' Belinda asked Nick.

'I'm flatting at the moment. Between marriages,' he said. 'Well, who knows, I might never have another one. It's not bad being fancy-free. I was planning to kip at Dan and Carla's tonight.'

'Have you got children?' Belinda asked.

'Ssh,' he said, and put his arm around her.

'You don't ask questions like that,' Carla called from the front seat.

Daniel was driving like a maniac, around the narrow winding road that led out to the coastal village at Makara. Yee-ha, he shouted over and again. 'This is fun. Aren't we having fun?'

Carla said, 'You don't have to get home for a sitter, do you, Berlinney?'

'No, but …' Carla had forgotten about the train Belinda was supposed to catch. Or had she ever told her? Belinda couldn't remember exactly what she'd said to anyone. Truth was a slippery substance and she couldn't always hold onto it. She wanted to be sick. If she could be sick, she might be able to stop what was happening, get out of this car, find her way back home, even though by now they'd travelled for miles, and the sea lay before them. She was afraid to speak in case she vomited before the car stopped.

The water lay unusually calm before them. The stars seemed as big as saucers and the moon that spread its rays over the ocean was huge. This was a rocky shore indeed, stonier than the one she grew up beside. She could see lights on above a porch, hear people singing at a party, their voices ringing out across the night. Belinda climbed out of the car and threw up, her feet crunching on the hard pebbled beach as she tried to keep her balance. She vomited and vomited until she was sure she must be empty of everything she had eaten for a week, her body heaving and wretched.

'It's okay, I'm holding you,' Nick said. 'Whoa, easy does it. It's all right,' he called out to the others, 'I'll look after her.'

He was holding her dress with its pretty braid on the sleeves in a bunch behind her back so that she wouldn't be sick on it. After she'd finished, he got his handkerchief out and wiped her face. He went to the water's edge and rinsed it and came back and wiped her face again. It stayed sticky with salt until much later, the next day. The next day? She had an idea that it was already the next day, that they had left the restaurant some time round midnight.

'We should take her home,' Carla said.

'I don't want her spewing in my car,' Daniel said, suddenly turning sour.

It was the throwing up that Belinda thought must have saved her from doing worse than staying up all night. Nick's hands were gentle yet firm as he held her upright, his saying it was okay when it wasn't, the warmth of him in the car that was still with her, had calmed her. He took off his jacket and put it around her shoulders. She suddenly wanted him to hold her. 'We'll walk,' he said.

He led her along the beach by the hand, as if she were a

child. In the moonlight, beyond a tidal stream that ran to the sea, stood a row of fishermen's shacks. There was a light on in one, flickering like a candle or a lantern. Far behind them, Daniel had shifted the car away from her disaster. He and Carla sat inside it, listening to music.

Belinda and Nick had come across a log washed up from the sea. He sat her down on it.

'You know, you need to have lived real life before you start trying to write it.'

'What makes you think I haven't?'

'So young, so pretty. You talked about suicide earlier tonight. In the play. What would you know about that?'

Belinda described to him then a very bad time in her life, after the birth of her first child, when she had thought seriously about killing herself.

'How would you have done it?'

'I was thinking about bridges over rivers, high buildings, that sort of thing.'

'Yeah. Yeah, I see. But you couldn't be sure with things like that. Pills or cutting one's wrists, I reckon. You have to get the pills first, of course, that can be tricky. Like guns, they're pretty certain, but then guns aren't that easy to come by either, unless you're a farmer or a hunter or something.'

'Are you serious?'

'I was. I've considered the options. I figured out I'd rather live. Are you happy now, Belinda?'

'I reckon I am. I mean, I've got everything. I didn't always.'

She didn't know how long they stayed and talked. She must have dozed off, encased inside the coat of Nick, the director. If he was cold he didn't show it. Along the beach, she supposed Daniel and Carla were sleeping off the drink because they didn't come looking for them. There was no point in worrying any longer about who was looking for her. At some point she thought Nick might have touched her breast but she could have imagined it. She would remember that he sank his face into the side of her neck, and kissed it. The moon faded to a faint white disc, and dawn light began to appear.

'It's five o'clock,' Nick said. 'Five in the morning. Do you often stay up this late, Mrs Anderson?'

'You make me sound like Mrs Robinson. In the movie, you know?'

'We should go home,' he said.

'It's weird, now that I'm here in it, it feels like it shouldn't end. The waves, the moonlight. This sacred night.'

'Louis Armstrong. You like jazz?'

'Yes, yes, I think so.'

'You only think so?'

'There's such a lot to learn.'

'This guy, Seth, he's a lucky man.'

'I'm not so sure. Look at this pickle I'm in. Yes, of course we should go home. If Daniel and Carla haven't driven off and left us.'

'They're still there. I'd have heard them leaving.'

'It would make the good opening shot of a movie.'

He laughed, deep in his barrel-shaped chest. 'You make me feel very young again, Berlinney.' He touched her hair.

'My mouth is so dry.'

'It'll be worse when you wake up. Tomorrow. Today, whatever it is. Drink lots of water. Just brush your teeth before you leave me, baby.'

'What? What did you just say? How can I?'

'It's a mondegreen. Just touch my cheek …'

'. . . before you leave me. "Angel of the Morning".'

'You're beautiful, you know that, don't you?'

'I'm not.'

'You are. Kind of unstructured, but beautiful.'

Belinda asked Daniel to drop her off at the end of the street. (This was a trick she'd learned long ago when she stole out of her aunt's house to go to dances.) Don Anderson was at the house waiting for her, his eyes red-rimmed with sleeplessness. A policeman was there taking notes. Maisie had stayed in the Wairarapa with the children, Seth had rented a car and was driving down from Auckland.

'How could you?' Don said, taking in the state of her.

The policeman closed his notebook, his expression amused.

When Seth arrived, some hours later, everyone else had left. She woke up and saw him standing at the bedroom door. Her mouth tasted like the inside of a sardine tin that had been left out in the sun.

'Where were you?'

He looked as if he'd been crying.

'I ran into Carla,' she said. 'I got drunk.'

'Why didn't you phone someone?'

'I was too drunk. I'm sorry, Seth.' She saw the yawning gaps in her story opening up before her. That was how it would have to stay. When she reviewed it, later on, she agreed with herself that it was so nearly true that it didn't matter.

'Carla should have rung someone.'

'I know. She was drunk, too. Seth, I've never been drunk before. It crept up on me. These years I've been at uni, I could have but I never did. You believe me, don't you?'

And Seth did, because he had to for both their sakes.

'Yes, of course I do, sweetheart.' He opened his arms and wrapped them around her. She was engulfed in his tenderness. 'I was so scared, Belinda, you've got no idea.'

'I have,' she said. 'Seth, I love you.'

'I know. Just don't ever do this to me again.'

'Will they ever forgive me? Your parents?'

He touched her clean shining hair, fresh from the long shower she had taken before she slept, the same place where the man, Nick, had touched it in the morning light on Makara Beach.

'Give them time. You know my mother, she'd forgive a rat for eating the cheese.' It was meant to be a joke, but she shivered inside his arms. 'Mum's crazy about you,' he said. 'My sisters are jealous of you.'

When all of this was in the past, meaning in a week or so, because life went so fast and she was so busy that there was no point in dwelling endlessly on things, Belinda felt some break in her heart, as though some linkage had slipped. Her perfect life, rescued from the disaster of her childhood by the simple serendipity of becoming pregnant to a good and kind man, had almost failed her. The rescue seemed more improbable than she'd ever acknowledged. She considered letting him make her pregnant again, or letting it happen through her own stealth, as if by giving him yet another child she would be giving him back that part of herself that had gone missing for a night. But that wasn't what he wanted. What he wanted was harder to give. All of her. She promised herself she would work on it.

The following month a letter arrived, offering her a commission to write a play for television. The letter was from Letitia, who'd taken over Daniel's job when his contract ran out and hadn't been renewed. Belinda would find this out later, after she had accepted the contract and begun working at the studios on the many rewrites of the play that were asked of her. The director was a woman, because the studio had had to review their gender policies. It didn't look good, all the men who were running the place.

When the letter arrived, Seth said, 'So what about your Master's? I thought you were going to enrol.'

Belinda told him that she needed some time out from study, and anyway the money she would earn would be handy for the mortgage, wouldn't it, and her hours were flexible for the children, unless there was a scheduled script meeting. They wouldn't need Maisie's help so much. Seth couldn't argue with that.

She saw Nick Draper in the corridors now and then, and he nodded to her in passing, as though trying to remember who she was.

The next time Belinda saw her, Carla said, 'So did you know Nick's having an affair with Frances, after all?' She said this in a pleased way, as if she wanted to knock a bit of stuffing out of Belinda. She'd been trying to avoid Carla, guessing that she was bitter that Belinda was now inside the studio and Daniel was not.

They bumped into each other again at the library. Carla was trundling along with a trolley-load of books and Belinda thought she looked tired, her blonde hair tucked behind her ears. 'You know Nick's gone back to his wife and kids, do you?'

Belinda was sure Carla knew perfectly well that she didn't know, and she didn't like the way Carla wanted her to care. The sisterhood was on shaky ground.

After some time had passed, Belinda was offered some work in the documentary unit, and her eye for remarkable detail in the most harrowing stories was noted.

# 7

# Walking the Line

# 1981

The door closes, the lock is turned, the cold floor of the cell confronts them. But they are many and have one another's warmth for comfort. They have chants in their throats that the police cannot stop because there are so many of them, handcuffed and bloody but still unbowed.

It is a late winter's day in 1981, as the Springbok tour grinds on and on. Belinda Anderson and her friends are part of the protest marches trying to stop the games. How long, oh Lord, how long, a newspaper headline asks, and it is what they ask each other every day: How long can this unrest go on in a country that prides itself on harmony and peaceful green fields? The streets are running with blood, the police are marching on the people. They're using their batons to smash in heads, the hospitals are overflowing, children are turning against their parents, and parents against their children. It is so nearly spring and the front gardens of narrow Wellington houses tucked cheek by jowl next to each other are illuminated by kowhai in flower. Such a nice afternoon, full of pale sunshine, to have gone walking through the streets. Although Seth is against the tour he is at home because someone must stay with the children.

*Amandla, Amandla! Ngawethu! Power to the people. The whole world's watching* — the chants going up, words bouncing around the concrete walls, the mists of their breaths rising and mixing with the smell of piss and old vomit. Belinda's eyes travel around the initials scratched in the walls. Even though it's still happening, she knows that it is history in the making, that outside there are cameras rolling capturing the chaos, the citizens at war. When she gets out she will report on it from the very heart of chaos.

'Where's Frances?' she asks Daniel. The friends have been trying to stay together on these demonstrations, so that they can help if any of them get hurt. 'Is she all right? I didn't see her. We haven't left her behind, have we?'

Daniel rolls his eyes. 'She didn't come today. She hasn't marched for a while.'

Carla makes a fingers-down-her-throat gesture. 'Not since the night of the Charles and Diana wedding party, when we were out on Molesworth Street. They all got dressed up in tiaras and big hats and drank champagne while they watched the wedding on telly in the middle of the night.'

'I'm surprised,' Belinda says, because even though she has never liked Frances as much as the others, she still has the capacity for astonishment when she discovers someone she thinks she knows well is so out of tune with her own views. Still it's hard to reconcile the image of a fancy dress party with what had happened to them in Molesworth Street right outside Parliament, the night the police launched their baton attack on the peaceful crowd, and blood ran on the pavements. That was a while ago now, when the tour had barely begun, this civil war barely declared. 'Frances couldn't have known what would happen that night,' she said, hoping to sound charitable.

'Oh, Belinda,' Daniel says, 'really, at heart you're the original naïf, aren't you?'

'Don't condescend, Daniel, it doesn't suit you,' she says crossly. 'Anyone would think you knew what was going to happen.'

Things have been tense between Daniel and Belinda since she turned down a job he was offering her with his fledgling independent company, but that's how it is. You can't be sure with Daniel that any job will last for long, and why would she risk the very good one she already has? She had been sent on a production course and was beginning to learn more about the industry. It was whispered in the corridors that she was a rising star.

Carla has completed an accountancy degree she started long ago, before she had children. Now she's a public servant accountant, her first foot on the promotion ladder already. She hadn't wanted to get caught today. Still, as she remarks, if they're going to sack public servants for protesting, the country will close down. There are thousands of them out marching. Carla used to look faintly Bohemian but these days her fair hair is neatly tied up, her demeanour changed. She wears dark suits to work.

As Belinda tries to make herself comfortable on the floor, she hears a man's voice saying her name.

In the paddy wagon that brought them to the police station, after they were dragged from the road, there were at least twenty people heaped together — writers, hippies wearing ponchos and jeans, a couple of gang members with tattoos on their faces, academics, businessmen who started the day wearing nicely cut Savile Row overcoats, and a woman in a lavender blue twinset and a pearl necklace. The smell of old tobacco, whiffs of marijuana, mingled with that of Chanel No. 5. They've been divided up and herded into holding cells, divided only by bars, that line a dimly lit corridor. Eight of them are crammed into the cell where Belinda finds herself. As she looks over her shoulder she sees an artist whose right hand has been trodden on holding up his fingers to examine them, a nurse with a bandage made from someone's handkerchief, a man squinting through the remaining lens of his glasses.

'Belinda,' the voice says, more insistently.

Belinda picks out a young man whose face she knows and doesn't know, a pallor beneath his stubble, his cow-lick sticking up in a way she half remembers, a hint of fear in his eyes. 'Grant,' she says. 'Is that you?'

'It is, it's me,' and her brother's voice is scared, just like when he was a little boy and used to get hidings from Charm.

'My little brother,' she tells Carla and Daniel, and Nick Draper, who has come with them, hanging in close with the group. He and Belinda are trying to sit back-to-back for support. Carla and Daniel pretend not to notice. Belinda and Nick, it is considered by the others, have a history.

'Well, how about that?' Carla says to Belinda. 'Did you two plan to march together today?'

Belinda and Grant hold each other's eye for an instant. 'Grant, are you okay? Have you been hurt?'

Around them people are quietening down as the reality of being in a prison cell begins to sink in.

'I'm alright,' he says. 'You?'

'Sore back, that's all,' Belinda says. The police who arrested her shoved a knee in her back, one on each side of her as they dragged her away. 'It must be ten years,' she says. 'More than that. I wouldn't have known you.'

'I saw you once, but you didn't see me,' Grant says. 'It was at Parliament when Kirk died. You were carrying a baby. You were with someone. Was that your husband? I was going to come over but I was afraid I'd lose my place in the queue. I was going for a mate who couldn't go. Besides,' his voice falters, 'I didn't know what to say.'

Belinda sees that night in her mind's eye, the queue stretching all the way across the forecourt and down the street, thousands of people waiting to pay their last respects in front of the flag-draped coffin.

'Seven years. It's seven years this week since Kirk died,' Carla says, beside Belinda. 'Big Norm would never have let this happen.'

'So it's seven years this week since we saw each other,' Belinda says to Grant.

'No, since I saw you. You looked happy. Dad heard you had three kids. Someone told Aunt Agnes.'

'It's Rob Muldoon,' Carla says, 'even his mates won't thank him for this. They wanted rugby, not riots.'

'How is the old bastard?' Belinda asks, and she and Grant both know it's their father they are talking about, not prime ministers present or fallen, although loathing for Muldoon runs like a tidal wave through the country. Nobody had expected to be beaten for walking down the street on a sunny afternoon, or sitting down in the middle of the road. Nor at twilight, when people of conscience were going home from work, that a friendly stroll would turn violent outside the very place where they had stood and mourned Kirk.

'Mad as a snake,' Grant says. 'They've locked him up and I hope they've thrown away the key. I left home as soon as I could. You know Charm died?'

'I saw it in the death notices. Good riddance. What happened?'

'Her liver crapped out.'

'You don't say. So, Grant, what about you? What have you been up to?'

'I went to uni.'

'So did I. I never saw you there.'

They are interrupted by the opening of the cell door. All eyes swivel around, an involuntary movement ripples through them as they half rise in anticipation of release. A policeman beckons the artist with the broken hand; the nurse is left behind. The door clangs shut again. A murmuring swell begins to fill the air as a Maori man in the cell next door begins a karakia, then someone starts to recite the Lord's Prayer, and Belinda finds herself praying along with everyone, even though she doesn't believe in God.

'I have to get out of here,' Daniel says, his voice feverish. 'They let that other bloke go.' His greying curls are sticky and a film of sweat has gathered beneath his eyes.

'All in good time.' Carla lays her hand on his shirt sleeve to calm him, but he jerks it away. She doesn't get it, he tells her, he has to get out of this fucking place. Now.

Nick looks worried. 'Cool it, man, they've started processing people now, they'll let us out of here soon.' Belinda had come on the march with Nick. He had stopped by her house that morning so they could walk into town together.

'Take care of her, won't you?' Seth had said at the doorway. 'I'm the one who should be going but nothing's going to stop Belinda. You know what she's like.'

When she glanced back, Seth was watching after them, a wistful expression on his face. She thinks he felt guilty. He is a scientist and has a paper to finish for another conference. It is about coastal and estuarine processes, and the effects of certain tides on marine life. Belinda loves him so much that her heart breaks when she sees him alone like this, except for Simone, who is standing close to her father and doesn't understand why her mother is going out again. Belinda is often going out. Really, she is the one who feels guilty, but although there are many things she can do, she can't write his paper. She thinks of herself more as the eye of a camera, someone who can see things that others cannot and translate them into film. This was what she had seen that morning: that Seth is afraid of losing her. She is afraid of it too, because she has discovered that it is possible to love two men at once. No, worse than afraid, she is terrified.

Nick and his wife, Esme, and Belinda and Seth go to restaurants together and to movies and plays. They have a season ticket at Downstage theatre, and they pool child-minding resources now and then. This is something that bothers Daniel and Carla because they've known Nick and Esme much longer and, as they say, have seen them through some rough patches. There are things they could say, but they wouldn't dream of it, of course. Esme and Nick have a toddler, a late surprise baby, who Carla says brought Nick back into the fold when he'd been straying. She didn't say who with but that's Carla, she likes to tell stories that are suggestive rather than precise. The other word for it is gossiping.

One of their number in the cell is a gang member, who introduces himself as Matiu. He offers to shake hands with them all and rubs his wrists where the handcuffs have been. At least they'd been on his wrists: in the melee Belinda's wrist had been handcuffed to Nick's ankle so that she had to crouch like an animal in the paddy wagon.

'Someone told the cops which way we were heading today,' Matiu says. 'The marshals had a plan to take us up a side street. They didn't tell us until we were heading off. But the cops were waiting for us. They knew.'

'You mean somebody narked?' Nick said.

'I reckon so.'

'Well, they must have buggered off when we got arrested.'

'They wouldn't have,' Matiu says. 'They'd have got arrested with us so they could keep going the next time.' He speaks with the authority of someone who knows the ways of the police and their informers.

'You reckon they might be in one of the cells?' Nick sounds

alarmed. The cell contains Matiu, the four friends and Grant, the nurse with the head wound who hasn't been saying anything, and a man called Phil, perhaps in his late twenties, wearing a green pullover, hand-knitted in cable stitch.

'Nick,' Belinda says, laying her hand on her friend's arm, 'we don't know that. There's enough trouble in here as it is.'

'Okay, Berlinney. You're right, kiddo.' Nick sounds tired. The little girl, Sarah, has kept him and Esme up in the night with a cough. He shouldn't be here. It's what they're all thinking: we shouldn't be here, look at us, arrested.

But for some of their number prison is more familiar. Matiu says: 'If I figure out who it is, I'll poke their eyes out.' He jabs the air with the first two fingers of his right hand, a sharp menacing motion that you'd be crazy not to believe.

Belinda senses fear somewhere in her vicinity, some small startled movement like an animal that has been caught in headlights. She thinks, that person is in here, near to me. She closes her eyes. Not Grant, please let it not be her brother. Down the corridor, in another cell, a woman begins to sing 'We Shall Overcome', but Matiu yells out that they've sung that smarmy one too many times today, they'll never overcome the fucking pigs and can't they change the tune? Then, with a sudden movement, he clambers to his feet and, out of nowhere, his voice swells into Johnny Cash's 'I Walk the Line', and for a few minutes the group is united in belting out the words they know. *Because you're mine*, Nick sings in Belinda's ear, and up and down the row of cells other voices join in. *I walk the line.*

Daniel tries to stand up but his legs give way on him. *I'm on fire*, he warbles, while Carla is clapping her hands in time. 'C'mon, everyone,' she calls out, 'that's more like it.'

The song seems to restore them for a few minutes, but again the group subsides into silence, broken by coughs and sighs, the clearing of throats. Matiu says, 'Well, we better get to the bottom of this. I reckon it's somebody in here. Who grassed?'

'I thought we'd moved on from that,' Nick says. 'What's the point? We're banged-up anyway.'

'Nah, mate, somebody needs a lesson in here. I'm just the person to give it out. Was it you, mate? Is that your problem, eh? Fuckin' nice windbreaker, fancy walking shoes — you one of those undercover blokes?'

'He works in television,' Belinda says. 'You're nuts.'

'Nuts, eh? You his missus?'

'Of course I'm not,' Belinda says. 'I'm just telling you where he works. I see him every day.'

'Leave my sister out of it,' Grant says, his voice going up a note. He's managed to find a pair of black-rimmed glasses in his pocket that make him owlish. Matiu mutters something to himself, but he lapses into silence.

'What did you do at uni?' she asks Grant, as quietly as she can because it's their business, but everyone can hear everyone else in the silences between. People are putting their heads on their arms as if willing themselves to sleep.

'Law and pols.'

'I can't see how I missed you.'

'I mucked round for a year or two. Did some labouring jobs. When did you finish?'

'End of '74. I was in a rush, with the kids. I went back later and did Honours, never have got round to my Master's.'

'I started later. I guess we just kept missing each other.'

Belinda sits thinking for a moment. She's been so busy that the years have melted away. He's seen her, he's walked past her and not known what to say, and she feels ashamed. 'So you're a clever bunny,' she says. 'Political science *and* a lawyer. You through?'

'Yep. Done and dusted.'

'A lawyer? You say you're a lawyer?' Matiu says. His tattoos

167

are carved on the backs of his hands and in deep gouge-like marks on his cheeks. He pulls at the frayed edges of his denim sleeves, his arms crossed. 'A lawyer who works for the cops, are you, mate?'

Grant seems to edge closer to Belinda, just like when they were little and she was his big sister.

'Grant's not that kind,' Belinda says.

'You're a bit of a fancy-pants know-all yourself, aren't you, lady? Well, what's to say it wasn't you? It doesn't have to be a man.' He nods his head in a knowing way. He smells of stale marijuana. 'Yeah, bloody clever theory that.'

The nurse says quietly, 'This woman was beside me all the way on the march. She couldn't have talked to the police.'

'Thank you.' Belinda touches the woman's hand, trying to express solidarity. 'Do you need a doctor?' she asks. The nurse shakes her head. She knows what she's doing; it's not serious.

It's past midnight. The cells are still full; people aren't being processed. It's as if they've been forgotten. Or, Belinda wonders, are they being taught a lesson? What will they be charged with? Disorderly behaviour, perhaps. But it was a peaceful protest, civil disobedience in the spirit of Gandhi — though, let's face it, they'd said some things to the cops that Gandhi wouldn't have said.

Phil needs to go to the toilet.

'They're not going to let you go to the little boys' room,' Matiu says.

The nurse tells him just to lean forward and take deep breaths and the need might pass.

'Our grandfather was a striker in '51. The waterfront lockout. That's thirty years ago. Things go in cycles, I guess,' Grant says to Belinda.

'Our grandfather? Our mother's father? How did you know that? Did Dad tell you?'

168

She guesses as soon as she's spoken that this is unlikely. Their father never spoke of their mother, as if she had never existed, as if they had come into the world like flotsam from the sea beneath the house where they grew up, washed up on the rocks. It wasn't until she got married that she'd even found her mother's maiden name on her birth certificate.

'No, of course not. Our old man didn't like the workers. He only pretended he did when he felt hard done by. I found our grandfather's name when I was doing pols. I had an essay to write on the lockout and I was researching the men on the Wellington waterfront. I guess it's in our blood, eh sis?'

'Why don't you shut up?' Matiu's head bobs up from the doze he'd fallen into. 'Anyway, you never did give me an answer. Was it you that grassed?'

'No,' says Grant, 'it was not.'

And Belinda believes him. She's looking straight at him and his face is clean of guile. Yet still she senses the frisson of fear in the cell that she'd felt before, and she finds herself glancing at the faces all around her. Nobody has moved a muscle. Phil has pissed himself. Daniel is blinking rapidly, as though he wants to wipe something out of his eyes but doesn't dare. And she knows. With a sense of weary, disgusted calm she knows who it is and wonders why on earth he would do it and if he is that broke that he'd take money, if that was what they were offering. Surely, it can't be, that Daniel has gone over to the other side, that he's a cop. She's afraid for Daniel because she thinks Matiu knows, too.

The door is being opened. They are being released. They are more trouble than they are worth.

'Man,' yells Matiu, when they're in the night air, 'I ought to be caged up with nice guys like you more often. They don't let me off that easy as a rule.' The last they hear of him, he is still singing 'I Walk the Line', the words echoing in the streets.

Nick hums it as he walks alongside her. Everyone has dispersed, said goodnight or good morning or whatever the hell it is, calling, 'See you next Saturday.'

Carla and Daniel have left hurriedly. Does Carla know? Belinda thinks not. Daniel wouldn't want her to. She decides not to tell Nick. There was a slight kerfuffle when a taxi came to pick up the nurse and the driver said if she was one of those scum-bag protestors he wasn't having her in his cab, but there was another cab close behind and they piled her into that.

When Belinda turns around to check, Grant is leaving. 'Grant, wait,' she says.

He hesitates and walks back to her. Under the street light, his face is pale and drawn. He swallows and says, 'Our father told us you didn't want to see us again. When you got married.'

'But that's what he told my mother-in-law. That you didn't want to see me. He told her I'd brought shame on the family.' She rummages in her pocket for a ballpoint. 'We should keep in touch. Here, give me your hand.' She holds his fingers steady as she scribbles her phone number on his palm. 'Ring me,' she says. Her head is bursting with questions.

'Sure,' he says.

Nick is waiting in the shadows. She drops a clumsy kiss on her brother's cheek, and watches him as he disappears into the night.

'It's time we were all home,' Nick says.

They're all walking some dark path, Belinda thinks. The marches have brought out the best and the worst in them all.

'Are we really marching because black people in South Africa are oppressed by white people?' she asks Nick. 'Or are we doing it for ourselves because we have stuff and things and good lives and we feel bad about it?'

'Is there any real answer to that? Why do I want to stop games of footy when I love them? I tell myself it's just a game, and then it seems like we're all in one big game, like kids. We're in this rage but some of it's fun, if we're honest.'

'Oh no,' says Belinda. 'Not fun. I didn't mean it that way. I believe in this. I mean, Nick, I *believe*.'

'But in what? You just said you didn't know.'

'That things are wrong. The government. Everything. That black people aren't allowed to play the game with whites. Yeah, I do know what it's about. We're all so fucked in the head, that's all.'

Nick puts his arm around her shoulders and pulls her towards him. They stand in the light of a street lamp. 'Remember?' he says. 'That night?'

Seth has never known about that night on the beach, and Belinda is sure that Esme doesn't either. It's not something you would tell your wife when you were in the midst of being reconciled with her. It's not even that important in the scale of things.

'Why can't we, Berlinney?' he says. 'Just once?'

'Because we can't.'

Another two days and it will officially be spring, but already the fragrance of new growth is around them in the dark, a magnolia blooming with its ghostly white cups in the shadows. They walk past the hospital, Nick still holding onto her, taking her hand as if they really were lovers, not just two people talking about it. Near the zoo a lion roars. This is what she and Nick do — they get lost at night and want each other and talk about it, but that's all. One day it may happen, but she can't imagine that far ahead.

# 8

# In the desert country

# 1982

The hairdressing salon that Nonie Shaw operates at the back of her house is closing for the day. Nonie has gone home to make dinner for her children because one of them has school choir practice and needs to get away early. She has left Janice in charge to sweep up and clean the basins.

The town of Turangi huddles on the banks of the Tongariro River. The water sweeps down from the mountains, on towards the great lake of Taupo, a shining sheet of water stretching into the far distance, where rich people come to fish and play. Yet, although the town has been designed with a central hub of shops and curving streets with nice footpaths, it's still what it is, a place where hard-up people live in small ordinary houses that all look much the same. The cul-de-sacs, designed by town planners, fill with mud and slush in the winter and dust in the summer, because they're still to be completed. On the fringe of this newly-arrived community, tracks curve through the bush to settlements nobody really sees — the camps, as they're known, where the Italian people live. It is the Italians who are rich although they wear their wealth quietly, sending the money back home. They've come to build tunnels that snake kilometre after kilometre under the earth, in the hydro-electricity schemes.

Janice knows the Italians well. Because of the fishing families she grew up with in Wellington, she knew without being told to say *Ciao* when the women came in and *Grazie* when they left and *How are things going?* in Italian, which they liked, because other people wanted them to say everything in English. Nonie says she brings business to the place, and now Janice has mastered some new phrases like *Come vorrebbe il taglio?* How do you like your hair cut?

What Nonie doesn't know is that Janice is seeing one of the Italian men. Nobody except her and Tommaso, who is also known as Tommy to the locals, know about this, and it has to stay a secret because she fears for her life if it gets out. Well, perhaps her friend Paola guesses, but if she does, she doesn't say anything. It's better not to know some things. Paola is Janice's saviour and she doesn't want to cause her trouble.

Janice isn't a hairdresser herself, although Nonie lets her put in rollers and do brush-throughs when the client comes out from under the drier, some blow-waving. She washes people's hair, too; they like the way her fingers linger on their scalp, the pressure she exerts at certain points on their head. They sigh and murmur things like *This is bliss*, their whole bodies relaxing as she releases them for a short while from their everyday lives. Once or twice she's done trims for the kiddies and Nonie says, Well, you don't really have to have a certificate to put on the wall, so long as the customer is happy, and she could probably teach her to do a few basic cuts. The way the business is growing she could do with the help.

Janice doesn't mind sweeping up other people's hair. She likes the mixed fur of blonde and black, brown and grey that mats the linoleum. There's something silky and still alive about it, people shedding themselves, transformed in front of the mirrors from frowziness to instant glamour, sleek or curled. People still want Afros and big fat perms. Janice's hair is curly anyway: she's been trying to straighten it for years without success. She knows girls who try to iron their hair to keep it flat, and now they have permission to be pretend radical, just like the sixties with their frizzy hairstyles, although mostly it's girls home from holidays in the city who are having them. There are still plenty of short bobs and older women who want finger waves. Nonie has dyed Janice's hair dark auburn, and changed its shape so it ripples in corrugated fashion almost to her shoulders, falling forward to hide the blemish on her face.

She's anxious to be away now, because it's nearly time for her to pick up her five-year-old daughter, Heaven, from the minder. Janice called her Heaven because when she first arrived in desert country, it seemed like heaven after a childhood she wanted to put far away, with a man who, it seemed, would be good to her. She loves the country in the centre of the North Island where there is tussock and few trees, just snow-covered mountains, crystal bright, and roadsides crowded with wild flowers.

For some time, after she left Wellington behind, she continued to believe in this heaven of hers. It wasn't the first black eye that changed her mind, nor even the tenth, or both of them at once, it was the time her nose slid around her face, the knowing that she would never look quite the same again when it was mended. But still, in Heaven, she can hold onto the memory of the sweet good times she and Darrell had before it all went wrong.

When Heaven was born she thought it might make him happy.

'You useless cunt,' he'd said at the hospital. 'Why couldn't you give me a son?'

She knew from that day on that her life had a purpose, a mission: to keep Heaven safe. In the evenings she would croon to her child *'Heaven is in my arms tonight'*. It had taken Paola to convince her that the only way to protect her was to leave.

There's an urgent tapping on the glass door, covered by the blind she has pulled down. Some people can't read a sign that says CLOSED. She smiles wryly. She can't read, or not very well. Janice stands quite still so that the person knocking will think there's nobody there, but they must have glimpsed a movement, because the knocking gets louder.

'Janice, open up,' says an urgent voice. Janice recognises it as Paola's, and calls out, 'Coming — hold on a sec,' as she hurriedly unlocks the door.

Paola throws herself into the salon and bangs the door shut, glancing behind her, fearful someone might be following. She carries a big brown paper bag, as if she's been shopping.

Paola is the Italian woman who saved Janice's life. It's three years now since she walked into the salon and saw Janice so battered her face was all but unrecognisable. Nonie had told her to go home, but going home would have meant going back for another hiding.

Paola had said, you have to come back with me. *I take you home. Get your kid and leave. Now.*

Janice remembers the ride in the Land Rover, bumping over potholes, down a dirt road called Access 13, through the scrubby trees that skirted the desert, the sign at the gate, deep in the fast of the bush: *Autisti Rallentare Attenzione Bambini Che Giocano* — Drive Slowly, Children Playing. And the next thing she was in Paola's kitchen of the tiny house she shared with her husband, Lorenzo, a red gingham cloth on the table and the gamey delicious smell of food cooking in the oven.

'You like *spezzatino*? What you call it, casserole? Wild pork, lots of herbs. See, I grow rosemary and thyme and sage. Is good. Tomorrow we eat real spaghetti, the company brings us in the things we need to live like Italians, olives, proper tomatoes in tins. We live good here in the bush. I get you a skirt. Women not allowed to wear trousers in the camp.' She gave Janice something to drink, a coffee made with sugar laced half-and-half with brandy. 'Give you strength.'

When Lorenzo returned he wasn't pleased to have a guest, a New Zealand woman who looked like trouble, but as Paola pointed out, why not? He was at work day and night, and there was nobody else to share the house with her. She got lonely, remember? They might have the food and the wine and yes, Lorenzo, you have drunk more than your share of the red wine today, but the two of them, they do not have much company. Janice felt the air heavy with decision. She would learn that men made the rules at the camp. Paola pouted and wound a hand round his neck.

'*Per favore*,' Janice had said.

Lorenzo appeared to soften a little, but he talked too quickly for her to follow what he said next, still not convinced. She thought it was about bringing a child there. Paola's face had clouded. In the end Lorenzo had relented. Janice could stay for a while, but not for too long. He knew Darrell, who worked on the diggers in the town; he didn't want fights from him.

Paola explained later to Janice that Lorenzo lived with a sadness she could not change. 'He wants a bambino but I don't make babies, I cannot.' They had married in Northern Italy some years before, and he had brought her to the camp as a young bride. 'He think the babies will come straight away, but so far nothing, you understand?'

Paola wonders if it is him that cannot have babies, but this is not a thing you can discuss with a man. He had taken to drinking far too much of the Valpolicella that the company provides. Two litres at the end of every shift. Paola had shivered, wrapping her arms around her body. As if that wasn't enough, he drank still more when he got home.

Janice considered Paola beautiful — eyebrows like the wings of a little bird, sweeping black hair that fell to her waist when she loosened it, full breasts that Janice sometimes glimpsed when she ran from her bedroom to the shower, dark nipples tilted upwards, a tiny waist. Her visits to the hairdresser were just to get her ends trimmed, to have her hair washed by Janice, and to practise her English, which was better than that of most of the women at the camp. She had gone to a good school, she told Janice. Some women in the camp weren't so friendly with her because they were from rural villages and she wasn't. And because she couldn't have children. They'd found something to criticise. She knew the men did, too.

It was in the camp that Janice met Tommaso, a single man, his body packed with sinew, covered with hair like a pelt when he took off his clothes, eyes like the bottom of a dark well. They shared cigarettes now and then in the big camp kitchen where the single men ate. He touched Heaven's head gently. The Italians liked children. Heaven was a cute kid, the women said, small for her age but strong, with hair that would be curly like Janice's own, and freckles on her pale pointed face. She was free to roam within the confines of the camp, although Janice was warned not to let her go too far away. There was a prison for dangerous criminals next door. Who knew when one of them might escape? That was their fear. They looked out for one another.

'You want to watch it with Tommaso,' Paola said anxiously, one evening when Janice had loitered too long over at the kitchen.

Janice said that she'd just been collecting Heaven, who ran after Tommaso, and he seemed like a nice guy.

'Tommaso would steal your eyeballs if he thought he could take your eyelashes,' Paola said.

177

'I don't get that,' said Janice. 'I've got nothing to steal.'

'You have a heart,' her friend replied. 'You should be careful.'

Nothing happened with Tommy while she was at the camp, but she knew he liked her. She wasn't a woman a man could safely go with.

Since then Janice's face has healed, she's returned to the town, though she would have liked to have stayed. Darrell has gone away, sending a message that he will kill her if he gets his hands on her again, but as the police were onto him, she'd got lucky for now. He hated her, the bitch, but she belonged to him so she better watch out.

Because Janice has nowhere else to go she stays in the company house where she and Darrell have lived since soon after Heaven was born. Before that they lived in cabins in camping grounds and for a year they rented an empty caravan when the owners got too old for the life. She's come to believe that she's safe, that because she and Heaven haven't heard from Darrell since the day she first went to the Italian camp, that he's gone for good.

Tommaso comes to the house some nights when Heaven is asleep. Janice dreams that he will marry her, but knows it won't happen. Already there's trouble for some of the wives the men have taken back to Italy. The families don't understand why they should take women from another country. It's worse for the Maori women who marry the Italians. Word travels when one of them comes back to New Zealand, unwanted in Italy. She comes home to her family, who live near the lake. Janice is white, but she has a child, and she isn't a widow. It wouldn't do. Some of the men are talking about staying behind in New Zealand when their contracts end, but Tommaso has a mother and father waiting for him to return. He doesn't say so, but she knows he won't let them down. He is their son, their first born.

'What is it, Paola?' Janice asks, when she lets her friend into the salon.

'There is nobody else to trust. You will help me.'

'With what? Has Lorenzo given you a hiding?' She thinks this is unlikely because Lorenzo is a man who sulks rather than beats, has a glowering hostility that has slid into contempt for Paola.

Paola takes deep breaths to steady herself. 'The company is sending all the men back to Italy. You know there are only a few of us left?'

'I do know that. Yes.'

Paola gives her a sideways glance. 'Perhaps you do.' She wears a kerchief over her head, tied at the back, a dark jacket and a long brown skirt that covers her calves. 'They call it the repatriation. Lorenzo has our tickets, we go the week after next. No, he goes. The thing is, I am not going back.'

At first Janice doesn't understand. 'You're staying here? Hey, that's great. I didn't think Lorenzo would.'

'Lorenzo will go back,' Paola says, her voice measured and flat, as if she's explaining to a child. 'I will not. Tonight the bus for Auckland passes through around seven. I want to be on it. I don't wish to look like old Paola, I want to look like new Paola.'

Janice's stomach lurches.

'What do you want me to do?'

Janice has done enough risky things in her life — running away from home when she was still supposed to be in school, living with a man she wasn't married to, having a baby, smoking a great deal of dope at one time or another, although not while she lived in the camp, and hardly ever, now that Darrell's gone.

'I am going to change my clothes. I have been up to Rotorua today and bought jeans, same as Kiwi girls wear. New jacket. Look, leather.' Paola holds up a black coat. It is as soft to the touch as a baby's shawl. 'See, I put these clothes on. I have been, too, to the Woolworth shop. There I have bought glasses.' The spectacles have big blue frames.

'You're not really going to do this,' Janice says. 'You'll still look like you. Well, sort of like you.'

'No, because now you are going to cut off my hair. Very short like that of boy.'

'Paola, I can't. You know I can't. Nonie would kill me.'

Paola fixes her eyes on Janice's, reflected back in the mirror. It's unspoken, but Janice knows that this is about payback, that she owes Paola.

Janice tries a different tack. 'You won't be able to stay in the country if Lorenzo goes. The company will tell the immigration people.'

'I have my passport.'

'They'll find you and send you back to Italy.'

Janice doesn't know how she knows this. But there has been so much talk of the conclusion of the contract, the last Santa Barbara festival to bless the workers, the end of the tunnelling and the return home. Lorenzo has made enough money to build a house on the edge of the Adriatic Ocean, where he and Paola and his mother and father and his sister who isn't yet married will all live. For those who are staying, there's paperwork to be done, immigration to consult. It's a process that will take time.

'Cut.'

Paola picks up the scissors and hands them to Janice. As she slides off her old jacket, preparing to sit in the chair, she reveals a new red silk blouse that shows off her curves. 'He will not find me. I will get a job in Auckland. After a while he will go back to Italy, you see. Then I will find people to help me. Those women's liberation people, what do they call them? They have houses. Refuges. I will go to a refuge and tell them they have to help me, I help other women, now it is your turn. I will be dead if I go back to Italy. Cut my hair, Janice. Now.'

'Okay, but I'll have to be quick. Heaven's minder'll be ringing Nonie soon to see where I am.'

Janice picks up a swathe of the glorious hair. It feels full of energy, pulsing, a living skein of black silk in her hand. The first cut seems like a blow she is inflicting on Paola, but her friend doesn't flinch. Janice can tell from the set of her mouth, the angle of her jaw, that she's going to go through with this. She cuts beneath the collar line, until the hair lies in her hand, free of its owner. She lays it on the counter with something approaching reverence. She has seen long hair cut before, but never anything like this.

'More,' Paola says. 'Hurry.'

Janice picks up the clippers and shears the hair up shorter, so that only a bang falls over Paola's left eye.

'That is good.'

Even as she speaks, Paola is stripping away her skirt, pulling on the jeans and leather jacket. Then she fishes for some lipstick and applies a generous slash of deep glossy red. Janice sees that she is a stranger to her, but so astonishingly beautiful that she thinks everyone will notice her.

'Your hair,' Janice says, holding it out.

'The hair is for you. Perhaps you sell it.'

'I couldn't. It belongs to you.' Janice hesitates. She knows she's not going to see Paola again. She loves Paola, she realises, with an intensity that's almost physical. 'It's part of you.'

Paola laughs, a deep throaty chuckle, as if she is already adopting some new persona. 'I am not a holy wafer,' she says, but this is lost on Janice, who doesn't know what this means. She holds up a set of keys. 'I am going to leave the keys in the Land Rover. It is in the car park near the grocer's shop. If anybody asks, you tell them you do not know where it is. You have not seen me. You understand?'

Janice nods in agreement. She is wrapping up the hair, looping it through in a knot so that it doesn't all fall apart, and slipping it into her duffel bag. She wants Paola gone, so that she can clear away all traces of her deed as quickly as possible. When Paola has left, she'll give the minder a quick call to say she's on her way.

At the doorway, Paola hesitates. 'You should leave, too. Soon.'

'With you?'

'Of course not. Hey, do not look like that. They would pick me up very quick if there was a little girl along with us. But I think you might get trouble soon.'

'Why? Paola, you'd better tell me right now.' The shoe's on the other foot now, she thinks. She's the one with the power now that she knows what Paola's up to. She has Heaven to guard and she will do what it takes.

Paola says in a quick frightened voice, 'Darrell's back.'

'Oh, my God. '

'Lorenzo saw him yesterday at the petrol station. He told him about Tommy.'

'What about Tommy?'

'*You* know what about Tommy.'

'Were you going to go without telling me?'

'I have told you. And now I am — what is it that you say? — I am out of it. Pick up your girl, Janice, and leave. Go while you can.'

Janice hurries now. She rearranges the counter so that it will be neat and ready for business when Nonie arrives in the morning. After a moment's hesitation, she takes thirty dollars out of Nonie's till, the bit of change that she keeps there. Janice has told her in the past that she's a fool to leave it there, but Nonie says easily, who would rob her, and it wasn't that much money. To Janice, thirty dollars is thirty dollars and will buy her and Heaven a ticket out of town, just like Paola. She's not sure where, perhaps to Rotorua, a town she knows from the days when she and Darrell used to ride the roads. She hasn't been further north than that.

The woman who minds Heaven for her is impatient for the child to be gone. She's in her sixties, heavy ankles, a not very clean apron tied at the waist. Her kitchen is steamed up from cabbage cooking on the stove top. It's past the hour when she likes to release the cork on a bottle of wine. Heaven stands at the door, already wearing her coat, and grabs Janice's hand. The kid always acts like she hasn't seen her mother for weeks and clings to her as if she's a lifeline to happiness.

They set off at a brisk pace, and even as they go, Janice is formulating a plan in her head about packing up as soon as they have eaten dinner that evening and being ready to go first thing. It's not that she owns much. The house was furnished when it was let to her and Darrell. There are some pots and pans she will have to leave behind, but she might be able to stuff some of the bed linen and towels into her suitcase. Otherwise it's just their clothes and Heaven's toys.

As Janice walks down the road with Heaven at her side, she sees a glow in the darkness that's falling over the town on this spring evening. The street lamps are coming on, poking fingers of light over the houses with their drawn curtains, tentacles of mist from the mountains descending and curling around the ragged attempts at vegetable gardens, illuminating the new paling fences. But this flickering brightness isn't the street lamps. A sixth sense tells her not to round the corner. But

Heaven pulls on her hand and it's too late.

There's a burning cross laid out on her lawn and a man stands in the shadows cast by the flames near her gate. She thinks, for an instant, that it's her lover awaiting her return. But it's too tall for Tommaso and she knows it's Darrell. Her feet won't move.

She gets to say, before the first smash of his fist, 'I'm over you, Darrell.'

'You belong to me,' he says. 'You'll burn in hell if I don't save you.'

The blows falling on her head are swift and sure. She's on the ground and a boot smashes the nose that has healed and is now broken again; she hears the crunch of leather on bone. Her eardrum shatters at the second kick. Janice throws her body over Heaven. All the time she screams, a long thin howl, the word 'help' over and again.

Another man appears from out of the dark; dimly she hears some methodical punches. She knows who it is but she won't say his name. The beating Darrell is receiving at Tommaso's hands is something she knows he'll never forgive. If she survives this round, she won't last another.

People are coming out of the houses to see what the commotion is about. In a few minutes a police car arrives, lights flashing. By then Tommaso has gone, and so, too, has Darrell. Then everything goes black as she slides into unconsciousness.

When she wakes in the hospital in another town, she asks, as soon as she can speak, where Heaven is. At first the nurse thinks that Janice believes she's dead. When she's able to explain, the nurse says right then, she'll get the social worker who's been dealing with her daughter to come and talk to her.

Heaven, it turns out, has been taken into care. They've been searching for Janice's relatives to see who can take the child in, but so far they've had no luck. Surely there must be someone who can look after her? Janice says she has a sister, but she's got enough kids of her own, from what she's heard, and anyway she's turned into a stuck-up bitch. Janice doesn't want her looking down on her. Besides, she wants to get out of here and get her kid back.

'It might take a little while to arrange,' the social worker says. She's an older woman, her manner formal, wearing a grey pants suit, her mouth a little scarlet bow. 'What did you say your sister's name was? Belinda Anderson? Funny, that name rings a bell. Pawson? Anderson? Oh well, it's hard to keep track of you all.'

'I haven't seen her in years.'

'Well, I could be mistaken,' says the woman, who has introduced herself as Miss Borrell. 'I thought I might have met her when I was working down south.'

'She's not getting my girl. Anyway, it's that Darrell you should be after,' Janice says. 'I've done nothing wrong.'

'Well, maybe not. Nonie says she forgives you for the money you took from her till.'

'Okay then. I was scared. I'm sorry about that.'

Miss Borrell breathes long and hard through her nose, pursing her mouth. 'The police found some illegal substances in the house where you were living.'

'Look at me,' Janice says. 'You think my life is a bowl of chicken soup?'

'What sort of life do you think you're going to give your child? Always on the run. You can't even read and write properly.'

'So what's that got to do with it? ' But it stops her and she looks down to the edge of the sheet, humiliated and sullen. 'Heaven won't get anywhere if she doesn't have me. She'll pine away and die. Please.'

'We're going to give you a chance,' Miss Borrell says, as if satisfied that she has the upper hand. Of course, she's known all along what was going to happen, Janice thinks afterwards.

The social worker explains how a protection order will be obtained, how Janice and Heaven will go to Auckland and live at a secret location, known only to the social workers. She advises Janice to change Heaven's name as it will show up too easily on the school roll. Janice, too, is advised to use a different surname. To all intents and purposes, she'll become a new person. She'll live clean of drugs, she won't drink or go to hotels, she won't try to contact the Italians who have said, anyway, that they want nothing more to do with her, she'll learn to merge into a big city and become unseen. She'll be happy and grateful. The last isn't actually said, but Janice knows that this is what's expected of her.

Later, a letter will be sent, addressed to Janice, care of the post office in Turangi, marked 'Please Forward' on the envelope. It reads:

> *Dear Janice,*
>
> *A woman I used to know a few years ago has been in touch with me (you can probably guess who this is). She wouldn't tell me what it was all about, because it's confidential and so on, but I gather you've had some sort of bother and she's worried about you. I'm sorry about this and hope it's not too serious. I've been pretty lucky so far, things have gone better for me than I expected. I've lost track of the family and I'd really like us to all get back in touch with each other. I know where Grant is now, and our big sister Jessie has her name in the papers, though she doesn't answer my letters. But I have no idea where you are and I miss you. I'm here if you need me, you only have to say.*
>
> *Love from Belinda*

The postmaster doesn't know where to send this letter. Eventually it will go to headquarters to be destroyed, along with other undelivered mail.

Janice changes Heaven's name, for now, to Paula. It keeps alive that brief flame of friendship she shared with the Italian woman. In time, she believes, her daughter will be Heaven again.

# 9

# All day at the movies

# 1992

In the still part of summer evenings, Grant Pawson would catch a No. 3 bus to Karori. One or two people who were regulars on the route would nod to him as if his face were familiar although they couldn't quite place him. He could be any almost-middle-aged man going home to his wife and family. At the stop before the turn-off to the cemetery, he alighted, walking briskly to his destination, briefcase in hand, suit coat unbuttoned, his tie, usually red-patterned, flapping if there was a breeze. To his left, as he entered the gates, lay a rose garden at the centre of radiating plaques for those who had been cremated, their surfaces so small that only miniature versions of tombstone inscriptions could be engraved on them. Beyond, on his right, as he made his way along the avenue that ran through the cemetery, was the Small Crematorium chapel. Its interior reminded him of little dark chapels in Europe, without the overwhelming presence of saints and martyrs bleeding in plaster, or the scent of incense on the air.

The cemetery covered a large tract of land, forty hectares in all, and housed, if that were the right word for it, more than eighty thousand human remains. To read the laments of the bereaved on each stone could take many months, if one was so inclined. Some famous people were buried there. Grant always hesitated before the tombstone of Labour prime minister Walter Nash, and that of his wife, Lot. A good man who shouldn't be forgotten. Grant sometimes plucked leaves or pieces of flowers off nearby graves and placed them on the stone. There were separate sections for Chinese and Jewish and Greek and other varieties of humanity, Roman Catholics and war veterans, and so on, and this refined Grant's search. He knew what he was looking for and none of these fitted, except perhaps Roman Catholics. There were nuns and priests mingled with worn-out workmen and women who'd died in childbirth, and among them there was the possibility of an acceptable find.

After he had visited his mother's grave, as he did on each visit, he would look for the graves of children, small graves tucked among the larger slabs, often right alongside them, as if keeping the grown-ups company. Sometimes he would find the name of a child added to the stone on a family plot, so that he could never take for granted that the larger monuments might not have one sad line added, recording the loss of 'dear Boysie' or 'our wee angel only lent'.

The cemetery had become crowded and now most of the burials took place at the cemetery along the coast road, where untouched land stretched far and away into the scrublands, but all of those graves were too new. So he continued to search among the tombstones that had gathered moss. And this solitary pastime, which may have seemed strange to anyone observing him, gave him an odd comfort, a sense of direction that made his everyday life, down the road at Parliament, seem tawdry and insignificant.

Often, as he was leaving towards dusk, he stopped at the rose garden and touched the plaque where Allan Johnson's ashes were planted. After his friend had taken his own life, nobody

189

had come forward to claim his ashes, and once a suitable amount of time had passed the funeral director had allowed Grant to take the urn. For some years it sat in the wardrobe of the apartment Grant rented in the city, until he first set off to travel abroad. He feared that he might not come back safely and that the ashes would be discarded, a macabre discovery for some unsuspecting future tenant. Grant had bought one of the little bronze plaques, so that Allan could be remembered in the rose garden, as if he had been a real person, not just the figment of Grant's imagination that he occasionally seemed to be, after nearly twenty years.

But he was close to exhausting the possibilities of the perfect match for what he was seeking at Karori cemetery. Soon he would have to get out his blue Peugeot car, with its sweetly purring engine, and drive to cemeteries further afield: the Taita Lawn Cemetery, or the one at Akatarawa in a bush-clad valley. And beyond those lay little towns, the out-of-the-way places where families moved on and children became history. There were all of those, beckoning to him. Sooner or later he would find the right one.

The house in Brighton Street had stood empty for two years when Grant and his sister Belinda Anderson came to clear it out and make ready for sale. He had rung and asked her to come down from Auckland to help him. Their father, who had spent the last part of his life in a secure dementia ward, had died five years earlier, although, as Grant remarked, he might as well have been dead for the last ten.

'Make that forever as far as I'm concerned,' Belinda said.

Although she was a small woman, she had a way of standing

that made her seem taller, her dark hair showing its first threads of grey. She cut an elegant figure, quite different from the last times he had seen her, wearing tight jeans over firm buttocks, and a colourful tunic picked up in a market in Paris. That city, he learned, was her destination of choice when she and her husband Seth travelled, although she managed trips on her own when her work took her there. When she travelled alone, she told him, she felt like someone who'd made it out of a falling-down house on the far edge of the world, overlooking a narrow but often stormy sea. Or, words to that effect.

Although there had been an exchange of phone calls, Grant had only met with his sister once since they'd encountered each other in the cell. He remembered that distant night, the way he'd walked home and turned the shower on full, sluicing himself down as he did when he was a boy, after a shift on the rubbish trucks, expunging the smell of filth. Afterwards, shocked, he realised there was something missing. He opened his hands and they were empty: the number Belinda had written on the palm of his hand had disappeared. It felt like an omen. For a long time, Grant couldn't bring himself to look her up in the phone book. She'd have decided he didn't want to be in touch, or, perhaps, that she really wouldn't want to see him again, like their father had said; that their chance meeting had been just that.

When he did find the number and dial it, she was away for her work, Seth said. His voice was cool. The husband, as Grant thought of him, someone he knew nothing about and couldn't visualise. In the end, she tracked him down. He was working for a law firm on The Terrace, not far from where he lived, and they met at a café. He sensed that her mind was on other things; there was something edgy and distracted about her, as she dissected a club sandwich with her fingers without eating, and let her coffee grow cold. There were things he'd wanted to talk about, but the moment didn't seem right for intimate conversation. After they'd asked each other about Janice, and neither had any answers, Belinda had announced abruptly that she and Seth were moving north to Auckland. It had been a sudden decision on Seth's part, but she was sure it would be good for her career. She said this without conviction, staring out into the street as if watching for someone. So the meeting was really about hello and goodbye, and how she must fly.

He'd had hopes for that meeting, but it seemed he was as much on his own as ever. The next time he called her was to tell her Jock had died.

'Oh goodness,' she had said, after a pause, 'I should come down, shouldn't I?'

'It's done and dusted,' he said.

'What do you mean?'

'I had him cremated this morning.' He didn't tell her that he'd had practice at disposing of people without fuss. 'It seemed the best thing,' he added, to soften what he'd just said.

'Are you okay? I mean, are you feeling awful? I'll come if you want.'

He hesitated again.

'The house is rented out, so there's nothing to be done really.' He heard her sigh of relief.

'Well then, thank goodness, and thank you, Grant. I'm off to New Caledonia tomorrow. I'd have put it off if you needed me.' Her voice was breezy. Whatever had troubled her when he last saw her must be in the past. In the background, one of her children called out that he was waiting for a lift into town.

He'd left it at that. His busy, bright sister with her family and successes.

The house had been rented out since then, until the last lot of people left when it had been too run-down for anyone to want it. A few pieces of furniture remained from their childhood, a couch with broken springs and rotted fabric covered with dog hairs, a gate-legged table where Belinda could still see her mother sitting with a book propped up in front of her while she peeled the potatoes. She often missed the eyes in the potatoes.

Grant's eyes followed hers. As if reading her thoughts, he said, 'I visit her grave now and then. I was up at the cemetery the other day.'

'That's good of you,' Belinda said. 'To be honest, I don't know if I could find it. Well, the fact is, I haven't been back since she died. And now that we're in Auckland . . .' Her voice trailed away. She shrugged. 'I've been busy, Grant, my work and three kids. I still remember her, though. I thought about her so much at the time it's probably why I got sent away. I set out to make Charm's life hell, you know that. Was she as bad as I thought or was I just in a funk because we didn't have our real mother to tell us what to do?'

'She was bad,' Grant said. 'But partly she was just thick, and we weren't. We scared the tripe out of her.'

'Put you off marriage, did it, Grant?'

'I got married.'

'You did? You dark horse. Are you still?'

'It lasted a year. Her name was Lizzie. I wasn't much of a husband.'

'In what way?'

'Does it matter? I wasn't the man she thought I was.'

'Meaning?'

A tense silence fell between them until Grant looked away.

'Okay, I'm sorry I asked. Where are you working?'

'At Parliament.' He'd brought a thermos of coffee and handed her a plastic cup. 'I hope you don't mind it black.'

'That's how I take it.' She gestured to the door where sun gleamed on the step. The morning was calm and the navy blue sea lay before them, the small huddled island of Tapu te Ranga standing in the bay, and beyond, on this glass-sharp morning, the snow-tipped mountain peaks of the South Island appeared on the horizon. Only a flock of gulls screeching with excitement as they swooped on a school of fish broke the silent day. Belinda sank down on the step, wiping perspiration off her forehead.

'So you're not practising law any more?'

Grant saw she wasn't going to leave it alone, the subject of his life. Her skills in asking questions were as good as his.

'I never did have a taste for courtrooms.'

'You were doing conveyancing work the last time I saw you. That's hardly *Twelve Angry Men.*'

'I had the chance to work for the Labour government. It was exciting at first. Now that they're out, I've finished up advising a broken-down politician from up North. Kendall, he was lucky he had a safe seat in the landslide.'

'Kit Kendall? He's to the right of Genghis Khan.'

'In a left-wing party. Don't start, I know.'

'I know his ex-wife, Rose. She's got a little film company.'

'So I heard. She makes dramas, doesn't she?'

'She tries, but the money's so hard to come by in drama.'

'Not your field?'

'I'd love to.' For a moment Belinda's voice was wistful. 'But, you know, I'm good at what I do. You can get finance for documentaries. My stuff actually gets made and goes to air. Rose Kendall might make it, she's smart and persistent, smarter than he ever was. He went off with an air hostess. She's probably smarter than him, too.'

'Not any more, she didn't have enough money for his tastes. He's off with another one now, or make that two or three. He does a great line with the ladies, I'll give him that. You should see his florists' bills.'

'And I suppose I'm paying for that with my taxes. Lordy, I do miss the Wellington gossip. But honestly, Grant, he turned into a lackey for neo-liberalism. Surely you don't like working for him?'

'Not really. I'm probably just addicted to politics. Lately I find myself asking, what's the point?'

'Seth's joined the Green Party. He's an environmentalist.'

'Good for him. The Greens have got a future, I reckon.'

'So, Grant, what about the people who're getting kicked out of state houses because they can't pay market rents? Kids are going hungry. What're you doing for them?'

'*I* don't make a blind bit of difference, Belinda. It's the free market. Of course I know what's happening, I see the letters that come across Kit's desk. Sometimes his constituents turn up at Parliament with their kids. They haven't eaten for days. I have to arrange for them to see him. You can't just walk up to Parliament and knock on the door any more. Not since the tour.'

'What does Kendall do?'

'He puts his head in his hands and says he's sorry it's so tough out there.'

'What do you do?'

'Take them over to the railway station, buy them a feed of pies and chips and put them on a bus back up North, or wherever they've come from.'

'Awful. Do you have to keep working for him? You've got all those quals.'

'Haven't you heard about the desks that have been cleared in Wellington lately? If you're a public servant, you go to work in the morning and somewhere round lunchtime someone comes around with a slip of paper that says you've lost your job, and gives you a green plastic rubbish sack. The rubbish sack isn't to be sick in, it's for your belongings. You've got twenty minutes to clear your desk and be out of the building. If you don't, you'll be trespassing. I know people it's happened to, and it's like their lives are over. This is the real world, Belinda.' His voice was bitter. 'I had hopes when I went to work for the Labour government. As it was then. I watched it fall apart. I worked for a good bloke but he lost his seat like most of the left when National came back. Kendall's been there for years, he doesn't deserve his seat.'

'Yeah, I know. Peter got his degree paid for, but Dylan's got to take out a student loan. Or rather we pay, because it's not fair that one didn't have to pay and the other does. And we've still got Simone to come yet. I should be working on something like this, a doco about what poverty's doing to the country. But I buy into making money like everyone who can.'

'I haven't seen any of your films.'

'Probably not. This and that. Mostly whatever pays the bills. I did take a doco our company made about coastal ecosystems to Europe last year. Seth helped me with that. That was pretty cool — very local, very ethnic. I love mangroves, those smoky grey plants with their feet in the water and their heads in the sky. They're art forms.'

Grant found himself chuckling.

'What's so funny? It was a real coup getting into Cinéma du Réel. Before that I just went to see how other people did that sort of stuff.'

'I'm not sure I'd spend all day at the movies watching those kinds of things. But good on you.'

'So what would you watch? Is that what you do, Grant, spend all day at the movies?'

'We should get this junk in the skip before we start on the basement,' Grant said, standing and collecting up their cups.

'It scares me, what we might find down there.'

'Just ordinary old junk, I guess. You didn't manage to track down Janice, I take it?'

Grant thought of her as the wayward one, although all his sisters had skipped off into the distance, one way or another.

There was Jessie, the eldest, the famous foreign correspondent in London who reported from exotic danger zones and never communicated with any of them. But that seemed to be what this family was like. He still couldn't think about Jan, though, without anguish, a sense of his own failure. She wasn't like the rest of them, just clever enough to get out to save herself. He was glad that the others had left, that they'd got out sooner. And here was Belinda, the middle one who had tried to protect them when they were kids, and had got banished. He felt a rush of warmth and unexpected camaraderie with her, as they worked together.

'Tried everything,' Belinda was saying, still talking about Janice. 'I even went to the Sallies. I'm sure she's alive — somebody would have told us if she wasn't. It's not as if either of us are hard to find. You've checked all the electoral rolls?'

'Of course. Perhaps Jan's not the voting type. I reckon we should do the basement first, get it over and done with.' He wiped his hands on his jeans, noting the grime with distaste. He saw the look on Belinda's face. 'She's alive, Belinda, I know for sure.'

'How?'

'I went to the police. They told me she was not deceased, that was the term they used, but they couldn't tell me where she was. Classified information.'

'Some sort of protection order?'

'I think so.' He didn't explain to her that he was used to doing searches for missing people, that he had spent many years in the pursuit of one particular woman, and it had become second nature.

The basement door swung on a rusty hinge. They had to crouch in order to enter the rancid space beneath the house. There were cartons of old newspapers, tins of dried-up paint, some rusted gardening tools, a lawnmower with the frame and some threads of a canvas catcher attached to it. They worked methodically, carrying the stuff to the door and stacking it outside so that it could all be taken to the skip at once. At the back of the basement, Belinda came across some cartons. One was filled with clothes falling apart with mould. She pulled out a disintegrating skirt. 'That was our mother's,' she said. 'I remember it, those taffeta roses. She thought it was romantic. Charm must have missed these.'

'Past saving.'

'I'm not that sentimental. Ugh.' She dropped it back in the box, then picked it up again, looking at something beneath. 'Strange.' She was picking up a damp shoebox that fell apart in her hands. Some objects fell out, a button, a man's pipe. 'I don't remember our father smoking a pipe.'

'It might have been her father's.'

'The wharfie we never met?'

'They lived in Kilbirnie, not far from us. Our grandparents.'

'All that time? That's so sad, Grant. I just never thought.'

Grant took the pipe from her and turned it over. 'Or perhaps it was her first husband's. Jessie's father.'

'Maybe. But this leather button, it's been in a fire. It's weird. I've got another one just like it in my button tin, not as burnt. I mean, it was Mum's special button.' She laughed uncertainly. 'It sounds silly. But I can see it now, me with the rows of buttons spread out on the floor. I remember Mum picking it up once. "Don't lose this one." That's what she said.'

'Junk now, I guess.' He held out a bag for her to throw them in.

'I might keep them,' Belinda said. 'Perhaps they mean something.' She hesitated over the pipe, then stuffed it into the pocket of her tunic, along with the button. She grimaced at the sight of her filthy clothes.

Grant shrugged. 'Our mother's secret life.'

They'd come to the last cartons. Belinda pulled the lid off another. 'Photographs.' Most of the pictures had glued together with the damp but in the middle of the bundle were some that had been preserved. She carried them into the light.

'Our dad took up nature photography. It got him out of the house and away from Charm.'

'They're not bad, some of these. Nice leaves and plants. A good eye for light.'

'They're all yours.'

Belinda was beginning to gather them up and say that no, thanks, interesting as they were she really didn't want any of these, when she stopped. Grant could see her face pale, her hand go to the edge of the door to steady herself. 'Oh, my God,' she said. 'No.'

Grant stepped over, curious. Even as he glanced down he tried to cover what was revealed, repulsed, his hand slamming down outspread. But Belinda had seen it. A picture of his sister Janice, as a teenager. She was naked, legs slightly parted, her face dour, eyes turned away from the camera.

'I'll take it,' he said, his voice sharp.

'Did you know?' she said. 'Grant, did you?'

'Some bad things happened in this house.'

'You didn't *do* anything?'

'I swear to God I haven't seen these pictures. I didn't know they existed.'

'But something was going on. You knew that, I can tell.'

'I was a teenager. He was a bully, a demented old bully. It started before I left home.' He touched his head. 'Besides, he had a wife. How could I be sure? It didn't *go on*, as you put it, while I was in the house.'

'That could have been me,' Belinda said, as if he hadn't spoken.

'I doubt it.'

'Why not? Was I being spared, getting sent away from home?'

Grant gave a weary sigh. 'He wouldn't have fancied you. You're too much like our mother.'

'That is so disgusting.' Belinda was storming around, grabbing rubbish to take to the gate, her shoulders beginning to shake.

'All families are tragedies, aren't they?' Grant said.

'How very Tolstoy.'

'No, that's not the way the book begins.'

'I fucking know how *Anna Karenina* begins, Grant. I've got a degree in literature. It's the same thing, isn't it?'

He hoped she would calm down, speak to him again, pick up where they had been during the morning, but her face remained set and closed. They carried the last pieces of furniture along the path in silence. She went back to the house to pick up her handbag and car keys.

'I'll see you,' she said.

'I'll have the lawyers get in touch when it's sold. I don't expect we'll get much for it.'

Her eyes travelled around the house, the bareness, the peeling wallpaper, the sordid secret walls. He saw her blink away tears, and for a moment he thought she would relent. This wasn't the way the day was supposed to end.

'Do what you can. We'll be well shot of it.'

He watched her walk back down the path and climb into her car, draw her seatbelt into position, and switch on the engine, without looking back.

As she pulled away, he shouted, 'You got lucky. You just don't know.' He knew she couldn't hear him.

He was alone again, like when Lizzie left.

He and Lizzie stayed together on and off for four years. It was marriage that undid them. Something had sparked between them the second time he saw her, at Allan's funeral.

After he'd seen her at the Newtown flat, staring at a wall with her made-up eyes and blank white face, the memory of her had remained compelling. He learned from Allan that her name was Lizzie. He found himself dreaming of her. In his dreams she was a wraith-like figure on the outside of something he couldn't see, looking in, holding out her hand, not motionless, as she'd been that night.

He'd gone to live in a student flat in Holloway Road the year after Allan's death, not that he intended to live in a flat forever. He enrolled at university, opting for law. The idea of striding around a courtroom had appealed to him then. His would be the voice of justice, the kind of person who got people like Allan off the hook, proved what a terrible mistake it had all been.

Perhaps even the screws thought Allan wasn't that bad. He was released early for good behaviour. Grant wasn't there to meet him when he got out of jail. That was something he would go on and on regretting.

Lizzie found Grant the day after Allan died. Nobody else was in the house. She stood at the door of the flat and said, 'Let me in.'

She was shaking, a slip of a woman with mascara running down her face. Grant had to force her hands down from her mouth to understand her, because she kept covering it as if she couldn't believe what was coming out. 'I found him,' she said. 'It was me that found him. In the woodshed. He stood on a piece of firewood, that's all it took for him to swing. He didn't need to do that. He didn't need to be dead.'

They arranged to meet at the crematorium where Allan would be disposed of, in a cheap wooden casket that slid through the doorway of the furnace, into the roar of flames. Lizzie had bought some flowers at a dairy, red carnations wrapped in plastic. 'He was all right,' she said. 'He was a pretty gentle sort of a guy.' She put them on the casket at the very last moment, because they nearly missed the cremation. There'd been a gap in the schedule and he was sent in early.

'How come they had a gap?' Lizzie asked. 'Did somebody not die after all?' She was wearing a black beret, and a long black dress with a pattern of gold flowers splattered over it, hooped gold earrings.

'Have we got time for a prayer?' Grant asked the funeral director. They couldn't let Allan go without saying something for him. 'Do you know the Lord's Prayer?' he asked Lizzie.

'Of course,' she said. 'What do you think I am?'

So they said it as one, then Lizzie stood up straight and began to sing 'Amazing Grace', her high notes sure and true, and Grant began to weep.

'What do you want to do?' he said, after they had been shown out, with more haste than ceremony.

'Go for a drink, perhaps.' Her kohl-rimmed eyes looked at him. 'Go on, I know you're not old enough to go in a pub. I'll buy us some booze if you like and we can take it back to your place.'

This way he learned she was older than him by some years. Old enough to go into the boozer and buy a bottle of wine. She had money, she said, waving away his offer.

Lizzie took her shoes off and lay on his bed. The bottle of Cold Duck was nearly finished, drunk mostly by her. 'Do you want to do it now?' she said. Her face had settled into something of the same expression he'd seen at the flat with the men.

Grant said that no, not now, that wasn't what he wanted, and he didn't.

'You don't fancy me?'

'It doesn't feel right today.'

He wouldn't ask her if she'd been with Allan; he preferred not to know. Besides, he'd never been with a woman, and he'd rather she didn't discover that either.

'Could I just sleep here a while?' she asked him, seeming to relax again, as if pleased by this response.

Grant sat watching her until around midnight. He saw the contours of her cheekbones, the tiny lines that had begun to form at the corners of her eyes, the small snorting intakes of her breath in the wake of the wine she had drunk.

Towards midnight she stirred. Her gaze was fresh and clear, her eyes grey pools, lit from within. 'I need to go now,' she said. 'The boys will wonder where I've got to.'

'Do you have to go?'

'Yes.'

'I'm here if you need me,' he said. It felt an absurdly grown-up thing to say. He was nineteen, living in a run-down house on the edge of town. In the sitting room there were sounds of revelry, a Friday night student gathering, or a bit of a piss-up. There was nothing he could offer her.

'Thank you,' she said. 'Thanks.' And kissed him lightly on the forehead. The room felt empty when she was gone.

A year would rush by without him seeing her, although she still came to him in dreams. At nights he worked as a security guard, and on the weekends he took on an extra job in a warehouse sorting deliveries ready for Monday morning. Some days he was so tired the words in his textbooks blurred before him. None of this stopped him from passing exams; the answers appeared before him as if his mind were a magnet that had drawn every word he had ever read into perfect patterns in his brain.

At the end of the long summer vacation he'd accumulated enough money to rent a room with a kitchenette and a shower, in an apartment block just off The Terrace. His own place. No need to pretend he was a regular guy, drinking beer and watching rugby on a scratchy television screen with the volume turned up loud. The building was old, but the floorboards were polished and there was a stained-glass window high up on one wall where sunlight shimmered through, creating patterns of colour. A memory returned to him, of his mother telling him about light that shone through windows of the house where she grew up, an old fragment of story that made the place feel like home.

This was where Lizzie found him a second time. He supposed it wasn't so hard to find people in Wellington, a small city where most people knew each other, meeting regularly on Lambton Quay. Both her eyes were blackened when he let her in. She was carrying a suitcase that turned out to hold all her clothes, and a duffel bag containing her make-up and a few books, mostly poetry.

'What is it you want?' Grant asked her. They'd eaten a packet of fish and chips that he'd hurried out to buy, half afraid she'd be gone when he got back, and half hoping she would, because he'd no idea what to do with his unexpected guest.

She scanned the room and picked up one of the books she'd unpacked, opening it, riffling through the pages until she came to something that caught her eye, and began to recite: '*Given here in this room the quiet / tilting of light through glass panes, / the tenuous skin of day / stretched out, nothing becoming something.* You see, it's perfect. Poetry makes everything whole.'

James K. Baxter, the vagabond poet, had died but his poetry still spoke to her, Lizzie told Grant, made sense of things. She'd lived with a poet for a time, when she was younger, before all this shit happened to her.

What sort of shit? What had taken her to the house in Newtown?

This was hard for her to explain. Some months elapsed before he extracted a story that he thought close to the truth. It had to do with a breakdown she'd had at school, cramming for her exams, a studious girl from a family up North who didn't value education. They expected her to leave school and earn her keep as soon as she turned fifteen, she explained. It was a constant battle just to go to class every day. By the time she was sixteen she was a nervous wreck.

'I ran away after I left hospital,' she said simply, one night, when she was sitting on the bed with her arms around her knees. 'And there was nowhere to go, and no turning back.'

Grant understood this. He'd done something similar and, on the whole, things had turned out better for him than they had for Lizzie. So far.

There had been more breakdowns, some men along the way and the poet was one of them, although, as the shit had been happening since Lizzie's school days, he wasn't sure where he fitted in.

'Things are going to be different from now on,' she said. 'I'll cut out the booze, no more bad blokes. Just you and me.'

The two of them together.

'Why me?' he said.

'Why not? I like you, just a steady life, that's what I want.'

His life took a different turn now. Lizzie got a job in a bakery, while he dropped night work. Between them they had enough to get by. She liked country and western music. Her favourite song was 'You Picked a Fine Time to Leave Me, Lucille', which she often hummed as she cleaned the apartment and cooked for them, something she did very well. She liked the movies, too. On days when they both had time off, they would go to the Penthouse in Brooklyn and watch two or three movies in a row. He held her hand in the dark, consumed with love for the pale intent woman seated beside him. His favourite movie was *The Day of the Jackal*, hers was *Badlands*.

Still, there was something missing. At first it was all right, but then it wasn't. They still hadn't had sex together. They didn't talk about it.

Lizzie began to bring home a bottle of wine most nights. It would be gone by the time they went to bed. She knew writers and artists who met at the pubs, usually at the Abel Tasman, with its turquoise carpet and faded orange-and-red chairs. She started catching up with her old friends, as she described them. Poets who had known her from earlier days dropped into the Tas. They quoted poetry and told yarns and shouted at each other until the pub closed at ten, when they lurched into the night, arms around one another, calling each other 'my dear boy' or 'my good fellow'. The women wore floating scarves and peaked caps. A youth with skin the colour of milk was cutting his teeth on his first acceptance from a literary magazine. It seemed to Grant that they had some kind of Jesus complex. They looked prayerful when they recited their poems; at other times they merely looked drunk. One man had a place in the country where they all gathered some weekends and lit giant fires in a paddock and anything could happen.

One night Lizzie climbed a tree and Grant had to coax her down as if she were a cat. The crowd joined in, calling 'Pussy, pussy', and Grant's cheeks blazed with shame. People had sex behind the hedges, and once Lizzie did so with an older poet, a man with a thick thatch of hair who, in his day-to-day life, was the managing director of an importing company. She was whinnying with pleasure when Grant found them. He stood very still until the act was finished, so that it wasn't until she was pulling on her panties that she saw him. 'It was nothing,' she said. 'Just a bit of fun.' Later, Lizzie said she was sorry, it had been a mistake. 'We can't go on like this,' she said.

Grant knew this. His grades had slipped. It was hard to hold onto the weekend job because Lizzie wanted to go to parties and he was taking time off because he didn't want her to go alone. A small treacherous voice in his head was reminding him of the way Charm had slid down the slope and fallen off at the end. He'd despised his stepmother, but he didn't despise Lizzie. He needed to hold onto her.

If she went to the parties alone, she might never come back. She'd slipped into his life. It would be just as easy for her to leave.

He woke earlier than she did every morning. She would be lying there asleep and he would watch her, her face on the pillow, a porcelain doll in repose. It came to him now and then that if he killed her he could keep her exactly like that forever.

He wanted to make love to her, but he couldn't.

It wasn't that he'd never experienced sexual desire, but when he lay beside her, images flashed before him — Lizzie in other lives — and passion died. It was as if, in this way, there were some honour between them. This was a secret notion he held close to himself, even when she suggested that he see a doctor, or a psychiatrist, or both. She had seen a few shrinks in her time and look at her, she was all right, wasn't she? It might work for him. But he wasn't ready to open all that strange secret part of his life to anyone else.

'Things'll be all right when we get married,' Lizzie said one day, as though the idea of marriage was always on the cards. This solution hadn't occurred to him, but it was something he was willing to go along with anyway. This way he would keep her.

'I'd like to meet your family,' Grant said. 'We should ask them to the wedding.'

'Just forget it,' she said. 'They wouldn't get it.'

'Get what?'

'I don't see your family guest list,' she said, silencing him.

They got married in a registry office with two court clerks

as witnesses. Afterwards they went to a Mexican café and ate a meal laced with chilli. Later that night, and much to his own surprise, things did improve. He was no longer a virgin. But in the days that followed, when he was not with her, he sat staring at walls wondering if she was at that very moment comparing him with others. One night she had cried out a name that wasn't his.

She said to him, one morning at breakfast, 'Do you think it was true, Grant, what the boys said? That night I first saw you.'

'What was that? I've forgotten.'

'I don't think you have.'

He knew exactly what she was talking about. 'I'm not gay,' he said.

'I think you were in love with Allan.'

He banged his fist down on his toast, scattering the coffee. 'Is that all you think about?' he said. 'Sex. Who screws who. I've never asked you, have I?'

'I didn't think you'd had sex with Allan. That's not what I said.'

'Look,' he said, his voice dull, 'Allan was my first friend. And you're my second one.'

She left straight after he finished his final exam. At least she had waited for that. There was a picture of them standing together, him in his cap and gown, holding the rolled-up scroll in his hand. They looked like the perfect young couple. He was twenty-three, Lizzie close to thirty. The day he found her gone, it was pouring, the Wellington wind lashing the streets, rain blowing in his face as he made his way up The Terrace. The emptiness struck him as soon as he entered the apartment. On the pillow where her dear head had rested beside his, lay a slim blue book of poems by Louise Bogan, an American poet whose work Lizzie liked. It was opened at a page with a marked line about never having a male friend who failed to see that love had to end.

Why not just say, a fine time to leave him? Never mind the cleverness.

A fine time, yes.

Her face would appear to Grant every moment that he wasn't busy in some way or another. Like his sister, she was gone without trace. Perhaps there were people who knew where she was, but, in his searches for her, he never came across anyone. He tracked down her family. The father worked in a Taranaki dairy factory, the mother was blowsy and careless. They hadn't heard from her in a long time. At first they didn't believe she was married. To prove it, he had to show them a copy of the marriage certificate he obtained, because Lizzie had taken the original with her, as if in doing so she could cancel out the truth of what had taken place.

He went to the house where he thought she had lived with Allan and the other men, although it was hard to be sure that it was the right one in the jumble of buildings so close to one another. A woman came to the door and said she had never heard of Willie and Snort and Ripper, and what sort of names were those anyway. She moved away from the door fearfully, looking about to call the police.

Grant stayed on in the apartment. The warmth of the sunlight streaming through his colourful little window cheered him, as if it might beam her through to him. He figured that, if he stayed here, Lizzie would know where to find him.

She appeared to him on street corners, and in pubs where he sometimes dropped in, just in case she might have joined the old crowd. For an instant, he would think he had seen her, but in reality, she was never there; her friends hadn't seen her there either. In time they would move on: poets had other lives and careers to pursue like everyone else, children to mind at home, or the old ones got sick and died. There was one who used a stick when he walked. One afternoon when Grant came in, he was sitting by himself, taking snuff.

'Hello, young fellow,' he said. 'You're Lizzie's boyfriend, aren't you?'

'I'm her husband. We got married.'

'Oh, dear boy, that was a mistake, wasn't it?'

'No. We were happy.'

'And now she's gone. Well, that's women for you.'

Grant hesitated for an instant. He might hear something he would rather not, but the opportunity seemed too good pass. 'I wonder if you knew who Lizzie lived with a few years ago? A poet.'

Grant wasn't sure whether the man had heard him or not.

'A vodka, dear boy. If you'd be so kind.'

Grant bought the vodka and a beer for himself. He was prepared to wait. The poet began a rambling story about his sailing days.

'Lizzie?' Grant said, when he'd heard it through.

'Oh, my good chap, I don't pry into people's private lives.' The old poet seemed about to fall asleep, a line of damp snuff trickling into his beard.

'I just thought you might know. I'm worried about her.'

'*Quem dues vult perdere, dementat prius*. You wouldn't know what that means, I suppose. The young are an uneducated bunch these days.'

'It means,' Grant said, ' "whom the gods would destroy, they first make insane". I learned Latin. But lots of kids could tell you that: it was in a comic book.'

'Really? Well, I didn't know that. You're an interesting

young chap after all. Another vodka, perhaps?'

'About Lizzie?'

'Oh, I've no idea about that, dear boy. No idea at all. You sure she didn't make that up? About the poet.'

He didn't know whether Lizzie was even alive. But somewhere, some day, he thought he would see her, that she couldn't just vanish. His rational self told him that she'd probably left the country. At other times, he wondered whether she was a mirage, had never existed at all.

The day that he and Belinda found the picture of their young sister in the basement of the home where they had all once lived, he saw Lizzie's face again, lost like Janice. Missing in some terrible private war.

So here it was, 1992. The effects of Ruth Richardson's Mother of all Budgets were described as Ruthanasia — killing people slowly. Designer-clad hosts and their guests talked about it at dinner parties in the capital city's fringe suburbs. They had rural holiday homes and, yes, they could see that some of their neighbours in the countryside weren't doing so well. But that was the way it was. You did what you could. You made policy. Grant found himself sitting down at the tables of Kit Kendall's wealthier patrons. They believed that there would be a return to the left, that what was happening was an aberration. He thought they were dreaming, that there were more years of pain to come, but he sat silent. His views didn't fit well with the drift of the conversation among the fluted champagne glasses, the white linen and silver, the lights of their chandeliers.

Fifteen years had passed since Grant last saw Lizzie. Along the way, he'd got caught up in the anti-apartheid movement, marched against the Springbok tour, oversaw from a distance the slow demise of his father, joined a chess club, worked out at a gymnasium five days a week and travelled once a year because he had money now, and nothing else to spend it on, hanging out in Florence, which he preferred to Rome, the Louvre in Paris, island-hopping through the Aegean Sea, or wandering through the British Museum. These distractions had carried him through the years. He had, too, begun his evening walks through the cemetery.

Kit Kendall, whom Grant worked for in Parliament, knew that Lizzie was missing. A woman from the SIS, the security agency, came to see Kit, to do a check on his staff member whose wife had been listed as a missing person by her parents.

'Why didn't you report her missing?' Kendall asked Grant.

'She wasn't missing, she left me,' he said, stubbornly.

'Can you prove that?'

'There was a note.' He had to produce the shameful message, the poem that proved nothing. During the interrogation he broke down in tears. They appeared to believe him. He thought.

There was a woman Grant met often at the cemetery, walking her spaniel. She allowed it to cock its leg and pee against headstones. Grant had found dog turds where she walked. He wanted to remonstrate with her. Maybe she hadn't owned a dog for long, didn't know the etiquette of dog walking or, indeed, was not very interested in it. It could be that she was minding it for someone. Every time he saw her, she was wearing the same light-coloured shower coat with a belt, a tweed skirt and sensible walking shoes. After several of these encounters, when she barely returned his greeting, he tried to avoid her, but in a few minutes she would reappear.

These hide-and-seek meetings continued for some weeks, until it dawned on him that he was being followed. He supposed she was looking for some sign that Lizzie might be buried in the cemetery. But wouldn't the records show that she was not? He had pored over burial records often enough. Perhaps she thought his victim might be buried under another name, that sooner or later some clue would give him away. People didn't just vanish, as he had thought a thousand times.

Or did they? For a long time Grant had been drawn to the notion of disappearance. If Lizzie could do this, perhaps he could, too. He might find her out there in space. Like the movies, the hero came to the rescue, snatching the lost woman from distress. Somewhere out there Lizzie might be in the badlands. He could no longer wait for her to come to him.

After Belinda drove away from the Brighton Street house, he saw that nothing in his life had changed, and nothing would if he continued to live in his skin as the person he was. She'd confirmed his suspicion that his existence was of no consequence. He'd nurtured a small hope that their reunion would open some possibility of family life. His image of himself as the kindly uncle seemed belated and silly. It had vanished, along with everyone he'd ever cared for. He was on his own.

One weekend, not long after this, he drove north towards the town where Kit Kendall had his electorate office, near the centre of the North Island. He'd been invited to join Kit and Amber, his latest wife, for golf and some fishing if the weather held. 'Come for a long weekend,' Kit had said. 'We can brew up a few ideas to hit this damn government.'

When Grant said 'Well, why not?', Kit had offered a high-five.

'We'll get those bastards,' Kit said, like an ebullient school boy.

As Grant drove north, he remembered that earlier on his sister Janice had lived in the area. The school she attended in

Wellington tracked her, after she ran away with her boyfriend. Not that she could be persuaded, or forced, to return. She'd reached both the age when she could leave school and the age of consent. But at least, for a time, they'd known where she was. He wondered what she'd made of the bare bones of the countryside, the dark red heart of the Desert Road. He hoped she'd been happy here, although he suspected not.

Glancing at his watch, he realised that he was hours too early, so, on an impulse, he turned off, following empty roads. He slowed the car when he came across a woman walking beside a long stretch of the highway. She carried a child on her back and looked exhausted. He pulled over.

'Do you want a lift somewhere?' he said.

The woman was perhaps thirty or so, dressed in jeans and a windbreaker. From the way she hunched over, bracing herself, he could see that her thin clothes didn't protect her from the chill wind that blew off the mountains. She viewed him with suspicion.

'I don't take lifts from strangers,' she said. The child on her back was no more than a year by the look of him, but a heavy boy.

'Fair enough,' he said. 'Is there anything I can do for you?'

The woman eyed him again and came to a sudden decision, abandoning caution.

As she settled herself in the passenger seat of the Peugeot, sliding the boy onto her lap, she said, 'I hitchhiked to town. It was benefit day yesterday. You know they've closed the post office, so I couldn't draw any money. I hitched to town this morning but then I had to wait because the queue was so long, and I missed the bus home.'

'Couldn't you have taken the bus this morning?' Grant asked.

'I didn't have any money,' she said patiently, as if this were obvious. She had a pleasant fair face, chapped a little by the cold, no make-up. The child had fallen straight to sleep. 'I had to collect the benefit before I had the fare.'

He drove on, until he came to a small town. Or the remnants of one. He saw the boarded-up post office building. He knew what happened next, after the closures. One shop after another shut its doors: first the little dress shop that carried hosiery and underwear as a sideline, the hardware store, the bookshop, then one by one the food shops, the greengrocer's first, then the butcher's, and so on, until there was just a poky dairy with a few tins sitting on sparsely stocked shelves. The windows of shops like this, and of the liquor stores that survived, were laced with wire barriers that made them look caged.

The woman pointed to a sign on the window of what appeared to have been a café. Happy Inn. 'That was mine once,' she said.

He wanted to offer her money, but he understood that she would have refused.

'Can you tell me the way to the cemetery?' he asked. 'If there is one.'

'Oh yes, the dead don't leave us,' she said, as she got out of the car, her laughter wry.

But she was wrong. A small headstone stood in the second row of ragged paspalum. The birth date of the child who had died coincided almost with his own. A boy, who had lived for just one week, in 1954. Alongside him, his parents lay buried. Joseph Higgs. Joe, the kid would have been called Joe.

He was taking Joe with him. Soon Joe wouldn't have a car, or an apartment on The Terrace or a membership to a gold card club, the way Grant Pawson did. But he would carry a new copy of his birth certificate.

Joe would be the risen man.

Who could tell, but that Joe might meet Lizzie. Like in the movies.

# 10

# Running in the dark

# 2000

The Hokianga, that was where Janice had had the best of times, the times she felt safe. It was a place that people called remote, although, as she would tell the women in the prison, it was only a four- or five-hour drive north of Auckland where a couple of million people lived. When they challenged her to describe it she found herself at a loss for words. She couldn't explain the light in the sky, the gold of the rippling sand dunes, ancient trees like gods, the sense of mystery and the wild unknown. She understood it, but she didn't have the language. 'I'll bet none of youse have ever taken the trouble to go up there' was what she said, brushing it off. 'You could get up there between breakfast and lunchtime. A late lunch. You ought to go.' And then she and the women would laugh because at that point in their lives they weren't going anywhere.

Those times up there in the Hokianga were what she liked to remember when she lay awake in the dark of her prison cell. Wiremu came from there, though she'd met him in Auckland, where he'd gone looking for work. At that time she was in hiding, but in the street where she lived nobody took much notice of you if you kept your head down. The apartment she and Heaven occupied was on the ground floor of a housing block owned by the state. It was a dirty hole when she moved in, with torn curtains and cockroaches in the bath. She assumed they'd crawled up through the plug hole. It took her two days of scrubbing and mending to make it fit for her daughter, but when it was done it didn't look half bad. It was on the damp side of the complex, and that was what she didn't like, that the sun rarely entered the rooms. The neighbours were all right. The social worker had told her she needed to take people as they came, there were Maori people next door on one side and Asians on the other, and did she have any objection to that, because if she did, she'd better get used to it.

'I reckon I've seen it all,' she told the woman. She went by another name then, calling herself Janice Smith. 'Ha, ha, that's really original, isn't it?' she said, but she couldn't think of anything else.

'It'll do,' the woman said, 'so long as we know where to find you.'

Wiremu lived with relatives in a house next door. The first time she saw him she was hanging out washing, while Heaven played in a little sand pit left by some previous tenants. They didn't speak that time. But he'd taken off his shirt, revealing a torso like that of a sportsman, though, as she would learn, he'd never played anything other than a bit of touch rugby at high school.

She saw him again the following Saturday afternoon, sitting on the doorstep. The light played on his body, as if it had had furniture polish applied to it. She felt the stirring of something she thought she'd left behind. The last man she'd had sex with was Tommaso, and that had been doomed to failure from the start. Tommaso could touch her buttons in all the right places and drive her crazy-as, but he was far away in Italy, and she was here. When she looked at Wiremu she shivered. Tommaso had given her a taste for dark nuggety men with hard muscles.

Wiremu said, 'So how's it going? You getting settled in there okay?'

'Not bad. Bit cold. How come you stole the sun?'

'Come on over. It's free.' He held up a pack of cigarettes and grinned, a big white flashing smile.

Janice hesitated. Heaven was sheltering behind her, pulling her cardigan around her. Since they left Turangi and all the trouble, the child was nervous of strangers.

'What you reckon, kid? You want to hang out next door for a bit?'

Janice squatted on the step beside him, while he cupped his hand round the flame of his cigarette lighter, lighting up for her. She drew in a long lungful of smoke and let it go, closing her eyes and turning to let the sun rest on her face. Heavy cooking smells drifted from the window of the house, meaty and rich.

'Nice kid you've got there,' he said, after he'd introduced himself. 'She looks smart.'

'She's nearly six. She knows all her letters,' Janice said.

Heaven's fair hair had curled into short ringlets. People remarked, when they went to the shops, what a pretty little girl she was. Janice liked tracing her eyebrows with the tip of her finger.

'You come from round these parts?' he asked.

'Just come here. I'm from Wellington, but that was a bit back. I've been here and there.'

'You like it here?'

'It's kinda lonely,' she said, throwing caution to the winds. She knew it sounded like an invitation. 'What about you?'

'Oh yeah. The cuzzies are good, but I gotta shit job. Not what I come for. No work up North, eh.'

His job was at the freezing works but he hated it, didn't like the smell, didn't like all the dead bodies of animals, and the sound of the railway that made his head hurt. He stood under the shower so long at the end of every shift to get the smell off him that there was no hot water left for the family. Besides, the works were laying off staff. He wanted to go back north, back to the Hokianga, only he reckoned it would make him a loser. They had hopes for him. He'd got his School Certificate, all that shit.

'You clever or something?'

'Nah, don't hold it against me. Look where it's got me. I had a job at the post office for a bit but the boss had it in for me. Black and white, you know what I mean? What about you?'

'I'm dumb as stink,' Janice said, lowering her head on her knees. 'I ran away from school.'

'Yeah. Well, you don't seem dumb. Look at that kid of yours.'

'I'm a hairdresser. Sort of. I can cut, but I can't do perms.' There was more she could tell him but she had learned to keep her counsel. There were some things you didn't tell people. Ever. She told him he could take some showers at her place; there was just her and Heaven. She was supposed to call Heaven Paula, but the kid never answered to the name anyway; it was a problem at school sometimes.

At first he was shy when he came over. He covered himself with his towel even before he got undressed, as if she hadn't seen him with his shirt off. 'It's okay,' she said, 'I've seen a bloke's bits and pieces before.'

He laughed then, said he figured she might have. Janice guessed he'd had girlfriends, but there were none in evidence now. Perhaps there was someone up North. She wasn't rushing it, although when he'd gone she felt clammy with heat. Heaven liked him, you could tell. She kept pictures she drew at school to show him.

The family put down a hāngi most Sundays, and they'd

ask her over. She got used to the taste of puha and pork, that's where she started to put on the beef, or should that be pork, she told the women in the prison. Never lost it really.

On one of those Sunday afternoons, the sky a bit overcast and grey, the family was talking about going inside, although that would mean it was time to start thinking about Monday and the working week. They'd downed a few beers, someone was playing a guitar and there was singing. Janice can see and hear it all even now —*Blue smoke goes drifting by*, the voices of neighbours along the street picking up on the words, beginning to harmonise, remembering the happiness she felt, a sense that things could still turn out all right.

That was the moment when she saw an aged blue Holden cruising slowly by and felt the sick jolt of fear. This was nothing new, old cars cruised around these streets day and night. But she got it, this one was looking for someone. Before she could duck or call out a warning — because the words froze in her throat — Darrell was among them, swinging an axe, catching her on the arm, blows falling on Wiremu's auntie as she tried to shield Janice and Heaven, Wiremu launching himself onto Darrell, one of the uncles taking the axe, the scream of sirens.

I thought they'd hate me 'cause of that, Janice told her new inescapable friends. A group of them sat in a circle, with a woman called Bev who described herself as a facilitator leading the discussion. What the discussion amounted to was them telling their life stories to each other. Spilling their guts, in other words.

Bev wore big black-rimmed glasses, a burnt-orange cardigan with a wide colourful scarf. Her hair was iron grey, as if she didn't mind that she was getting old. She was a nice enough woman, Janice thought, though she'd held back until the last to tell her story, hoping she could avoid speaking. Too much grief in the past, too much she didn't want to say. But when it came to her turn, the other women glared at her, as though she were a coward, a cop out.

'It's all right,' Bev said, 'you're among friends.'

Janice wasn't sure about that. There were some mean bitches in here. But once she began, she felt compelled to go on. 'Next day, when everyone's been stitched up, Wiremu comes over and says, You can't stay here, and I'm ready to leave. Come with me, up home to the Hokianga.'

The Hokianga was where Janice lived for eight or so years, she lost count exactly, tucked away in the wilderness to the north of the harbour, a place reached by winding gravel roads, ravines falling away at either side, a settlement where the sun shone hard and hot day after day in summer, and mist closed in when it rained in the winter, so that you couldn't see your hand when you held it in front of your face. It was like the time when she lived in the bush with the Italians in the south, only there were no frills, no fancy Italian food, no doctors on hand.

When Janice arrived, Wiremu's mother, Mere, looked her up and down. Her eyes were full of reproach for Wiremu. 'So is this my hunaonga? Plenty of others you could have had.'

Wiremu shook his head.

Janice wasn't meant to understand but she got the drift.

'You been married before, girl?' Mere said. He'd warned Janice that his family were Catholics.

When Janice said, no, not married, Mere looked as unhappy as if she'd said yes. 'You've been living with men.' It was a statement, not a question.

Wiremu said, 'She's taking some time out. You can see she's had some damage done.'

'From what I hear there's more than her been damaged. What about my sister? She's in the hospital down South.'

'I know,' Janice said. 'I'm sorry. I didn't do nothing.'

'Auntie's going to be all right,' Wiremu said. 'She wasn't cut bad.'

221

'I don't want you bringing fancy city ways here,' Mere said. She was speaking to them both. 'No booze, none of that other stuff, you know.'

'No trouble, Ma,' Wiremu said. 'Honest. I come back home for peace and quiet and some of your good kai.'

Finally, Mere said to Janice, 'Well, I suppose if you're good enough for my son you're good enough for me.'

The subject of marriage never came up again.

Janice gave birth to her and Wiremu's son, who they would call Patariki, with the help of Mere and the women who lived there in the bush. The electricity, fed with a generator, had gone on and off while she was in labour, so that she gave birth by the light of kerosene lanterns. Patariki looked like a small dark eel when she first held him, with a shock of black hair standing on end. He was a tough little guy. He needed to be. The roof of their house was all but caving in; winter draughts leaked around the windowsills. There were no locks on the doors — that went without saying because people came and went in one another's houses. Wiremu got some seasonal farm work for a time, but he had to travel so far to the jobs it wasn't worth it. At least they managed to save for a new corrugated-iron roof; it made a difference. They put a roof on Mere's house, too. Mere said, that girl of Wiremu's, she's a hard worker: it was high praise.

They grew vegetables, and some days they would get in one of the old cars at the settlement and drive out to the coast to catch fish and collect kina. Once a month, when their benefits were due, they went to Kohukohu and caught the ferry over to Rawene to buy supplies, have takeaways for a treat. Heaven, and later, Patariki, caught a bus to school.

'Often as not,' Janice said, 'they'd come home and tell me they missed the bus. No good giving them a hiding, wouldn't do no darn good. Wiremu says to me, What's the point, they ain't never going to be the prime minister. We were so darn happy, you wouldn't believe. Well, I think Wiremu was, even though he reckoned he'd missed a bus or two of his own in his day. His uncle come up once from Auckland, in his ute. Wiremu borrowed it off him and took me all the way to Cape Reinga. We got to that place where the two oceans meet and you can see the walls of water smashing up against one another. It's the place where the spirits fly off when you're dead. Wiremu says to me, One day you an' me will be gone and we'll be off over the sea. And come another time, the children will follow.

'I said, Heaven too? Though that wasn't fair 'cause Wiremu always treated Heaven like she was his kid. Still, I could see stuff going through his head. He says, Heaven will find her way. I didn't know what he meant by that, but I let it go anyway.

'We come to Kohukohu one day, just to stock up on a few odds and ends — it's only a little store there. Some cars had just crossed the water from Rawene, taking the short road up through the bush to Kaitaia. And this day, there's Darrell, large as life. I saw him before Wiremu did. I felt the bastard in the air, like a bad smell. I thought they'd have put him away for good, running round with an axe like that, but no, he's out, done his time again. He's driving a nice car, not new but quite flash. I think he might not recognise me, it'd been so long, and I looked pretty different, you know, I'm big eh, big puku, and I've got muscles from all that work in the gardens, my hair tied up. But he knows me. He says nothing. I say nothing. I think perhaps he'll let it go. I get into the car with Wiremu, old banger it was — we used to just drive them till they stopped and leave them where they were. Somebody always found another one. But this car, it's pretty darn slow and old. Darrell must have been just hanging back, you know, letting us go on ahead, leading him right along to our house.

'He pulls up. I tell my friends, get inside, don't talk to him, he's a bad man. Darrell says to Wiremu, All right, I know you.

But this time I'm here on business. You got what I'm after? Man, we got no drugs here, Wiremu tells him. But Darrell doesn't believe him. He goes back to the car. I call out to Wiremu, Look out, here's trouble, but Wiremu is faster than him, he's got the shotgun he used to keep by the door. Darrell sees it. Okay, man, I'm out of here. Easy. And he backs off, just like in the movies. I figured he had a gun of his own but he wasn't going to try anything on. We had a couple of smokes to calm our nerves, you know what I mean, and tried to figure out what would happen next.'

'He came back?' one of the women ask.

'Nah, not that I know of. But people started looking at me funny. It was one thing for Darrell to find me in Auckland, but another thing that he'd tracked me up there in the bush. A couple of weeks later, Wiremu up and died. Yep.' Janice fell silent, her eyes filling. 'Yeah, well. I can tell you I loved that guy. An aneurysm, the doctors said. Well, why couldn't he have had his aneurysm a couple of weeks earlier if he had to have one?'

Janice's voice was bitter. 'I knew soon enough what they were thinking. After the tangi, nobody's talking to me. I figured it out, they reckoned I brought a curse on that place. They weren't interested in what the doctors said. So that was that, you might say. I headed off, finished up South again. Sulphur Town. The kids seem to be okay about it, although I could tell Patariki was pining for the Hokianga. Mere tried to stop him leaving but he was my kid. And then of course good old Darrell turned up, too. He found me soon enough. Same old same old.'

Annabel Rose was studying the brief of her case for the day. She gazed across the still waters of the lake towards the island at its centre. Her breakfast lay untouched in front of her on a circular glass-topped table with delicate wrought-iron legs. The table stood on a wooden deck painted white, adorned with white ceramic plant containers. Bright green herbs, flourishing mint side by side with parsley, were planted in one and a white-flowered camellia in another. Every aspect of her house was designed to reflect what she saw as her own personality, cool and light on the surface, steel beneath.

A familiar sound broke the train of her thought, the faint crunch of gravel beneath the tyres of a Daimler moving smoothly up her driveway. The beautiful pale grey sedan was a recent model, around about 1998, purchased not long before she met its owner, Harold Penny. He kept a special spray in the glove box to maintain its new leather smell. Harold said that, as the millennium rolled around, just months away until they became citizens of the twenty-first century, the car would become redundant. Everything of the past thousand years would suddenly fall out of date. He said this half in jest, but there was an edge to it, a reflection of how they all felt. Annabel herself felt some slight unease, a misgiving about the future that she hoped would be resolved when the round numbers had all rolled over and it could be seen whether their computers were still working or not.

Harold, His Honour, Judge Penny, to be more accurate, unsheathed himself from the car and sauntered over, his hand raised in greeting.

When Harold visited her, he closed his eyes for a moment as if refreshing himself from the world beyond. He was a tall, thin, slightly angular man with a high domed forehead, hair beginning to thin around his temples, a long face, heavy curved eyelids, only a slight fullness of his mouth displacing the symmetry of his features. His clothes were chosen with care by another woman. His socks were made of silk that outlined the boniness of his ankles which, Annabel happened to know, were cold when he first got into bed, however warm the weather might be outside.

'Should you be here?' she asked.

Neighbours did notice that the judge's car cruised up the widowed lawyer's drive. A shame she'd been left so young, they said. One of them had remarked, at a barbecue, in a seemingly casual way, how nice it was she had someone to keep an eye on her.

He made a small shrug of denial. He would be presiding in the district court later that day, hearing the case of the woman on whose behalf Annabel was appearing: Janice Pawson, up on charges of selling cannabis from her home, charges she flatly denied. Her children, a young woman with the unlikely name of Heaven, and her half-brother, Patariki, had already pleaded guilty to lesser charges of possession. The girl got some periodic detention, the boy, a minor, was cautioned. Annabel couldn't understand why people gave their children names like Heaven, redolent of the seventies and hippy communes and drugs. Little wonder they got mixed up in this sort of stuff. Heaven and Patariki had insisted, when they spoke to her, that what had happened had nothing to do with their mother. At the time, Heaven was living in a house on the western side of town with a boy called Rob. Heaven had some tinnies in her knapsack when she came over to raid her mother's pantry.

'We were being a bit naughty, that's all,' she told Annabel. 'I know we were stupid. It wasn't Mum's fault.'

Patariki was at home when she called and she had given him a couple of joints. But deep in the recesses of the house the police had found some rolled-up twenty-dollar notes, the giveaway sign of the dealer. Planted, that's what Janice Pawson said. The police didn't like her.

'Why wouldn't they like her?' Annabel asked.

Although Annabel knew about Darrell — she'd acted for Janice before when she'd had trouble over him — she'd had no reason to dislike her. Darrell was known to the police. He gave them serious grief, escaping from holding cells and going on the run, a serial criminal who threatened to blow their brains out if they got close enough to him before he was captured. It had never happened, but there was always the chance that some day he would make good his promises. He was also the father of Heaven.

'I don't think she's guilty,' Annabel said.

'You have to say that,' Harold said, taking a piece of her uneaten croissant and nibbling an end off it.

'She wants a jury trial.'

'Oh, she'll cave in.'

'Seriously, Harold. Why would she if she's guilty? She's had a tough life, she's on legal aid. And she's been inside for nearly nine months already. Of course it would be easier for her to plead guilty and get it over.'

Harold stood up with deliberate care, so as not to knock over the little table, and walked inside, opening cupboard doors. He knew where things were in her house.

'Shall I get you another croissant?' Annabel called, not really listening for his answer.

She was doing a mental summary of Janice, an overweight woman with cropped hair dyed black, a scuffed denim jacket worn over a colourful T-shirt, tight jeans and boots. She had silver studs in her ears and sported a tattoo of a dragon snorting fire on her left forearm. Or, that was her when she first sought Annabel's help over a tenancy agreement that had gone sour. She got evicted from properties because, she claimed, Darrell rang up and told lies about her to whoever her landlord happened to be at the time.

The last time Annabel had seen her, she was wearing an

orange jumpsuit, prison garb, on remand in Auckland. Yet the woman she saw in the prison had a quiet certainty that she found convincing. Could be Darrell had got in and planted the money, Janice had told her, and if it wasn't him then it had to be the cops and nothing would ever surprise her. Not any more.

Harold returned, bearing a cup for himself. 'Not unless you decide you're going to eat this after all.' He poured coffee and spread fig jam on pieces of her croissant. 'So why don't you tell her to plead?'

'Suppose she does and it all turns to custard? I don't know how long you'd give her.'

'No,' he said thoughtfully, 'you don't, do you?'

'Harold,' she began. But he wanted to change the subject. His wife, Fleur, was going to visit their children in Australia, she'd be away for a fortnight. He and Annabel could get away together for a few days. He needed a break and so did she. She got too involved in her cases, she couldn't make everyone's life perfect. Where would she like to go? To the lakes at Nelson, or down to the Wairarapa and do the wine trail? She ought to think about it. He got up again, smoothing crumbs from his suit.

'By the way, that girl Heaven, she's running with Sergeant Coleman's boy. I should have put her away, too.'

Annabel stared at him. 'The boy Rob she's living with? Is that what this is about?'

'Jack reckons his boy's getting drugs from her. At least we can shut down the supply chain.'

'If Coleman's boy wants dope he'll get it from somebody, Heaven or no Heaven. Anyway, she's a nice enough girl. Very attractive.'

'Really? That may be so. But.'

'But what, Harold?' Annabel had learned long ago to listen to what came after the 'but'. Harold, however, was silent, not offering the clue. She had to say it for him. 'So Janice and her family are an embarrassment to the cops?'

'They want her inside for a stretch. The girl's talking about going up to Auckland to be closer to her mother.' He kissed her forehead. 'We get shot of the lot of them.'

He reversed down her driveway at speed, a small flurry of pebbles skittering in the wake of the tyres.

It was Belinda's daughter Simone who found Janice's name in the newspaper. Sleek and shiny Simone, who was still living at home, even though she was twenty-five. The paper was in a pile left in the laundry cupboard for recycling and the item was a paragraph in a side-bar about crimes in the provinces. 'Don't we have an Auntie Janice?' she asked her mother.

Belinda leaned over her shoulder and her eyes widened. 'How old is this newspaper?'

Simone turned it over to read the date. 'It was back in April.'

Simone was an advertising copywriter who went to work in the city. I shouldn't make home so comfortable for my kids, Belinda said with a laugh when she talked to her friends. I can't get rid of them. The truth was she liked them all around her. Dylan still kept his room the same as when he was a teenager, coming home to crash more often than not, although officially he lived in a flat with a group of young men his own age. He could play a conch shell or a guitar with equal ease; on the weekends he played rugby. His boots, discarded from the winter season, were in the clutter of shoes at the doorway. He worked at the museum, with its columns like the Parthenon, restoring collections. Dylan's passion was archaeology; he travelled to Greece once a year. Only Peter, the eldest, was independent, a quiet man, never quite at home around his siblings, in a way Belinda couldn't explain to herself or to them. He'd left home when he was twenty-one, as soon as he graduated with a commerce degree, and had worked in a bank ever since, wearing a suit and tie every day.

Home, the place that Belinda kept so cosy, was a villa in Grey Lynn, with lacy wooden fretwork decorating the verandah. It stood on a rise that sloped down behind the house. In the spring, lavender flowered in the front garden, sunflowers in the summer. The back garden was planted in vegetables, tended by Seth, and there was space for hens. The interior of the house was made colourful with bright rugs, deep couches, a rosewood sideboard laden with large blown-glass objects that shimmered in a multitude of hues. As the journalists who came to interview Belinda would write, you could see the eye of the film maker at work in the composition of her surroundings. Seth worked from home as an ecological consultant. The move to Auckland, taken when the children were all at school, had suited them. Belinda was still in demand in the screen industry, still making documentaries, many of them overseas or in the Pacific. She showed her films in Toronto and Stockholm, in Sheffield and Prague. Her favourite approach was dramatised accounts of events that had changed history, both great and small. She believed that truth was best served by the camera's eye, that she was in some sense a recording angel. Somebody had to tell it the way it had once been, where they had all come from.

And how it was had just entered the pretty, organised chaos of their lives: her sister was in prison.

'I need to make some calls,' she said. 'Seth, can you turn that television down? Puh-lease.'

Seth was parked on a sofa. 'Hush,' he said, his face glum, as he hunched towards the screen, intent on the rugby. Belinda paused to watch for a moment. Those flashing young thighs, such gorgeous blokes she'd say, joking again, my middle-aged lust. New Zealand was losing over on the other side of the world in Wales, the unthinkable happening. It was a replay of a game that had taken place the night before, and he was analysing the disaster frame by frame.

Seth loved rugby now that he was older, just as his father had. Don would have been proud of him. It had been hard for Seth, coming from a family like his, to stand up and oppose the tour in '81. It was the only subject that ever caused a rift between her and Seth's parents. They, the kindest people in the world, who had saved Belinda and given her a life, couldn't understand what had got into her, going off on demonstrations. For once her mother-in-law Maisie had refused to mind the children.

Simone said, 'Mum, what are you doing? You don't see her, do you? Perhaps it's somebody else with the same name. Anyway, it was months ago, she's probably out by now. Mum, you can't.'

Belinda's mouth was set. 'It's time to mend bridges in this family.'

'Do you and she hate each other?'

'No,' said Belinda. 'No. We just didn't look after her, that's all.'

Simone looked at her curiously. 'I thought you lost track of your family.'

'True,' said Belinda, 'but I think it's time to find them again. This one, at any rate.'

Although the rugby was lost, at least, as Seth said, just weeks later we've got a change in government. It was as if life could go on, although the way the country had been in mourning, that seemed doubtful for a while. Labour was back in at last, Helen Clark was the prime minister and, soon after the rugby disaster and the elections, the millennium came around and the numbers rolled over without the world ending.

'Where have you been all these years?' Belinda asked, when she was seated opposite her sister. Janice was dressed in a strange puffy garment. Her face had a weathered look about it, making her seem much older than forty-three. Prison guards watched, their eyes flickering over them in constant surveillance. Belinda hadn't been prepared for the physical nature of the search she had undergone before she was allowed to enter. It was worse than airports. She kept her hands in her lap because every time she moved them, a guard came to attention. She supposed they were waiting to see if she had anything to slip to Janice. In this place, who she was counted for nothing.

'Now you ask,' Janice said. Her gaze wasn't particularly friendly.

'I knew you were alive. Grant asked the police to find you once, but they said they couldn't say where you were. I wrote you some letters but you never replied.'

'I never got no blimmin' letters,' Janice said. But she sighed, seeming to relent. After all, she had agreed that Belinda could visit.

'You're owed some money from the sale of the house in Brighton Street.' Belinda felt she was babbling, as if money were the important thing, although she could see that for the moment it might not be.

'Go on? How about that?'

'So you ought to know about that. But I wanted to find you anyway, honestly Janice.'

'I was living up in the Hokianga,' Janice said.

'I've been there often,' Belinda said. 'Magic place.'

'You have? So you've been around, Belinda.' There was an unexpected touch of irony in Janice's voice as though, perhaps, she did know something of her sister's life. 'My boyfriend Wiremu used to read the fish 'n' chip papers to me.' She laughed, a short rough sound.

'I've been a few places.'

'Oh well. You've seen all the sand dunes? Neat, eh? And the mangroves.'

'I made a couple of movies up there. One was about those mangroves, and later on one about De Thierry, a sort of a documentary about his failed settlement plan, you know.'

Janice gave a wry smile. Beneath her scars, her face was still crooked the way Belinda remembered it. 'You'll know all about it, then.'

'I don't know anything,' said Belinda, recognising her mistake. It had taken her two months of negotiating with the authorities to get permission to visit Janice. The first time she tried they had reported back that Janice didn't want a visit, but then she'd changed her mind.

'Ah well, you always were the clever one,' Janice said. 'Never mind, you couldn't help it.'

'It was Jessie who was clever.'

'Oh yeah. I don't really remember her. Oh well, you're forgiven.' This time she did smile, a grin lighting up her face.

'Why did you leave the Hokianga?'

'Oh heck, Belinda, I'd have still been there if it hadn't been for Darrell. You know about Darrell? My first boyfriend?'

'The one you ran away with?'

'That's the one. Frying pan into the fire. He's Heaven's dad. But she turned out all right. She's a real good kid, Darrell or no Darrell.'

'Aunt Agnes mentioned him once, but I never heard about Heaven.'

Janice's face curled with disgust. 'Old bitch.'

'She took me in,' Belinda says. 'She wasn't that bad.' She was surprised to hear herself defending her aunt.

'She kicked you out, I heard,' Janice said.

'True. Eventually.'

'She got you away from our father. She left me with him.'

Janice waited to see what effect her words would have on Belinda.

Belinda flinched, unable for a moment to reply. Images from the house in Brighton Street still stung behind her eyelids at unbidden moments. Since she and Grant had made the house ready for sale, it had become a persistent setting for a nightmare, a place where evil had been done. Often, in her dreams, the landscape was hazy, as it was on some summer days in her childhood, when there were gorse fires on the hillsides, the edges of the houses blurred, and smoke drifted over the sea towards the mountains on the other side of the strait. Through the haze their white caps glowed, as if floating in space.

There was something else she could not eradicate, the face and naked form of her sister who, like all her family, had suffered in that house. Only Janice had suffered more than all of them, in a way that made Belinda recoil.

'I didn't know about our father,' Belinda said at last. 'Not then. I'm sorry.'

'Sorry. That's what they say.' Janice looked around at women sitting on plastic stools, divided by low tables from their visitors. Belinda recognised the face of a murderer whose case had been in the papers.

Janice's eyes followed hers. 'You don't want to stare, Belinda. They'll scratch your eyes out before the screws get to you. They don't care, 'cause they're in here for a long time. Anyway, I thought Darrell was all right — he was good to me at the beginning. But I got it wrong, you wouldn't believe.' She pointed to scars on her face. 'I got flattened that often, it took me a while to figure out how bad he was for me. It was the Italians who got me out of it.'

Janice told Belinda, then, about the Italian tunnellers and Tommaso, who was her second love (or perhaps, really, her first one), but he'd gone back to Italy and, besides, he'd figured that Janice would never be free of Darrell so long as that man was alive. He would always make trouble.

'And he has?' Belinda said.

'Oh yeah. I keep thinking he's out of the way, but he isn't. But I'd found Wiremu, or he'd found me. He turned out to be my real one. I could never look at another bloke.'

Janice was embarking on an account Belinda sensed she had told before. As she listened, she knew this story was not a gift; it was a burden that Janice was bestowing on her.

She thought, I owe her this.

'Darrell gets put in jail,' Janice was saying, as she came to what seemed to be the end, 'and then he's out again and I'm on the run because he always catches up with me. Running away, moving, my whole life I've been running. It's like you're in the dark, not knowing where you're going to end up next. And then he'll find me.'

Belinda felt her own shoulders bowed. Nothing could shift the weight of what she had been told.

'What happened to Grant, anyway?' Janice asked, at last.

'I don't know. I haven't seen him in years.'

Belinda was ashamed she'd quarrelled with Grant. What had she been thinking of, that morning? She'd driven away from the house, leaving him sitting forlornly on the doorstep. When she got as far as the seashore, she'd pulled over and turned back. Grant was already gone. Since then, she'd tried to reach him, phoning, writing to his last address, both to apologise and to ask him to help her find Janice.

'Did you and him have a fight?'

'It was my fault.'

'What happened?' When Belinda remained silent again, Janice stared at her with clear candid appraisal. 'Was it about me?'

'I said he hadn't looked after you. You know, protected you from our father.' Belinda's voice was choking.

'Oh, my goodness,' Janice said softly. 'Oh my. What did you think Grant could have done?' She glanced at her hands, the short chewed nails, revolving her thumbs around each other. In the room, a child cried, wanting to stay with its mother as visiting hour drew to a close. The sobs rose to a long wail of despair. 'Grant's mate got done for drugs, just like me. Did you know that?'

'No. What happened?'

'I heard about it just before I ran off from home.' Janice stirred and shifted her position. 'His name was Allan. I heard he topped himself. After he came out.'

'Oh, no.' Belinda's voice was soft. 'You wouldn't do anything like that, would you?'

'Me? Don't be silly. I've got the kids. I wouldn't do that to them.'

The guards were checking their watches. 'You've been on remand for a long time. What happens next?' Belinda asked urgently.

'Oh yeah, well I'm waiting for sentencing now. You know, you done the crime, you do the time.'

'You pleaded guilty?'

'Yeah.'

'Is it true?'

'No.'

'Then why? Jan, why would you do that?'

Janice sighed and turned away. 'It's complicated.'

'You need to fight. Have you got a good lawyer?'

'She's all right. Her name's Annabel. Legal aid.'

'I can get you a better one. If she's not doing her job. Jan, please, I want to help.'

Janice stood up, as if ending an interview. 'I gotta go. You don't understand. I'm hoping for home detention. I've gotta keep my little girl Heaven out of trouble. She's running with shit, they're dragging her down. I can't see the kids, they're not allowed to visit me because of their convictions. I could be in here another year waiting for a jury to hear me. This way, well, you see what I mean. I can look after her, she can come and live with me if Housing'll give us another place. I lost my house by the way. That's what they do, they even chuck you out on the street before you've been found guilty. Heaven and Patariki are staying with her rotten boyfriend. He acts like a goody-good but man do I know bad when I see it. '

'Is he a gang member or something?'

'I wish. Well, perhaps you could look at it that way. His old man's a cop. The kid's as bent as a bobby-pin but he's sly. His dad thinks the sun shines out of his arsehole.'

'I'll come again. Is there anything you need?'

'Some money for a phone card. You have to give it to them at the desk. Seeing as I've got an inheritance, eh? How much, Belinda?'

'About a hundred grand. With the interest. Our father left you a bigger share than Grant and me.' Belinda felt herself blushing.

'Did he now?'

Belinda turned at the door and waved to Janice. Her sister hadn't moved. The guards were hustling her. 'See you next time, eh?' Janice called.

Belinda drove south the day Janice's sentencing was supposed to take place. She was being transported south the day before and kept in a holding cell overnight. Belinda had to change a day's filming schedule and that had created chaos, but now that she was in it with Janice, she felt committed. Seth said he didn't see what she could do to change things and how did she know what Janice had been up to in the past, how many convictions she already had. (Two, it turned out, both for shoplifting, nothing for drugs.) Seth couldn't help wondering if she'd been growing stuff up North — you heard enough stories.

'She's my sister,' Belinda said. 'You'd do it for your sisters.'

He hardly need remind her, he began, and stopped. Seth's sisters won the upright citizens' awards, real or imagined, hands down. No contest. Belinda didn't mention her trip to her children, not at this stage.

The courtroom was a long wood-panelled space, designed to make people think it was user-friendly, with a high red wall behind the judge's seat. There were bright blue chairs for the lawyers at their tables. Belinda didn't feel comforted. Men roamed the corridor outside wearing dirty jackets and torn jeans; stripped of their patches they still spoke of gangs. A smell of stubbed-out cigarettes and stale marijuana hovered in the air. Girls with blank eyes leaned against the walls. A woman of indeterminate age who had arrived in the back of a police car as Belinda pulled up outside the courthouse lay on the floor, refusing to enter the courtroom.

'Stand up, stand up, Nance,' shouted the court attendants, trying to get her to budge.

'I can't stand up,' she mumbled. She had slender white hands and a mane of dishevelled brown hair. From her position beneath them, she flashed a cell phone. 'I dialled for an ambulance, see? I'm sick.' Someone swooped to remove the phone. 'It's not right, I shouldn't be here,' she cried.

None of them should, Belinda thought grimly. Low-life and sorrow, poverty and pain, and many more Maori faces than white. Among them, she saw a girl she thought pretty: blue-eyed with small regular features, her fair curly hair streaked with purple. Beneath her left eye a delicate row of dots had been tattooed, smaller than the tips of flower stamens. Belinda found her face compelling. The girl was with a tall rangy Maori boy, a teenager, Belinda guessed, his hair pulled up in a topknot on his head, a tattoo on one cheek. Both of them wore carved bone pendants. They leaned into each other, before entering the court, then sat down near her in the gallery.

Janice appeared, her face stony and set. Her eyes flicked towards the young people and then she stared straight ahead, her hands folded. Belinda understood, with a sudden charge, that she was sitting two seats away from her niece and nephew. Her flesh and blood, whom she could reach out and touch. Silence had been called in the court.

Judge Penny wasn't sentencing Janice after all, that day. It turned out he was merely giving a pre-sentencing indication. A woman stood up at her desk at the front of the court. Her name was Annabel Rose. She was skipping-rope thin and as ripe as a peach ready to fall, so flawless and yet so fragile in her appearance that Belinda was afraid she might break. It seemed Ms Rose was objecting to this delay in the proceedings.

The judge listened to her with glistening attention, his large handsome eyes resting on her as she waved papers before him. He looked patient and resigned.

'Thank you,' he said. 'I appreciate your attention to the detail of this matter, Ms Rose. I should point out that I'm looking at a starting date of two years and three months imprisonment. There's a twenty-five per cent reduction in light of the prisoner's admission of guilt, so let's say one year and eight months. However,' and he raised his hand, to stop the lawyer from commenting further, 'it may not be in the best interests of justice to confine Ms Pawson indefinitely. I consider the prisoner in need of rehabilitation. I'm considering a lengthy period of home detention, during which time she will be required to undertake counselling. I take it Ms Pawson has an address where she can be detained?'

'My client has had her tenancy agreement with Housing New Zealand terminated,' the lawyer said. 'I'd have to confirm a suitable address for her.'

'I see. Thank you, Ms Rose. The prisoner is further remanded in custody.' He checked some notes in front of him, and provided a date for the next hearing, three weeks from then. Belinda thought she must be imagining it, but she could have sworn he smiled.

She heard the sharp intake of breaths from the young people beside her. The boy called out, 'Mister, how long do you want to keep her banged up?'

A court attendant appeared and grabbed the boy she took to be Patariki, and yanked him from his seat.

The judge looked up. 'If there are any further disturbances in this courtroom, I'll have those responsible detained. Do I make myself clear?'

Belinda followed the pair into the corridor. The girl was crying.

'Excuse me,' Belinda said. 'I'm Belinda.'

Heaven and Patariki turned to her in bewilderment.

'I'm your aunt.'

Patariki said, eventually, 'Well, we did hear there were some aunties. Kia ora, Auntie.' He put his arm around his sister, brushed hair back from her face.

At this point, they were joined by Annabel Rose, her creamy face flushed. Belinda offered her hand and introduced herself. 'I think we should talk,' she said.

In a side room that Annabel found for them, Belinda said,

'Do *you* think Janice is guilty? If you don't mind me asking.'

Annabel studied her carefully groomed fingernails. 'I can't change what she's said.'

'But it's not the truth.'

'Truth. It's always an interesting concept,' Annabel said. 'You do understand that she could stay in prison another year waiting for a trial if she'd pleaded not guilty? I couldn't guarantee she'd get bail.'

'Her sister will take her,' Annabel told Harold. 'She was there in the courtroom. She makes films. I've read about her in the newspaper.'

'It sounds like a fairy story,' her lover said, appraising the pinot noir she'd poured for him. 'Elegant,' he remarked. 'Quite intense. The wine, I mean.'

'The sister's for real. I recognise her from her pictures. She's very well thought of in the film world.'

'I saw her in the courtroom, I know who she is.' He turned his glass around. 'I'd say this is a Canterbury grape. Quite distinctive, don't you think? Have you thought any more about where you'd like to go? We could track this vineyard down.'

When she didn't reply, he said, 'Look, sweetheart, it wouldn't work. Wealthy fairy godmother turns up and saves the day. How long do you think it would last?'

'It turns out Janice has some money sitting with a lawyer in Wellington. An inheritance.'

'It's not going to buy her freedom. She's a drug dealer.'

'Harold.'

'She might be your cause, but I have to uphold the law.'

'What about justice?'

'You want to think her innocent because she's strung a

good line. And now she's got a glamorous sister. You know your client's run with a scumbag all her life. I've put her old boyfriend away more than once.'

'Then you know she's been trying to get away from him for years. You can't hold him against Janice.'

'Violent criminal. I've sentenced him more than once. That family's what it is.'

What had happened in the past could hardly be held against a whole family, Annabel argued. He wasn't a part of them now, hadn't been for nearly twenty years. Harold said Darrell would always be part of them because he was the girl's father.

Annabel tried changing tack. 'You're not allowing for the time Janice has spent in prison.'

'Aren't I? Oh dear, my mistake. I just want them out of town,' he said with finality. He checked his watch. 'I should get going. Fleur's having her golf buddies over for drinks.'

'I thought you were staying over? I've made coq au vin.'

'Sorry, sorry, I forgot to tell you. Fleur left a message with the secretary just as I was leaving.'

As he pulled on his leather driving gloves, Annabel said, 'So what if it's Coleman's boy that's providing the drugs? Have you thought about that?'

He gave her a long, cool stare. 'You're getting emotionally involved, Annabel,' he said. 'It never pays.'

'So,' Belinda told Dylan, 'you need to clean out that room of yours because your aunt will be sleeping in there very shortly. Don't argue, you have a room of your own in another house.'

'She can have my room,' Simone said. 'I'm moving out.'

Belinda appealed to Seth. 'You know it's the right thing to do, don't you?'

'No,' Seth said, 'but I'm resigned. If you think it's worth our kids leaving home on account of a whole bunch of people they don't know, you go right ahead.'

'She's my sister,' Belinda repeated. 'Why don't you come to the prison and meet her? I can arrange it.'

'I can wait,' Seth said. He shut his study door. Seth, who was never angry. Or was he? Sometimes, these days, Belinda didn't know. A simmering vein of resentment surfaced at unexpected moments. Did he look back and think he could have done better? she wondered now and then. The thought terrified her.

Contemplating the whole thing this way and that, lying awake dry-eyed with exhaustion, Belinda found herself agreeing with Annabel Rose, that truth itself was a slippery customer — an interesting concept. Janice had no doubt used a few drugs in her time. Possession, for sure. Dealing? Could it be true after all? Belinda's head hurt when she thought about it too much. It wasn't something she wanted to talk about to Seth or the children.

The atmosphere at home was cool. Simone was looking for a place of her own, but the rents were high. This was the hardest part for Belinda, Simone not really talking to her. Doing the 'pass the butter stuff', the dialogue the scriptwriters struck out. Mothers and daughters — it was tricky, according to her friends, but it had never been that way with her and Simone. Simone was like a friend who happened to live with her, and now there was a horrible distance between them. Dylan hadn't been home for a month. Seth said he supposed they were all going to appear in a 'happy families welcoming the prodigal sister back' documentary. He'd been invited to a conference in San Francisco and he'd be out of it for a month, so that let him off.

'It's not an experiment,' Belinda said. 'I don't know what else to do.'

Janice was still in prison a month later. Probation had been to visit the house to make sure that it was satisfactory: it had to be within range of their monitoring systems for Janice's ankle bracelet when she was released. On the sentencing day, their report hadn't arrived at the court.

'What's happening?' Belinda asked Annabel Rose. 'Has the judge got something against Janice?'

'The judge is neutral, he doesn't have feelings for or against the accused. This is routine. ' Her voice was stiff, her face puffy, as if she'd been crying.

Belinda wondered if there was something the woman wasn't telling her.

'I so want Mum to be out,' Heaven said to Belinda. They were sitting at a café on the lakefront, surrounded by a busload of tourists. On the water, wild black swans circled for remnants of food, arching their necks, their beaks flaring. Small vents of steam escaped along the waterline. 'I've got to get out of this town.' There was desperation in her voice. Patariki had already left, gone up North to stay with his grandmother.

'Annabel said you had a boyfriend here.'

'I want out. He won't let me go.' Heaven had created a perfect origami bird from her paper napkin. She was wearing a crimson top made of soft material that hugged her breasts, gold studs in her ears, a spiral tattoo on her inner arm.

'There's nothing to stop you, surely? I'll take you back to my place if you need a place to stay. '

'I can't. Rob, that's my boyfriend, or he used to be, he's like my dad, real controlling. My counsellor says girls like me go after people like their dad, it's a cycle you have to break — you know the shit they talk. So how would I know? I never lived with him since I was little.'

'But you remember him?'

'Well, of course I remember. He's been in our faces all the time, except for those years we lived in the Hokianga. You should have seen the things he's done to Mum. First thing I remember about him is fire. Fire burning in front of our house in Turangi. I was just a little kid. He's like a devil.'

'I see — I think,' Belinda said, although she knew that her camera's eye failed her here. Heaven had seen things she hadn't, and they were terrible. The girl looked tired, almost old, or perhaps it was just her expression. 'So what about Rob?'

'Yeah. What about Rob? He keeps saying if I leave he'll tell his dad about more stuff my mother's supposed to have done. Like that she was growing stuff up North. And if he did that, they'd send people up there to search for dope.'

'Would they find any?'

The girl shifted uneasily in her seat.

'Not that I know of. There's dope everywhere, Auntie.' Avoiding the question. 'You've got kids, you must know that.'

'Dear God,' Belinda said. 'Have you talked to Annabel about this?'

Heaven took a deep breath. 'If I tell you something, you promise you won't tell?'

'Well,' Belinda said uncertainly. But she saw she was about to lose the girl if she didn't agree. 'All right, I promise.'

'It's Darrell, my father, who's giving Rob the shit. You know, the drugs. All sorts of junk. '

Belinda took a deep breath. 'Then why haven't you told Annabel that?'

'Because the judge would just say it was us.'

'But, Heaven, you don't know what the judge would say. This needs to be sorted.'

'No, you don't get it. The judge will do what the cop wants him to do, which is to get rid of us. The judge owes Rob's dad. His missus, Fleur, got pissed when she was driving. The judge talked Rob's dad out of charging her. And Annabel, well she's the judge's girlfriend.'

Belinda felt herself quivering with rage. 'This is monstrous. It's a total injustice. We have to do something about it. I'll see a lawyer in Auckland.'

'Auntie, nobody would believe a word of it. Basically, you could say this family's stuffed.'

'I need to talk to your mother about this.'

'She knows enough. You promised me, Auntie.'

'Jan, it'll be all right,' Belinda said, on her next visit to her sister. 'They can't keep you in here forever.'

Janice shook her head. She looked exhausted. She had a fat lip and a bruise on her forehead. The murderer was in an animated conversation with a woman with a shaven head. The woman called Nance whom Belinda had seen in the court down South was now on remand. She was talking to a grey-haired woman who wept. Belinda thought it was probably her mother. It turned her heart over.

'Jan, who's done this to you?'

'Nobody. I fell over,' Janice said.

'No you didn't.'

'Keep your voice down, Belinda.'

Belinda guessed then that Janice would always keep her mouth shut — it was what she'd been doing for most of her life. She couldn't wait to take Janice home, introduce her to new beginnings, get her family back together. They would be proper sisters.

'Whatever happens to me,' Janice was saying, 'you'll look out for Heaven, won't you? She told me you've been good to her. I'm allowed to talk to her on the phone twice a week.'

'You'll be able to look after her yourself soon,' Belinda said.

'Will I? Oh I don't know, sis. I could have done better. She's got brains, but I didn't even make her go to school up North. I'm so dumb, I didn't think it was worth bothering about.'

'Jan, stop talking like that. Heaven's crazy about you, she thinks about you all the time.'

'Yeah, she's a good kid. You know, I had two convictions before this. They were both for pinching clothes for her. I wanted her to look nice.'

Belinda said then that she knew what it was like, to have a daughter you loved so much it was like pain. Janice would be able to buy nice things for Heaven with the money put away for her, get a decent place to rent, stuff like that.

'The money. Yeah, I meant to tell you about that. I don't want it.'

'Don't be silly.'

'I'm not. You know where it came from.'

'Our father.'

Janice gave Belinda a long sideways look. 'He was Grant's and my father. He mightn't have been yours. Perhaps you got luckier than you know.'

'I don't believe I'm hearing this.'

'Well, you never know, do you? It might have just been something he made up. One of the sweet nothings he whispered in my ear. I said to him one time, Why me, why not Belinda? And he said, 'Cause you're mine, all mine, and she's not, same as Jessie. He said our mother was a dumb slut.'

'I can't think about this now.' Belinda felt sick.

'You should be happy. Anyway, it's dirt money. I wouldn't touch it with a barge pole.'

'You'll get over this,' Belinda said. 'You'll come out of here, and live with me until you get the bracelet off, and you and the kids can start over.'

Janice's voice was dreamy. 'Up North, we had these tin roofs.

I remember one night me and Wiremu were laying awake, just chatting you know, holding hands under the blanket. It started to rain real hard, the way it does up there. I said to him it sounds like a movie. Like *Butch Cassidy and the Sundance Kid*. I saw that in Wellington, a long time back.'

'A soundtrack to a movie,' Belinda said. ' "Raindrops Keep Falling on My Head" — I can hear it.'

'They were good times. We didn't have nothing and if you saw the way we lived, rusty old cars and junk and just surviving, you mightn't have thought it. But it was good.'

'It'll be good again. Promise.'

'I just don't know how much longer I can do this. Anyway, thanks for coming.'

'I've put the money in for the phone card,' Belinda said.

When she left she turned, as had become her habit, to look at her sister. Janice stared after her, her face not tough at all, just wistful.

Janice didn't kill herself. It wasn't like that. The call from the prison came late at night. She was in hospital with pneumonia and was asking for Belinda. When she arrived, Janice was hooked up to tubes and drips, her face ashen. She'd had the flu, a nurse told her, and it had got onto her lungs. They were doing all they could.

'Heaven's on the way,' Belinda said, squeezing Janice's hand.

'I know,' Janice said. 'I can see her.' She opened her eyes once, blinked and she was gone.

Her little sister.

Looks like she just gave up, the nurse said.

# 11

# Home truths

# 2012

Belinda is searching for a recipe her daughter wants. It's more years than she can remember since she's made her mother-in-law's fudge pudding, the one with cake floating on chocolate sauce. The children said it was their favourite dessert when they were little, but then it was Maisie, their grandmother, who made it for them. Whenever Belinda speaks of her mother-in-law she gets a catch in her throat. Maisie had stood beside her, loved her, helped her to care for the children who appeared with alarming regularity — three in the first four or so years. They were careless then, she and Seth, their lovemaking tumultuous and frequent, and when it was over, as often as not, they would look at each other and say, We didn't use anything. Oh my God, you don't think there'll be another baby? And there would be. Though Seth urged her to persevere, the pill didn't suit Belinda; it took them a long time to get birth control sorted out.

And now Maisie is dead, has been for many years, and Belinda is a grandmother. One day her daughter Simone had come home and announced that she was marrying a stockbroker, a man from the city. This shocked Belinda and Seth, although it was hard for either of them to express, even to each other, just why the idea of a money man in the family should unsettle them so much. They supposed, they said, when they were on their own and the big old house was silent, that it was just that most of those people were right-wing. They said 'those people' in ways that others spoke about people of different races or religions. We're being prejudiced, Seth said, he mightn't be like that at all. Besides, we're being hypocrites, aren't we? We're hardly poor. When Belinda thought about it, Seth never had been. All the same, Belinda had said, we should watch out for landmines.

Simone married Vaughan beside a lake in a vineyard on a gentle summer evening. She wore a satin dress that glided over her spiky hip bones. Every table was decorated with bunches of cornflowers, as if a whole field of them had been stripped. The guests danced by the light of flaring lanterns until moonlight took over. Simone is in her thirties now, and the mother of two sons, although she still looks like a model. Politics are never mentioned when the family meets, which is enough to tell her parents all they need to know. Their son-in-law always greets them with perfect courtesy, a certain gaiety in his manner as if they're old people who need to be humoured a little. This bothers Belinda, who is about to turn sixty and as busy as ever, and Seth is only five years older. Their conversation is about the children, what private schools they can gain admission to, the traffic, always the traffic, and, of course, the showing of digital images of their travels. Vaughan and Simone spent three years in Paris before the children were born. Simone's voice has developed a texture with slight French inflections.

'I keep promising the boys Nana Maze's fudge pud,' Simone says. 'You must have the recipe somewhere.' Her shoulder-length hair is coloured a delicious toffee shade. She is wearing layered clothes in pale and dark grey shades, black sneakers with white laces and no socks, showing her sexy ankles.

'I can't think offhand where I might have the recipe,' Belinda says. 'You can probably find one on the internet.'

'Oh yes, but that's not the real thing, is it? Didn't she leave you her recipe book?'

Belinda remembers then that, indeed, Maisie had given her the book, in the days when she knew the end was near. Her husband, Don, had died, the house in Masterton with the big garden had been sold. Maisie lived alone in a small apartment in Wellington so that she could be nearer to her daughters. She was pensive when she explained this to people. Belinda and Seth had moved away and she would have liked to be near them, too, but she couldn't be in two places at once. It was, as it turned out, Belinda who stayed with her in the last weeks, when Maisie didn't want to go to the hospice, not yet. Belinda was free at the time, and Seth's sisters had busy lives, full-time jobs.

'I threw out so much stuff,' Maisie had said, 'but I wondered if you might like this? The girls thought it a bit tatty. I think they meant grubby.' She had laughed as she said it, but the book was fingermarked with what might be butter smears or golden syrup, crackling with crumbs of brown sugar, smudged with vanilla. 'You know, if ever the children want some of the things I used to make.'

To please her mother-in-law, Belinda had said that yes, she would love to have the book, that she would make something from it when she got home. Maisie had put her head on Belinda's shoulder then and wept. 'I'm not ready to leave everybody just yet,' she said. It was just that her heart was failing her and it was a matter of time. 'Just like Don's,' she said, 'and I never climbed on any roofs.'

It came sooner than any of them expected, days later.

After the funeral, when Belinda returned home with Seth, there was the usual pile of mail waiting, bills, fliers from land agents offering to sell her house and a letter with vaguely familiar handwriting. She'd been away for longer than she expected. There were voice messages to be answered and shooting schedules to arrange. Someone wanted her to go to Thailand to an award ceremony the following week and she had tickets to book, the usual whirl.

'I think I've still got Nana Maze's book,' Belinda says. She knows it's not with her other recipe books because she uses them often. Maisie Anderson doesn't figure among Julia Childs and Elizabeth David, or the new healthy Asian lifestyle recipe books. There's a drawer in a spare bedroom where Belinda has stuffed things she still feels sentimental about — the children's reports, their first drawings, things like that. She rummages around beneath piles of paper, and there it is, Maisie's book.

She carries it in triumph to the kitchen.

'*Voilà*!' Simone cries.

As Belinda relinquishes the book, she feels a pang of guilt. She wants to hold onto it, to make some of those old sludgy recipes the kids loved, like a real grandmother.

Simone flicks through the pages. 'There's some old letters here, Mum,' she says. 'Naughty, who didn't pay their bills? You didn't even open them.'

Belinda picks up the spilled mail and shuffles through it, stopping at the letter with her name on the envelope. She knows the writing. Why didn't she recognise it when she poked these envelopes inside Maisie's book? She tries to stop her hands from shaking. 'You can have the book,' she tells Simone. 'Nana Maze would have liked that.'

After Simone has left to pick up the boys from school, she sits at the table and opens the letter.

> *Darling beautiful very married Berlinney,*
>
> *How are you? I'm writing to tell you that I'm now an unmarried man. Believe me, I tried to stay married, to do the right thing, but it has never*

*worked. I was on a plane that nearly crashed not*
*that long ago, or that's what the passengers thought.*
*Everyone was screaming and calling out the names*
*of the people they loved. And I found myself saying*
*yours. Berlinney, if I was going to die you're the*
*person I'd want to see last. I knew, even before the*
*plane landed and the pilot had made all those calm*
*reassuring noises that everything was normal, I*
*knew it wasn't, or not for me. I was overcome by*
*the most overpowering feeling that I must set myself*
*free from Esme (and perhaps set her free from me).*
*This isn't a mid-life crisis — I'm almost past the*
*middle already.*

*I've walked all over the city, here in Wellington,*
*and I see you everywhere, in all our old haunts. I*
*want us to be together. Could you make this break*
*with your life and start anew with me? I would*
*care for your children, I would do whatever it*
*takes, but I can't face the rest of my life without*
*knowing where I stand with you.*

*With all my love,*
*Nick*

A letter written a quarter of a century ago. A proposal of sorts.

She hears of Nick from time to time. He is alive. She thinks he's remarried after a divorce she heard about on the media grapevine. There was a time when she thought she couldn't live without him, but it passed. What would she have done had she read this letter at the time? She's glad she has been spared this choice. The days when she caught herself thinking about Nick simply moved further and further apart. She is as whole, in this fractured steamy life, as she ever can be.

Nevertheless, an unexpected thorn of grief pricks her, a sudden rawness stirs around her heart.

Curiosity was what led Belinda to her sexual encounters, she thinks. Although wasn't it like that for everyone? Didn't everyone rage with lust? She needed so badly to know what it was like when she was young. Some of the girls at school slept with boys and got away with it. One of the prefects slept with a married man whose wife had complained to the school, and the girl had been expelled. (Belinda rages when she thinks back on this, the unfairness of it.) She felt like an outsider in those days; she was the girl who lived with the weird old aunt and didn't have pretty dresses for school dances. Boys, those other girls assumed, wouldn't look twice at Belinda.

But they did. They pashed her behind the bike sheds and in the shelter sheds, feeling her breasts and pushing their thrusting busy fingers inside her, one of them leaving a huge love bite on her neck that she could barely hide. She took to her bed for a couple of days while it subsided, and told Aunt Agnes she was sick.

Her aunt had groaned and rolled her eyes. 'Well, you have to get used to having your periods, you want to be thankful you get them,' she said. 'If you ever fall, it'll be the last sight you have of me.'

Belinda remembers the way she lay in bed hoping her period would come because she wasn't exactly sure what had to happen in order to fall pregnant. She didn't like to ask anyone at school because they would think she was odd, not knowing, and because what she did was a secret. The names of those boys who sweated and groaned against her have all but vanished from her memory. But back then, she knew that, sooner or later, she would have to find out what happened next.

At a dance, one night, she had seen an ordinary enough man, older than she was, but there was something about him that she liked. He asked her for the supper waltz and then if he could have the last dance with her, and take her home afterwards. In the back seat of the car, it had begun the way it had with the boys at school. His fingers unhooked her bra and his hands were on her breasts, then they moved down to her panties and pulled at the elastic. She wrapped her legs around him then, and felt her body saying thank you as he entered. It seemed perfectly natural and not difficult at all. Her ardour seemed to briefly startle him, the way she came so quickly and cried out.

The young man's name was Seth, a university student. He didn't come home to Masterton very often, and there were weekends she couldn't get away to the dances without her aunt knowing. Aunt Agnes disapproved of dance halls. Their encounters were infrequent, perhaps every two or three months. Once he appeared with a girl who turned out to be his sister. He pretended he and Belinda didn't know each other that time, offending her. Of course his sister knew who she was because they had gone to school together. His sister wasn't one of the girls who slept with boys. She would go on to be a debutante, in a white gown that was like a precursor to a wedding dress. He didn't even ask Belinda for a dance.

'I'm sorry,' he said the next time he saw her. 'I don't know why I did that.' She knew, though; she wasn't good enough for his sisters. When they began to make love, he said he was sorry again. 'We need to be careful, I forgot to bring a rubber,' he said. He began to withdraw but it was too late, and it was, for her, such unbridled pleasure. Afterwards, he stroked her hair and whispered how much he liked her and how pretty she was. He wasn't sure when he'd be back, but he hoped she'd be around.

And then he vanished.

It wasn't as if they'd talked much. What they had in common, at that point in their lives, was a yearning for each other's bodies. She had discovered his second name and the house where his family lived, and sometimes she would walk past in a way that she hoped might appear accidental if she was spotted, hoping to bump into him. It didn't happen, and after a while she had to stop because the baby she was expecting was beginning to show. Soon, Aunt Agnes would send her away to live on a farm and tell her never to darken her door again.

Later, after she and Seth had been married for some years, and were the parents of three children, she began to wonder what it would be like to sleep with a different man.

She sits at the long rimu table where she and Seth and their children have sat so many times, the letter in front of her. The night she and Nick began their affair really started six or more years before they realised it, in the sense of sleeping together. It had been going along in its own way for all that time, a courtship of sorts. One night, they had stayed up on a beach, and talked about their crazy dreams. She was twenty-four. Nick was free, or so he said. His wife, whom he had left, was a short plump nurse with a Yorkshire accent and big eyes she surrounded with dark eyeliner. Nick had met her on an overseas trip, studying film direction, and persuaded her to marry him and come to New Zealand. He felt responsible for her, he said, although Esme seemed good at looking after herself, a woman with a sharp tongue and a quick comeback.

Nick was there for the taking then. She remembers the way her bones ached for days after that night, a shrinking down into herself, like coming down with an illness. She told herself it had come about from being on the cold beach all night, but really, it was fear. She was afraid she was falling in love. There was so much to lose if it were love.

Nick went back to Esme. The old friends continued to

gather as if nothing had happened, or if it had, they hadn't noticed. Daniel and Carla, Nick and Esme, Belinda and Seth (although Seth would become a friend later, by default, because he was married to Belinda). Belinda slept with two or three men, because she was truly curious. They were men she didn't expect to see again. There was a director from Birmingham who'd come out to New Zealand to work on a one-off project; they had a frantic encounter at the wrap party in an office at the studio, with the door locked. Belinda was fairly drunk at the time. Afterwards she didn't remember much of it. There was a writer she had met at a pub with a film crew up north; she rather fancied him. As it turned out he lived in Wellington so she did see him a few more times, and the sex was different, more measured, with lots of romantic platitudes. At some point she became concerned that he might be getting too interested in her, which had never been her intention. Just as she was worrying about how to get out of this, the writer began an affair with a pale stick-thin woman called Lizzie, which hurt her pride because she hadn't got in first with ending it.

And, just when Belinda had thought her sexual curiosity sated, and the seventies were over, and promiscuity was becoming less relentless, she and Nick found themselves alone in the countryside one day. She'd been to see Maisie, in shock after Don had died of a heart attack just weeks before, staying overnight to help her clear some of his clothes, which her mother-in-law didn't want to do on her own. Seth was coming up at the weekend to go through his father's workshop tools. On the way back she stopped at a roadside stall to buy apples. And there was Nick, buying apples, too.

'Berlinney,' he said.

And 'What are you doing here?' they both said at the same time.

'Darling,' Nick said, in an astonished, joyful way. His eyes were alight with happiness. He had been over to the coast to check out a possible location for the job he was working on. 'Just park your car down the road,' he said, as if it were all decided, and she would go with him.

She followed him, parking as he had instructed, got into his car as though she were sleepwalking, as though something calamitous and inevitable had finally struck her.

Nick drove through the light of autumn, past apple orchards where perhaps their apples, abandoned at the stall, had come from, past the new olive groves that people were planting, as if they lived in the Mediterranean, past vineyards full of ripeness and the turning colour of the leaves, until they came to a deserted road, more of a track really, leading to paddocks. They made love in long grass, full of dandelions and sticky seedheads and the deep autumn sun shining in the lengthening afternoon.

'I love you, Berlinney,' he said.

'I know,' she said. 'I know.'

'What are we going to do?' he said.

'This, just this,' she said.

Seth was the one who saved them all. Reliable, good Seth who has never let her down. Or not that she knows about, although rumour had it that he got fed up with her antics at one stage and had a fling. She prefers not to think about that. The lid is best kept on some pots.

The year that Belinda and Nick decided they really were in love, Seth was working with a team of scientists who were testing the effects of nuclear radiation in the Pacific's coral reefs. Their findings were making world headlines. Seth often looked at the end of his tether, white-faced and stressed from the intensity of the work. There was venting in the seabed where bombs had been tested in the past. It took a long time, he explained to Belinda, to gauge the effects of the tests that had occurred years before, and it would take many more years, beyond their lifetimes perhaps, to know what the outcome of it all might be, what might bubble up from deep below the surface. But it was important to find out what they could, to let people know what they might expect, how their health might be affected, what fish from the sea would be safe to eat in ten or twenty or a hundred years' time.

The bird life worried him the most. Seth had a thing for birds. 'The sandpipers,' he said, in a voice of anguish. 'The fruit-doves, so few of them left.'

Belinda looked at him in his walk-shorts and long beige socks that reached to his knees, his sensible brown leather brogues. He was like a boffin, and she felt a yearning anxious love for him that had nothing to do with Nick. (Nick wore blue denim jeans and a leather jacket.)

The government professed a lack of interest, or so it was read. Muldoon was still in charge then. As the year ground on, they were haunted by bright images of nuclear explosions and desolation in their wake. All the talk was of nuclear-powered frigates from America bearing down on New Zealand. In August, word came that the USS *Texas* would arrive in Auckland. The government wouldn't step in and refuse entry to the port. Protest was in the air again. Belinda and Nick and Daniel and Carla joined a group planning anti-nuclear protests in Wellington. Belinda was never sure where Daniel stood on confrontation with the government. She'd suspected him of betrayal in '81. But that was all it was, suspicion. They were friends. Weren't they?

'Seth, you have to come with us,' Belinda said. 'We're doing it because of you.'

'No, you're not,' Seth said. 'You're doing it because you like demonstrations.'

There was a bitter edge to his voice.

'That's not true.'

'If you'd told me you were doing it because you wanted to save the planet from devastation, or because of our children, I might've thought about it. Just don't tell me you're doing it for me.'

'Why are you so hostile?' Belinda shouted. 'You know what I mean. That I believe in the things you believe in.'

Seth was quiet for a moment. 'Well, if you're sure about that, perhaps I will come.'

She was sorry then, but he probably knew that, she decided afterwards. It meant that she wouldn't be alone with Nick, or that there wasn't the potential to slide off at the end of the demonstration with him. His wife, Esme, didn't approve of demonstrations, so she wouldn't be there.

The protesters had made grotesque masks that they handed out to the marchers. Someone had made a papier-mâché Statue of Liberty wielding a nuclear-armed missile. It was carried at the front of the parade. Seth joined in, in full voice with all the others, marching beside Daniel and Carla.

*Two four six eight — We don't want your nuclear bait!*
*Two four six eight — You can keep your nuclear freight!*

They were pouring up Hobson Street towards the American embassy. Someone with a loud-hailer broadcast the news just through that a protester had got on board the *Texas* and tied an anti-nuclear banner around a chain. There were shouts of joy up ahead. Nick and Belinda had slipped further back in the line.

Nick said, 'Esme knows.'

'How?'

'She heard me talking to you on the phone.'

Belinda looked up ahead. Daniel and Seth seemed to be having a private conversation amid the bedlam. Nick's eyes followed hers.

'Meet me in the Basement,' he said.

The Basement was a café beneath street-level on Lambton Quay. It was a good place to hide out if you didn't want to bump into people. Belinda peeled off at Hobson Crescent and doubled back into the city.

Nick joined her in the café a few minutes after she arrived. The room was noisy and thronged. The background music was Split Enz — 'I Got You'. There was an electric beat in the air.

'What's Esme going to do?'

'Well, it's more about what we're going to do, isn't it? I mean, I've left her before, you know I went back for the kids.'

'Yes. I see.'

'I might have to sort a few things out before I go. Esme thinks she's got the drop on me at the moment. You?'

'I don't know how to leave Seth,' Belinda said, beginning to cry. 'I guess I'll have to.'

'Don't look,' Nick said, so quietly she could hardly hear him, 'Seth's here.'

She did look all the same. Seth was standing at the top of the stairs leading down into the café, his mask hanging absurdly round his neck. He turned and walked away.

He wasn't at home, when Belinda got back. He didn't come home until four in the morning, his face like chalk, his body shaking with cold. It had started to rain and his coat was damp. Belinda was sitting at the kitchen table, her head in her hands.

Seth sat down opposite her, watching her as she cried. There was still a long time to go before dawn.

'I'll make you a hot drink,' she said.

'Soon,' Seth said. 'We need to talk.' He leaned over and took her wrists, laying her hands flat on the table between them. 'I will never lose you,' he said. 'Understand that. I mated for life. I've arranged for a transfer to Auckland. For all of us.' He sat back and watched her.

Belinda wiped away snot with the back of her hand, incredulous. 'How could you have arranged all that tonight?'

Seth shook his head, exhaustion overtaking him. 'Oh, it hasn't just happened. You've been a bit distracted lately. I haven't had a chance to mention it.'

'What if I don't come?' she said.

'Well, sooner or later you will. When Nick's gone back to Esme half a dozen times. I'll still be waiting.'

She thought she saw a sliver of light in the sky, clearing rain. 'You won't tell Maisie about all this?' she said at last. 'I wouldn't want her to know.'

It didn't end right away. Thinking back, it limped away. There were stormy encounters in hotel rooms, days of weeping, Belinda's work in abeyance. Later, a weekend in Paris when their paths crossed, not quite accidentally. They stayed in a cheap hotel. Nick was restless in bed and perfunctory in his love-making. When they checked out, he fumbled his wallet.

'I'll go halves,' she said.

'Hush,' he muttered. 'They think we're married.' He handed over cash.

Outside in the street, Belinda said, 'They don't care whether we're married.'

He looked away. 'Esme checks the credit cards.'

She remembers how they sat in La Rotonde, a few hours before he was due to catch a plane. He held her hand across the table in mute apology. He was changing, she thought, older, but then weren't they all. It was November; yellow chrysanthemums stood in *jardinières*, looming like gold lanterns in late afternoon mist. The next day Belinda was going to Spain to meet a woman

262

who wanted her to work on a project in Tahiti the following year, Nick to Amsterdam hoping to locate funding for a project. She had a sudden stricken thought that if anything happened to her, Nick would be the last person to see her, the person who would have to talk to the embassy, to talk to her family, to tell Seth that he had met her on the other side of the world. The idea filled her with horror. At the Métro station Nick said, 'Well, off in different directions again.'

He kissed her forehead, and she thought then that that was the end at last. One of those things you just know. Or it was for her. (The trip to Spain would go well, her reputation assured by the film made in Tahiti.) After he had gone, she kept walking on, through Montparnasse to the cemetery. She stopped and put a rose on Simone de Beauvoir's grave. Her daughter's namesake.

She doesn't know whether Seth knew any of this drawn-out sorry ending. She hopes not, but supposes that in some way he did. All through the years, she has seen his eyes follow her, and she believes that, in spite of everything, she is loved, if not altogether forgiven.

The letter before her fills her with a sort of weary disgust. It had taken Nick two more years to leave Esme, and he must have known by then that she, Belinda, wouldn't go back to him. Not ever. Nick was a person who couldn't leave well alone. He would be an old man now. This is something she finds difficult to imagine. Yet she is shaken.

The search for the recipe book had stirred up another memory. Her sister's words, in the prison visiting room where she had had her last proper conversation with her, are a refrain that has haunted her. Janice had suggested they might have different fathers. Was it possible that her dreamy, unwell mother had children fathered with three men, rather than two? Belinda had examined her birth certificate, but Jock Pawson's name was written there large. His and her mother's marriage certificate showed their wedding taking place eight months before her birth, something she hadn't registered until she had subjected the documents to that later scrutiny. It still didn't seem possible.

She returned to the room where the chest of drawers stood. The room once occupied by her son Peter was stripped bare of any sign of its previous inhabitant. There was a coolness about the room, something Spartan, like Peter himself. He never came back to stay at the house, and she never offered it to others to sleep in. The distance between them was hard to measure. In her heart she suspects that it is something to do with the time they lived apart after he was born. She's never told him this, and she doesn't believe Seth has either. It's there in some secret reserve of her own.

'I know I was born on the wrong side of the blanket,' Peter had said once. Such an old-fashioned phrase. She can't bring herself to tell him how nearly he was brought up by strangers, how at the last moment she had retrieved him. Would it have been better if she had told him? It seems too late now. Peter saved money from the job at the bank, and then, out of the blue one day, announced that he was enrolling at St John's College in order to become an Anglican minister. No, that wasn't right, he was a priest. But a priest who could marry. He had been called by God.

When Belinda had asked him why, he'd shaken his head and shrugged. 'I liked going to church with Nana Maze' was all he said, implying it was really none of her business.

He had married a parishioner in his first congregation, a young woman from the Philippines. They'd all gone to Manila for the wedding. There, Peter had seemed alive and free, as if overtaken by some hitherto unseen rapture. She has heard the expression 'God's thumb print' and she's not sure what it means, thinks that it might even be a place, but it occurs to her that Peter might have had the thumb print placed upon him. She believes he is happy. He has two children, who visit once or twice a year, although they don't stay long. Peter has told them he will pray for her and Seth.

In the bedroom, there's something she's searching for, yet she still can't quite figure what it is, what connections might be made.

Heaven had gone with them to Manila, an unexpected addition to the family. After Janice died, Heaven stayed in the room that Belinda still calls Dylan's, next to Simone's. Dylan hadn't taken his stuff out of the room and Simone hadn't left home right away, as she had threatened.

It was Janice's funeral that had brought them together. Patariki had phoned her from the Hokianga after his mother died. 'The elders say they want her to come home and be with my dad,' he had said.

'Aren't they still angry with your mum?' Belinda asked.

'They never were,' he said. 'They were just afraid, but they're not any more.'

Seth was overseas when it happened. Simone said, 'Mum, you can't do this on your own. I'm coming with you.'

Then Dylan said he would go, too, and Peter, whether he wanted to or not, saw that it was his duty to come. 'It'll be different,' he said, but Belinda knew that anyway. At the very last minute, Seth arrived after all. He had caught a flight from Los Angeles the night before. So he knew that it mattered.

They had all driven north together, through the little town with railway tracks running down the main street, past abandoned dairy factories, and the meatworks towns, past gum trees and jacaranda in bloom, beyond the ghosts of tractors abandoned in paddocks, and on into the countryside where the seal on the roads ran out into gravel and the bush pushed in, as if ready to swallow up the car.

At the marae, Heaven and Patariki greeted them as they shed their shoes at the door of the meeting house where Janice lay. Her coffin was open and her face was peaceful, her hair arranged around her face to give softness to its contours, a little glitter sprinkled on the collar of her dress. Women wearing wreaths of leaves in their hair sat and fanned Janice's face.

The ground beside Wiremu's grave had been opened up to receive her. The women spoke of Wiremu as Janice's husband. When the coffin was at last lowered into the earth, and keening rose all around her, it occurred to Belinda that her kid sister, who had seemed ordinary and difficult, had brought them to some new knowledge. There was a priest and prayers, yet part of her thought that Peter was right, there was something that spoke of strangeness and difference, and she was moved more deeply than she could have imagined. He surprised her by standing close. She glanced sideways at him and saw a blister of tears on his cheek for this unknown aunt. He made the sign of the cross and moved away.

It was after the tangi that Belinda asked Heaven if this was where she was planning to stay.

'I guess so,' the girl said. 'There's nowhere else really for me to go.'

'What will you do?' Belinda asked.

Heaven seemed nonplussed. 'I'll find something,' she said.

Simone did something surprising then, although, when she thought back on it, Belinda could see that the charged atmosphere of the tangi had transformed them all from their everyday selves. She stepped forward and put her arms around Heaven. 'Cousin,' she said. 'You're my cuzzie.'

Heaven rested her tear-stained face against her cousin's shoulder.

Simone said, 'You can come home with us. Mum and Dad won't mind.'

'Really?' Heaven scanned their faces, gauging their expressions. It occurred to Belinda, then, that she and Seth hadn't done such a bad job with their kids.

'I need to stay here for a while,' Heaven said, 'be with Mum and my nana and the aunties for a bit.'

'Give it time,' Belinda said.

Later, Heaven caught a bus to Auckland, turning up in a taxi at the house in Grey Lynn. Dylan had gone by then, but Simone and Seth seemed to accept her presence as if she had always lived there, as if she fitted.

Heaven took a tourism course while she lived with them. Now she operates her own small company in the north, started with money that Janice had inherited from the faraway Brighton Street house. When she can, she employs her brother Patariki, because it's hard for him to find work, the way it is for everyone up there. His share of Janice's money has been put in a trust for the time being. It's just that he doesn't want to leave the Hokianga and the marae where he grew up, not yet anyway. She's not to worry, he'll find his feet. Dylan emails Heaven pictures of the places where he's doing archaeological digs. She should run a tour to Greece, he says. Very cheap. Very beautiful. The best. He is in love with a Greek woman called Cosima. He can't imagine ever coming home, and Belinda can't imagine that he won't.

Belinda continues to prowl around the house. First, though, she tears Nick's letter into little strips and pours Janola over them so they will bleach. She wraps them in newspaper and puts them in the rubbish.

She is restless and can't calm herself. It is more than the letter from Nick. She goes back to Peter's room, and this time she knows what it is that she is looking for. In the drawer sits a small plastic bag which she has been meaning to throw out. It contains the singed leather button and the man's pipe found in the basement of her early home. They are still wrapped in her handkerchief. She doesn't understand why she has held onto these items. Perhaps it's her eye for unusual detail, which has been a hallmark of her work. Now she takes them out and places them on the bed. Underneath the bag sits the tobacco tin of buttons, rescued from her mother's belongings. She gets that out too.

Belinda opens the tin, and there it is, the other button. These things, the buttons and the pipe, have meant something to her mother. As Grant had said to her that day at their old home, they may have belonged to Jessie's father — or even, she reflects, be a remnant of a grandfather she never knew — but she has no way of knowing. It had shocked her, long ago, to discover from Grant that her grandparents had lived in the same city and they had never known them. Had her mother been so ashamed of her marriage to Jock that she hadn't returned home? Or had he, for some perverse reason of his own, forbidden it? He seemed to have had a hold over their mother.

That evening, over dinner, she says to Seth, 'There's something I've never told you. About what Janice said to me. She thought that she and I had different fathers.'

Seth put his fork down carefully. 'It wouldn't surprise me,' he says.

Belinda looks at him in astonishment. 'You've never said.'

He shrugged his shoulders. 'A hunch.'

'Wishful thinking?' she says, and laughs. She sees that he's serious. 'I've got these bits and pieces. It seemed crazy to keep them, but I did.'

Seth listens, nodding his head as she explains how she found the pipe and the buttons, how all her mother's belongings were destroyed, except these things in the huddled cobwebs under the house.

'We'll see if we can get some DNA from it,' he says. 'If you're happy with that?'

Belinda agrees that this is what she would like. It occurs to her that Nick's letter, shredded in the bin, has been the key to some mystery, that might or might not be solved, but at least she has seen it for what it is. Her mother, like other women, had secrets. She is no different herself.

It's just that secrets have odd ways of surfacing.

# 12

# The Light healer

# 2013

It's always there, the immensity of the sky, and the light of each day. When Joe Higgs is shepherding sheep, he sees light reflected on grass, and on the water of the lakes in the southern landscape where he works, and lying on the mountain snow across the plains. He has been drawn to the sky all his life. It has been so near and yet it eludes him. In the mornings he waits for the first instant, what he has heard described as the green light, the flash between night and day, when dogs begin to bark. He looks towards the sunlight with relief that he's alive to see it again, or on gloomy days he finds a dark pewter gleam among the clouds. At night he's overwhelmed by the red ink lights that flame across the horizon. He has seen, too, the Southern Lights, the electrically charged aurora that turns the sky into a blazing green and pink quilt drawn to the magnetism of the earth, into that area in space where the magnetic fields meet solar winds.

It's white light that fascinates him most of all. He has read a definition of it which says, in effect, that it's a mixture of lights with differing wavelengths in the electromagnetic spectrum. But when he looks at a white sky, such as occasionally appears soon after dawn, it is like a white linen sheet on which the history of the world might be written, before it dissolves into an aching tender blue. There have been songs and stories written about white light. He has heard people talk about it in a spiritual sense, too, as a place of purity that the soul enters after death. He is curious to know whether he will experience it and, if he does, whether he will remember it in an afterlife.

Joe lives in a workman's cottage, a place one might think of as drab were it not for the countryside surrounding it. It is furnished sparsely, with a wooden table that looks like an object a high-school student might have made in a woodworking class; two straight-backed chairs and an easy reclining chair, a book shelf, a computer on a small desk, an aged television set, a single bed with a good-enough mattress. He has bought his own because his back gives him trouble some days. He hopes to stay on this farm for a long time. His gun leans against the laundry tub at the back of the cottage. In the winter he shoots rabbits, a good time to catch them when the grass is sparse and they have to forage longer in the open. Joe shelters behind a beard that has sprouted like a pelt the colour of mouse fur, the hair thick and fine. In his late fifties, he is in better health than when he was a young man.

On his day off, usually taken on a Thursday, he drives his ute into Twizel and changes his library books. It takes him a week to read the four he chooses: one thriller, one book about science, one travel book and a manual about computer technology (he has some trouble keeping up with the rapid changes that occur). At the same time, he chooses four modern novels for Margaret Fraser, the station owner's wife. She says his choices are always better than the ones she makes for herself. She reads the reviews in the Christchurch paper and the *Listener* and likes to keep up as best she can, but you can't read everything, can you, so she depends on him. Once she was a dental nurse at one of the local schools. Her marriage has given her land and money but not a great deal of happiness, he suspects. Fraser's family has been on the land for six generations. There are ways of doing things that a girl from an Auckland suburb will probably never learn.

Joe has worked on the farm for some years, and Fraser and his wife trust him. After a polite knock, he can go into the kitchen and put her books on the counter, without further ado. Sometimes she makes him a cup of tea and they sit down together and talk about books. And the stars. Margaret likes the night sky. They have this in common, a love of the heavens. Sometimes, he can see that she catches herself in surprise, talking to him the way she does. He thinks she would be in her late forties; the children had all but grown up when he first arrived at the station, a greenhorn who could hardly lift a loaded wheelbarrow, let alone a stranded ewe.

It's on one of his visits to the library that he sees the poster about the light-healing sessions that will take place in one of the local pubs the following Thursday. The poster isn't actually in the library, but pinned to a back wall. When he enquires about it, the librarian he speaks to says that it's not the kind of thing they like to advertise. 'You know, alternative medicine, it's not a community activity we support.'

'I can't see why not,' Joe says. 'It might do somebody good.'

'Unorthodox practices. They claim to heal people. We'd get into trouble if someone failed to seek proper treatment for an illness.'

It's on the tip of Joe's tongue to say that he doesn't understand why the library stocks books on religion if they won't advertise light healing. As far as he's concerned God is alternative medicine. Not that he knows what this healing practice entails, but he has already decided that he's going to find out. He knows the hotel, not a bad watering hole. Some days on a Thursday he calls in for a cold lemonade before heading home.

He doesn't plan to tell anyone what he's up to, but when he

delivers her books to Margaret, he can't help himself. Besides that, he'll attract attention, driving off into the night without some excuse. It's not the kind of thing he does. Joe is a man who keeps himself to himself, not one who frequents the pubs. He drinks very little, a glass of pinot noir at the station Christmas party perhaps, which raises an eyebrow or two. Most of the station hands drink a long cooling lager.

'Perhaps you could tell the boss that I'm going in for a game of chess,' Joe says. The boss, that's what he always calls Fraser, preferring not to address him as Mr Fraser, or as Stan, which he has been invited to do. He calls Margaret Mrs Fraser.

'I wish I could come with you,' she says, and her voice trembles. She has kept herself in trim. She turns over a book. Her slim hands are worn, her nails unvarnished but manicured. He wants to touch their small white crescent moons. It's not as if he hasn't thought about taking her against a red barn wall. It's a long time since he made love to a woman. From the way she looks at him he knows she wouldn't mind either, that her knees would buckle a little and her back arc against the wall. She'd get no tupping from him. He doesn't plan to get himself killed by Fraser. She's the kind of woman who would fall in love and go around all dreamy-eyed, and her husband would smell the heat on her.

When the following Thursday comes around, Joe nearly doesn't go. He has been to town once that day and the thought of another round trip of forty kilometres or so is unappealing; in the morning he will have to be up at five for a muster. But the morning had been one of those pale white dawns, the sort that lingered, setting him on edge for the day. As he thinks back to the calm, clear morning he knows he won't be satisfied until he finds out what the light healing is about. He might be healed in some part of himself.

It's a quiet night in the hotel, just half a dozen patrons standing at the bar in the lower level. There's an upstairs space with tables. On busy nights, this is where food is served, but the town is so quiet you could drive a flock of sheep down the main street and nobody would notice. He wonders if there's no light healing after all, but the bartender motions him to the stairs leading to the upper level. In the corner of the deserted area, three men are gathered. One sits facing the other two. They have a contraption pointed at the seated man. It brings to mind those photographers of the past who set up their cameras on tripods and covered their heads with a cloth. The seated man is very still.

Joe sees that this man has a bright white light beamed on his forehead. It is about the size of a two-dollar coin, perhaps a little bigger.

'Do you mind if I watch?' he asks.

One of the men behind the machine waves in assent, and Joe takes a seat in the corner. The man looks peaceful, his eyes closed, as though he were receiving the light into his head. Several minutes pass, until the light is switched off. The man opens his eyes as if recovering from a trance. 'Thank you,' he says. 'I feel better already.'

'Just take your time. Take it easy,' one of the projectionists says.

'What is it? The machine?' Joe asks.

'A light box. LED. It's brighter than an ordinary lamp. It sends out ten thousand lux of light. A lux measures the intensity of light passing through a surface. Very therapeutic.'

'I know about that,' Joe says.

'You do? Well, mate, you want to try it?'

The man, who has introduced himself as Claude, is small and dapper with a slim moustache, like a magician. This bothers Joe, but the man who has just undergone the light therapy seems in good shape. His assistant looks more rugged, with a bushy beard like Joe's own, wearing a Swanni and boots.

'Right,' Joe says, and takes his place on the chair facing the light machine.

'Cost you a hundred. You all right with that?' Claude says.

'Sweet as.'

The machine begins again. Joe can't feel the light there, but he knows something is happening. He feels tranquil as if the very core of him were being reached. It is a frightening feeling and yet he feels at ease.

There's a slight commotion in the bar downstairs. A group of people have come into the bar, asking for a table where they can have a glass of wine, a bit of finger food if there's anything going — just some hot chips would do. Everything in town seems to have closed up for the night. Joe closes his ears to these voices. If he concentrates, he doesn't need to hear them at all, they can become just a blur at the far edge of his consciousness.

The next minute, the group comes up the stairs and settles at the corner table where he sat earlier in the evening. Focus, he tells himself, just focus.

All the same, he can't help but overhear the conversation. It's a group of film makers on location to shoot a documentary. He hears a woman's voice talking excitedly about the beautiful visual composition they were making. Something to do with Central Otago's lakes and waterways, with a dark underside of pollution. 'We just have to get to some of those runholders, get them to talk,' she is saying.

Joe freezes; this is a voice he knows. He opens his eyes. There are some women wearing skinny jeans and bright tops, men in denim, some with their hair tied back in ponytails like girls.

'Keep your eyes shut, mate,' Claude says.

The woman's voice says, 'What's going on here?' She has a slim behind, grey hair fashionably cut in a wavy bob.

Claude says, 'Nothing to worry about.'

Then the woman says, 'Grant, it's you, isn't it? Grant, I've been looking all over for you.'

Joe feels himself flinch, willing it to be so momentary that it won't show. But she's walking towards him and he knows that she knows. He jumps to his feet, fumbling in his pocket for a roll of notes.

'A mistake,' he says, thrusting the money in Claude's hand. 'I'm Joe,' he says, as he heads for the exit. 'Sorry, ma'am.'

As he takes to the stairs, two at a time, past a barman carrying a tray bearing a plate of chips, and a dish with the unmistakeable pungent smell of fried onion, he hears someone say, 'That was Joe Higgs. That's his name, that's just Joe.'

Does he imagine it, or does he hear someone say that he's a quiet old coot, keeps himself to himself as a rule? It's what he would expect to hear of himself.

He is trembling as he starts the ute, worrying that the woman who has spoken to him might try to find him. As he hurtles along the road he feels a sickening bump, and another one. Dead rabbits. He slows down. There are eyes like pinpricks in the dark. They're pests to be shot, but still he feels like a murderer, cutting them down like that.

Days pass and he begins to believe that the danger is past, although he's overtaken by a feeling of gloom. The skies have been overcast all week. Then, around about Tuesday, the clouds lift and the morning is the way he likes it, a bright white-gold building up to a smashing day. Fraser appears at his door on his quad bike.

'Mrs Fraser would like you to call in later,' he says. His manner is cool, his eyes appraising.

Joe knows straight away that it's not good news. So long as she's not one of those women who starts telling their husbands about their fantasies. Perhaps he flatters himself, but he can't think what else could bring about this request or why Fraser would look at him like that.

She sits at the table in her dining room, not in the kitchen, so he knows this is to be formal. There is a dresser lined with fine china and old silver. Her hands are in her lap, and she's not really looking at him. In front of her lies a folder of papers.

'What is it?' he says. 'Mrs Fraser. Margaret.'

'There's been a woman here,' she says.

Immediately, he guesses, but he waits for her to tell him.

'She was looking for a man called Grant Pawson.'

He takes a deep breath. 'Oh, Grant Pawson,' he says, trying to make his voice easy. 'Yes, I knew a fellow by that name once. Reckon he owes money, people are always after him.'

'She saw someone at the hotel last Thursday night. She thought it was this man she's looking for. Only they said his name was Joe Higgs. They said it was you.'

He shook his head. 'Well, fancy that. Fancy that I should be mistaken for him. He must get around, this fellow Pawson.'

Margaret Fraser has opened the file in front of her. Her computer sits beside her, a little cloth protecting the high polish of the table. When he went to work at the station, Joe had had to provide a lot of details about himself, his IRD number, a copy of his licence, even his passport because, as Margaret had explained at the time, they'd had a chap who stole some valuables — some Oriental ivory, a lovely piece of jade. They didn't find out until he was well clear of the place, by which time he'd done a runner overseas. Well, he would have fetched a tidy sum on those items. This was when there was still money in antiques. Of course, she could see that Joe wasn't like that, but her husband said they must be very careful in the future.

'My papers are all in order,' he says.

There's a pained expression on her face as she studies the file. 'There was another Joseph Higgs born the same day as you,' she says. 'In the same place. The same little town.'

'Well, I never knew that,' Joe says. 'But thank you for telling me anyway.'

'He had a brother. I've tracked him down. He told me about the little boy in the family who died.'

Her expression is intense, but it's not desire she's feeling. It's pity perhaps, that's the kindest way he can interpret it, but more likely it's a mild contempt. 'You haven't asked me who the woman was. The one who came here.'

'Some busybody,' he says, getting to his feet. She won't get anything from him.

'She says she's your sister,' Margaret says. 'Belinda. Does that mean anything to you?'

He has his back to her. 'Nothing,' he says. 'No, can't say it does.' His head is full of pain; light is burning into his brain.

'What will I tell my husband?'

He hesitates at the door and turns back for a moment. He remembers the face of his mother, the same helpless, uncertain expression when she knew she was beaten.

'Tell him I'm on the lookout for that fellow Pawson,' he says. 'I'll talk to him in the morning. Thank you.' He bobs his head like one of the servants in the period dramas he sees replayed on television now and then.

It is a reprieve, the best she can offer him. One more night to gaze up into the stars, the cool, deep, sparkling dark. One more morning to catch the first light of dawn and all that radiance.

# 13

# The beautiful flower

## 2015

The long garden at the back of Belinda and Seth's house has been terraced. Here, not far from the heart of the city, they still have their quarter-acre dream. As Seth has grown older, he has turned increasingly towards tending the garden. The top terraces have been planted with small hedges to create garden 'rooms' where they entertain friends and hold family barbecues. Further down, he has planted New Zealand native trees along one boundary fence. In autumn he climbs up ladders to trim them with a chainsaw in order to keep them from shading the neighbour's garden. Belinda gets anxious when he's up the ladder, wielding the angry machine.

'Please *promise* me you won't go up there when I'm not around,' she pleads.

On the opposite boundary, he grows a strip of gladioli and dahlias that bloom in summer, planted in memory of his mother. Granny flowers they might be, but he loves them. Besides, he says, they're back in fashion. The central terraces between these boundaries are planted with citrus trees, a plum tree and vegetables. Seth collects manure from the fowl house to feed his plot. He has four Black Orpington hens and would love a rooster, but roosters aren't allowed inside the city limits. He loves the dark plumage of the breed, with its green sheen, the black beak and eyes, the bright-red comb. They are the hardiest kind of hen, he says, charmed by the way they chuckle about their business. Good-natured hens, he tells Belinda. But, also, he rescues commercially raised caged birds so he can give them a better life. There are two of them, spongy-looking creatures with sparse white feathers and swollen pink bottoms. They seem to blink perpetually at the light and lose their way. If ever a hen is going to find a gap in the fence and wander onto a neighbour's property, it will be one of the freedom hens. Sooner or later, all the others will follow like Judas sheep behind their leader. Seth calls them Bundle and Squat.

Belinda likes the hens, too, although if Seth is away sometimes she forgets to feed them if she's in a hurry, and then she spends the whole day fretting about them being hungry. She wonders if Seth will be able to tell, which of course is absurd, but it's almost as if the birds can talk to him.

It's on one of these mornings, when summer is on the rise, that Belinda remembers, at the very last moment before she drives off to a meeting, that this chore has still to be done. Seth has flown to Sydney for a meeting of his own and will be away for two nights. He is off to present a paper at a symposium. Although he has officially retired, he's still in demand, a mine of knowledge. Travel to these gatherings of his colleagues invigorates him, reassures him that his life's work hasn't been in vain.

Belinda is wearing a lime linen suit and chartreuse Italian leather shoes with high heels. She parks the car in the driveway and runs back towards the house, thinking that she should change her shoes. When she glances at her watch, it's clear that if she's to survive the traffic and make the meeting on time, it's best to make a dash for it down to the garden shed, grab some grain and fling it to the chooks without further ado. Her phone rings when she's in mid-stride. *Yes, yes*, she says, she will be in soon. *Start* without me if I don't make it in half an hour. Make *sure* lunch is organised. It's on the edge of the lower terrace that her heel catches and she's falling. She's falling through a space that she knows, as the day will wear on, is short but it seems to take forever for the impact to happen. The snap of her leg is a broken stick, a sharp tiny refrain, the pain a black fire of agony that shoots through her body. Her phone has flown through the air.

At first Belinda can't believe her predicament. Her mind is focused on dealing with pain. She hears herself groan, and a tight little voice that isn't her own, or not that she recognises, cries *help*. Her vocal chords seem to be wedged in the back of her throat.

There's silence all around her, except for the disturbed cackle of the hens. The end of the garden is bounded by a high wooden fence that borders a driveway. The neighbours at the rear are out of earshot, unless they happen to walk down their drive, perhaps to collect mail from the box at the gate. It's on this account that Seth has chosen the site for the hen house. Belinda is utterly alone, although this takes a few minutes to register. Here, close to the centre of the largest city in the country, she is on her own. Her phone rings from inside the foliage of a budding dahlia bush, some metres away, or that's where she thinks it is. It's set to 'Don't Worry, Be Happy'. When she tries to move in the direction of the ring tone, it's impossible. She can't move. At this point, Belinda lapses briefly into unconsciousness.

When she comes round, the sun is beating in her face. Someone will come soon, she thinks. The people at the meeting will wonder where she is. But she doesn't know them well, and besides, she discourages people from ringing her at home. It's now some time since she's made a film of her own; rather, she's consulted by others on matters like technical skills, production problems, raising money. Belinda has become one of those go-to people who has contacts in the industry. The team will think she has been delayed, or that there is some emergency that has taken precedence. Well, they would be right about that. They will, perhaps, have been calling her not once, but several times. The phone continues to ring on and off in the dahlia bush. In the sun, one of the buds has begun to unfold. Her leg, waxed, tanned and silky, throbs with a steady incessant pain; she sees how it has begun to swell.

'Help. Help me,' she croaks. The thinness of her voice is terrifying.

At some point, she believes she hears a neighbour walking down the driveway behind the fence. The person doesn't hear her feeble bleats. She wriggles out of her suit jacket and puts it over her face, to shield herself from the sun. In the dim light beneath the fabric, she tries to work out what she can do, or whether there's anyone who might have been calling on her that day. Simone often comes in with the children after school. But the house is locked. Belinda's car is in the driveway but that wouldn't signify anything, the garage door is closed. Simone might assume that Belinda had been picked up and had left the car out. Her thoughts become more and more convoluted. She's wracked with thirst, yet at the same time shivering in the heat.

Hours pass. If nobody comes, she could be here all night among Seth's carrots and lettuces. The petals of the dahlia flower are unfolding. She remembers that it's called 'Tutti Frutti', one of Seth's favourites, a coral pink cactus flower, the first dahlia of the season. The scents of mint and rosemary waft from her herb garden. Remember me. At funerals, baskets of rosemary have been passed around so that the congregation can put sprigs on the casket. She thinks that if she lies very still and tries to gather her strength, she might be able to drag herself to the dahlia and find her phone. After a time, she begins to cry, not sobbing because even the movement that causes is enough to rally the pain, but letting the tears trickle down her face and over her neck. The hens squawk in bursts, hungry and angry because she's there but won't feed them. Surely someone will hear the racket they make.

It occurs to Belinda that if she could open the gate they might get out, as is their wont since the freedom chooks appeared. She remembers Seth telling her that Squat is broody at present, but Bundle is out and about. One of the neighbours would be sure to notice if they appeared on their doorstep. They always come fussing over when it happens, protective of their gardens, the mess the hens make on their immaculate paths. The latch is almost within her grasp. She reaches for it with her fingertips, thinks she has caught it, but the gate swings an inch or so back and doesn't move again. The effort is too much. As she subsides, she understands how weak she has become.

Just when she thinks the heat so unbearable that it will get her if nothing else does, a cloud passes over the sun. Her watch tells her that it's three o'clock. Six hours have passed since she fell. Another hour passes and she knows Simone won't be coming. More clouds have massed, threatening a change in the weather. If she's not fried she'll be drowned. Rest, she tells herself. Gather strength, carry your leg to safety if you have to, two hands and one good leg.

The next hour is dream-like, a kind of half-sleep in which faces gather around her. They're looking down at her. All her children. Her and Seth's grandchildren. None of this is fair. Belinda thinks she has done the best she can, all things considered. Sure, she's made some mistakes, but who doesn't? There have been losses and gains. She's in the back seat of a little car in the countryside again, pushing aside Maisie Anderson's gardening gloves as she makes love with her son. He could have abandoned her, but he didn't. He could have treated Peter like Jock had treated her and Jessie, unwanted cuckoos in his nest. But Seth didn't. If anything she is the one who has had the troubled relationship with her older son.

She has surprised herself, the way she behaves over Peter. Although there has been a thaw between them, there are some distances that can never be recovered, she has told herself. And here, in the garden where she may well be dying, Belinda thinks about a woman she never knew, the woman who was, briefly, Peter's mother. Over the years, she has tried hard not to think of her, not to conjecture what she might look like, and, most of all, not to imagine what she gave to Peter that was so special.

When he came home to her and Seth, he was a crotchety baby. Colic, Maisie had said, but she looked anxious. Just a change of routine, the Plunket nurse said, as if it were nothing. Belinda had phoned the social worker who had organised Peter's return and asked if perhaps she and the other mother might meet, only to be given a frosty refusal. 'Have you no idea how that poor woman feels?' the social worker had said, putting Belinda in her place. As if she were still a delinquent teenager, not a married grown-up mother. And it is this idea, about how the other woman felt, that she has refused to entertain through all the long years since then. Why would she? No, that wasn't right. How could she not have done? Her failure, staring her in the face. Now, she wonders if the woman is still alive and whether she'd had more children. And would Peter be the same kind of person had he grown up with her? Surely it can't be possible that he missed his other mother, that he misses her still? *You will never know*. Like a story or poem she read him in one of the countless Dr Seuss books. She can't remember the rest of the quote, something about *the value of a memory*.

Seth stood by her through all that and has stood beside her for forty or more years. He has put up with her absences and betrayals, the days when she's somewhere else in her head. That's Seth, rarely unkind. What will he make of her dead? She wonders if he will deliver a eulogy in which he bares the truth of what she's really like. Perhaps Seth couldn't describe who she really is. Nor could she describe him.

There's nobody to tell what she's just figured out, that she and Seth know each other for dear life, and don't altogether know each other at all. Perhaps that's what it's like with most couples. She has read recently in the newspaper that couples who describe themselves as happily married might be divorced a year later, that happiness isn't necessarily a guarantee of living happily ever after. How strange. She doesn't think Seth would leave her now. But she might be leaving him. This may be what's happening to her right now: she's dying and leaving him, the way Janice left, simply not able to stay alive any more. And Grant had left. Not that she's convinced Grant is dead. She believes she has seen him.

And there's an irony about all this. There's her sister Jessie, who deserted the family when she and her siblings were still children, a woman who had become famous for her exploits gathering news in the world's hot spots, but couldn't face the past. Now Jessie was coming back. She had emailed Belinda just the week before. Snatches of the message spool through her head. *I hadn't realised that you were the Belinda Anderson who made that splendid film about the aftermath of testing in the Pacific. I should have known.* Well, yes, you should have, Belinda thinks. Jessie hasn't even bothered to find out what Belinda has done with her life. Thanks for nothing, Jessie. When Simone was little Belinda had persuaded her to write a letter to her famous aunt, but there had been no reply. A few years ago, Jessie had been in New Zealand for the funeral of a friend and had written to suggest a visit, but Belinda was about to go to a film festival. That seemed not to have registered either. *I would very much like us to meet again*, Jessie had written. On the way to New Zealand, on this visit, she was planning to stop over in Cambodia to spend time with her daughter, whose name was Bopha. Jessie had adopted her after the civil war. Later, Bopha had elected to return to her country and help with its rebuilding. *Bopha means 'beautiful flower' and she lives up to her name. I would be honoured if you would agree to meet me. I have so many questions to ask.*

Belinda can't get the letter out of her head. She has a few questions of her own. Like who belonged to whom in our family? What do you know that I don't? Tell me about our mother, the things I never knew about her. You, of all of us, knew her. Don't tell me about your beautiful flowers. Tell me why I share the DNA of a stranger I can't even begin to trace. *I would be honoured if you would agree to meet me.* A wheedling note there. The cheek of it. How arrogant the woman was, expecting to turn up after all these years and pick up the reins again. Because that was what Jessie was like when they were children, the person in the driving seat. Besides that, Belinda had read plenty about this flower of Jessie's. Jessie had written of the girl often enough, the way she had plucked her from the cesspits of human trafficking in the midst of a war. This was false modesty, the notion that Belinda wouldn't have followed her grand life story spread through columns of newspaper space. Or rather that, in spite of discovering her talents as a film maker, she still doesn't think of Belinda as very clever.

Her rage is unreasonable. Really, it's a nice enough letter, but it's come too late. Belinda will be dead before long. She will glower at Jessie from her coffin without an inch of forgiveness. But her anger is healthy: it revitalises her for a few minutes. The dahlia is fully in bloom now, glowing with colour in the muted light. She remembers that the dahlia is the national flower of Mexico. She was always good at Trivial Pursuit. The children had grown frustrated in their efforts to beat her at the game. The dahlia is the beautiful flower in Seth's garden.

The hens appear to have retreated indoors, as if they've lost their expectations for the night, and accept that the morning might bring a better day. Only an occasional sighing squawk emanates from their house. The air has grown cold. A few drops of the rain, augured by the dark, rolling clouds above, splatter her. She gives herself up to the rain. The phone rings again. *Don't worry, be happy.* She's lost count of the number of times it's rung. Simone, her own gorgeous daughter, for sure. She often rings after dinner when the kids are doing their homework. Or Seth, calling from Australia. He calls her quite frequently these days when he's away, now that they live alone, just the two of them, in the big house.

It might just be the phone company offering her a deal. They do that in the evenings. Another call. *Don't worry* ... Soon the battery will run out. Dylan ringing her from Athens with an invitation to his wedding? That seems unlikely, too. He could see his mother breaking plates, and he didn't need that, was what he'd said the last time she'd asked. This had offended her. 'He wouldn't get married without us, would he?' she'd said to Seth. Seth had said, 'Look, it's not that important. I'm no Zorba the Greek. I'd be lost at a Greek wedding.' But Dylan is, she'd said stubbornly, yes, Dylan is that kind of person.

It will have been a long meeting, the family will say to themselves when she doesn't reply. She's gone off for drinks. God knows she'll probably be on the town half the night with nobody to go home to. Trust Mum to forget to switch on.

The rain doesn't last long, but a mist seems to have formed in front of her eyes. She's losing it, she knows, her sanity slipping away. Belinda would have liked to say goodbye to her children. She's angry all over again that this is being denied her.

A late watery sun re-emerges, daylight-saving prolonging the hour, though the light is going, and she's wet through. Nearly eleven hours since she fell. It's now or never if she's to save herself.

Belinda levers herself onto her elbows, heaving in her effort to roll over. Her scream startles her, a prolonged shriek, as alien as her trembling whispers of the morning. As she falls back, engulfed in a new and vicious pain, she thinks she sees a movement at the top of the garden.

'Hello, is there anybody here?' a voice calls. It's Peter.

'Here, I'm here. Peter, help me.' Perhaps his voice is just another manifestation of her failing mind. But she sees his unmistakeable figure, looming above a low hedge.

'Mum, what are you doing there?' He's leaping down through the terraces, his white clerical collar gleaming in the dying fall of the light, his suit coat flapping behind him.

He kneels beside her, one hand on her pulse, the other holding a cell phone, speaking rapidly, calling an ambulance. His expression is distraught. 'An emergency, yes, she's in shock. I'd say needs oxygen, yes, something for the pain. Oh God, hurry please, she looks awful.' He slides the phone into his pocket. 'Hold on, Mum. How long have you been here?'

Belinda is barely able to answer, her voice just a croak. 'I don't. Know. Morning. Long time.'

'Come on, Mum, come on, don't leave me.' His voice is full of anguish.

'How?' she whispers. 'How did you find me?'

She's only partly listening as he explains how Seth has been phoning to let her know he was coming home a day later than scheduled, some change in the timetable. And when he couldn't get a reply he'd rung Simone and asked her to come over and check on her, but she was at a parent teacher evening at the school and she'd rung Peter. Here he is. And she thinks, in some clouded part of her brain, that he has said it at last. He needs her.

'I thought there was nobody home. I nearly fell over one of your bloody hens. I was figuring out how to get it back in the run.'

Bloody. Fancy that, Peter saying 'bloody'.

'Bundle,' she says. 'She must have got out after all. I think I was asleep, Peter.' He holds her hand tightly. The wail of a siren draws near; soon there are lights, torches in the dark, people bearing a stretcher, a mask placed over her face. 'You'll feed the hens, won't you?'

'In the morning, first thing.'

Belinda's phone rings once, then stops. 'My phone,' she sighs. 'It's there. In your dad's dahlia.'

'I'll find it later.' His grip on her hand tightens.

'But you'll tell him, won't you? I so wanted him to see it, his first dahlia of the season.'

'You'll tell him yourself, Mum, you'll see.'

Peter rides in the ambulance with her, smooths hair from her forehead. A needle has been inserted in her arm. Above her mask, she sees that his face has lines around his mouth and that he's still frightened.

'My boy,' she says. All the years have vanished. He must surely feel that immense surge of love filling her. She puts her free hand out to touch his face. 'Such a beautiful boy. I won't —' she says and stops.

He leans to catch her words. 'Won't what, Mum?'

The morphine is stealing through her veins. She might yet survive.

'I won't go away, Peter. It won't happen again.'

# 14
# The book of leaving
# 2015

'They said we'd find you here.' The speaker is a tall, thin woman, stylish in the way she dresses, but old beyond her seventy or so years. She leans on a wooden-handled cane. A puff of wind would blow her away, Belinda thinks.

The man at the table in the zoo café looks up slowly, taking them in, the muscles in his face not appearing to move. He has thick, neatly cut, grey hair, a grey moustache clipped in an exact line above his lip. Beside his cup there is a monocular that he has been using to observe the pygmy marmosets in the cage alongside the tables. Belinda has watched him through the glass as she and her sister Jessie mounted the stairs. She saw him, seemingly immersed in the activities of the swinging creatures, mothers with babies borne on their backs. It takes her a while to get up the ramp on her crutches because one leg is encased in plaster, by which time the man has turned his attention to their arrival.

He stands up to face them. He wears a collar and tie beneath a green cashmere sweater, trousers with knife-sharp creases, polished brogues. 'The smallest monkeys in the world,' he says, gesturing towards the enclosure. 'Quite a primitive species. Did you know marmosets don't have wisdom teeth? They've got claws, not fingernails.'

'Grant, it is you, isn't it?' Jessie says gently, trying to stop this flow of information.

'Yes,' he says, 'it's me. At least I think it is.'

'Have you got someone with you?' Belinda asks. She sinks into a chair opposite her brother.

'No,' he says. 'It's all right, I'm not rabid. They know where I am. I didn't want you to meet me at the hospital, that's all. I'm learning to live in the world again.'

'Do you like it out here?' Jessie asks.

Grant seems to sigh. 'Joe Higgs liked the world. I'm not sure it's got room for Grant Pawson.'

'Jessie's come down from Auckland to see you,' Belinda says. 'She's going back to London tomorrow.'

She feels as if she's speaking to a child, not her brother Grant. It's like talking to a stranger. She remembers when she was young, just setting out on her career as a film maker, seeing the series of plays that are etched on her psyche. *Talking to a Stranger*. Judi Dench, Maurice Denham. She can't remember who else starred. What she remembers is the pain of a family in the act of disintegration. 'Gladly, My Cross-Eyed Bear'. It's here, her own family drama, one she will never make. Grant had tried to reinvent himself as someone who didn't belong to their family, taking on another identity, choosing to be someone else, until it all fell apart around him. This is where madness lies, she thinks. In the end, whenever the end comes, we can only be ourselves.

Jessie is talking again. No food for her but do either of them want something? Her hand holding a menu is almost translucent in its thinness. She has come on a day between dialysis sessions. Her whole journey from the other side of the world has been timed with careful planning to allow her to travel. She had arranged private care in advance for her stay in

New Zealand. Her daughter, Bopha, hadn't wanted to leave her, but she had promised her husband Tan, back in Cambodia, that she would return soon, not leave him and the children alone for long. Bopha had met all the family, except for Grant, and she and Dylan have only met on Skype, but they have promised to stay in touch. Belinda was surprised how well the two of them seemed to get along. It was Bopha to whom Dylan volunteered the information that he and his wife Cosima were coming to New Zealand. 'Time she met the outlaws,' he had said, referring to his parents. 'Hey, I've just spoiled the big surprise.'

Belinda is finding it hard to concentrate on the conversation that's evolving between Jessie and Grant. Young children jump and shout, high on the pleasure of their outing to the zoo; others are cranky and tired. It surprises Belinda these days, the way mothers allow their children to run riot in restaurants. It was something that her mother-in-law, Maisie, disapproved of, and Belinda had made sure that her children never did this.

Jessie, on the other hand, is smiling. 'Remember how you kids used to play up when our mother took us to Kirkcaldie's for afternoon tea? I could have died of shame. You used to bang your fists up and down on the tables, and blow sherbet all over each other through straws.'

'We didn't,' Belinda says. 'You're making that up.'

'No, she's not. We did do that. You were the worst of the lot,' Grant says.

'Ouch,' says Belinda, but she feels happier. Grant is remembering, something the hospital people had said he didn't seem able to do, when they first called her, to tell him that he was a patient. At least he'd asked for her, that was something. His next-of-kin.

He and Jessie are talking about refugees, about all the places in the world where people are displaced and homeless. 'What can people do about it?' Grant asks.

'I'm not sure,' Jessie says slowly. 'I think we stop trying to save all the world and focus on what good we can do for one another in the space we occupy. We become cells of good living, as best we can.'

'But you wrote about the world's problems,' Grant persists.

'I tried to tell people what was happening, that's all.' Her voice was wistful.

Jessie had covered conflicts in Somalia, Rwanda (barely escaping with her life in a helicopter, while tides of people clambered to ride with her, their dark hands reaching out and imploring), Afghanistan, Iraq, Burma that is now called Myanmar, where she'd snatched moments with Aung San Suu Kyi while she was under house arrest, the genocide in Cambodia. It was only in Cambodia that she'd allowed herself to become involved, in a personal sense, when she'd taken Bopha, who, in time, became her daughter. Bopha could have led a professional life in London, but chose instead to return to Cambodia. Each step was a small one. Sometimes, Jessie said, Bopha and Tan felt their steps had a hollow ring, in a country that had had its heart emptied. Perhaps, she says, it might add up to something bigger in the long run, but that is one of the lessons you learn, that you do what you can and hope that the good will outlast you. It was too easy to be overwhelmed.

This conversation is of the kind Jessie has been having with Seth, about the environment, over the past week. At times, Belinda has felt on the periphery. The two of them seem in tune with each other, and now it's happening with Grant, her strange lost-and-found brother.

Jessie looks over at Belinda, touching her hand lightly. 'Recording angels, you and I.' So that Belinda feels part of the dialogue again.

But she sees that Grant is drifting, his eyes beginning to cloud. He is weary of the world and its politics. 'Such desolation,' he remarks, tapping his fingernails on the table. His hands are neatly groomed and pale, but they carry scars, reflecting years of hard manual work on a farm down South. Belinda knows that's where he tried to take his life.

'I'll go soon,' he says. 'What brought you back anyway, Jessie?'

'I'm dying,' she says. 'And yes, I should have come before but I didn't.'

His eyes are following the marmosets again. One mother carries twins on her back, yet she leaps from branch to branch like spindrift in the air. Beneath them a giant green iguana has curled itself around a log. Do any of these creatures, Belinda wonders, believe that their temperature-controlled cage is really the Amazon?

'Did you ever find out anything about those bits and pieces under the house?' Grant asks Belinda, almost as if Jessie hasn't spoken.

At first she hesitates, thinking that he's talking about the picture of Janice. He knows that Janice has died. Belinda had asked the doctor to tell him this, if it seemed appropriate, because she thought it was something he'd want to know. But it's the box of their mother's belongings he's talking about, not something she'd planned to discuss. She thinks that what he doesn't know won't hurt him. But he's onto her.

'You did, didn't you? What about that pipe?'

'I had it tested for DNA.'

'And what did you find?'

Belinda takes a deep breath before she speaks. 'Inconclusive,' she says. 'It must have been under the house a long time.' She knows he doesn't believe her.

The mothers and their children have mostly taken their leave. The café is quiet. 'I'm sorry you're sick, Jessie,' Grant says, as he stands up. 'I hope you don't experience pain.'

'Nor you, Grant,' Jessie replies gravely.

They all stand up then. 'We can walk back with you to the hospital,' Belinda says.

He nods at her leg in its plaster casing. 'I don't think so. Besides, I want to walk on my own. It's such a good day for it.'

And he's right. The sky is duck-egg blue, just the faintest breeze stirring the magnolia trees along Roy Street, the last of the season's flower cups shining among the leaves. It takes Belinda back to nights she has walked along here after a protest march with friends whose names she barely registers now. Well, some of them she remembers better than others. They're part of her history. Old times. Some of them good. She would rather be where she is now, her place in the world.

Grant nods at the marmosets. 'Families,' he says. 'They're families all right. Nice if you've got them.'

And then he is gone, walking briskly into the sunlight.

'I'll never see him again,' Jessie says.

'I'm not sure I will either,' says Belinda.

'Why did you lie to him?'

'Who said I did?'

They have reached the rental car Jessie has hired. Belinda isn't sure that Jessie should be driving, but she has insisted. She presented her international licence without batting an eyelid when she signed for it. She's driven all her life, she tells Belinda afterwards, drove all the way through the Khyber Pass from Pakistan to Afghanistan in the 1960s, over the mountains, when she was just starting out as a journo. Those were the days, before the mujahideen. She'd got away with it without wearing a burqa. Ye gods, though, it was a long way down the side of the road, deep ravines below. But beautiful, so beautiful in the mountains. When it's time to stop driving, she will. That time hasn't come yet.

Belinda busies herself with levering her leg into the vehicle and finding the catch for her seatbelt. Jessie pulls out and drives straight ahead and up the hill, over the road that leads back to the sea. It seems to Belinda that her sister is driving with reckless abandon, swirling and swooping around the corners.

'I get it,' Belinda says. 'Your life was more exciting than mine.'

'You seem to have had your fair share of adventures.' Jessie's voice is dry.

They crest the hill and begin the run down Sutherland Road that leads to Lyall Bay if they turn left, or back towards Island Bay, if they make a right. To Belinda's relief, Jessie turns left. She has no wish to go back to Brighton Street. They park and watch the lazy surf, the long line of the beach, the black heads of distant surfers riding the waves.

'Different lives,' Belinda says.

'I think you got the lucky life,' Jessie says.

'You do?' Belinda looks at her, surprised. 'You left us, Jessie. You left us with Jock and Charm. We were children.'

'How old are you, Belinda? In your sixties. You're not a child any more.'

'They took away everything that was our mother's. Grant and Janice never got over it.'

'I know. Look, Belinda, what was I supposed to do?' For a moment, her voice turns defensive. 'Besides, I didn't know Jock would marry Charm.'

'Do you remember our mother? I should be able to, I was old enough, but I can't get a handle on her any more. Stupid, I know.'

Jessie's voice is gentler. 'I do, yes. Some days, well, you know, when I'm having my treatment, I see her face. She was quiet and dark and read a lot. She was a librarian when she married my father, Andrew Sandle. I remember her as always being a little sad. Although at first she seemed happier when we lived down south, in the tobacco fields.'

'What do you mean, lived in the tobacco fields? I never heard about that.'

'Where she met Jock.' Jessie told her, then, about the summer in the heat, when she and Irene lived the life of casual labourers, in a little hut and where, as a child, she'd been allowed to live wild and free. And then she came back to the pipe, as if some image had been illuminated for her. 'Tell me about that pipe Grant was talking about. Come on, what did he mean by that?'

So it was Belinda's turn to explain, about the day that she and Grant had found the items under the house in Brighton Street.

'The DNA told you something, didn't it? I could tell by the look on your face,' Jessie says. 'Something you didn't want to tell Grant.'

'I'm not sure what. It's possible it belonged to someone who was my father. It seems Jock wasn't. I didn't think it was the moment to tell Grant that. Hey Grant, I'm your half-sister. You thought you had sisters? But look, we're just the remnants, the leftovers from our mother's life.' Belinda waited a moment, before going on. 'Jessie, do you happen to remember a jacket with leather buttons. A man's jacket, I'd say. Someone who smoked a pipe?'

Jessie shakes her head. She's starting the car, turning around, preparing to drive back after all. 'I can't leave without saying goodbye to the island.' She drives more carefully now, back along the edge of the sea — Lyall Bay, Houghton Bay, Island Bay. Belinda tells her about the last time she and Grant and Janice saw her mother, how Grant thought that Clean Linen Bay in the hospital was like these bays, without the water. Funny little kid, and now look at him. It'd break your heart, wouldn't it?

'You go up to the house if you want,' Belinda says. 'I can sit on the sea wall for a bit.'

'No, I'm done with it, too.' One or two fishing boats that have stayed behind that day bob in the quiet sea. Tapu te Ranga Island lies in front of them, almost but not quite within swimming distance when they were children, its rocky shore uninviting.

'There was supposed to be a woman living there in a cave at one stage,' Jessie remarks. 'I never found anyone who knew about her. Perhaps it was a myth. But I see the Italians are still here.'

'They were good to us kids. After you left.'

'They were good to me, too. Antonio was a nice guy. The night of our mother's funeral.' For a moment Jessie stops, appearing to remember something, as if she might tell Belinda, and then decides against it. Her face softens in a way that makes Belinda fleetingly wonder whether Antonio might have been a lover. It's not for her to ask. It doesn't seem possible.

'Well, he was kind,' Jessie adds, after a momentary silence. It's the pauses in a conversation that have always fascinated Belinda.

'Did you ever meet our grandparents?' Belinda asks.

'Of course I did. I lived with them until I was six.'

'We kids didn't meet them. I never saw them.'

'They saw you.'

'When?'

'More often than you thought.'

Belinda closes her eyes. That trick of hers, to see things in pictures, the flashes of recognition when she least expects them. 'Mum's funeral?'

'Yes. But, later, they watched out for you. Perhaps you never knew.'

'What will happen, Jessie? When you get back to London? You'll be on your own.'

'No, I won't. Bopha will come. When I need her.' Jessie

glances at her watch. 'We should be getting back to the airport soon. So, Belinda, were you not going to tell me about these things that you found? And the DNA test?'

'I've been thinking about it. I was waiting for the right moment,' Belinda says. She sees how tired Jessie has become. She wonders whether they'll make it back to the airport. Her sister reaches for a bottle of water and drinks deeply.

'But soon you'll run out of moments. Tomorrow night I'll be off.' She doesn't need to remind Belinda that the morning will be taken up with her treatment, enough to get her back to London. Jessie's hand rests on the gear shift. 'There was a fire at the tobacco fields,' she says. 'A night or so before we left. A man died. Not an old man. I think he was a foreigner.'

'Did he wear a jacket?'

'It was summer. I can't remember. It was something our mother wanted me to forget. He used to come to our hut, and she was pleased to see him. Jock was courting her then, if that's what you could call it. I used to get into trouble a bit and Jock would come over and tell her to keep me in order, or that was his excuse. But this other man used to come when the workers went to town on a Friday night. Yes, I do remember that.'

'Did you see the fire?'

Jessie gazes out to sea, to the island, to the birds wheeling overhead. She puts her hands on the steering wheel, and grips it tightly.

'I would have said no if you'd asked me yesterday. I've put it out of my mind, the way our mother told me to, for the past sixty or more years. But I see it. I do see the flames. The great arc of electrical fire from the kiln. Bert trying to put it out.'

'Bert? Was that his name?'

'It must have been. I'd forgotten. I can't be sure, but I think he smoked a pipe. I was only little. There might be some account of that fire somewhere. Old newspapers, that sort of thing. It might be worth you doing a search.'

Belinda says nothing. She wonders if she'd been the cause of her mother marrying Jock. It might have been like that. There's a whole new road to travel, the lives of her brother and sister to fathom, people for whose lives perhaps she is responsible. It's true, she's had the lucky life.

'There was singing. The Maori workers from up north were having a singalong. It was getting cool that evening. In spite of the summer heat, some nights got quite cold out there. Yes, a cold, starry night. I can feel that.'

'So he might have been wearing a jacket?'

'He might,' Jessie agrees.

They sit together in silence. The street behind them winds up the hill to the house they both knew long ago. Jessie reaches over and takes Belinda's hand in her thin fingers. 'There's a poem that Neruda wrote about guilt. He thinks of himself as guilty for having hands yet not having made a broom.'

'I know that poem,' Belinda says. 'He asks what good his life would be if he only watched the stir of grain, and listened to the wind and never gathered straws that were still green on the earth.'

'But Belinda,' Jessie says, 'whatever our mother did, *she* did, not you or me. You and I, we've made a few brooms.'

Songs, poems. The lines we live by, Belinda thinks. Even the lines of television plays, although she's not sure it's the moment for this either, any more than it seemed the time to tell Grant about her parentage. But it comes back to her, the last line of the play she had liked so much when she was finding her way towards her life. The mother who says at the end: 'Somebody hold me'. It's all anyone can do, she thinks, to hold one another, to make it through to the end, as best they can. Yes, lucky, that's her. Touched by fire, but still going strong.

Belinda holds her sister's hand. Tomorrow Jessie will fly

off towards the night, across blazing cities and cauldrons of darkness.

She is leaving.

# Acknowledgements

I thank the following for information and support during the writing of this book: Bev Brett, Sharon Crosbie, Judith McCann and Jeremy Salmond. Kate Melzer, Rod Fry and Margaret Woodley provided invaluable research about the Motueka tobacco fields. Ian Kidman makes everything work while I write, and thanks never do him enough justice. Thanks, as ever, to my brilliant editorial team: Harriet Allan, Leanne McGregor and Anna Rogers.

My thanks to the James K. Baxter Trust for permission to quote from Baxter's poem 'Breadboard and Knife' on page 216. The poem referred to on page 221 is 'Juan's Song' by Louise Bogan, and the poem described on page 319 is 'Guilty' by Pablo Neruda (1973, translated by John Felstiner).

Two books consulted provided invaluable background reading. They were: *The Golden Harvest: A History of Tobacco Growing in New Zealand* by Patricia K. O'Shea (Hazard Press, 1997) and *Panguru and the City: Kainga Tahi, Kainga Rua* by Melissa Matutina Williams (Bridget Williams Books, 2015).

This is a work of fiction and any resemblance to real people living or dead is entirely inadvertent, although you will find a few characters walking through several of my previous novels.